Always And Forever
+ Ten Years Later

JAMES PRINCE

Order this book online at www.trafford.com
or email orders@trafford.com

Most Trafford titles are also available at major online book retailers.

Printed in the United States of America.

ISBN: 978-1-4907-2529-1 (sc)
ISBN: 978-1-4907-2528-4 (e)

Trafford rev.   04/03/2014

 www.trafford.com

North America & international
toll-free: 1 888 232 4444 (USA & Canada)
fax: 812 355 4082

Always And Forever

05, 16 2009

CHAPTER 1

*T*he least I can say about our story is, it is a bit uncommon.

They were two young women who were absolutely inseparable and this since there early teenage years. They told each other then; this was for always and forever, that nothing and nobody would come between them and their friendship will never be broken by anyone.

One of them with black hair and a very soft white skin has on herself some beautiful round and fair size breasts. They are firm and they could feel my eyes and my hands, I was sure of this.

She is my height, thin without being skinny, a person very enjoyable to hold in my arms. I strongly fell in love with her the first night we danced holding each other closely and tenderly on the dancing floor. I fell in love with her in the first hour we met right there on this floor. This was the very first time I felt this way, which I think they call; love at first sight.

Neither one of us didn't care, not even a bit about the rest of the world at this time. The music was soft and we were both in another world, so much we could make love right there and then on the dance floor among everybody. I have never felt this way in my whole life. To my surprise, when she opened her mouth, she said: 'You'll have to dance with my friend too.'

I was expecting something more like; your place or mine? I told her right away.

"I only want you, I only want to dance with you, I only want to make love to you, I only want to live with you." "You don't know what you're talking about. You hardly know me." "Maybe so, but I know what I want in life and I mainly know how I want her to be, this is what I found with you." "I appreciate what you're saying, but give yourself some time and in the mean time dance with my friend, would you please?" "Then it is only to please you. What is her name?" "Her name is Janene." "What is she doing in life other than being you're best friend?" "She's a nurse at the hospital." "And you didn't tell me what you are doing?" "I do the same thing at the same place." "Interesting! You girls work the same hours?" "Not always!" "OK then, introduce me." "Let's go."

The crowd was dense and we had to push one another walking to make our way through to their table.

"To tell you the truth; I would rather take you to my bed than dance with you're friend." "Wait, you'll see. We have a lot of time, the night is young and we only had a few dances."

Once we got to their table I thought I was in some kind of a dream. I was facing at this precise moment what I thought was the most beautiful woman in the world. The most pretty blond girl who existed on the face of the earth. They are just about the same size, but totally different one another in look. Her friend was sitting down with a man quite a bit older than her. She introduced him to me right away.

"Hi Danielle, you seem to have fun? Let me introduce you to this man. His name is John. He is a trucker and he travels across the country."

"Nice to meet you John, I know you know my brother." "Yes, yes, I know him well."

So, I said hi to him too and I shook his hand.

"Janene, I have a very nice young gentleman to introduce to you too. I don't know yet what he's doing in life, but I can tell you he's the best dancer I happened to dance with and you absolutely have to dance with him. He can dance anything you want too. Janene, this is James."

"No, no, I'm just a very ordinary dancer. Hi Janene, nice to meet you." "Very nice to meet you James!"

This is what she said shaking and holding my hand in an unusual way. I felt a bit bad, because just a few minutes ago I was telling the one I thought was the woman of my life that I love her. Who could imagine such a thing? Not that I was also in love with Janene, but I was definitely blown away by her beauty. Janene got up and she asked Danielle to follow her to the lady's room.

"Where did you find this phenomenal guy?" "He was back there against the wall, hoping I supposed a pretty girl will smile to him.

He seemed very gentle to me, so I smiled back to him and I found myself happily cuddled up in his arms. I believe I'm in love with him already and he feels the same way with me." "But, you just met him. I can't blame you I admit, he is very attractive." "This is what you think too?" "Usually you don't have the same taste than me." "Usually you pick ordinary guys." "It's true that James is special." "What are you going to do with John?" "Which John?" "The one you've got sitting down at your table." "Ho, this guy, he is boring. You've got to get rid of him. He doesn't know how to dance and he would always be gone on the road somewhere. Besides, I don't like to travel in big trucks."

"Here is what were going to do. You're going to dance with James and stay on the floor for as long as you can. I'll sit with John and yarn until he's bored enough to get the heck out off our air. What do you think of this?" "It seems to be a good idea, but it's going to be very boring for you too." "What can't we do for our best friend? Just bring me James back in one piece, that's all I ask." "Ok."

During this time I was bored to death with John who had nothing else to talk about than his truck and his delivery on time and how important it was. It was a real small world for a guy who travels across the country. I had only one thing in mind and this was to find myself into Danielle's arms again. The wait felt like a cold shower after such a nice time I had just experienced with her. John just spent I don't know how much time with the most beautiful girl I have ever seen and all he had in mind was his darn truck. No wonder Janene tried to get rid of him. I just hoped he didn't cost me to lose Danielle for the evening. I was relieved when I finally saw them coming back to the table. I was afraid they wouldn't come back because of him.

"Here you are the two of you. I was getting a bit worried." "No, no, James, you'll have to know how to wait." "This is true Danielle; especially if we are sure we are not waiting in vain." "Don't worry James, when we find gold, we keep it preciously. I think I found some tonight." "Ho yea! I hope you're right, because I think I found a treasure too, one I wouldn't want to be too long without." "James, if you want to please me now, you're going to take my friend to the dance floor." "Are you sure you know what you're doing? I could make it a habit, you know?" "I hope so James, she is my best friend."

At that moment I had shivers. I was scared of what I just heard. Many questions came to my mind. Does she want to get rid of me already when she seemed to be so fine in my arms? Does she want to test me by pushing me into her best friend arms? Such a beautiful woman! Does she want to push me away, because she's interested in somebody else? I looked at her intensely and I asked myself if I should simply refuse to go away. But how can I say no to someone I love and refuse her anything in such a short time? There was almost a supplication in her voice and Janene seemed to be so impatient to get on the dance floor with me. Maybe Janene just wanted to get away from this guy, the trucker. Maybe she's interested in me too, when I think of the way she held my hand earlier. There was one thing I knew for sure and this was I didn't have much time for all the answers to my questions. What to do? I said; see you later Danielle and I took Janene by the hand and I brought her to the dance floor.

I was a bit upset I most say. The band was playing a cha cha, a music that puts me in a mood for dancing very quickly. We danced it with conviction and so we did with the next piece of music, a fast rock & roll.

"Wow! Danielle was right, you know how to dance." "Sure, a little! We should go back now and try to get our breath back." "There is no way, unless you are suffering." "I'm fine, but I don't want Danielle to think I already abandoned her, especially with such a beautiful woman and with her best friend above all. It's not that it is not fun, but are you always this skintight?" "It's been long since I had the taste to hold someone like this."

"You're only an hour late and everything could have been totally different, if I met you first. I have to admit that you are very pleasant and extremely pretty, but I'm in love with Danielle."

A mambo followed and I asked her if she knew how to do it, hoping her answer would be negative.

"Sure, it's my favourite dance." "No luck then, it's my favourite one too."

There were very few people on the floor and only another couple knew how to dance it. People all around us were watching with envy, I could tell. As soon as the music ended, they applauded to the point it was almost embarrassing. Janene jumped to my neck holding me tight, kissing me and saying she couldn't dance like this since she had her last dance with her dance instructor six years ago.

She had on a very pretty white dress with red buttons and shoes to match it. I thought at this moment it was possible I could fall in love with her also. She had a nice sun tan on a beautiful skin, her hair is like gold and her eyes are of the nicest blue. She could, I'm sure make thousands of men dream of her. Her breasts are a bit smaller than Danielle's, but firm and pointing up. Her bump is neither too small nor too big and her waist could make all the models of the world dream of it. It was enough to wonder why such a beautiful young woman was still single while thousands of men would like to marry her. It would be hard for me to dance a slow dance with her without being tempted to put my hands on those cheeks.

Thinking about slow dance the musicians thought it was time to slow down and it was a real sentimental one. I was lost in my thoughts with my observations about the one I was with on the dance floor when I remembered I was forgetting the one I love. I felt bad and ashamed of myself.

"Janene, I have to join Danielle now." "No way, there is no way I'll let you go before we finish this beautiful slow. Besides, Danielle will join us as soon as she got rid of this non sense guy at our table." "I don't understand; if you don't like the guy, why don't you just tell him to go away?" "It's not this simple; he is her brother's friend." "Ho, I see, she feels obligated. But if I understand well, you girls have tricked me into this."

Time went by and I found myself stuck in her arms surrounded by a couple of hundred people tight together on the dance floor. With her whole body Janene firmly stick herself against mine like a leech and I decided to give her a sample of what it could be like between the two of us if it was possible. She took one of my hands and she pulled it down on her bump, which seemed to me in fire. My member got bigger and I started to sweat and this really made me uncomfortable. At the moment when I was going to push her back, Danielle joined us.

"How are you doing the two of you? I'm please to see that you're doing well. Danielle put her arms around us and held us from behind me and the three of us finished the dance this way. Not only she pressed herself against me, but she also pulled Janene towards me, pinching me feverishly between those two pairs of wonderful breasts like a meat sandwich. Believe me, this was something to warm me up, to say the least. We finally got closer to the end of this wonderful and memorable evening, one I'll never forget for as long as I live.

Nevertheless, I was not yet at the end of my sweats. I was not scared about my health, because I was definitely in good hands with these two lovely nurses. I'm a guy who is strongly built and in a super good shape physically, but I had again a fair number of questions concerning these two girls.

What were these two beautiful young women really looking for? Are they single or married? The reality is not always what people say. That they were nurses I had no problem to believe it. The fact they were best friends was not very hard to believe also, but was there something more? Two of the same sex who goes together now days is not this rare and it is the same with the bisexuals. Usually women are looking for taller guys, which is not my case. I have no complex about it, because there is not much a tall guy could do that I couldn't. The fact is there are a lot of women who married tall guys because they were tall and handsome and they cried bitterly. The look and the height of a person don't guaranty happiness. Women especially should remember this. I have to stop questioning myself I suddenly realized.

I have to live the good time when it's there otherwise, I'll never see it. I still didn't know what they had in mind for the rest of the night. I knew though that what I had was better than I could ever dream of, that thousands of men would dream the same thing, the same luck.

"What are we doing from here Danielle?" "What about you? Do you have any idea?" "All I know is I'm not quite ready to say good night just yet." "Me neither James!"

"Me neither." Janene said! "What do we do then?"

"Janene and I have a large apartment, something to drink and something to eat and we invite you if you like to come?" "I have a fairly nice house too with three bedrooms, a sauna and a Jacuzzi, so what now?" "We invited you first, are you coming?" "Not yet, but I will I'm sure. How could I refuse such a nice invitation? Sure, I'll come, I'm following you. Don't drive to fast; I don't want to lose you.

Danielle you should give me your address and your phone number just in case something happened, we never know, you know?" "this is true too but, I think the hazard made things right so far tonight." "It's true, but I don't want to take any risk." "Here James, see you in a bit."

The two of them gave me an unforgettable hug followed by a kiss and I went toward my car right away. They went to their car too and it seemed to me they got into a deep conversation as soon as they left me.

9

I started the vehicle right away and I drove it and parked it just behind their car. They got going and I followed them. They still seemed to me in a big discussion and I hoped they were not going to fight over me. Ho how much I wished I could hear what they were saying. The worst that could happen as far as I was concerned is that one of them was jealous. It's possible I told myself, but yet again, I question too much. Happens what happens, I'll go to the end of this adventure.

In the mean time something was going on in the other car.

"Janene, you have never liked the guys I was interested in or the ones who were interested in me." "It's true, but you have never met someone like him. He is very gentle and polite, he dresses nice, he dances magnificently and he's got a new car, which means he's got a good job." "You forgot he's got a house too. He seems very strong for a little guy, did you notice this too?" "This is true. When he held me in his arms, I felt he was holding me good, that I was not going to fall. He is special this one, there is no question about it. You seem to love him a lot, but I know I could love him too." "One thing is sure and this is I don't want any competition between us and no jealousy either. We never had and we cannot let this happen." "Danielle what ever happens, you'll always be my best friend." "You will too Janene!" "What are we going to do then?" "We shared him so far and it wasn't too bad, what do you think?" "I think it was super." "He didn't seem to mind this either." "He was rather unwilling to stay on the dance floor with me at first." "What happened after?" "I held him back like you asked me to." "Rascal, it wasn't too hard for you, was it?" "It's probably the nicest mission you asked me to fulfil for you. He worried a lot about you though. I even believe he is in love with you. I had a hard time to hold him back, you know? I think he danced with me to please you. He was quite afraid it could displease you to stay on the floor with me. Should we keep sharing him?" "Yes! You'd do anything for me and I'd do anything for you, why not? We'll see what he thinks of it."

The two of them gave each other the high five in agreement. I followed them in an underground parking lot of a large condominium building where I parked in a guess area. They gave me another warm hug and I could see by their smiles, they were pleased with my presence.

'Come James.' Danielle told me. They grabbed my arms, one on each side and Danielle said; 'Let's take the elevator that will take us to the sixth floor.'

It was obvious they were not women who live in misery. It was late in the night and we were alone, so they weren't shy to take turns in kissing me all away up to their floor.

It was obvious too they didn't invite me just for a quick coffee or a cup of tea either. But what ever happen I was ready for anything, any eventuality. Both of them were showing me their interest and I could appreciate this just as much from both of them even though I think I was in love with Danielle. I was like the words of a French song from Dalida which says: 'Happy like an Italian when he knows he'll get some sex and some wine.'

Maybe I wasn't on the seventh heaven, but I'm sure I was at least on the sixth. We got out of the elevator and they invited me into a superb and luxurious condominium. There is a forty-eight inches TV in a greatly furnished living room. They guided me to a very comfortable sofa and Danielle asked me.

"Would you like something to drink James?" "I will only if you girls take something too. I would like another long kiss from you Danielle though." "Hin, hin, if you kiss me, you'll have to kiss Janene too and the same way." "What? What is this plot?" "It is very simple James, it is this or nothing, but the choice is yours." "What is it? A kissing contest of some kind?" "No, it is just we shared you all evening and we both found this very enjoyable. It is also that we both would like to continue, because we both love you very much." "Well, I was expecting almost anything, but certainly not this." "What were you expecting exactly James?" "I . . . , I Was expecting maybe to finish what I started with you Danielle." "And when did you plan to finish what you started with Janene?" "There, well I'm sorry, but I didn't plan anything at all about this. What if it goes farther than kisses?" "We are willing to share everything, if you agree of course." "What would happen if I only have enough for one?" "When there is enough for one, there is enough for two. You know the dictum, don't you? If you can only give us one portion, I'm sure we will be satisfied with it." "You're serious?" "Yes! If you can give me just half a portion and half a portion to her, this will be fine too. Better yet, you could make love to Janene tonight and to me tomorrow." "And you seem to be very serious?" "You're right, you can bet we are." "You girls being nurses, can you get me the blue pills at a better price?" "If this becomes necessary we'll take care of it, don't worry, we're not nymphomaniac. We don't want to kill you or hurt you in any way, on the contrary. We'll take care of you like a baby, our baby." "Wow! I'm simply astonished. Forgive me, but I have a bit of a problem to digest all this. Where are we starting?" "We made you sweat tonight, let start with giving you a nice hot bath." "Here we are, I'm already in hot water. What a start!"

This made them laugh a good shot.

"Can you assure me there will be no jealousy ever?" "Yes we can." They both agreed with a big smile. I started to sing a song I know, which made them laugh even more. Let go to swim my sweethearts, let's go all swim together."

When I entered this room I found out it wasn't an ordinary bathroom. It was as big as a normal bedroom, a room that is ten feet by twelve with a tub six feet in diameter and at least two feet high. When I entered I said;

"But this is not a bathtub, this is a swimming pool."

The two of them were undressed in no time leaving me with no choice. I had to move and there was no time to waste. I have to admit that I was still in an emotional shock. I had a hard time to believe that I wasn't dreaming on one hand and on the other I couldn't keep my eyes off those two beautiful nude bodies. I was totally in disbelieved and yet you know what they say; yes, seeing is believing. I don't think a million dollars would have made me any happier.

"Come on, jump in James, we're going to take care of you." "You too Janene, get in here."

Danielle got comfortably behind me while Janine took place in front. It was unbelievably enjoyable. I have never live through such a pleasurable thing in my whole life.

"Tonight James you can only look, you can not touch."

"Do you agree Janene?" "Everything is fine with me Danielle."

"Just a minute there, this is not only mental cruelty, but it is also physical cruelty." "What are you complaining about James? You're not well with us?" "I am extremely well Danielle, but it is nevertheless very cruel to look at those beautiful breasts in front of me and so close and not being able to touch them. Besides, I feel yours in my back without being able to see them. Come on; let me touch them at least once." "What do you think Janene? Should we let him?" "It's alright with me if you don't mind." "If this will please both of you then I will not intervene. Just once then!" "I think I will make this just once last a very long time."

While I was playing with Janene adorable breasts and looking her straight in her eyes, Danielle grabbed me and started to mass gently but firmly this thing that was ready to explode at any time. At that precise moment I was confused, because I wasn't sure if I loved one more than the other. Then came the crucial moment when there was no way I could hold back any longer. I was still holding those beautiful things in my hands when the explosion occurred. There was some for everyone, especially for Janene who was in a position to get the most of it. She had some in her hair, in her face, in her eyes and if she'd opened her mouth at that moment, she would have been the first one to taste me. The only time I remembered I was this generous with this liquid is when I was only fourteen years old. It was then my first sexual experiences.

"It looks like you got an eye on me Janene?" "You're right love, I got some everywhere. You're a real seafood James." "It's good?" "It's salty." "Ho yea. I hope you like salt." "In a matter of fact, I'm presently ashamed to say it, but I do." "Good!"

I gently pulled on those two beautiful breasts and brought her closer to me and I gave her a tender long kiss.

The ejaculation seemed to me endless to the point I started to have a bit of a pain in the back of my head that I couldn't explain. I also felt a bit weaker and it scared me even though I was in good hands. I finally left Janene breasts and I turned around to face Danielle. I asked her if I could only touch hers once also and I gave her a long kiss. She knew I was pleased with the pleasure she'd just gave me and I appreciated it. During this moment of exaltation Janene pressed herself against me and she ran one hand in my hair and tried to resuscitate me with the other hand. Then I went to sit behind Janene and I asked Danielle to pass me the shampoo.

"Danielle, we're going to give this beautiful blond girl a lovely bath, she really needs it, do you agree?" "Of course!" "You wash her hair and I'll take care of the rest, OK?" "Alright, wash everywhere, don't cut the corners." "Don't you worry, I always try to do things right." "It's very nice to discover you James." "You like this?"

I took a bar soap and I started rubbing her back from her neck to her bump, what gave her shivers over her whole body. After rinsing her I went to the front where I let my hands slip from her throat to her pubis. I spent a lot of time on her breasts again. Danielle who didn't miss a thing said:

"Hey there, we said only once, you're cheating." "Not at all Danielle, I don't touch now, I wash."

I let my hands travel all over her whole body and from time to time I also passed the back of my hand between Danielle's legs. She didn't complain about this one. Then I came back to Janene and this time I went where it teases the most, but then it was more than shivers, it was wiggles. I would go as far as saying, it was torture. I have to say that there I was cheating a little bit when I let one finger slipped in the opening of her intimacy. Her whole body was telling me; give me more. I muttered to her ear: "Sorry, I can't go any farther, I'm not allowed." "This is enough for me."

14

Janene said getting up very suddenly. I understood there was a bit of frustration in her voice. After she got up she dried herself and said:

"I'm going to wait for you in bed."

"Do you think she's mad?" "Janene mad, never! Hungry maybe, but not mad." "Well, I'm glad to hear this. I'm going to wash you quickly and we should join her before she falls asleep." "I agree." "Is she going to eat something?" "What she's hungry for you don't find it in the cupboards and neither in the fridge." "I see, it's got to be my fault then. Let's hurry before she's cooling off."

We quickly got out of the tub, dried each other and walked rapidly to the bedroom. Janene was lying down naked on the bed, smiling and absolutely dazzling. She had one hand on one breast and the other one near her velvety pubis. Danielle who was holding my hand pulled me towards Janene and said:

"She's first, she works tomorrow."

When I got close to Janene, I started to caress her with all of my knowledge hoping it was good enough for the situation. I will only know if I can get her to have many orgasms. Her pubic hair was so blond it looked almost invisible. I spent a long time kissing her deeply knowing she was burning with desire. When I came down on her body I noticed Danielle beside us had taking a similar position Janene was in when we entered the room. I went directly to the goal and I let my thirsty tongue and lips do what they were dying to do for many hours then. She didn't waste any time for coming again and again. She's going to drown me I thought, but she was so delicious I didn't dare to stop. Finally it was Danielle putting one hand in my hair indicating it was time for me to stop. I got on my knees and Janene did too in front of me, kissing me and she said with tears in her eyes:

"It's been five years James, you are marvellous. Thank you." "There is no problem sweetheart. You're welcome, anytime."

Danielle was about to cry too and I even think she shed a few tears. I stretched myself down between the two of them without a word for few minutes and then Danielle whispered:

'James, she's sleeping. I'll cover her up and we'll go lay down in the other room.'

I was almost sad to leave her behind. I came very close to come another time during this last workout. After Danielle had covered Janene she took me by the hand and led me to another room almost as luxurious. Just the bed is a bit smaller.

"Are you too tired now James? If you want to sleep I would understand." "We'll do like Janene if you want, we'll come first. We'll have a lot of time to sleep tomorrow."

We rolled down the blankets and we jumped in the bed.

"Do you know that I'm waiting for this moment since I lifted my eyes on you?" "Without lies?" "Of course, I never lie." "Never?" "It would have to be a real uncontrollable situation." "Can you give an example?" "Sure, let say I am a cop and I see someone who is ready to jump down a bridge, because he or she wants to kill herself and I ask her to come down saying with a lie, she wouldn't be prosecuted. It's a good lie or a necessary lie, I should say." "Can you give me another example?" "Not now sweetheart! Right now I want to caress you until you fall asleep." "Alright, this is alright with me."

I gave her the same treatment Janene received.

"Are you feeling good enough for a complete session?" "I certainly am, but I'm not a cheater." "I see that revenge is sweet to James' heart." "It is not revenge darling, it is faithfulness." "I agree, because I know you're right. I think I would have loved it." "Janene too! Wait till tomorrow, this way no one could say I got you the first day we met." "I want you so much." "Me too, believe it!" "Its true that many people think it is wrong for a woman to give herself to a man on the first date." "Personally I think the decision belongs to the two people involved and so are the consequences. You know that we never know; I might just be a guy who goes to the brothels." "No way, not you!" "There are good looking guys who are timid and go to those places."

At the same time I sat beside her and I said:

'Don't you worry, this is not my case.'

I kissed her one last time and we fell asleep in each other arms. It was our first night of love and I didn't forget the least detail. At around noon, Janene came to join us and she said:

"I see that you guys deserted me." "Hi you!" "Good morning to both of you!"

"You were sleeping so well, we didn't want to wake you up." "It's true that I slept like a baby who makes it through the night. I'll have to be put to bed some more this way. I'm going to take a bath, I feel sticky." "Put enough water for two, I feel the same way."

"Go ahead girls, I like to sleep another hour if you don't mind. Don't let me sleep any longer than this though."

Danielle gave me a little kiss on the mouth and she went to join Janene in the bathroom. I was thinking about the whole evening and the night. It's not a dream, they really are here. I also new they weren't lesbians, because it would have been impossible for a lesbian to see Janene in the state she was, laying on the bed naked and not touching her. Then I fell asleep again. In the mean time these two women had another plan in mind.

"Do you think it is possible Danielle?" "Of course it is. I think I have enough now." "Are you sure?" "Yes, I am."

They came to wake me up at two forty-five, just before Janene departure for her work. Janene came to give me a hug with a kiss and she quickly left. Danielle came to sit beside me on the bed and asked:

"What would you like to eat?" "It depends." "It depends on what?" "Well, if we're going to make love for the rest of the day I would certainly need a couple of eggs." "Are you sure eggs are good for this?" "This is what they say. Do you know anything better?" "I will ask the doctor. How do you like them?" "Over easy with a pair of white toasts and a cup of tea with one sugar and no milk. I can do them if you like." "Give me a chance to try first and if you don't like them, then you can make them yourself." "Go ahead then, but I have to warn you, I'm the worst client for the best cook." "What do you mean by this?" "I mean I don't eat everything, everywhere, anyhow. I'm very fussy

17

and on top of everything I have allergies." "We'll learn to know you. I'm sure there will be compensation for the inconveniences. Things will work out." "I appreciate your understanding, thanks." "Breakfast is ready." "I'm starving, I didn't eat anything in the last twenty-four hours, besides you girls." "I'm sorry; we didn't offer you anything to eat." "On the contrary, you offered me what was the best, but not for the stomach. Mmmmm, they're good, exactly the way I like them. What about you, you don't eat?" "We ate while you were sleeping." "Why didn't you wake me up as I asked you?" "We both decided you needed a good rest and well deserved." "I see, this is nice of you. Thanks for the breakfast." "Ho, you're welcome."

We talked about nothing and everything and then the phone rang at around five thirty. Danielle picked it up.

"Hello!" "Hello Danielle, I can't talk to long, we're expecting an emergency at any minute now, but the result is negative. Say hi to James for me." "I will. This was fast, thanks."

Danielle put the phone back on its cradle and she seemed worried." "You've got bad news?" "No, on the contrary, it's good news." "Why do you looked so worried then?" "I'm always like this when I have to take a quick and important decision. This was Janene. She said to say hi. You had enough to eat? Do you want some more?" "No, this was plenty, thank you." "What would you like to do now?" "If you could lend me a tooth brush and tooth paste, I'd like to brush my teeth and rinse my mouth, then I'd like to wash a bit." "Go lay down a little and I'll run a bath." "I'm I dreaming or you're always this sweet?" "It's nice to be ourselves for the person we love." "You love me, is this true?" "I don't lie either James."

I took her in my arms and I strongly kissed her. Then I threw myself on the bed and she went to the bathroom. When she came back to tell me it was ready, I was already dozing. She helped me getting up by pulling on my arm and I went to jump in the tub. When I finished brushing my teeth I came back to the bedroom to find her lying on the bed. She was the most desirable and me, well, I was naked like a worm.

Sorry no, all I was wearing were my glasses. I came closer to her and I started undressing her. With all of my heart I wanted to make love to her. With something else too, but I wasn't sure it was the best thing to do."

"Can you explain to me how it is possible to love a person or two so much in such a short time?" "No, in fact, I was asking myself the same question." "I want to make love to you, but I think I should be tested first." "Why, do you think you might have a disease?" "I don't know; I've never been tested for this." "I have to tell you James, I'm a virgin." "Seriously?" "I'm very serious." "Who could have believed such a thing? And you're twenty-four?" "I have never loved someone enough to give myself to him until now." "There is also the risk to get pregnant. I don't have any protection. I never thought myself to get in this position." "I thought a nice looking guy like you would have sex every time he's going out." "This is the first time I go out in two years. I went out last night because it was a special occasion." "And what was the occasion?" "It was my birthday." "Seriously? It's true, you don't lie. We'll have to celebrate this, how old are you?" "I just turned twenty-seven." "Happy birthday then!" "Thank you!" "I want you to make love to me now." "Now?" "Now!" "Don't you think I should be tested first?" "Well, it's done." "What do you mean, it's done?" "I mean it is already done. Janene and I are asking you for forgiveness, but Janene brought a sample of your sperm to the laboratory and when she called earlier it was to tell me the result was negative. You have no disease." "But you girls stole from me." "I rather think you gave it to us." "And how? I've never come this much since I was fourteen or fifteen. Well, this is good news, but what to do to avoid pregnancy?" "Don't worry; I'm not in a dangerous period right now. Like one could say, go in peace or come in peace." "Ok then, may peace be with us."

During the time of this conversation my hands didn't stop undressing her and they were all over her shivering body. I felt the tension going up every time I was approaching her breasts and her low belly. It has been a long time since I was with a woman, because this is not something I give to everyone. I got on top of her and I kissed her tenderly while holding her left breast in my hand. With all my heart I wanted to give her the maximum of pleasure. I don't think I left any part of her body untouched. The hardness of her nipples was telling me a lot about the way she felt. She was all mine soul and body and I was fully aware of it. I made her come many times orally and I suddenly felt the need to position myself in her wonderful love nest, because I was ready to explode at any moment. I got on top of her again and in one time, two movements, three shots in, it was gone. My fear was founded, because one more time I came prematurely. The engine that is supposed to give the most part of the pleasure and satisfaction to your partner just lost the best part of its power. Luckily the power lasted just enough to give her another orgasm.

"I'm sorry, but I wish I could hold it a lot longer." "Don't be sorry James, it was so good." "Believe me, it could be much better. I got to find a way to make it last a lot longer for both of us." "I believe and I trust you." "If you want, we can wash and start all over again." "I'd like to just lie beside you and chat. I feel so great in your arms and I love to hear you talk." "What do you want to talk about?" "Nothing and anything and what ever comes to your mind." "I wonder what Jeannette Bertrand would think of our story, a triangle." "She would probably be scandalized." "I don't think so. Do you know she had a radio sex talk show for a long time?" "I didn't know this." "I heard her say once on the air that more than fifty per cent of the sport world, more than fifty per cent of the artistic world and more than fifty per cent of the clergy was homosexual." "This is a lot of people. I didn't know this." "I am both ways since last night." "Ho no, don't you tell me you're bisexual." "Don't make me laugh; I'm a guy who loves both of you. It's quite an experience and I hope it's not a one night story, because ladies, I'm deeply in love with both of you." "Don't mock me James, it would hurt too much." "I don't mock you Danielle, it's not my style, seriously, I love you and I believe I love Janene too very much. It makes me feel strange to say this though, I feel a bit like cheating on both of you." "You must not feel guilty about this; we put you in this position and this is what we wanted." "When did you plan this plot?" "Last night! I always knew I could share anything with Janene, but I never thought she could love the same man. This is the first time she likes my partner. It is actuality the first time she pays attention to anyone in five years." "What happened to her?" "She had a deep deception, but I'll let her tell you herself." "Sure! I'm sorry, I just wanted to understand. You girls are serious, you don't mind the triangle?" "If you agree, we we'll be happy about it." "You didn't even ask me what I was doing for my living." "This is because we don't need your money." "I'm touched, really. So, it means when a woman asked, it's because she need support? I don't need your money either, I make a good living." "What are you doing for work?" "I'm a journeyman carpenter, I build houses." "Janene and I talked about having a house built sometime on a big lot and we want at least three bathrooms. If you ever build our house, just be sure of something; we don't want any favour, meaning no discount. We won't want to use you." "What ever, we'll talk about this when the time comes. What time is it?" "It is near midnight. We should dress up; Janene will be here within twenty minutes. I spent a very nice day with you James, I'm very happy. I'm going to make tea and a snack for all of us." "Danielle, tell me that I'm not dreaming. I have trouble believing in this much happiness." "If you're dreaming, I'm dreaming too, but trust me, I really lost my virginity today and I think it couldn't have been with a better man. I always knew it would happen with a good guy." "I'm glad you waited for me."

With these words Janene was opening the door."

"Hi the two of you. How are you doing?" "We are fine. What about you? Did you have a good day?" "Yes! It was funny; most of them thought I won the lotto. In a way they were right. Only the doctor guessed the right thing; I even think he is a bit jealous." "Jealous or not I want a hug and a kiss from you and I'm not ready to let you go just yet."

I took Janene in my arms and I hold her real tight for a long time while I kissed her deeply. The idea was to taste her beautiful mouth, but also to make sure there was no jealousy between these two young women that I was then in love with. Contrary to what one could expect Danielle was happy for both of us. It was almost disarming. Everything happened so fast I had a hard time to assimilate all this. I hate jealousy and I hate cheating too. Both of them can ruin any relationship. It is jealousy which pushed Cain to kill his brother Abel.

"You know what Janene; it was James' birthday yesterday." "And we got the gift; it's not really fair, is it?" "On the contrary, you girls made my best birthday ever. I still can't believe it. Tell me it's not going to end tomorrow."

They looked at each other and then Janene said:

"Could you really believe we want such happiness to end for us? We have to find a way to make this situation last forever." "We can not forget that the rest of the world will judge us very severely."

"We don't give a shit about the rest of the world. Do we judge people who sleep around left and right even married people?" "Don't get mad Danielle it is just a reality we cannot avoid." "Trust me James, we'll find a way. Where there is a will there is a way."

"Ho, I trust you and I'm sure that between the three of us we'll find a solution and a way to be happy in this dirty world."

"Well, I'm tired, I'm sleepy and I'm going to bed. I'll see you tomorrow. Good night James!" "Good night Janene! Don't go to bed too late."

Danielle gave us both a hug and a kiss and she went to bed. I excused myself to Janene and I followed her to the bedroom where I helped her to get in bed. I also gave her a tender kiss and I told her that we'll see each other in the morning. After I covered her nicely with the blankets I left the room. I fear the worst Monday in my life was coming up for me. Back to the kitchen Janene started to clean the dishes which were used during the day and I asked her:

"Where is the tea towel?" "There it is beside the fridge, but you don't have to, I can handle this." "Take advantage of me, it wouldn't happen this often, especially not with two women in the house. Let me do it, you already have a full day work behind you, besides, I like to be near you. I spent most of the day in bed." "You had a good time?" "I had an absolute gorgeous day." "I was forgetting, happy birthday."

This is what she told me putting her arms around my neck and kissing me with her languishing lips and her delicious tongue.

"What do you want to do James, watch a movie or go to bed?" "I better go to bed, I have to work tomorrow." "Ok then, let's go."

After taking a bath we walked to her bedroom where she opened the door and turned on the light and then I stopped her. I took her in my arms and I brought her to the bed, which seemed to be really nuptial. She was all smiles and inviting, so there I gently laid her down. We undressed each other looking in each other eyes. I put little kisses all over her face and then down on her breasts and then finally all over her body. She did the same with me, which brought us both to a complete ecstasy. We gave ourselves to one another in a very complete way. I thought we both just found the kingdom of heaven. 'Who when he had found one pearl of good price, went and sold all that he had, and bought it.' See Matthew 13, 46.

We fell asleep in each other arms and we woke up at seven-thirty in the morning. Danielle who woke up and felt lonely came to join us at four, but she was very careful not to wake us up. To this day I wonder if there is anything scarier than the thought of losing such happiness. Janene who was still in my arms kissed me saying, good morning.

"Wait a minute beautiful; I have bad breath in the morning because of my sinuses problem. I'll go wipe my nose, rinse my mouth and I will be back in a hurry. Wait for me."

"How did it go?" "He was super Danielle, I'm so happy. How did it go for you?" "It was good, but not extraordinary, although I think it was my fault." "I told you before, remember? The first time we are scared it might hurt even though it's not always the case. It depends a lot on the man delicacy and gentleness." "You must be right, because everything was fine until the penetration. I just felt a little pinch and this put an end to the pleasure immediately." "Welcome to the deflowered girl's club my dear friend. It will be better next time. You'll have a chance to catch on with me, because on my next long weekend of four days I'll go see my parents and tell them about our new man." "You don't think you should wait a bit longer, especially if you want to tell them the whole truth? You know, if you want it or not our families will put some shadow on our happiness. None of them will understand what we are living through." "What ever they say Danielle, none of them can stop me from living this wonderful new life and I hope it will be the same for you." "Always and forever, only death can stop us."

The two women were doing high five and laughing when I entered the room.

"How are you doing both of you? I'm I interrupting something?" "On the contrary, you are our continuation, but what took you so long?" "Ho, I made a few phone calls to prepare my men for work and free myself until noon. This is what you girls make me do." "Janene will go away and let us alone for four days soon." "She leaves us already; I'm going to miss her. Not that it is any of my business, but where will she go?" "She's going in Gaspé region to visit her parents." "Ho yea, I hope she's not going to tell them about us. I think it's too soon."

"It's not too soon if we are all sincere and serious." "I am." "Me too!"

"Which means it's not too soon. I will tell them next week."

We all gave each other the high five followed with a kiss.

"I don't want to tell you what to do Janene, which means I will talk to you in parables as for which concerns your parents. You know that gas was very high lately and people didn't really have a fit about it. Do you know why?" "Why gas was high or why people didn't have a fit about it?" "Why it didn't have a fit about it. You see, when Jos Clark raised gas by twenty five cent a gallons a few years ago, people was scandalized and his government was brought down. Last summer gas went up eighty cents a litre, which is three dollars and sixty cents a gallon and there was no crisis. Today gas came down to ninety cents a litre and people go fill their tank in a hurry and with a smile. I just want you to think about this, hoping you will understand on time. This is an eight hundred miles trip return, so I hope you're going to take the train." "I had in mind to go with my car." "Think about it, two days to travel and two days to rest, it doesn't leave you much time to visit." "On the train it's tiring too." "But at least you can sleep on the train." "I'm going to miss my car." "You can always rent one." "Not in this part of the back country!" "Don't you parents have a car? All I'm asking is that you're coming back in one piece. You know that there often are some very bad winter storms in March and bad enough to close the roads, don't you?" "I'm glad you're concerned, but what ever I decide, I'll be careful."

"Hay, both of you, you must be getting hungry?" "Yes Danielle, you must be the most motherly of all of us. That's alright, this way I won't miss my mom too much." "You're not living with your mom anymore, are you?" "Are you kidding me? I left home when I was sixteen. Do you want me to make you some granny's crepes?" "What is this?" "Good crepes I learned to make from my mom. It's one of my specialities. I love them a lot with pole syrup." "What is this again?" "This is another one of my specialities. I like it better than maple syrup." "Wow, this must be good? Another time, because you won't have time to make your syrup this morning."

They had their nightgowns on and all I had on was my underwear, so I had to dress up not to show at the table half naked.

"We have corn flakes, some rice krispies and oatmeal, all of this is good for your health." "Do you have some fresh white bread?" "Yes! Why?" "This is what I would like with milk and sugar." "This is another one of your specialities?" "Nothing is special about this, but I like it." "You're funny."

We took our breakfast talking about all kind of things but nothing in particular. I had to hurry when noon came though, because I had no choice, work was out there waiting for me. I wouldn't have felt too good either with these two pretty women until I was shaved again. So I kissed them both with passion and I promised them to come back as soon as possible.

Please James; before you go give us your phone number." "Here it is." "What is the name of your company?" "It's called; Reliable Constructions and Fiab Enterprises." "This sounds reliable." "It is and so am I. I'm sorry, but I have to go, see you soon sweethearts."

I left them, but not without having a feeling of emptiness. I had just spent two days extremely enjoyable and fully appreciated. Only one thought came to haunt me and this was concerning polygamy, knowing it was forbidden and illegal in Canada. I knew too it is allowed in certain religions, but I'm totally and definitely against any kind of religion. I just knew this won't be easy. I knew too that in Utah there are a few sects where it is permitted, but again it's not Canada. We are not at the end of our troubles, I thought. I had to stop thinking about this for a while. Just as I was thinking about those things, I heard on the news that two men just got arrested and charged with polygamy near Vancouver. It was as if someone wanted to tell me; it is best you think about it very carefully my friend. I will have to follow this story from a close range, I told myself. I heard much later they were acquitted. This was kind of a relief to me.

I had some business to take care of. I had men to put to work and the customers rarely understand you being late no matter what the reasons are. Even though I have good workers the boss is the boss and he is the one to blame and the one to congratulate, but above all he has to be responsible. At that point I haven't had the time to delegate work or any body to replace me.

On my way to work that day I heard on the radio that two men, two church leaders near Vancouver just got arrested and charged for polygamy. I thought the timing was quite strange, to say the least, since I was wondering how in the world I could marry the two women I was in love with.

CHAPTER 2

"Hello boss! What happened? You have never been late in two years?" "Well, I kind of celebrated my birthday this time." "Ho yea, happy birthday!" "Thank you. Is the drywall in?" "Not yet, but the windows and doors are inside the three houses." "Well, we are going to install them this afternoon then. What about finishing trims, are they in?" "No, they should be here very soon though." "That's good, let's go to work now."

I finished this day which seemed endless. When I arrived at my house my mom and one of my sisters were there waiting for me.

"What happened to you? I tried to phone you for the last three days." "I'm sorry mom, I should have called you." "You're not reasonable. Where were you? You weren't home." "I wanted to get away from everything and then I forgot everything even my birthday."

"She was this pretty?" "Yes Céline, she is pretty and very pretty, believe me. I'll tell you about it another time."

"You were not at work this morning either and nobody knew where you were." "I just about called the cops on you, you know?" "Ho, I wouldn't have like this mom. I wouldn't have wanted to be disturbed, especially by the cops. You'll have to get through your head mom that I'm old enough to live my life the way I want it no matter what you think. I didn't want to worry you, it's just that I was too captivated and I didn't think about calling you or anyone else, that's all." "You must have a thousand messages on you voice mail." "I would like to invite you for supper, but I have nothing ready. If you want to I can take you to a restaurant." "It's not necessary; our supper is ready at home. Happy birthday son and make sure I can talk to you on your birthday next year." "Thanks mom."

"Happy birthday brother and be careful." "Thanks Céline, I'm going to call them all now. It's going to take me a couple of hours." "For sure!" "Again, I'm sorry, forgive me. I'll see you soon."

Both mom and Céline took off and I went to listen to my messages.

"Happy birthday James, it's your little sister Marcelle."

"James, it's me, your mother, call me as soon as you can."

It's me, your sister Céline. Happy birthday brother.

"Happy birthday little brother, it's me, Francine."

"Happy birthday James, your sister Diane here."

"Happy birthday James, it's me Carolle, big kisses for your day."

"James, it's me again, your mother, give me a call."

"Happy birthday, it's me, your friend Murielle."

"Happy birthday, it's just your brother."

"It's me my love. I miss you already, Danielle who miss you a lot. I kiss you. Bye!"

"Here's Rolland. I have details to discuss with you. Monique wants to change the colour of the cupboards. Give me a call if you can."

This went on for another twenty minutes. We still like to know who called and who didn't. The thing is I had something else than the birthday wishes on my mind. Even so I had to make at least twenty phone calls to thank them all for their wishes. None of them though could have wished me a birthday like the one I just lived through. Although, the more I think about it the more I get scared. Me, who is ordinarily never scared of anything, I was afraid to have to move out of my country, afraid to be obligated to join a religion to be able to marry the women I love. I was also afraid that one or the other or even the two of them get discouraged from the troubles which were awaiting us, but it was also in my nature to trust in life, in my destiny that served me good so far.

After an hour and a half I was finally done with those calls and I received a call from Céline who was intrigued with what was going on with my life.

"Hi you! You're finally done with your phone calls?" "Finally, yes!" "I tried to call you many times already. For what I concluded, you had a nice weekend?" "Very nice! Thank you. It was beyond all expectations Céline." "I understood that you met someone?" "Not one, but two!" "Two what? I didn't met one, but two women and I don't want to talk about it on the phone." "I understand. When can I see you?" "Give me a minute to check my agenda. Wednesday if you want, I'll come and have supper with you." "I got that, come right after work." "I'll be there, good night."

At ten thirty that night I was in bed and I tried to sleep, but it was useless. Everything I lived through in the last three days was flashing back in my mind. I know very well that I need sleep to be able to function properly the next day. At twelve thirty I got up and I decided to make a phone call.

"Hi, Danielle here!" "Danielle, it's me and I need a nurse, I cannot go to sleep and I don't have any sleeping pill." "It's you, my love." "Do you know another way to make me go to sleep? I'm a person who needs his seven hours a night to function properly the next day." "I think you did pretty good in the last two days." "Did you have a good evening?" "Yes, but all the girls asked what's happening to Janene and I." "We can read happiness and distress on people's face; you know this, don't you? You're happy and people can tell. I'm happy about it." "Well, I'll let you go, I understand you need to sleep. You can make yourself an herbal tea and read until your eyes can't stand it anymore. This will help change your mind." "Well, thank you and say good night to Janene for me" "I will tell her" "Good night to you too, I love you both and I kiss you."

It was two thirty when I finally gave up thinking about all this. I felt like I slept bout ten minutes when the alarm clock woke me up at seven thirty. I felt very heavy and I dragged myself to the bathroom where I got better after a hot shower. I took a quick breakfast and I went to work where there were many tasks waiting for me. When noon came I free myself from my workers to make an important phone call.

"Hello! Is this you Janene? How are you?" "I'm well and what about you James?" "I'm fine, thank you." "Could you finally sleep?" "Yes, but just a few hours. I miss the two of you." "We miss you too. I'm leaving Thursday morning for Gaspé." "Already?" "This is me, I don't drag things." "Do you really think you're doing the right thing?" "Don't worry; I know what I'm doing." "I would like to spend a night with you before you leave if you like of course?" "Of course I want; it will be wonderful if you can." "I will wait for you in the same parking lot when you come home. Is Danielle home?" "No, I'm sorry, she's gone shopping." "Well, say hi to her for me and I'll see you Wednesday night. I got to go now, I love you and I kiss you like you know how, bye."

Wednesday at five thirty I was entering my sister's home at the set time, but I just knew it was mainly to satisfy her curiosity. She welcomed me with a hug and a kiss on each cheek. Her favourite meal, meat sauce spaghetti and matched potatoes were on the menu. If there is one in my big family who can understand my situation without judging too much, she's the one. We ate and then I helped her to do the dishes. Then started the bunch of questions.

"Now James, you're going to tell me what is going on with your life. I have to admit, I'm very curious." "Before I say anything, you'll have to promise me to keep all of this for yourselves." "I promise. I understood you met two different pretty women. Don't tell me you don't know which one to choose from?" "If this was the only problem, there would be no problem at all." "What do you mean by that? I don't understand." "I didn't make two encounters, but rather one encounter of two gorgeous women. Not only they are very pretty, but they are also very kind and intelligent." "What are they doing for a living?" "They both are nurses at the hospital." "You're going to be in good hands." "Who are you telling it to?" "But the thing is, I am already." "Already? What do you mean?" "I mean I am already in their hands." "You didn't waste any time." "You're mistaking, they didn't waste any time. I just let them carry me in a whirlwind of incredible love and a new world of extraordinary happiness for me." "Would you have changed to the point of accepting unfaithfulness now, you who were disgusted by it?

I'm still disgusted by it Céline, it is just there is no unfaithfulness at all." "You'll have to choose between the two of them or cheat on one or the other." "This is what is nice about the whole thing, I don't have to choose and I don't have to be unfaithful. I love them both and they are both in love with me." "Now you're playing with my nerves. You're mocking me, right?" "Not at all, I'm telling you just the way it is." "Now I'm lost. I don't understand a thing you're telling me." "Let me start all over for you. The two of them are best friends, they fell in love with me and I love them both, it's this simple." "Han, han, it's not simple at all, because soon or later jealousy will kick in and this will be a nightmare for all of you." "I checked this out already, they are happy for one another each time I kiss one or the other." "And you are flying like a bird." "Apparently the male bird only has one female in his life." "What a story! What are their names?" "One is called Janene and the other one is Danielle. Tonight I'll see Janene, because she's leaving tomorrow for four days. She's going to see her parents and she will tell them about the three of us. Then I'll have four days to get to know Danielle a bit better." "Now, do you understand why it's best not to talk to anyone about all this, for now anyway?" "It might be best not to talk to anyone ever about this." "The truth will come out soon or later." "I think you're not at the end of your troubles brother." "I think so too, but I also think it's worth it." "I hope so for you." "For what they both said, it wouldn't even matter if I was naked like a worm." "You hit them right in the eye like bull's-eye." "You don't know how right you are. I'll have to go soon, they finish working at midnight." "Do you mean you already sleeping with them?" "Yes, it was love at first sight for all of us." "Be careful, it could be hit and hurt at first sight too." "If it's always like last weekend, it will be just marvellous Céline, take my word for it. I never imagined something this great. I got to go now; I wouldn't want them to wait for me or to worry." "So, you're really in love with them. Good luck!" "Thanks and good night." "Good night too and thanks for coming." "It was my pleasure, thanks for supper too."

I got in my vehicle and I travelled towards my love ones' place. Streets were deserted and this allowed me to get there a bit earlier than they did. While waiting I relaxed by listening to a few good songs on the radio. As soon as I saw them coming in their little car I got out of mine and I locked the doors, then I walked towards them in a hurry. Janene came out of the car first and she jumped in my arms. She held me real tight like she hasn't seen me for ages. She kissed me in a way I could tell she was really in love. When she finally let go I looked her straight in the eyes and I said:

"Hello Janene." "Hello James."

"Hello James." "Hello Danielle. How are the two of you?" "I think Janene was a bit afraid not to see you before her departure." "Why was she afraid? I only have one word." "Yes, but as you know anything can happen." "This is true, but we can't always be afraid." "What about you James, aren't you afraid sometimes?" "You're perfectly right, I'm afraid even at this moment that all of this could just be a dream." "I'm afraid too that this could fall apart." "Don't fear Danielle, I love you both and I don't think anything could change this." "I hope you're telling the truth James and this from the bottom of my heart." "We should go up there now; you know the walls have ears, don't you?"

Danielle was a lot less enthusiastic that night and I came to the conclusion it was because she knew I was spending the night with Janene. She always been the same to this day, she doesn't want to get in the mood when she knows it's not her turn to have sex. I can understand this. I told them I couldn't stay up too late that I have to work in the morning.

"I got to get up early too; my train is leaving at nine." "Then we should take a quick bath and hit the bed right away." "You don't want to eat anything?" "Nothing from the cupboards anyway, I had a big meal at my sister." "You two go ahead, I'll take mine later; I have a lot of time."

Janene went to the bathroom and I went to sit with Danielle in the living room for a few minutes.

"Yell at me when it's ready Janene." "Don't worry, I will."

"You look like you're not feeling too good Danielle? Is there something wrong?" "I always worry when Janene leaves by herself for a trip." "Ho, that's what it is, mother hen. Janene is an adult full of good senses and I think you're worry for nothing." "I know what you're saying, but it's beyond me, I can't help it." "If you want to, I won't leave you alone and I'll come and spend time with you." "Well, I hope so."

"It's ready James." "I'm coming."

"Are you going to bed right away?" "No, I'm not sleepy and I'm going to watch a good movie." "See you later then; I'll come to say good night."

I ran to the bathroom and I jumped in the soapy hot water with whom I believe to be the prettiest woman in the world. Of course, after I was undressed.

"Man, this is hot. How can you?" "We get use to it very quickly." "If I was a rooster you could pull the feathers out off me very easily." "You are our rooster, but we won't pluck you, don't worry, at least it's not our intention."

I shut her mouth with a deep kiss while I was holding her tightly in my arms. Then I washed her from head to toe taking my time on the spots which please both of us. When she felt clean enough she did the same thing to me. What a pleasure! Great happiness! I suggested we make love right there in the water and she sat right away on what she loves particularly. I tried with all my strength to hold back, because I wanted the pleasure to last for her especially and for myself too, but unfortunately, the stupid thing exploded way too soon. I was certain this time she wished the love making would have last a lot longer. I knew then I had to find a way to fix this situation before it cause emotional trouble for both of us. It's true it was all new for me. It was also true she is very pretty and drives me crazy sexually, that she excites me to a very high level. It was true that with Danielle it was very tight and stimulating. It was true too that I wanted to give both of them way more pleasure, at least as much as they can endure. As soon as tomorrow, I told myself, I'll make an appointment with a psychologist.

"Janene, working at the hospital, you must know a psychologist?" "Yes, I know one, it's a she. You have a problem?" "Yes, I have a holding back problem." "What do you mean?" "I just wished I could have held it back another twenty or thirty minutes longer, don't you?" "Yes, but I thought it was normal. You're young, I'm pretty, it's all new. I think it could get better with time." "I don't want to wait any longer. I want to give you both a lot of pleasure, not in a year or so. I want to give you a lot of pleasure as soon as possible." "What a caring person you are. I love you so much James. I am in love with you and I know I will be happy with you forever." "I love you too Janene and I don't want this to stop ever. I think we should go to sleep now."

We got out of the tub and having dried each other, Janene put on her nightgown and I put on a large towel. Then we went to say good night to Danielle.

"How's the movie?" "It's good." "Do you mind put it on pause for a minute? I would like to say good night to you in the proper way." "Sure I can."

"Good night Danielle, sleep well." "Janene, I will take you to the train station tomorrow morning." "Is this true, I'm so happy. Don't worry, everything will be fine." "I know, but you know me, if something bad happen to you." "I'm telling you, nothing bad will happen to me." "I know you're right, I worry a lot." "What was to happen to me happened last weekend and I'll let nothing and nobody changing a thing about it, believe me. I'm gone, good night."

Janene went to her bedroom and I wished Danielle good night my way. Then I went to join Janene who was not ready to go to sleep just yet. So I gave her the oral treatment, which became sort of one of my specialities. She's doing not too bad either. This gave me another erection even stronger than the first one, which allowed me one more penetration, more satisfying for both of us.

Morning came very quick though for the three of us who were around the kitchen table at seven fifteen. Our mother hen had already prepared a bunch of things. Coffey, tea and toasts were already served. It is surely different for me who leave alone for more than eleven years. I sure can appreciate it even though I had no complaints to make about my lifestyle.

We mainly talked about Janene's trip and how she should tell her parent about us. I told them about my conversation with Céline, which went pretty well. From one thing to another it was time for me to go already, but it was not without a bit of sadness. I don't like tears and neither difficult separation. I gave them both a hug and a kiss, saying I'll see them soon. It was hard. Only Janene was smiling and she said with a good reason:

"Hey, you guys, I'm not going to a funeral and I'm not going forever. I'll be back Sunday night, I promise." "Have a good trip Janene. I'll see you when you're back." "Well I hope so, I'll be fine."

"Have a good day Danielle. If you want to, I'll come back tonight, so you're not too lonely." "I would appreciate it, but only if you can." "Of course I can. Thanks to God; I don't have any other women."

This made them laugh a good shot and it was quite good at that moment. Then I slowly went on my way. Danielle took Janene to the station and I went to work. Janene who seemed sure about herself had butterflies in her stomach anyway, but I knew she could take care of the situation. She told us that what ever they say, it wouldn't change a thing about her position regarding our relationship. When the night came she phoned Danielle and she phoned me to say she had a very good trip. She also said that her parents were in a good mood to this point. She said she will keep us informed as things go. At twelve thirty that night, I was back with Danielle.

"You're still sad; you're not reasonable, do you know this?" "I just hope her parents won't be too hard on her. You know, people in the back country don't think the same way we do." "I know, but Janene is a big girl and I'm sure she could handle them." "You must be right and we should go to bed and talk until we fall asleep. I appreciate you to come and be with me, you know?" "Yes I do, but all the pleasure is for me. I love being with you. When do you have a weekend off again?" "At the end of this week, I'll have two days off." "This is great, I never work on Saturday and I have all my weekends off normally. I only work Sundays if it's really necessary." "Are you from seven days Adventist?" "I'm against all religions and I think it is the largest slavery ever invented. Some people kill in the name of their religion and a lot of them believe it's the will of God." "Is it possible they can be this dumb?" "Yes, if this is what they have learned from their spiritual leaders and they are bad enough to do it.

They have killed Jesus for the same reason." "You seem to know what you're talking about." "Are you religious yourself?" "Janene and I are catholic from birth, but we're not practising. I don't know what really happened, but we both stop going to church." "The routine can become boring. I was born catholic too, but just like little puppies, one day my eyes were opened and I never went back. Puppies take about twelve days, it took me eighteen years." "But you believe in God, don't you?" "Me and God are one." "The priest in my dad's village would say you just have blasphemed and my dad too." "It proves only one thing and this is they don't know the word of God. Do you have a Bible?" "Yes, it's there somewhere on the bookshelf." "You should read John 17, 21-23 as soon as tomorrow. It is and it was one of Jesus prier that we become one with God." "Why not doing it now? I am curious and I would like to sleep well." "Alright, but we have to be reasonable, I work early tomorrow."

She got up and she went to get the Bible, Louis the Second, which is my favourite.

"Let me look here, you said John?" "John 17, 21-23." "Let me read this for a minute. But you're absolutely right James." "One of the greatest and possibly the most important message from Jesus is in Matthew 24, 15. 'The reader will understand.' It's a bit more specific in the French Bible. It's said: 'May the reader be careful when he reads.'

This means the traps are in the writing, in the Bible. There is where we have to look and no where else." "But James, the Bible is the book of the truth." "Yes Danielle, but it is the truth about the lies too. I will explain this to you another time, if you want.

This is what I like to do on Saturday, the last day of the week, the Sabbath day, the day of the Lord." "Why not on Sunday?" "Because I don't want to contradict God who said in his law; 'Keep the last day of the week holy.'

Not the first day, but the last day of the week. You can read it in Exodus 20, 8-11. There is a great promise to the one who obeys the law. I don't want to contradict Jesus either, who said that not the least stroke of a pen will disappear from the law for as long as the earth and heavens exist. It's written in Matthew 5, 17-18." "Let me see. But this is all true. Wow! This is something. But, this is not what we were taught. We were taught that on Sundays you will keep serving God." "There you are. What is Sunday?" "The first day of the week." "A four year old child could tell the difference. I made a little song on the subject." "What is it?" "They deceived me; they lied to me on the Sundays morning. They deceived me, they lied to me and I didn't take it one morning. The Lord said the Sabbath day is Saturday, the last day of the week. I wonder for who is the Sunday." "Hay, this is cute." "Thanks Danielle. I'd like to go on for hours, but I need to sleep now. One more thing Danielle if you want?" "Go ahead, I love this stuff." "Are you serious?" "This bore and shock most people." "Not me, I like to discover and I like the truth." "Well, I'm glad it doesn't fall in deaf ears. If you want to next time you talk to your dad ask him if he calls his priest father." "I'm sure he does, but why?" "Because Jesus told his disciples not to do it. Please read Matthew 23, 9, would you?"

"'And call no man your father upon the earth: For one is your Father, which is in heaven.'"

"Wow! My father will surely fall on his bump." "Ask him just to see his reaction." "I will." "I can't wait to see yours." "My what?" "To see your reaction following the reaction of your father. I kind of know what he's going to say." "Ho yea, and what is it?" "I'm not telling you. I'm going to write it down and hide it; then you'll see it after you talked to your dad." "Alright, I'll call him this weekend." "We got to sleep now." "I feel so much better now James, it was really good to speak with you. I'm not sad anymore and my worries went away. I was a bit depressed, you know?" "Yes I know, but the word of God is very powerful. I have a favour to ask you." "What is it? I'll help you if I can." "I would like you to get me an appointment with a psychologist at the hospital." "Do you have a problem we should know about?" "I have a problem you both know about." "I don't understand. What is it?" "I just about always have a premature ejaculation and I want to fix this problem and soon is not soon enough." "I'll do better than this, I will require for you if there is a method or medicine and I'll let you know. What do you say?" "I say this is wonderful. Thank you very much. Good night Danielle." "Good night James, I love you." "I love you too."

After hugs and kisses we fell asleep and we woke up at seven in the morning. After a good breakfast I left her to go to work.

In Gaspé near the village where I was born myself, it was a total different story. Janene was discussing with her parents, especially her mom who cries very easily and can get very hysterical.

"Mom, Danielle and I know each other for more than fifteen years now and were going to get married possibly this year." "You and Danielle are getting married? Tell me that I'm dreaming, this has got to be a nightmare. A lesbian in my family! Danielle dragged you into this? I just know you weren't born like this." "Be careful how you talk about her mom, she's my best friend and she always will be."

The mother, Anne Marry started to cry and her husband Rene asked Janene to go take a little walk outside to give him time to calm down his wife.

"You're not going to cry all day, are you? We only see our daughter once or twice a year and I would like this to be a bit happier." "If she's going to marry another woman, she's not my daughter anymore." "Come on, calm down, would you? You're saying stupidities. Janene will always be our daughter. I trust her, she's very intelligent and I will always love her what ever she does with her life." "What are we going to do? The news will spread all away around here. What a scandal! Everyone will look at us like dirt." "You always exaggerating things; we're not the first ones and we're not going to be the last ones either, believe me. My dad often said: 'Life is high on legs.' Which probably means anything can happen. Janene is coming back, stop crying, would you?" "How could we congratulate her like we're supposed to do?" "We'll do our best."

"Janene, my sweet daughter, did you rally think this over? I want you to know that what ever you do, you'll always be my favourite girl." "I know, I'm the only one you have." "Yes, but I'll always love you." "I know dad, you're an angel, I love you a lot too." "When do you plan to get married?" "Probably in the summer, we didn't choose a date yet."

"Can we ask you not to spread this around here?" "You can, but it is useless, because news have no frontier nowadays. Almost everything is known the same day." "We have to keep this secret Janene, keep a lid on it." "What about you mom, can you keep the secret? I'll bet you'll be the first one to talk about it."

"It won't surprise me either."

"Are we invited?" "Of course you are; we're not this wild. Does this mean you're accepting the situation?" "Do we have any choice?" "Now that you are settled down, I'm going to tell you the whole truth." "You're not going to tell us that you're going to create a club of these girls, are you?" "Don't be ridiculous mom; it's a whole different story." "What are you going to tell us now? I think I heard enough for today."

"Would you keep it quiet for a minute Anne and let her say what she wants to say?" "Danielle and I are getting married alright, but it's not to one another. We are both getting married to a man." "So you're not lesbians then?" "Neither one of us is. It's not because we don't sleep around left and right with all kind of different people and because we love each other that we are necessarily lesbians. I know they catalogued us this way because we are best friends and we live together and we are still single at twenty-five, it's unfair." "But why did you say you were?" "I never said such a thing mom and this was your own conclusion. All I said is we were getting married and it's true, but I never said we were getting married to one another. It is possible though that we're getting married the same day." "It's kind of strange you both found someone to marry at the same time." "Danielle was just an hour ahead of me." "This is very strange! What is the name of yours?" "His name is James Prince. He's a real prince." "Why didn't you bring him over?" "He's very busy with important work." "What is he doing for a living?" "He builds houses."

"This is a good trade and it is good everywhere." "You got it right dad. He's a great man and I am deeply in love with him, otherwise I wouldn't even be here, especially not at this time of the year."

"Danielle also found someone? What is his name?" "This is the whole point mom, he's the same man." "What? You both love the same man?" "Yes mom and Danielle found him. We're both deeply in love with him and neither one of us wants to let him go. No one of us wants the other one to suffer from his absence and this is why we decided to share him like we always shared everything before." "Wow! This is quite some news and it's much more acceptable than a marriage between women. But you girls are going to kill the poor man." "Don't worry mom, we are nurses and we will take care of him. He didn't complain so far, on the contrary." "You guys are going to meet some troubles along the way with the authorities." "We know all about it. It's crazy, isn't it? A man can have fifty girlfriends across the country and have hundreds of kids with them, who will become the state kids for most of them and this without been bothered by the law, but if a man has two wives and a dozen kids that he's taking good care of, he's a criminal." "You got to remember that he could be charged for alimony." "Not necessarily!" "What do you mean?" "I mean the father can't be charged if the mother declares the father unknown on the birth certificate." "He would have to be not too paternal." "Dogs don't care about their pups and they are ready to serve females any time and anywhere. Our man is not like this, he's a good man who will take care of us and he will do anything to make both of us happy."

"Well Janene, we just got to congratulate you and wish you the best and a lot of happiness. If you need anything, don't hesitate to let me know." "We have all we need dad, we only needed understanding from both of you. Thanks dad, mom! Unfortunately I have to leave tomorrow; I'm working on Monday morning. I hope there is no storm in the forecast. It is important that I'm in, otherwise there will be some surgeries postpone and it could cause people's death. Almost all hospitals in Quebec are short of staff, mainly doctors and nurses." "You deserve all the best Janene no matter how you get it." "Make sure your car start in the morning dad, I can't afford to miss the train, you know?" "I know, don't worry sweetheart, you'll be there on time. Sleep well." "Thanks for everything dad."

The first obstacle of our adventure was now behind us, so we had to concentrate on the next one. The three main reasons for divorces in life are money, children and religion. I didn't worry about money, because they had enough for all their needs and both of them had a job security and well paid above all. They were assured also of a good pension at the end of their mandates. I was making a good living myself even though the risk is a lot higher in business. It's not always easy to force someone who doesn't want to pay to do so, although I was not worrying about my financial situation. I wasn't too much worried about family either, but I still needed to know Janene's intentions on this. I also needed to know which were her views on religions. As far as Danielle is concerned everything was settled. I knew there is no more motherly than her and I knew too that she likes my way to see things about religions and the slavery they impose. I was not too worried about Janene either on this subject, because I had an ally with Danielle on my side. I was really happy with Danielle's reaction, because I'm always pleased to tell someone about my Bible discoveries. On Friday night I was back again with Danielle to spend the night. To this day Friday night is always my favourite, because no matter what I do, I always have the next day to recuperate, being the day of rest, the Sabbath day. It is for me a day of rest and I had in mind to continue what I started with Danielle, meaning, instruct her about Jesus' messages. I don't know exactly why, but this makes me particularly happy to do it even if the person I'm talking to is not too receptive.

"Hi you, how are you doing tonight?" "I'm very well James and you?" "Me too Danielle, since I have a day off tomorrow finally. We can make love all night if we want to; we have all day tomorrow to get back on our feet. Do you have any news from Janene?" "Not much, it was bad reception on the phone. She'll be here on Sunday. If you don't mind we'll go take a bath and then go to bed, I got a surprise for you." "Now you got me curious, what is it?" "Well you'll see." "Ho, come on shoot; don't be cruel by keeping me on a hook." "You got to wait James, its something I have to show you." "And you can't tell me what it is?" "You know that patient is a virtue." "I'm not too sure to be very virtuous, you know?" "I won't tell you anyway, I'll show you later." "Let's hurry then." "James, we have all night for ourselves." "You're right, I'm sorry, but I'm still curious." "I'm pretty sure you're going to like it." "Let me soap you all over, would you?" "I was wondering what you were waiting for." "I was kind of distracted by an intriguing woman who likes suspense. You like this?" "I love it." "Good, because it's a job I like to do." "Ho, this is a job now." "I hope I'm doing it right?" "You too good, I'm about to come." "Let yourself go, we have all night. Hooooooooooooooooo, too late, you got me."

She held me real tight for a long time and I understood that she appreciated it.

"Let's dry ourselves and go to bed, Ok?" "Hold me tight, my legs are weak." "Don't worry; I can carry you if you want?" "I don't think it will be necessary, although it could be fun."

"And up we go. We're going to bed pretty princess with your prince." "Yes M. Prince! Wow, you're not very big, but strong like Hercules." "You're as light as a feather." "One hundred and twenty pounds, a feather?" "Well, maybe two!" "Ha, ha, ha, very funny." "Lift up the blankets, would you?" "Here we are." "Down we go, let me taste this thing now." "No James, it's my turn to give you pleasure. Lie on your back and let me do it, alright?" "Mmmmm, I'm welling to, but I'm not used to it." "You'll get used to it, believe me." "I don't mind trying. Mmmmmm, mmmmm, it's good, so good. Watchhhhhhh. What did you do? Everything suddenly blocked." "It works. Let me do it again if you like it." "If I like it? But it's superbly good." "Now you taste a bit salty, a little bit like oysters." "I hope you like them, because it's so gooddddd. Watchhhhhhhh! Everything blocked again." "It works well." "But what are you doing?" "I just follow the psychologist's instructions and it works." "It's a nice job." "It's a real pleasure." "All the pleasure is for me." "You're wrong; I got really excited doing this." "So, this is the surprise you had for me?" "That's it." "Now I know why you didn't want to tell me." "Do you want some more?" "As much as you want to give me sweetheart. Mmmmm! Mmmmm, it's so good. Mmmmm! Watch! Mmmmm! Watch! Your trick is good; I managed to hold back twice." "Now I'm all excited." "Ho yea, I'll fix this for you pretty princess, you'll see."

I managed to make love to her for at least thirty minutes and I could hold back the ejaculation as I wanted to, which I could never do before. She counted four orgasms and I stopped only because she wanted to. It's was only then I let myself go. I never experienced such a pleasure in my whole life. The pleasure to give pleasure to the one you love is tremendous. I cannot say any better, it's tremendous.

"I never though it could be this good James." "Me neither!" "Wait till Janene hear about this." "Please, don't tell her anything; we'll get her the surprise." "She won't believe her own ass." "You're quite funny too, when you want to. Tell me, what did the psychologist tell you?" "She said; 'you could do it yourselves or you could do it with your partner. The guy can masturbate himself or she can masturbate him and when he's ready to ejaculate you strangle the penis right under the head, this will block the flow and after a few good practices the guy learns to do it automatically.' I can tell that you learn quickly, because you succeeded on the first time." "Ho, I'm sure we're going to need a few more good practices just to make it perfect." "You enjoyed this, didn't you?" "I just loved it." "I wonder why so many women don't want to hear about oral sex, it did excite me so much, I was ready to come even before you touch me." "We're going to have to find a way for you to hold back too." "Very funny!" "Apparently half of men love it a lot like I do and the other half simply hates it. I wonder if it's because they don't really like women or if it's because half of the women are not eatable." "What do you mean by this? Not eatable!" "Well, I mean girls don't all taste good; some women are sweet like you and Janene and others are rather sour. For me, if you were sour even though I love you very much I know I couldn't. I would just bring up. It would be real sad, but I wouldn't be able to. It could make two people very sad." "So, Janene and I are very lucky?" "I think the three of us are very lucky. Well, all this is appetizing. Aren't you hungry?" "Do you want to eat me?" "A little bit later if you don't mind, right now I'd like a few toasts and a cup of tea." "I just hope I'll have the strength to get up." "I can help you if you like or I can carry you one more time?" "It's alright; I'll be fine, thank you." "It's already pass four, we'll have to sleep a bit." "I thought I heard you say that we have all night?" "You can talk; you can hardly get up to make a few toasts." "I really feel weak and I didn't even have a drink." "And look how young you are." "Don't forget, it's only my second time." "Ho right, I forgot, excuse me?"

We took a little snack and then we both went back to bed and we woke up to the sound of the phone at one in the afternoon. Danielle answered it to hear the sweet voice of Janene.

"Hello, Danielle here." "It's me, how are you?" "I'm very well."

"James, it's Janene." "Let me talk to her, would you?" "Here!"

"How things on your side?" "There is still a lot of snow as usual to the height of the roof." "It was not the best time of the year to go in this part of the country, this is for sure." "It takes what it takes. The storm is out of the house too. I got to tell you that I understood your parable just in time." "I'm glad, because this means you will understand all the others too." "What this means? Is this another parable?" "No, but Danielle will talk to you about it when you're back. It's nothing really, don't worry. Alright, I'll let you talk to Danielle now. See you soon, I love you." "Me too."

"Hello! Danielle, I will arrive at the station at four tomorrow." "I will come to get you, but don't forget your cell phone."

"I will come too Danielle."

"James will come with me Janene." "This is wonderful. Alright then, I'll see you tomorrow." "See you, I can't wait."

"While I'm on the phone, I'll call my parents." "That's good; I got to go to the washroom anyway."

"Ring ring, ring ring. "Hello!" "Is this you dad?" "Danielle, my sweetheart, it's been a long time since we heard from you. How are you?"

"Joanne, it's Danielle, pick up the other phone."

"I am marvellously good daddy. I met a very fine young man and I'm just crazy about him." "Wow, for a news, this a big one coming from you. Usually you're not so quick when it comes to men." "This is because this one is rather special." "What is he doing for a living?" "He's a houses builder, a contractor." "It's a good trade and it's good everywhere." "But dad, I called you for an all different and a particular reason." "Ho yea! What is it?" "Do you still have your Bible?" "Ho my God, it's been a long time since I took it. I leave father st Germain read it to us every Sunday." "You've already answered one of my questions." "Give me a minute or two and I'll go get it."

"Hi mom! How are you?" "I'm fine Danielle, but I have to tell you to take your time with your new boyfriend. Some times it takes a long time to get to know a person, you know?" "Not this one mom! This one you know him when you meet him."

"I'm here Danielle with the Bible in my hands. What do you want to know?" "Do you want to open it at Matthew 23, verse 9?" "Give me a second there. Sweetie, we cannot talk about those things." "Why not dad? Should we destroy the truth or simply hide it?" "You, you've been talking with a Jehovah witness, haven't you?" "Not at all dad, but I talked to someone who seems to know about the truth. Do you have a piece of paper and a pen? It will be good for you to take a few notes." "Yes, I got this right here near by." "Go read Exodus 20, it's the law of God and take a special look at the verses 8-11 and then go read Matthew 5, verses 17 and 18. Be really careful when you read this, would you?" "You know we were worn that we could go crazy by reading the Bible, don't you?" "Was this said by a psychiatrist or by a priest?" "It was a priest of course. But you have to be careful to whom you talk to sweetie. There are trouble makers out there. All this can drive a person crazy, you know?" "Well, it's true it is disturbing to find out we've been lied to for years, especially by those who condemned us to hell for lying. If leaving the religion because I was lied to is crazy, so be it, I'm crazy too. Jesus told us that it was better to lose one hand than to burn completely in hell; maybe it's better to lose my mind too. Do you believe in Jesus Christ Dad?" "Of course I believe in him." "Do you believe more in your religion than in Jesus?" "The church is infallible Danielle." "I believe the church has infallibly lied to people and the proof is right there in the Bible. I'm sorry, but I will take the word of Jesus and the word of God before the word of any other one. If you believe in Jesus go read Matthew 24, 15 where it said; "May the reader be careful when he reads.

'Seek and you shall find.' Jesus said in Matthew 7, 7 and because I love you so very much I want you to look for and to find the truth the church has hidden from us." "But you've become a real priestess Danielle." "Don't insult me dad, I love the truth." "Well, I didn't want to insult you sweetheart, I just think you are a good preacher, that's all." "I'm going to let you go now. It's not to cold up there in the North?" "We had worst believe me. Take good care of yourself sweetie." "You too, I love you both. Bye!" "Bye sweetie!"

"Did you fall asleep in there James?" "No, I was just resting while waiting for you." "It's true, it's the Sabbath day." "You should come and join me; it's nice in the water." "Do you think it's wrong for us to sleep together?" "Well, it depends." "It depends on what?" "If you sleep with me because you love me and you want to be my wife, then you have not sinned. You simply became my wife. Go read how Rebekah became Isaac's wife in Genesis 24, 67." "I'll do it as soon as we get out of the tub." "It's the same way Joseph, father of Jesus took Mary for his wife." "What do you think about priests, friars and nuns who don't get married?" "I think that if they don't get married to please God, they have made an enormous mistake." "Really?" "After God created man, He created a woman, saying it was not good for a man to be alone. This is still true today. He told them to be fruitful, to multiply and to fill up the earth. I don't think God is for abortion and neither for celibate. It takes a man and a woman to multiply. God made us to his image, meaning creators. This is the reason why he made sex so enjoyable. Some priests condemned my mother to hell for avoiding pregnancy after having thirteen kids and all of them avoid multiplying by not getting married. For her last baby it was almost suicide or attempt murder and mom was even pronounced dead at her delivery, but God by miracle brought her back to life. The baby only lived twenty-three hours. My mom's mother died with twins baby girls in her belly, because her priest told her she has to do her duty. A nurse kept her warm until the doctor arrived to give her a cesarean. One baby girl lived a whole fifteen minutes and the other girls lived a whole twenty minutes. Her doctor told her before she couldn't have anymore children, because of the asthma she was plagued with. My dad's mother died of similar reasons. The results were that my parents have hardly known their mothers and I never had the chance to know my two grandmothers. Today doctors decide without consulting priests or pastors, which is slowing down the killing of so many women and children. Now when you read John 8, 44, it is written: 'He is a murderer from the beginning, he is a liar and the father of lies.'

Does this remind you of anybody?" "The church, the religions!" "Let me tell you that you're on your way to become a great disciple. Maybe we should get out of the tub now, the water is getting cold." "How do you do it? I could listen to you for hours." "This is only because you love the word of God too." "But you know all those verses by heart." "I love the word of God too." "But, how come you know all these things? How come you know so much?" "It's simple Danielle, I follow Jesus of Nazareth, the one who was crucified and I follow the God of Israel, the One who created everything. Now if you translate this in French you will read; I am Jesus of Nazareth and I am the God of Israel. I mean in French I am and I follow translate the same way (Je suis)." "But you don't mean to say that you are God." "I would never say such a thing, although according to what Jesus said and what Christianity teaches I am God's brother." "You are God's brother? Ho, come on now James, this is beyond understanding. You don't think it is a bit pretentious?" "Not at all sweetie, it is only the truth according to the Bible." "I never heard such a thing." "You've never heard the church is teaching that Jesus is God made man?" "This I heard, yes." "Now if Jesus is God and the same Jesus surely didn't lie when he said that the one who does the will of his Father in heaven, this one is his brother, his sister or his mother. You can read it in Matthew 12, 50." "Let me see this. But you are absolutely right. If Jesus is God and the one who does the will of his Father, what you're doing, is his brother; then you are God's brother." "Exactly!" "People will say you are crazy to say such a thing even though it's true."

"I can also tell you that I heal people and I resurrect them too." "This must be another one of your traps?" "There is no trap like you said and always remember one thing, I love the truth." "But I cannot follow you dear." "This will come. Go read Ezekiel 18 completely and you will find out two very important things. First we are not accountable for the sins of our parents and neither of our first parents (Adam and Eve, the original sin) like the Christian church made us responsible for and we are not responsible for the sins of our children either. Jesus healed the sinners by teaching them the word of God and he resurrected them by leading them to God and away from sin and from religion. This is what he did then and he continues to do today. This is what I'm trying to do too. The medicine is the Word of God. This is also what I'm doing with you." "It's true that I have a lot to learn and I don't know much about God, but because of you, all this is changing now." "We're having a good start. It's five, are you making supper?" "I don't work on the Sabbath day anymore if I can do otherwise and I don't really feel like cooking." "The Sabbath will be over in one hour, but if you like I can take you to your favourite restaurant." "Ho, this would be so sweet." "Let's go and later on we can maybe go dancing for a bit." "This would be sweeter yet." "Let's get dressed and get some fresh air."

So we went out for supper and we talked about all kind of things. After supper we walked until the time of the dance arrived. We danced and we danced until we were out of breath. That day was for Danielle and me another one of a long journey of complete happiness. A couple of weeks later her father called and mentioned that he began to have doubts about the religion and the teaching of his church. The good seed was planted.

The next day Janene came back from her trip very happy to get back with us. Danielle who loves the word of God as much as I do didn't waste any time to start teaching Janene. Janene understood very quickly what I meant when I mentioned another parable. There is something else she understood very quickly too.

"You must have met with the psychologist, because since I came back from my parents you make me come like never before?" "I didn't, but I learn to listen to her anyway." "How did you get the information?" "Danielle got it for me and she gave it to me in a very special way. The important thing is it works."

We live very happy every day for many months and one day Danielle noticed a change in her hormonal system.

"James, I need to talk to you about something very important." "Alright, what is the problem my love?" "I don't want you to feel obligated in any way, shape or form, but you're going to be a father in seven months. Well, this is a wonderful news sweetie. Did you tell Janene too?" "Not yet, you're the first one to know it beside my gynaecologist." "How could you ever hide this from your very best friend?" "I just found out about it myself. I think it's also time to talk about having a house built, because I don't want to raise our kids in a small apartment. I want him to have a place to run and to play." "You're absolutely right, but this conversation concerns Janene too, you know?" "Of course it is, but I wanted to know your reaction first." "Danielle, my love, I'm ready for this day since the first time I laid my eyes on you. You must have noticed that I never took any protection to go with you." "I thought you just relied on me to avoid pregnancy." "I mainly relied on you to decide when you want to start a family. I've been ready since the beginning." "I love you so much and I always knew you were the man I needed." "You mean that you both needed." "This is what I was saying." "When can we continue this conversation between the three of us?" "Next week we both work day time; we'll have all the evenings to discuss everything." "This is wonderful. Then tell me, did you do it on purpose?" "What do you mean?" "To get pregnant; did you do it on purpose?" "Let just say I was ready for it and I wasn't careful anymore." "I was under the impression you were looking for me a little more often lately. This is going to bring some major changes in our lives; you're realizing this, don't you?"

"You said you're ready and I have been too for quite a while so, there is no problem." "There is one anyway." "What is it?" "I don't want the baby to be an illegitimate child, a state child, we got to get married." "I just don't want you to feel obligated, you know?" "I don't feel obligated at all, but you see, all of my parents' children were called and treated like bastards in the village where we grew up and I don't

50

want this to happen to my children." "Why? Weren't they married?" "They were married alright, but it was just like they weren't." "I really don't understand." "Well, the priest of the village as usual called for my parents' birth certificates from where they were from and from where they were baptized and all that, but when he received them, it was not mentioned they were married. The stupid man didn't bother talking to my parents about it either. My parent's witnesses were still alive fortunately, but for us kids, the wrong was done." "What happened to you?" "We were jeered for almost our entire school time." "This is terrible and so unfair." "What can you do, the church is infallible." "Poor you, you kids had an unhappy childhood." "Yes, but I'm happy about it now." "How can you be happy now for having been unhappy when you were young?" "Because, this lead me to look for and to find the truth I know today and I can share it with you and with all the people I meet. Believe me, there is no greater feeling. I am free like the wind, free from any slavery. Even if you were the only one who listens to me, it would be worth it." "You're an incredible good soul person my man, you know?" "If you say it I want to believe it." "What else can you tell me today about the lies and contradictions you found." "There are big and obvious ones. Take 3 John 16 for example. It is written that: 'God so loved the world.'

Well, God so loved the world that He asked his people to retrieve from it, that the world is the way of perdition. It is written that He sacrificed his one and only son, which would mean that Jesus is his first born. Now we can read in Luke 3, 38 that Adam who was born four thousands years earlier was also the son of God and would also be his first born. Now it is written that Jesus is God's only Son when it is also written that Adam is the son of God. Somebody somewhere lied. It is written in Genesis 6, 2. 'The sons of God saw that the daughters of men were pretty and they took them for wives among the ones they chose.'

Now, this means the angels were also sons of God and they obviously like sex too. Now if you go to Deuteronomy 32, 19 and read; 'The Lord Almighty was angered with his sons and daughters.'

51

God has many sons and many daughters.

I am his son too.

What is surprising me truly and the most Danielle is the fact I never heard anybody talked about this before. Think about all the teachers, the searchers, the pastors, the scholars, the preachers, the priests, the bishops and the infallible popes and more who are and were on earth.

The Bible is the most sold book in the world, for what I heard. Is it possible so many billions people were blinded this much?" "Maybe it's because the time wasn't yet come or worst yet and this scares me a bit, maybe everyone who talked about it was killed like Jesus." "You got a point there. It's not at all impossible, because Jesus predicted this. Now, remember I read the sons of God, the angels took the women on earth." "Yes, why?" "Well, God was so mad about this that He almost destroyed the whole earth with the flood and almost all the people who were on it because of their actions." "Yes, but this seems to me quite fair." "Who do you think the sons of God were then?" "I would think they were bad angels." "This is what I think too. But I still don't see where the problem is." "You see, God condemned and almost destroyed the world and its people because of the bad angels who slept with women and bare children to them and He would have done the same thing with Mary, the mother of Jesus?" "This means we were lied to about the conception, the birth and the death of Jesus." "It is an absolute abomination in a holy place, in the Bible, which Jesus talked about in Matthew 24, 15.

The end is near by, believe me. Jesus to be the Messiah has to be fathered by one of King David descendants and not by a Holy Spirit that was not yet in the world according to many verses in the Bible. See the Acts 2, 2-13 and John 15, 26.

My God, James, this means we are at the end of ages." "This is why we have to make disciples of all nations and teach them everything Jesus has commanded. Look in Matthew 28, 19-20." "This is a lot of dough."

"Yes and I hope to be able to multiply the bread like Jesus did." "You have already started James." "I'm going to start a chain letter coming from a Jesus' disciple and send it around the world to wake up a few people who will read it, hoping they too will multiply the bread of life." "Well, this is enough for me today." "One more question if you allow me." "What do you have in mind?" "The baby and the baptism!" "You're asking me what I think of it?" "Yes! Jesus was circumcised at eight days old and he was baptized when he was thirty years old. I think we have to believe in God and know about Him before we can get baptized. There are a lot of babies who were baptized and turned out to be real devils. Jesus said the children already belong to the kingdom of heaven and nobody can answer for others. John the Baptist said he baptized with water, but Jesus who is more powerful will baptize with fire and with the Holy Ghost, but both of them did it to bring people to repentance. You can see this in Matthew 3, 11 and Matthew 4, 17.

So we agree the baby will be baptized if and when he decides for himself. Right now you are being baptized with the Holy Ghost, the word of God." "This is a lot of stuff." "You do well to stop me when you have enough. You know that I'm in it for the rest of my life. Good night my sweetheart." "Good night my man."

A few days later we had this famous discussion about the new life that was ahead of us. Even though the child was very welcome he was going to change a lot of things in our lives and habits.

"We're going to need a big house." "Yes Janene and I think we should build it in the country to avoid gossips and tittle-tattles of the town. It's going to be a lot of talks as soon as somebody sees me kissing one and the other of the two of you."

"Janene and I don't give a shit about what will people say." "You will change your mind when they attack the children." "I didn't think about this aspect." "What do you suggest?" "I think we should be looking for a big acreage or even better a nice farm around here not to far from town. To tell you the truth, I would like to raise a few animals beside the children of course." "We didn't know this side of you." "Well Danielle, you should know by now that I am full of surprises. I hope it's not too disappointing." "Not at all, in fact, I think you have some very good ideas."

"What do you think Janene?" "I think we have a man who amazes me more and more every day." "Me too! So what are we doing?"

"We look for a little farm even if there is nothing on it." "I agree." "We could build one or two or even three houses according to our taste and finances." "We could also build a duplex where everyone could have is own quarters. You could travel from one flat to the other instead of one room to the other."

"Can I make another suggestion?" "Of course you can, you are the corner stone of our life." "I suggest we build a triplex where each one of you would have her flat attached to mine situated in the middle of the two of you. One would be on the right and the other one on the left. It will be a picture of the three of us." "What a marvellous idea!"

"Myself, I want three large bedrooms, a large bathroom and another one medium size, a large livingroom, a large kitchen and a large dining room." "This will be good for me too."

"I can build the size you want. This is going to be a castle. We can only afford it if we build in the country." "You're right, I vote for this."

"Me too!" "Then we all agree. It's going to be expansive." "Do you have any idea?" "It's going to be between four and five hundreds thousands dollars if I build it." "Our condo is almost paid for and it's worth a bit better than two hundreds thousands and we both have a little more than one hundred thousand each at the bank." "My house is all paid for and I presently have an offer of one hundred and eighty thousands, besides, the guy is getting impatient. So, this means the money is not an issue." "How much time do you need to complete the work?" "From five to six months, but I have to finish all the contracts in course first." "How long will this take?" "I'm pretty sure it will take between thirty and forty-five days. This is if I postpone one house, which is not too much in a hurry." "This means our house could be ready for the coming of our first born." "Chances are pretty good." "Ho, this would be so great." "Don't choke me Danielle, like you said; it is a lot of dough. Multiply darling, multiply, we need it." "In the mean time we have a marriage to attempt. Would you have time to take care of the marriage preparations Danielle?" "Yes, Janene will help me and I don't see any problem for now."

"Talking about multiplications, I'm getting old and you can't put me on hold, because I want four children at the very least." "Are you sure three bedrooms will be enough Janene?" "We'll set two girls in one room, two boys in another; papa and mama in the third one, it should be ok. We could always finish the basement later." "Then everything is fine. With the two of you and all my work, I'll be very busy. Can you also keep an eye on properties for sale? Maybe we should put an ad in the papers specifying what we're looking for. If we buy a farm that nobody wants, it should be cheap. All is really matters for us is that it is not too far from town, from your work. This reminds me that I have a hard day work tomorrow, I should go to bed. It's your turn tonight Janene, don't wait too long if you want your candy." "If I miss you tonight, I'll catch you in the morning." "As you wish then! Come on; give me a hug now before I disappear in the dreams of the night."

I thought they needed to talk between themselves and I didn't want to be in their way for this. Besides, a night without sex was almost welcome for me. At this stage of our lives our families had so, so accepted our living situation. One thing was still bothering me though and this was the question of polygamy. I knew for sure they both wanted to marry me. We had to find a solution to this problem and this was coming pretty urgent. So, I got on the internet searching for some answers. On the Mormon side I found a lot of answers on Christianity and gospels, but nothing at all on marriages as if this was taboo. I think I will have to go meet one of their ministers in person to get some answers from this side. The unique thought of being obligated to be part of a religion, no matter which one, makes me sick to my stomach. There is one thing Jesus said and I cannot forget in

Matthew 6, 24. 'No man can serve two masters; for either he will hate the one and love the other; or else he will hold to the one, and despise the other. You cannot serve God and Mammon.'

So, this means I cannot serve a religion, a church and serve God. I choose to serve God, so, no religion for us.

I'll have to find a different way. As far as I am concern, deep inside of me, I am already married to each one of them as much as Solomon was married to his seven hundreds wives or King David who walk according to the heart of God.

"So, you're going to get married before me." "James is insisting we get married before the baby is born." "It would be wonderful if we could get married the same day." "I don't think there will be an easy way though. No matter what happens Janene, you will never be left aside or behind. I don't think it is a question of heart for James, but rather a question of legality. He loves you just as much as he loves me if not more." "Poor guy, it must not be too easy for him all the time. I trust him; he seems to always find a way to do things. Did you think about how many kids you want?" "Not really, I just want to take this one at the time." "It's wonderful the way he plans to install us in a sort of a castle away from mean people and evil eyes and ears." "I also think it's going to be wonderful to live on a small farm which we own. It's going to be just wonderful for the kids too and they'll have everything to be happy. Are you serious when you say you want four children?" "I can't be more serious than this." "Between the two of us we could have a dozen kids. It takes the two of us to equal his mother." "Can you imagine thirteen kids, the same woman?" "No! This is not for me. Doesn't it scare you a bit too all the knowledge he's got on the Bible?" "A little bit, I have to admit, knowing that not this long ago people like him were accused of witchcraft and were burnt alive." "Luckily it's not like this anymore." "I'm not so sure about this." "Stop right there, you're scaring me." "There are murders in the world we'll never know how it happened and neither why. Louis Riel is one of them and all we know is how he died, but why, it is still a question mark in the mind of a lot of people. They sure got rid of him. He must have known something they didn't want him to talk about. His wife became a very young widow and his kids were young orphans." "How did he die and why?" "They accused him of treason, but James things he too had a lot of knowledge about the truth and he made the mistake to talk with his friend, a bishop about it. James things he might have been a trader to his religion when he found the truth, but not a trader to the country as he was accused of. The judge asked him if he had a last wish before the sentence and he said: 'My wish your honour would be to separate from Rome for it is the cause of divisions in the world.'

The six juries were Christians and so was the judge. This was enough to declare him guilty. This was the end of the poor man. He was hanged and the truth was choked with him for another hundred years or so." "But this means James' life only hold by one tread." "Don't be scared, everyone's life is hold by one tread, yours and mine too, but at least his life is worth living." "He has a physical and spiritual strength, which is out of the ordinary and he will know how to spread the truth safely. He did it so far." "This is true and because of him we are not as ignorant as we used to be. What ever it is, we should go to bed now." "It is not two o'clock, is it?" "Yes dear, it is very late." "We only have five hours left to sleep. We should set up two alarm clocks. Good night!" "Good night, sleep well."

"Janene, Janene, it's time to get up, you're working this morning." "Whatttttttttt? I want to sleep." "It's almost seven; you got to go to work. You stayed up late, didn't you? I got to go now, have a good day." "Byeeeeeeeeeeee!"

"Danielle, I got to go and leave you handle Janene, she's got a hard time to get up. Have a good day." "You too my love."

CHAPTER 3

I went directly home and I phoned the foreman to delegate enough work for the day. Then I took my breakfast and after I sat at my drawing table to put on paper what I had in mind. It was not too easy to concentrate on this important work, because the phone wouldn't stop ringing. Three of them were potential customers who insisted my company build their house. The only problem was the timing, because I was not available before August, unless I hire more staff. Staff you cannot keep an eye on constantly could be very dangerous. I already lost a lot of money with subcontractors who didn't really care about the job well done or not. Those are life's lessons you don't want to forget too easily. It's better to make a little less money than to lose some. Do, undo and redo are expensive matters. After all it's better to do later what you cannot do now. Who has ears to hear can hear! Despite everything happened at the end of the day I had quite a bit done. Only a few details were missing to complete the plan. Of course I had still a lot to discuss with my two adorable women, but I was sure it would only be insignificant details like the colour of the walls and the cupboards. I was done with all the calculations as far as what this famous house will cost, but I decided not to talk about it until I have everything on hand. I learned the hard way that it was best not to talk to your customers about prices until you can show them what they are getting for their money. Ho sure, my customers this time were my own wives, but nevertheless, it was their money which was involve in this project too. They both wanted something big and I think they're going to have something grandiose. The size of this house will be 5472 square feet, beside the garage underneath and the two basements. I built a seven suites building once that was smaller than this house. What ever my ladies want, I want it too. We still had to find a piece of land to build it on. At five to five the phone rang again, but this time it was the wonderful voice of the mom to be.

"Is this you James?" "Is this me you want to talk to my angel?" "Nobody else! Supper is ready and the table is set, we are waiting for you and you cannot refuse." "I need a bit of time to wash and shave and I'll be right there." "Don't take too long, it's good when it's hot." "I'll be there within a half hour." "See you soon, I love you." "I love you too."

I rush to the bathroom, because I didn't want to let these two wonderful women in waiting for they don't have this many occasions to reunite all three of us this often for supper and talk. They often have to take turns at nights and evenings at the hospital. Thirty five minutes later I sat down with them at their table.

I had anticipated an evening of discussions about the house and maybe where we could build it and all that, but it was completely different. I couldn't believe it when I heard:

"Happy birthday to you, happy birthday to you, happy birthday dear James, happy birthday to you."

There were about twenty guesses hiding in the bedrooms. They came out at the moment the desert was served. My mother and a few of my sisters were some of the guesses who answered the invitation. Danielle's parents, some of their friends and some co-workers were also invited to the party. I'm not too crazy about this kind of surprise parties, but nevertheless, this one was important for what was coming down the road. I was very happy to finally meet Danielle's parents. They sure had a lot to say about the catholic religion and they had a lot of questions about the lies in contradictions, which could be found in the Holy Bible. They were asking endless questions and I had to be almost rude to get away from them and to introduce them both to my mother. I wanted to get near Danielle who herself had a bit of a problem to get away from the young doctor. Janene seemed to have a good time with my sisters who wanted to know how she was coping in our three ways relationship. I was really concerned about the young doctor strange behaviour. He was the type of men who likes to blame and to lecture others. So I invited Danielle to follow me to a bedroom for a few minutes.

"Danielle, is there a problem with your doctor friend?" "He never acted like this before." "Do you know what his problem is?" "I'm under the impression he knows about Janene and I with you." "But even if he knew it all, this is none of his business at all. Are you sure there is nothing else?" "I think he is a bit jealous of you and he would like to be in your shoes." "My shoes are way too small for him, but this is not the question, he seemed to be pestering you for the last half hour." "He is in a position to cause me a lot of troubles at work." "You're not going to give to blackmailing, are you?" "It is not my intention, but anyway, I love my work." "I don't think you should jeopardize your happiness for your work." "Don't worry, I love you and you'll always be my priority." "I knew it, but it's always nice to hear it. Do you want me to talk to him?" "No, I will just tell him what I just told you and if he doesn't get it, then you'll talk to him yourself. Are you alright with this?" "It is as you wish sweetie, but as far as I am concerned, he's not welcome to my party. I'll be happier if you ask him to leave." "I'll do it and forgive me for inviting him." "It's not your fault if he is an idiot. We should go before they all wonder if we are making love." "Frankly, it wouldn't be this bad of an idea."

We got out of the room to everyone's wondering eyes, but the doctor had already excused himself and left. I think he sensed the hot water and guessed what was going on. I just knew then this was a story to be followed. I knew too I'll have to clear things up with my two lovers. The party had started early and had to be over early, because almost everyone was working the next day. At ten all the guesses were gone and we had to pick up all the glasses and dishes which went to the dishwasher. All the empty bottles and cans went in the boxes, which I'll have to take to a bottles depot.

"No point asking you darling if you liked your party or not." "It was a surprise party with a few surprises, but my birthday is only next week." "We have something else organized for next week and this is why we chose tonight where we could bring in a few people." "I thought your parents were very nice, interesting and interested." "They love the truth just like me and this makes me very happy."

"I wish I could say the same thing about mine." "Maybe this will come some day Janene, but one has to love God and his word more than himself and mainly more than his religion."

"Tell me Danielle, what the heck happened with Raymond?" "I kind of understood that he wanted to make me understand something about you Janene, as if he wanted to cause trouble between us." "I know what his problem is." "Tell us, what is it?" "Last year he was after me and I think he is after you now. He thinks James is cheating on you with me. I made him understand I wasn't interested in him at all and I think you should do the same thing if you're not interested in him." "Me, be interested in him? I rather die. Neither him or anybody else, I have the man I want."

"Tell me Danielle, why did you invite him exactly?" "Well, he was quite gentle and he basically invited himself. I know he doesn't have this many friends and I gave up. I'm going to put him in his place as soon as tomorrow." "Good, this is enough talking about him, what would you say if we go to bed now? Who's turn?"

"It's still mine, but Danielle needs you more than I do tonight. She's sad and she needs to be taking care of. I had a very good time with your sisters James. They were very curious to know how you could satisfy both of us and they found it very strange there was no jealousy between Danielle and me. I think I convinced them, at least this is the impression I got." "You're wonderful. I love you and good night."

"Good night Danielle and take advantage of it." "I will put all my heart to it as you would yourself. Thanks!" "You're welcome, but not too often."

"Don't worry Janene you will lose nothing by waiting." "Sleep well on Thursday, because I'll keep you up all night on Friday." "It's promising."

After a bit of cleaning up, we all went to bed. I watched Janene pull away from us with a bit of nostalgia, I have to admit, but I also knew I was not losing anything by getting between Danielle's legs.

"You're not too mad at me?" "Neither one of us have anything to blame you for my love and who knows, the future will tell, it might be one of the best things you've ever done. I mean, inviting him. I don't understand, but if you say so, it's got to be true." "Now, enough talking about all this, keep quiet and let me love you my way, alright? And try not to scream too loud, Janene needs her sleep." "When I scream it's because it's so good I think I'm going to die." "I want to make love to you so much; I want you to be touch. I'm telling you with no lie; make love to you till you die. I put these words in a song one day." "I'd like you to sing it to me sometimes." "Not now, right now I'm hungry." "Help yourself, the meal is ready." "Hum, the fruit is juicy and delicious."

I made love to her until the middle of the night hoping the walls of this building had not too many ears and that Janene had earplugs. Both Danielle and I had a hard time getting up that morning. It's not easy for me to stay in good mood all day in those days, but when I seemed to lose patient, I only have to think at what kept me awake and everything is alright again.

Danielle didn't waste any time confronting Raymond, the young doctor, who is almost always on the same shift than her at work.

"When you'll have a minute Raymond, I need to talk to you." "I have time now; let's go to the conferences room. You look gorgeous this morning, what did you have for breakfast?" "The same thing as usual, but I made love almost all night with James and I'm pregnant with him, this might be the reason I look like blooming. Can you tell me what your problem was last night? Do you realize you spoiled our evening? I didn't appreciate it at all." "I'm sorry, but it wasn't my intention at all." "Tell me what your intention was exactly?" "Are you sure your James is completely honest with you?" "There is no man on earth who is as honest as he is. I don't mean to hurt you, but let me tell you one thing; you can't hold a candle to him." "This is yet to be proven." "For you maybe, but to me it's all settled." "I think he's cheating on you with Janene. One thing is sure, Janene is crazy about him and it's obvious to everyone." "Who could blame her? He is a wonderful man and handsome above all." "It doesn't bother you he could be cheating on you with your best friend?" "Janene is the most faithful friend I could get. She's a friend whom one could say; always and forever." "If it's the way you see things, I have nothing more to say." "I sure hope you won't say anymore on this matter, do you understand me?" "This is clear enough, thank you." "This is all I had to say, good day."

She went out of the room leaving him thinking behind her, but yet she wasn't completely convinced this was enough for him to get rid of his obsession.

On my side after checking on my jobs and seeing the work was going on normally, I went back to my drawing table to work on my dream house, which got me more and more excited. I was also dying to let my girls know about it.

Only one thing worried me a little, the cost was going to be higher than I previously estimated. They both saw big and I designed big. The total link of this house will be one hundred and fifty-two feet long. Such a house in the city would cost at least twenty thousands dollars a year in taxes alone. At three thirty in the afternoon I called at the condo to let them know I will be having supper with my mom and that I will come to see them at around nine in the evening. Mom still thinks we're wrong to live like we do.

"Are you conscious that you're going to have the whole society against you?" "This is not true mom; there are communities in Canada where men have more than one wife and many children." "It is still not accepted very well." "All it matters to me is that I'm in good terms with God." "God gave Adam only one woman and she was named Eve." "Well, God couldn't have been boning Adam completely just after making him to give him more wives. I'm sure it was painful enough as it was. Some day we'll know how many wives Adam and Jesus had." "Jesus didn't have a wife." "I'm not so sure about that." "What make you say such a thing?" "First in John 3, 2 a Pharisee, man of the Law came to Jesus and called him Rabbi. I just happen to know that to be a Rabbi a man had to be thirty years old, have ten followers and to be married." "This is beyond me." "You also know there were many women who followed and served Jesus. Did he really need this many women to serve him, he who didn't even have a home, a place to rest his head? Besides, they discovered Jesus' tomb lately and the name of Mary Magdalene is inscribed on it. For this to happen she had to be either his sister or his wife." "This is only a supposition for now." "Maybe so, the truth will come out sooner or later. Jesus said it himself. Take a look at Matthew 10, 26. 'There is nothing concealed that will not be disclosed, or hidden that will not be made known.'

There is another very important thing I have to tell you mom and this is Jesus had at heart to do the will of God, the Father Who is in heaven. One of the first will of God for men is to be fruitful, to multiply and to fill up the earth." "It was also said that each man should have his wife." "This is yet better than to say: 'If you don't marry you do better.' Or yet to say like Paul did: 'I wish that all men were like me.' No wife and no children! We'll have to talk about all this another time mom, I told the girls I would be there by nine and this doesn't leave me much time to get there."

What surprises me the most in the conversations with almost everybody, including my mom, it's the fact they have swallowed the lies with mouth full, they have digested them with no problem and I have to give them the truth in very small amount, with a little spoon and yet this has to be done with a lot of precautions. It's true though that the truth is a medicine to their sickness, their handicap. There was a good reason for Jesus to say in Matthew 10, 8. 'Heal the sick.'

It is also true that a sick person who knows he's sick is not as sick as a person who is sick and doesn't know it.

It was already nine fifteen when I got at the apartment's door step. My two charming women were waiting impatiently. For Danielle it was to tell me about her conversation with the young doctor and for Janene it was to tell me about the four properties she found, which could be very interesting to us.

"I think Raymond got the message now. You should have seen his face when I told him we made love almost all night and I was pregnant with you." "He didn't suggest abortion, I hope?" "No, but I'm sure it is not because he didn't want to. I think he will leave us alone from now on." "Let's hope so."

"Janene, you seem anxious to tell me something. Do you have some good news?" "Yes, since we talked about it, I'm dying to know where we're going to live and where we're going to have this dream house built." "Well, I'm almost done with the blue prints and I'm pretty sure you're going to like it. I spent almost the whole week working on them." "You really have our happiness at heart, haven't you?" "My sweethearts, it's the only thing which matters to me as far as you are concerned." "What a charming man you are. It's my turn tonight, but you're not going to make love to me." "Did I do something wrong?" "On the contrary, but I'll make love to you. You'll get the full treatment." "This is promising, I can hardly wait."

"Would you stop the two of you, I'm going to come just by listening to both of you."

"I'm sorry Danielle, this was not my goal." "I know it, but it's just like watching a sensual movie with my favourite actor." "You're not going to play with yourself, are you?" "I rather wait than to feel too lonely."

"That's enough, let's get back to our business." "I found two different five acres pieces of land, one old abandoned farm on which run a little river. There are also a ruined house and a ruined barn just good for firewood." "Do you know how far this one is from town?" "Just a minute, I got this here. It is at eighteen kilometres from the town's limit." "Is it too far for the two of you?" "Not for me!"

"Not for me either, besides, we can travel with you many times."

"I would travel farther than this to reach the dream house. There is a big problem though." "What is it?" "There are a lot of scrubs growing back and more than three quarters of the property are forest like." "Maybe we can turn this to our advantage. Do you know in which zone it is located?" "Yes, it is in an agricultural farm zone and I was told it will most likely never change." "This is good news." "What do you mean?" "This means it will never be anybody too close to us." "That's true too; we could be like in paradise." "This way we could at least choose our neighbours." "We could also make a little beach with the river." "This is not so sure." "Why?" "Because the governments will have something to say about this." "On our property?" "Yes! All the rivers, the creeks, the lakes and so on belong to the governments or are under their jurisdictions. Maybe there is a natural little beach and this they can't do anything about it." "Let's hope so. The best news about this one is I think at a very good price." "Here comes the killing question! How much is it?" "Twenty thousands! When you compare this one to the five acres at fifty thousands each, I think it's cheap. This one has one hundred and sixty acres." "This is probably because the five acres are zoned commercial. And what about the forth one?" "It's a newer farm with a house almost new, a big barn, seventy cows and a big bull. They are asking three hundreds and fifty thousands dollars for it. There is also a huge German shepherd which comes with it." "Are you interested in this one?" "Not really!" "Do you have a phone number for the little farm?" "Yes, the old man lives in Quebec city." "Do you know if there is power around this property?" "Yes, it is written the power is accessible and the road is cleaned year round.

Well, I don't know what you girls are thinking, but I sure would like to walk this one soon." "You know James that we trust you for this kind of things." "Give me this phone number Janene and I will call tomorrow morning and this is only because it's too late to call tonight." "All of this wood doesn't scare you?" "On the contrary, I love it." "Can you tell us why?" "What if I keep it my secret for a while?" "We don't have any secret for you." "Ho no, and what about my birthday party? Wasn't that kept secret?" "Yes, but this is not the same thing." "On the contrary, it's exactly the same and it's getting late, we should go to bed now." "I'm surprised you took this long, I began thinking that you forgot." "Such a great invitation, no way Jose! Give me a few minutes first; I will put Danielle to bed."

"I got to tell you Danielle, I'm very proud of you." "Can you stay for a few minutes more? I'm so excited and I would like to be released a little bit." "I can't be long." "Don't waste any time talking, go right ahead." "Try not to scream; I don't want Janene to think she lost her turn again." "Go ahead, pleaseeeeeeeees." "Juicy like you, it's impossible. Good night!" "Good night! Now I'm going to sleep nicely."

I went to the bathroom to clean up a bit and then I went to join Janene who also made nice plans to make me happy. To say happy is to say too little, because I have to admit it, I'm experiencing something that is beyond happiness. I also think it's beyond every man's dream.

In the morning right after breakfast I dialled the phone number which Janene gave me.

Hello!" "Hello" "Talk louder my earring is not too good." "I called to find out about the little farm you have near Trois-Rivières." "It's for sale." "I know and I'm interested. This is why I called you." "You have to be very interested, because I'm too old to travel this far just for a ride." "I would like to walk it to see what you've got." "You will have to walk alone, because I can't drag myself anymore." "That's alright. You only have to show me the directions. When can you come this way?" "I can be there on Sunday if it's nice out there. I can be there around noon." "Bring all the necessary papers, because I'm very serious."

"What is your name?" "My name is James Prince." "Mine is André Fillion. We need a place to meet." "Do you know where the Grandma Restaurant is?" "I was there quite often and on top of everything, it's on our way. I'll be there at noon on Sunday, if I'm still alive." "Come on now, don't play games on me, I want you to see what I'm going to do with this property." "You sound like a gentleman and I can't wait to meet you." "See you on Sunday and be careful."

I went to my construction sites that I've kind of neglected these last few days, duty demands. Everything seemed to be alright, so after discussing a few details with the foremen I went home to finish the plans for the mention. I told him that we most likely going to have a triplex to build and that we have to finish all the going work first. He seemed to be happy to have work guaranteed for most of the year. I also knew he would tell all the other workers.

At noon all the plans and blue prints were finally done and ready for the demand of the permits, just a question of being legal. I still needed to get the property registered in our names to complete everything. I was sure hoping this wouldn't delay the beginning of the work. I already knew that except for a major problem, it was the piece of land I was hoping for. After a good dinner I went to present the plans at the building office, telling the people the plan of the land will be there shortly. I just knew I was saving some important time by doing things this way. I also made an appointment with the surveyor who assured me he will be there when I need him. I was completely ready for this wonderful project. It is not the biggest of my career, but surely the one I'm the most proud of to this day. The main reason is very simple; this house won the first price for the house of the year in Canada. The price included a trophy and a wonderful cheque of one hundred thousand dollars. It helps a bit to get rid of a mortgage. At first I wasn't too sure if I should accept it or not, because I wanted to keep our place as private as possible. After some discussions with my women, they came to the conclusion and they insisted that I should benefit from the product of my imagination. Then I took arrangement with the association to limit the propaganda.

From one thing to another things were rolling pretty fast and the girls asked me to go wait for them at the same place where we met a year ago, day for day, because they wanted to renew this wonderful night we had then. So, I put on the same suit and I went to lean on the same wall I did a year ago when Danielle first talked to me.

A few women came to ask me to dance, but there was no way I would miss the moment when one of my ladies was going to show up. One of them said to me;

"What's the problem, I'm not good enough for you?" "That's not it; I'm just waiting for the femme fatale." "Be careful, she might just be fatal to you." "The ones I want I would die for her anytime." "Maybe you're too romantic for our times." "Maybe so, but this is the way I like it."

"May I invite you for a dance sir?" "You sure can pretty lady."

"So, this is it, you like blonds?" "Only if they are fatal. This one is so gorges, she's a killer and I would die for her."

"What is the problem here?" "Ho, I refused to dance with her and she's not too happy about it. You sure took a long time both of you. Where is Danielle?" "She is sitting down at the exact same place I was sitting last year." "Did she found a thick truck driver too?" "If he wasn't so thick, I might have left with him." "What would you have missed?" "Stop, I don't even want to think about it. I had such a wonderful year of happiness with you and I meant to tell you while dancing." "I have a hard time believing that you could be happier than I am Janene." "You'll have to dance with my best friend too, you know?" "I just can't refuse you anything my sweetie; this is how much I love you." "Where did you learn to speak to women like you do?" "I learn day by day as I live with the two of you.

I'll have to invent a three way dance partner, because, when I'm with one of you I miss the other one and I hate to leave her waiting."

"You really love us both, don't you?" "I love enormously both of you, yes. Let's go meet Danielle now."

There were just as many people as last year if not more and again we had to push our way all the way to the table. Danielle was sitting down with her brother and his girlfriend Sylvia. She had saved us two chairs, which shouldn't have been too easy with this kind of crowd. Normand, Danielle's brother called me the seducer, which is really not the case.

"You seem to have fun, the two of you?" "Yes, we're having a good time, but there are a bit too many people here to my taste."

"I found out you build nice houses James and I want to have one built eventually." "I don't want you to think that I'm rude or independent or anything like that Normand, but you'll have to contact me at my office for this, because I never mix pleasure with business."

"You were right Danielle." "I told you brother, I know my man."

"This is a nice cha cha Danielle, do you want to dance?" "Nothing would please me more right now." "Are you sure about this?" "Between you and me, just say almost nothing."

Then the band slowed down a little bit to play the very first piece of music we danced on last year.

"Did you ask for it?" "No, I thought maybe you did." "Maybe it's just a fluke or Janene did." "It doesn't matter; it's just as good as the first time. May we live these moments over and over again like tonight, for it was the beginning of a wonderful adventure. We have a whole life ahead of us and I will do my very best to make it as interesting as possible." "I have to admit that I am a little concerned about the marriage." "What are you concerned about sweetie?" "I'm not worried about my marriage to you, but I'm afraid you might have a hard time to marry Janene once you're married to me." "It's very possible that your worry is founded, but what ever happens, I consider myself already married to both of you before God and nobody can change this. Papers are only formalities." "I love you so much, it's almost unexplainable." "I know exactly what you're talking about." "Then we understand each other." "I can't wait to take you to bed, do you know it?" "I felt it." "Did you like it?" "As usual, I'm always extremely fine in your arms." "Are we going home early?" "Go dance with Janene another time, she too love to dance with you." "I love dancing with both of you."

The crowd was still very heavy and I was telling myself that if there was ever a fire, we would be cook like rats. I would be absolutely powerless in such a mob. All it would take is that an idiot starts yelling; 'fire, fire,' even if there is nothing at all for the crowd to panic. It's my love for the two of them that inspired me to stay away from these high risk places. There is nothing as scaring as the thought of losing your loved ones.

"What is the problem James, you look so worried? Are you alright?" "I'll explain it to you later if you don't mind."

When we got to our table Janene was gone. Danielle asked her brother if he knew where she was gone, being herself wondering about it when Janene suddenly showed up. Janene looked quite upset and she was followed by a man who was apologizing all the way to our table. As soon as she was close to us she turned around to face him and yelled loudly; "Get the F out of my face before I use my claws on yours." "I didn't wa . . . ." "Go away I told you."

I got up to face the man and I told him looking him straight in his eyes and I said; "You've heard the lady, so go away while you still have time." "Alright, alright, I'm leaving. No point yelling so much."

"Calm down now Janene it's over. What the heck happened to make you so mad?" "He didn't want to let me go when I wanted to. He forced me to insist and I don't like to be forced in what so ever." "I kind of understand that a man would want to hold you back on the dance floor. The least we can say is he's got good taste." "Good taste my ass, I can't be forced and that's all." "Would you like to go somewhere else?" "No, I just want to dance with you again, would you?" "Of course I would, but only if you calm down. I'm a little scared of your claws." "Very funny, let's go."

We danced a mambo, a tango, a nice samba, a Rumba and we were just starting a nice slow when I felt a touch on my left shoulder. I kept dancing anyway, but that touch became more and more insisting.

"James, it's him again." "Keep dancing and pull yourself back a little, would you?" "What are you going to do?" "Just trust me, you'll see. Keep your eyes wide opened and at the same time he'll put his hand on me again, pull yourself back very quickly, ok?" "Ok!"

I was waiting very patiently for the moment he was going to touch me one more time and when he did it, Janene who did exactly as I asked her to do, pulled herself back quickly and at the same time I grabbed the fingers of this man who found himself on his knees making all kinds of faces. A few people started to scream and within a few seconds a couple of doormen were on the spot too. One of them asked Janene what happened and with no hesitation she told him this man was harassing her. The two men grabbed him and showed him the door, which will be banished for him for a couple of years to come.

"You will never cease to impress me, will you?" "This is not something I like to talk about Janene, because this is my strength. The surprise and the fact my enemy doesn't know what I'm capable of are my trumps. You see, this guy didn't have a clue of all this and he was taken by surprise. He is almost twice my size and he thought he had nothing to fear. Now I just hope nobody will talk about this at all. What if we get out of here now?" "He might be waiting for us outside." "Don't worry, he had his lesson. The world is full of this kind of hazards; we just have to be ready for them."

I walked Janene to our table and then I took off for a few minutes, because I wanted to know this man's name. I went to talk to the doormen who took care of this individual and they said they couldn't tell me his name.

"If this man is a treat to my family, I have the right to know what his name is. If I have to call the police to find out who he is, I will."

One of them knew me enough to know that I won't hesitate a single minute to do it.

"We don't want to get the police involved in this, just for such insignificant matter. It's never too good to get the police involved for our reputation. His name is Bernard Sinclair." "Thank you!" "You never learned it from us." "That's fine, I got what I want."

I quickly went back to our table to find all of them in a passionate conversation.

"Where did you go? You seem concerned" "I just needed a little information, that's all. I think we should go now. Are you guys hungry? Maybe we could go to a restaurant." "Thanks the same, but we have prepared a little snack at home before we left, if you're interested naturally." "That's fine with me, let's go. Ho, one more thing before we go; make sure no one else but me is following you."

We drove home without any problem. They had prepared everything before they left and this was the reason for them to be a little late at the dance. They had organized a birthday like no one else has ever done, I'm sure. On the table there was everything you can imagine to please the mouth. Suddenly Danielle got up and went to run the water in the tub.

"Do you remember last year?" "I will never forget it for as long as I live." "We would like to repeat it just in case it happens some day. We just want to refresh your memory." "Which one will get the shower this time?"

"It's Danielle's turn." "Don't tell me you still need a sample of my love for the laboratory. You're the only ones with whom I sleep since I met you." "No, we trust you one hundred per cent, but Danielle doesn't know what it's like to be showered this way. This will be fine if she likes surprises, because it goes without warnings. Go slow Janene, I got lots of time and tonight I do more than just look."

For the rest you already know what happened, because it's the same thing than last year. When the morning came at around ten, I turned on the TV to get the last news as I almost always do.

"Oh my God! Oh my God!"

I returned very quickly to the bed to talk with Janene.

"Let me sleep a bit longer, would you James?" "Janene, there is bad news." "What is it?" "The guy we had trouble with last night, he was arrested." "You call this bad news. It's good for him, he deserved it." "He returned to the club with a gun, I think he was seeking revenge. I think he was looking for me." "What?" "He was looking for us." "He's crazy; they are going to lock him up." "I'm not so sure about that." "What are we going to do?" "For as long as he is in jail there is no danger, but when he's out, that's another story. I don't think he knows where we live, but then again, we don't know for sure. I have to go to the police station to find out more about this. By acting like he did he made death threats. Do you realize this? He will get a few years. I'm sure too that there were a lot of witnesses. His name is Bernard Sinclair." "I think I know this name." "Try to remember, every detail could be important."

I got dressed and I went to the station to find more on this case if it was possible.

"Can I speak to the officer who is on Sinclair's case please?" "Do you have a special reason for this?" "I have a reason to believe he was after me last night." "What is your name?" "My name is James Prince." "This is not what he told us. He told us he was looking for the doorman who bullied him." "Alright, maybe I made a mistake. Excuse me!" "There is no problem."

I returned to the condo, but I was certainly not convinced of what I just heard. There was something very suspicious about the whole thing and I knew I had to keep my eyes opened and my ears alert.

"Girls, it's me, are you up?" "James, is that you? We might be in danger." "What makes you think of this?" "Did you say his name is Bernard Sinclair?" "Yes; why?" "He might just be Raymond's brother, doctor Raymond Sinclair's brother." "So this means it wasn't just a hazard last night, maybe it was a plot for revenge. I think you girls should think of moving out of here. They both know where you live and this place is not secure for you anymore. It's best you put this apartment for sell as soon as possible." "Where could we go?" "My place is very modest, but I have room for both of you and it will be safer." "If it's good enough for you, it's good enough for us." "It is only for a few months, our new house should be ready for September. If you pack everything, I could use my men to load the truck. You could be out of here in a single day even if it's hurting. You'll have to be careful at all time though; you know this, don't you?" "Yes, we know. You said the new house could be ready within six months?" "Yes, I already asked for the permit." "But you need to have the plan and blue prints." "I presented them with the demand of the permit already. I spent the whole week on this project." "What a sweetheart you are." "Do you want to see them?" "You got them?" "Of course I do, I made them. Just wait a few minutes, I'll get them." "You too be careful." "Don't worry, I will be."

I went to my vehicle to get the plan and I came back quickly.

"It's me girls, you can open. Take a look at this." "What a beautiful thing. You made this?" "I did." "But you're quite an artist." "I only designed what you asked me. All you have left to do now is to choose the colours and the furniture to decorate it. Here is the floor blueprint." "It's even better than what I had anticipated. There is a very large kitchen with a kitchen Island and a large number of cupboards. A large living room just like I like it. Three big bedrooms! What is this?" "There is a bathroom between each bedroom." "What a marvellous idea!" "There is an insulated panel in each wall. This is the same material they build freezers with. If you want to know how efficient it is, you just have to put a battery operated radio on high volume in a freezer and shut the cover. Danielle especially really needs walls like those." "Look at the size of these windows. The balcony makes the whole link of the house. How long is it?" "Fifty-eight feet long!" "It's almost a race track. Kids will just love to ride it with their bikes." "After what happened last night at the club, I think I would like to have a dance floor in one of the basements, with your permission of course. Take your time and discuss it between the two of you. You've got six months to make up your mind. It would also make a nice place for kids to play in on the rainy days. The heat system is of many pipes running in the floor where hot water is circulating all the time. Each place will also have a slow wood burner just in case the power goes off for some reasons. This system will function the same way a conventional hot air system operates. Only it will operate on batteries. The batteries system will be able to operate and supply us with all the power we need for a whole week before the needs of a generator. The walls between my place and yours and the floor between the garage and my place will be done with reinforced concrete capable to resist a medium size explosion. We never know what can happen with cars. There is a fan system also capable to send all the smoke outside in case of a fire. The walls and the communicating doors are also fire proof. There is an intercom system in the whole house which works together with the sound system. You might lose the sight of me, but not the sound of me. Inside each window there is a blind that shuts down as soon as you turn the light on." "You're not serious?" "Ho yes, I am. These windows are also eat efficient, just like the back window of your car. Instead of cooling off the house they help heating it in the winter." "This is completely genial." "Of course there is a vacuum system in the whole house. I will have a cold room at the end of the garage and also a place to put fire wood. Each one of us can enter our own place from the garage. That's about it. Ho yes, each bathroom is big enough to include your laundry machines or if you like it better, I could install them in your basement. If you choose the latter one, I will make a shoot for our dirty laundry that we're going to keep within our family, I'm sure. I will find a tub like you have here if it is what you want. Why are you so quiet?" "It's simple, we are stunned. Everything is there, there's nothing to add and nothing more to say. How do you do it? It is totally genial." "Come on Janene, it's just a house. You like?" "If we like it? Do we have enough money for all of this?" "I think so." "What is the big number?" "I got it here somewhere. It is a bit more than I initially thought. It comes to five hundred and forty seven thousand and two hundred. You don't pay anything for the garage because it's under my quarters. Each of your shares comes to two hundred and eight thousand eight hundred." "We are ten thousand dollars short and we don't have the land yet." "You both have an excellent job and the banks will go out of their way to lend you the money. We'll talk about this later, if you don't mind. For the land you don't worry, I'll buy it, in fact I will meet tomorrow with the old man. I got to meet him by noon and I will have diner with him at the restaurant. I will walk the land and I will take a decision afterwards. If I like it I will buy it, but I will put your names on the contract as owners as well. It will be ours at even shares. All I ask is the right to use it my own way." "I see no problem with this."

"Me neither." "So we all agree." "Tell me James, why are you doing all this?" "Everything I buy since we are together would be considered equal share from the court point of view anyway if we ever separate, might as well do it now." "God has reunited us and no one will separate. It's there for better and for the worst." "You will have to come and sign for the permits too, because we will be owners and responsible for each of our quarters and it's better this way." "But we still don't have enough money for all this." "Is this what you want?" "It is a lot more than we were hoping for." "Are you absolutely sure?" "Yes, we are." "I don't think so. Sure, also mean sour in French. But I know that you are both very sweet." "Ha, ha, ha, very funny!" "Here is what I suggest you do. You have between the two of you four hundred and ten thousand and you need four hundred and thirty thousand, is that right?" "That's right." "Then you need to go see your bank manager and borrow each of you a big one hundred thousand dollars." "What?" "You heard me. Never let yourself go dry if you can do otherwise.

Desmarais made himself a multibillionaire with bank's money and you can do the same. Banks lend up to ninety and ninety-five % on properties and in your case you would only borrow a lean thirty per cent from which you will only use ten per cent for your actual needs. You keep approximately ten thousand in you bank account for your own needs and place the rest at fifteen per cent for a loan that cost you five per cent, which is the rate of the preferential customers. This way, instead than paying for a loan, you get paid for it." "But this kind of deals scare me." "Even if I take responsibility for anything that could happen?" "Well then, I close my eyes." "Make an appointment quickly with your bank manager and I will take care of the rest. So, you had fun? Me too, because I don't work on Saturday. What do we have for supper?" "Are you hungry?" "A little!" "Everything will be ready in five minutes. I too don't like to work on Saturday. I got everything ready yesterday." "Do you have a good movie for the evening? I would love necking with both of you tonight." "This can be arranged my man, but maybe you'll find us a bit sticky." "That's good. Sticky yesterday and today and forever, stick with me girls, I love it."

I'm not too sure if it was because my women were toady and charming, but I didn't find the movie interesting at all. They kind of brought up the temperature and something else too.

"I'm not too sure where I'm at right now, who's turn is it?" "It's Danielle's. Go ahead, don't waste any time, I want some too." "Well ok, then Janene would you run the water in the tub, we will need it and this way it will go faster."

"Come Danielle, don't let Janene wait too long, she seems to be very hungry."

That was very quick indeed, because we were both ready to explode right from the beginning. Then we jumped in the tub where we soap each other lovingly.

"It's your turn tonight to get me for the night, are you going to wait?" "If you're not too long, I'm going to watch the movie we were supposed to watch all together." "Then I'll come to watch the end of it with you. See you in a bit, I love you."

I went to spend thirty-five minutes with Janene and when I left her she was contempt and ready to sleep for the night. I watched the rest of the movie with Danielle, which was not so dull after all. Afterwards, we went to bed and continued what we had started earlier. I was very satisfied with myself on that particular Saturday, mainly because I succeeded to make them forget about the tremendous threat that was hovering over our heads with the Sinclairs.

The next day at noon on that Sunday I met with M. Fillion just as planned, a man that you wish you always known and have as a friend. After a very good meal at the restaurant we got into my vehicle and he guided me to the property I was interested in.

"I wish I was still young just to walk with you in that wood one more time. I hope you brought a gun with you. You might encounter some wolves, we saw some before, you know?" "Yes, I thought of it." "This nice piece of land wouldn't be for sell if only I could walk like I used to. You must know this." "Do you know your neighbours on both sides?" "Yes, they are good people and they too are getting old." "Do you think they would sell their properties too?" "I'm sure they would sell if they could. They tried to sell before, but no one wants those abandoned farms so far away from everything. Besides, they're not profitable. You can only starve to death on a farm like these." "You're not a very good salesman, are you?" "I'm honest and I tell things the way they are." "You said there is a little river on this land, didn't you? Is there any fish in it?" "My friend, I ate a lot of good trout." "Is there enough water to make a little beach?" "It's already there just natural and there is about six feet of water. It's also there I took all the nice twelve inches trout." "Is there *any* deer on it?" "I promise you'll never have to go anywhere else to hunt." "Interesting! You said you want twenty thousand for this land, didn't you?" "This is the asking price, yes." "How is the entrance situated, North, South, East or West?" "The entrance is south. How important is this?" "To me it is. Did you bring the land title?" "Yes!" "Is there any chance or I should say, any risk I get lost in this wood?" "Not really. There is a road on each side and a very good fence at the end of the property. You can't get lost, you go all the way up North and come back all the way South, simple as that." "It should take me a few hours." "If it wasn't for the undergrowth on the road we could go all the way with your vehicle." "I'll have a lot of cleaning up to do if I buy. You can wait for me in the vehicle, I'll leave you the keys so you can listen to the radio and if you get cold, you can start the van."

When I enter the wood it was nice and sunny, but without any warning and all of a sudden, it started snowing to the point I couldn't see neither the skies nor the ground. I was gone for more than two and a half hours when my old friend began to worry seriously. I start to pray that he doesn't leave the vehicle on the spur of the moment out of compassion to come to my rescue. It's always easier to look for one person than to look for two and besides, for him to walk in this weather condition would have probably killed him. But he did what he should do and this was to blow the horn until he sees me. The least I can say is that he was quite relieved to see me again. I could hear a lot farther than I could see.

I was out of the bush, but not out of the storm yet. In no time at all there was more than eight inches of snow on the ground. My father often mentioned the March snow storms. Luckily I had good tires and I had a front wheel drive vehicle. I was also convinced I would have to buy a tractor as soon as possible. The problem was to turn around without getting stock in that deep snow. My fear was founded, because after I backed up while turning, I got stock really good to the point I couldn't move either way.

"Hope you have a shovel. I'm not very strong anymore, but maybe I can push a little." "It won't be necessary, I got what I need." "Do you really think so?" "No, I'm sure." "We'll see."

I then got out and took the shovel to clear the snow that was up to the bottom of the doors and was blocking the wheels. I put the shovel away and I got back in, but that wet snow made it so slippery that there was no traction at all.

"You'll need me to either push or to get behind the wheel." "Even if you get behind the wheel, you would have to stop to pick me up and we would be at the starting point again. I got better than this."

I got out again and I put what I should under the front wheels and I came back in again.

"Hold on, we're on are way." "Oh, you believe that?" "Yes I do." "I'll be damned. What did you do?" "I just put a shingle under each wheel. Once you're gone, you just can't stop, you have to keep going. You just have to put the rough side down of those shingles, so they don't slip and the trick is done. It's cheap and very efficient and it's not worth stopping to pick them up. They are also very thin and slide easily under the wheels." "Don't say anymore, I'm convinced. We sure learn at all ages, don't we?" "How good are they to open the roads in this part of the country?" "We never had any problem with that. You might just have to call the council if you're not happy with what is done." "You can not drive back home in this kind of weather and you can stay at my place tonight, this way we could see the lawyer tomorrow." "Does it mean you're buying, but you couldn't see it all?" "I saw what I needed to see and I am happy to take it away from you." "Don't tell me you found gold." "Gold wouldn't make me as happy as this property will." "Well! It's true that you were serious." "Are you coming to my place?" "I don't want to disturb. It would be better than at the hotel, I think." "It settled then. I'll take you to my place and then I'll go pick up a couple of my friends and I'll be right back."

So I took him to my place and I told him to make himself at home. I then went to get my two favourite girls, mainly because I didn't want them to be left alone for the night knowing perfectly well they weren't safe in their apartment.

"Hi, it's me." "It's you James? We were worried about you with this snow storm outside." "And I was worried for you. You are coming to sleep at my place tonight, because I don't think this place is any longer safe for you." "Really, you believe that?" "Yes I do.

This Sinclair who was looking for us the other night will still be looking for us." "But you said he was in jail." "He can be out of it as soon as somebody pays is bail and this could be sooner than we wish for. As far as I'm concerned he might be out already and I'm not ready to take any risk with your wellbeing. Did you pack your things?" "No, we didn't think it was this urgent." "Listen girls, this guy came after

81

us the other night with a loaded gun and you don't think it is urgent."
"How did it go on the property? I don't think it was too easy with
this snow storm." "I had enough time to see what I wanted to see and
I'm buying it. The seller is at my place waiting for us." "You left the
blue prints over here, do you want them now?" "Yes, I need them.
What time are you working tomorrow?" "Janene is working daytime
and I work in the evening." "We don't have solid proof, but I'm pretty
sure they are going to harm one of us and yet maybe every one, so
take what you need for the night and we will come to take the rest
tomorrow. Don't you worry; I'll take care of everything. Danielle, as
soon as tomorrow you should advertise the condo and it should go
very quickly, because there are not enough on the market. You should
contact your bank manager as soon as you can also." "I will." "Are
you ready?" "We are." "Let's go. Let me go down first and see that
everything is alright. I'll let you know through the intercom." "Forgive
us; we didn't think it was so serious." "It's my fault, I didn't want you
to be too worried, but the danger is real. When an individual is crazy
enough to enter a bar and threats to shoot someone, it's serious and we
cannot take it too lightly." "Now I'm scared." "It's better that you are
scared a bit and careful than not scared and too boldly, but everything
will be fine, I'm sure. You'll have to be careful at work too, we don't
really know what doctor Sinclair is capable of." "It won't be easy; he's
always working directly with us." "Keep your eyes opened, that's all.
Alright, I'm going down. See you in a bit."

Everything went fine that night and so were the next few weeks.
We got home to find my old friend sleeping on the couch in front
of the TV set. It must have been a very long day for him with all the
stress of the day on top of his trip from Quebec City.

We let him sleep until the supper was ready. I offered meat sauce
spaghetti to my young ladies and they accepted that with a smile
knowing very well I was the host for the evening. It was an ancient
meal served in the modern time. You should have seen the eyes of the
old man when he saw my two beautiful guests.

'I'm I still alive or dead and in heaven? I got the impression that I am in front of two angels.'

He gave us a good laugh. He was old maybe, but not blind and he knew how to appreciate the beauties of this world. He also seemed to wonder what I was doing with two of such of beautiful women. I didn't feel the need to inform him about it. Once we discussed the price of the land and we came to an accord I showed him the plan of the house we intend to build on his property and he could not believe his own eyes. Since he was such a poor salesman I decided to sell myself this piece of land to myself. He came down to ten thousand dollars, but I made him a cheque for twenty thousand. One more time he seemed all confused and he still wondered if he was still a member of this world. I also paid for the registration and all the other expenses and I wanted him to be able to cash his cheque the same day, but the notary public said no.

'The money will be deposit in a truss account and will go in M. Fillion's account as soon as we know the tittles are clear of liens and the land really belongs to him and only him.'

Andre quickly understood it was the normal procedure. Everything went on the same day anyway. It was obvious that he really loved this property and the only reason for selling was because he could not take care of it anymore. He was one of the rare chosen people to be invited at the inauguration of our house.

"I'm almost eighty and I never met someone like you. There is something with you that is not like everybody else." "Maybe it's because I walk with God and God is with me." "Ho, Him, I don't really believe in." "Maybe you don't really know Him." "We were told He sees everything, but you didn't see your way out of the snow storm." "Did I get lost?"

"No, but it's most likely because I blew the horn." "I would say that He gave you the occasion, the opportunity to make yourself useful for someone in distress even at your age, you who is getting weaker and sometimes thinks he's good for nothing." "It could be one way to see things." "Where do you think our thoughts and our ideas come from?" "I don't really know, but they most likely are within us." "On the contrary, I know for sure the spirits are speaking to us and some of us know how to listen and others don't. Some of us listen to the good spirits and others listen to the bad ones." "Where did you get such information?" "In Matthew 16, 17, Jesus said to Peter: 'Blessed are you Peter, son of Jonah, because it is not the flesh and blood that revealed this to you, but my Father who is in heaven.'

And then practically in the same conversation Jesus said to Peter again: 'Get behind me, Satan, you are offensive to me for your thoughts are not from God, but from men.'

"Never in my whole life had I heard someone talk like you do." "This is just because you didn't listen to Jesus. Many people think they are atheists because they don't believe in religions and in men who are supposed to tell the truth and this without making sure those same men are really from God. The ones who lied, especially about the word of God are not from God, but from the devil and they are numerous like the sand by the sea." "Nice meeting you James, it's a real pleasure to do business with you."

This is what he told me shaking my hand warmly. He took off afterwards but sadly I could tell. I wished I could spend more time with him, but I had many more things to do. I couldn't wait to join Danielle who had a lot of things to do on her own. I also went to the police station to find out the last move in the Sinclair affair. There is when I found out the criminal was out on bail already and paid by his brother, the famous doctor. I was pretty sure he was going to try something else again, but I had no Idea what to expect. I met with Danielle at my place at lunch time.

"How did it go at the bank?" "Pretty good I think, he said it will be no problem. Are you too busy to kiss me today?" "I'm so sorry, but I have so many things on my mind at the present time. I still have to go rent a truck.

"I gave it a lot of thought and I don't think it will be necessary." "What do you mean? You don't want to move to my place anymore?"

"That's not it, but I don't think we need all of those things. You have basically everything we need right here. We could just take the food and a few other things we need, but for the rest, it could just stay in place. You know as well as I do that a furnished apartment sells easier than an empty one." "You might be right. Let's forget about the truck and we can move the little you need in my van. Did you put the ad in the paper?" "Yes I did, in the paper and on the internet." "This is a very good idea. Did you talk to Janene?" "Yes, she's fine. How are things with you?" "Fine, the property is ours." "Is that right? I'm so happy." "M. Fillion is on his way back home." "He might just be a bad salesman, but you are a bad buyer; you lost ten thousand dollars by your own fault." "How much did you ask for your condo?" "Two hundred and twenty thousands." "What would you say if someone would pay it without asking any question?" "It would be wonderful." "This is it, do to others what you would want others do for you." "This is another good lesson!" "It's free." "What do we do next?" "You have two hours in front of you, might as well go get your things at the apartment." "Ok, let's go." "I got to call the foreman to cancel the moving assignment." "The real superman is not in fiction, it's you." "Ho, come on, don't embarrass me, ok? I don't do anything that is not normal." "But you do so much; no one ever saw something like this." "You're exaggerating, let's go."

As soon as we were back with all their things they needed, Danielle went to work. She certainly wasn't in an enviable position. Anybody can say what he wants; it's not easy to pay good for the bad we get, to turn the other cheek and to forgive the one who despise us. She had to be strong to go through this. We couldn't even talk to anybody about the whole situation for fear to be sued for defamation. The situation wasn't easy at all. Then I went to my construction sites to find out the work was in good progress. Raoul, the Foreman met with the new owners who all seem to be happy with our masterpieces.

I didn't stay there too long, because I wanted to be home to welcome Janene to her new living quarters. After I informed her of all the activities of the day I went to make supper.

CHAPTER 4

"*W*hat are you making?" "I'm making a fricassee. Did you ever hear of it?" "Yes, but I don't remember having it." "I like Africa, see." "You must since you're making one." "Did you ever go to Africa? Africa, see!" "Ha you! Comic, very funny.

You'll have to show me how to do this, so I can make it for you some day." "First I fry some beef cubes or ground beef in a large frypan adding salt and pepper. When it's done at seventy-five per cent I pour the whole thing in a large cauldron. I put a glass of water in the frypan and this too I put in the big container to get everything that gives taste to the meal.

Then I add water to make half of the container and I add salt and pepper.

Then I leave everything boil for about twenty minutes and during this time I go prepare the vegetables I like, starting with the carrots, because they take longer to cook. Then I peal the potatoes and I add them to the meat with a bit more salt. I leave the whole thing boil for another ten minutes and I go prepare the dumplings. One cup of flower, two soup spoons full of oil, one an a half soup spoon of magic powder and you mix the whole thing adding milk as you go until the dough is done but still thick. With a large spoon you put the dough on top of the rest and leave it cook until the dumplings are all up to the cover.

Bingo, the lady is served." "Wow, this is good." "I just love those dumplings, especially when they are well done, so if you don't really like them you can leave them to me."

"I think Danielle and I are lucky, you're a good man to marry, a good catch." "I don't think it will be easy even If I love you with all my body, my heart and my soul. No matter what, I'll do everything possible for this to happen, but I tell you right now, there is no way for me to join a religion, because it would mean making a deal with the devil to me. Solomon was the wisest king on earth and he had a fabulous wealth, but he lost everything because he prostituted himself to the foreign gods and religions of his last wives. With the help of my true God I won't do the same mistake." "Are you telling me you're not going to marry me?" "Not at all, I'm telling you that I'm not going to join any religion even though I love you with all my heart." "The most important is that you love me. All I know is I couldn't live without you." "I couldn't live without you either." "No matter what, if you get rid of our problems the way you got rid of this big ass hole the other night, everything will be fine." "I wish I could be as sure as you." "Why? Is there a problem?" "He's already out of jail, because your doctor bailed him out." "The son of a b . . . . What are we going to do?" "We'll have to wait he compromises himself. Unfortunately until then we won't be able to react." "In the mean time we have to live in fear and uncertainty every day." "Exactly! We don't know what they'll do next." "You said they?" "Yes, I think the doctor might be just as dangerous as his brother, maybe even more." "Does Danielle know it?" "I told her to keep her eyes opened at all times." "Changing the subject, how did it go with the property?" "It's ours. I bought it today and everything is finalized." "Is that true? Ho, I'm so happy. This means you will start building our house very soon." "I will as soon as the ground is defrosted. I will buy a backhoe to remove the snow and I will install an eating tarp, one of my inventions to defrost the ground.

I can't wait to see how it will work." "A backhoe, that's a lot of money, isn't it?" "It's nearly one hundred thousand for a new one, but I have a lot of work for it with the excavation plus all the undergrowth. There is a mile of road on both sides to clear plus a half mile at the end of the property and we cannot stay in the country without at least a tractor. A backhoe is a lot better and it's a machine that will pay by itself. I paid my excavator almost twenty-five thousands a year in the last three years. This kind of machine is good for at least thirty years. Believe me, it's a good deal." "Are you sure you're not going to be short of money for the house though? According to your numbers you basically build our house for the cost, without any profit." "Where did you get this information?" "You left the blue prints at our place yesterday and we asked another contractor how much it would be, because we thought you didn't estimate this house high enough. The other contractor said it wasn't the final price, but it would be at least seven hundred thousands. There is a difference of more than one hundred and fifty thousands." "Well, I didn't want to make any profit with my spouses and I'm sure if I need any help, you both going to be there for me. I also made all the calculations and I'm sure if I'm short of a bit of money there will be friends to help me out. My quarters are not very big, which means it doesn't cost a heck of a lot and this house here will pay just about everything including the backhoe." "I think you are a business' genius." "I'm not too sure of this, especially according to Danielle and M. Fillion." "What make you say this?" "I paid twenty thousands for the property, but I could have got it for ten." "What is the matter with you?" "He was vulnerable and I didn't want to take advantage of him." "It's all to you credit and I'm sure God will return it to you." "Now I know you know Him well. I don't know how it is for you, but I'm extremely tired." "Come and lay down, I'll give you a massage." "Your hands are incredibly soft. It's very nice." "James! James! Are you sleeping? No treat for me tonight. There is no treat, there is no treat, there is no treat for me tonight. I hope I wouldn't have to sing this too often. Well, I guess I'll put a movie on then."

Janene fell asleep too on another couch in front of the TV set. She covered me up with a bedspread. It was the first time in a whole year that I couldn't satisfy one of them, but believe me, it was not without any regrets.

Since there is a reason for everything, the only fact she was near the door allowed Janene to wake up quickly when Danielle arrived. She had forgotten to take a key for the house. I had shivers just thinking she just might have decided to go sleep in the condo all by herself if she couldn't get in. I took advantage of the situation to warn her again to not ever take any risk. I would rather lose a window.

"What is James doing on the couch?" "He was extremely tired and he fell asleep right there. I thought it was best to let him rest." "Make sure you're not going to kill him with love making Janene. I know he's strong, but control yourself, would you?" "No Danielle, I didn't get any treat tonight, but it's not because I didn't want it." "He should go sleep in his bed, he would be more comfortable." "He sleeps so well, I think it's best to let him stay there."

They both went to bed without any treat that night; although I went to join Danielle at four thirty in the morning, but I was very careful not to wake her up. When we did wake up, Janene was already gone to work.

After breakfast Danielle went on the computer to read her Emails. There were a big number of messages and most of them none senses as usual when suddenly her eyes stop on one a little more interesting. She yelled for me to come to take a look on the screen which scared me at first.

"What's going on Danielle, you've scared me." "Nevermind; just read this. 'Very interested in your condominium, please don't sell before I had a chance to see it. If it is still available, I'll take a plane tonight and I will meet you tomorrow at noon. I'm waiting for an answer, Laurent.'

"What do you think of this James?" "He might be a potential buyer. What are you waiting for to give him an answer? Make sure you don't let him think you absolutely have to sell." "I'll let you read my answer before I send it, what you think?" "As you wish sweetie."

'The condo is still available, but the demand is very high in this town. If you are very serious and I can put my trust in you, I'll wait until tomorrow noon before I make any decision, Danielle.'

"What do you think of this James?" "It's perfect, it's short and it let him believe that if he really wants it, he is better to move fast. This is what you need to send him to get him to move. Send it, we'll see what happens." "It's gone. Do you have anymore tea?" "Yes, I'll bring it to you right away. Do you want any biscuits with it?" "That would be nice, thank you." "Here, the lady is served." "You are a treasure." "Ho, come on now, that's nothing." "You have no idea what it means for us women, do you?" "Ho yes, I do." "Alright, tell me what it is then." "It's a jar of good treats which I can stick my face into." "That's pretty well it. Hey, come to see this, I got an answer."

'Give me the name and address of your bank and I'll send you five thousands dollars to the desk in your name. If I'm there on time, this money will go as a deposit towards the condo, if not it will be just a gift to you, Laurent.'

"Internet is unbelievably quick. Give him the OK and we'll go to the bank to see if the money is there."

Danielle gave him the answer with all the information he needed for the transaction and then we went to the bank.

"You don't really have to come with me James." "Ho, you think so? What if it was a set up? What if it was one of the Sinclairs who wrote to you?" "Gees, I never thought of that. We don't really know who's this offer is coming from, do we?" "From now on I'll be your bodyguard. I'll take you to work and I'll pick you up after. If I say get down, you hit the floor, if I say run, you run, understood?" "Yes, it's very clear." "We can't even go to the police without being laugh at. We can only count on us and on us alone." "I understood, I understood, let's go." "Prevention is better than cure even for a special nurse like you."

So we went to the bank as planned to find out the money was there as agreed. This scared me even more, because I said to myself, if this guy is ready to lose five thousand dollars to ambush Danielle, this means he'll go to any link to hurt her.

The next day a man in his sixties showed up at the indicated address where he came down of a white limo. He was a giant built, like a football player. He must be six foot six or more and weights at least two hundred and fifty pounds. He asked right away to see the condo, telling us he was in extreme hurry.

"Hi, I'm Laurent." "I'm Danielle and this is my husband James." "Please, let's go see this thing right away, would you?" "Yes, it's on the sixth floor."

All four of us went to the elevator. His chauffeur who is just as huge was following him just as if he was his bodyguard. I wondered if they were from the mafia or else from the government, which is about the same. One way or the other the situation was scary. As soon as they got in, they went all around the apartment searching the closets, testing the beds on and under and all of this without saying a single word. I was thinking I might have to use my marshal art when suddenly Laurent opened his mouth to say:

"What would say if I give you three hundred thousands for the condo and all the furniture? You would just take your personal belongings." "I would have to talk to my partner."

"No, we agree sir."

"But James!"

"We have a deal sir." "Laurent Charron is my name. Alright then, my agent will contact you within two hours. I want to move in no later than tomorrow. You will give him the, all the keys please." "He will get them sir and all the personal things will also be out of here by midnight. Is this good enough?" "This will be fine. Good then, we have to go, good day." "Good day sir.

They went and I had in front of me a lady who was really concerned, completely disconcerted and with big questioning eyes.

"But James, Janene will want to kill me." "Why? Is this to make her more money in one hour than she makes in a whole year? I don't think so." "But we should talk to her first." "This man had no time to waste, it was then or never. How much did the furniture cost you?" "About fifteen thousands if I remember well." "That's what I thought, but he's giving you ninety thousands for it. I don't know his reasons and I don't think I want to know, but this man is in extreme hurry to find a place and he wants it all furnished and both of you are richer by seventy-five thousands." "You are the one who deserves it, I would have lost it." "Surely, if you'd insisted to make him wait and this is why I stepped in. Forgive me!" "Forgive you for what? Making us richer? What would we do without you?" "The exact same thing you were doing before." "Before, I don't want to think about it."

We went home to wait for the phone call that was important to us. It was not very long. Within fifteen minutes we had an appointment at the lawyer's office.

"Where are the papers for the condo?" "They are at the lawyer's office." "But where are your copies?" "They are there at the lawyer's office. We thought it was the safest place to leave them." "My God but!" "What is the problem?" "You better pray for this man to be an honest man." "Why? He is a lawyer." "Danielle, if this man wanted to, this condo is already in his name and there is absolutely nothing you could do about it." "This is impossible." "Ho yes it is. I have known a notary public in Victoriaville who was dishonest and I had to pay the interests twice on the land.

I took him to court to be told by the judge that he was sorry for my lost, but because I had no proof I paid the first time, I had to pay again. The judge said that I most likely paid them, because the interests are usually paid before the principal and I had my receipt for the principal payment. The lawman said I didn't need a receipt, because he was going to write it in the contract. There you are, he was a lawman. I heard much later he was barred from office, but this never gave me my money back." "This would be quite a shot to gain seventy-five thousands in one day and lose three hundred thousands." "Don't laugh, it's very possible." "I don't, I'm rather nervous." "Papers like those you put them in a safe either at home or at the bank, but never, never in a place where you could never see them again. Janene and I trust this man." "It's alright to trust people, but it's not right to put yourselves in such a vulnerable position. Take for example, what could happen if this man died and the one who took over his practice was Doctor Sinclair?" "We might lose everything. You're right again." "Of course I'm right. Don't you ever do anything like this again. Let's hope everything is alright; otherwise our beautiful and gigantic project is gone with the wind. I hope we'll be there before anyone else to ask for the papers. Don't cry Danielle, but you have to understand that most of the business people of this world take advantage of the vulnerability of the weak." "I know; I saw what would've happened to the poor M. Fillion if you wanted to." "Here we are. I beg you darling, what ever happens, stay calm, would you?" "I will be, don't worry." "Let's go."

We went in and even though we were twenty minutes ahead of time, they were already waiting for us to come in. This was good news, because it meant we were still in the picture.

"Everything is fine Danielle." "Are you sure?" "Yes I am."

No point saying she was quite relieved to hear this. Everything went smoothly and all that was missing was Janene signature. As soon as we were out of this building I called Janene on my cell phone.

"Here's Hôtel Dieu hospital." "Hello, may I speak to Janene please?" "Just a minute!"

"Here is Janene." "Hi Janene!" "Do you have a few minutes?" "It's you James. Is everything alright?" "Yes, everything's fine. If I wanted to buy all your furniture, how much would you sell it to me?" "I don't know, I never thought of it. I was with Danielle when we bought it and I think we paid around fifteen thousands." "How much would you sell it to me?" "I don't know, ten, twelve thousands maybe." "What would you say if I can get you ninety thousands for it?" "I'd say that you're mocking me." "Not at all, do you know where the Tremblai lawyer's office is?" "Yes, it's there that we got the contract made for our condo." "It's sold and I'd like you to meet me there after work, would you?" "Of course I will, but are you sure?" "Yes it's sold, all is missing is your signature." "I'll be there." "How is it at work?" "Everything is fine with me, but you know who is working tonight." "Alright, I'll tell Danielle. You'll have to work a few hours tonight too." "That's fine, I feel good. I had a full night sleep." "I'm sorry; I didn't want to let you down." "You needed your sleep, it's understandable and forgivable." "See you in a bit. It might be possible I meet you when you come out, because I'm taking Danielle there to work. Bye!" "Bye!"

Once I had driven Danielle to work, I went to the Tremblai's office to wait for Janene who was in shortly after me. As soon as all the papers were signed and that we had all the documents in hands, I asked Janene to wait for me outside for a few minutes. She seemed a bit confused with my demand, but she nevertheless left me alone with the lawyer.

"M. Tremblai, you are a serious lawman, aren't you?" "I think I am, yes." "How is it then that you left these two girls without any protection?" "They were under my personal protection and this from their own demand M. Prince." "What could have happened if you'd died and the one who took over your practice wasn't honest?" "All this are only suppositions." "Yes, they are suppositions that could have lead to the lost of three hundred thousands dollars for these two women and this is unacceptable.

You have the obligation to protect your clients against everyone including themselves." "Will this be all M. Prince?" "That's all, but don't force me to come to testify against you M. Tremblai, because I will without any hesitation."

Janene who wondered what I was fabricating behind her back kind of forced my hand to know what was going on.

"Because of his way to do business you both could have lost everything and this is five years of your income." "But we asked him

to keep our papers safely, because we didn't know where to put them."
"It was his professional duty to protect you against yourselves. It's easy
enough for anyone to say: 'Put them in a safe at home or at the bank
or else make a copy of it and leave one at your parent's home. It makes
me mad just to think you could have lost everything when you deserve
the best possible security.

Enough of this now! What if we go get the rest of your personal
belongings? We only have a few hours ahead of us and we have to give
them the keys before eight o'clock tonight." "I can't believe this, ninety
thousands for our furniture. Is this all real? Are you sure that I'm not
dreaming?" "It's written in black and white on your contract and the
money will be in your bank account within a day or two, plus the
contract will be put in a safe place, believe me. Danielle wanted to talk
to you before giving him an answer, but the buyer had no time to wait,
it was kind of then or never situation, there is when I stepped in and
decided for you." "You did the right thing, but why didn't Danielle
took the decision herself?" "She's got a lot of respect for you. You girls
are so closed; it's something I never ever heard of in my life." "You can
say it again; it's just like; always and forever."

We picked up a dozen cardboard boxes and we went to pick up the
rest of their things at the apartment. Afterwards, we brought the keys
to the person responsible for them.

"I can't believe how quick this condo was sold. Maybe you should
get into building them." "I would need a few millions for this, which
I don't have and besides, the risk is much higher." "You must be right
and besides, the houses you're building are so much nicer." "You think
so, really?" "Yes, ours will be so beautiful; I can't wait to live in it." "It
will come. I will begin the excavation next week sometime." "But the
ground must still be frozen." "The ground is defrosting as we speak
where the house will be built." "Already? You must be working even in
your dreams?" "It's in my dreams I find my directions." "What do you
mean by that?" "I'm telling you that God is talking to me and guiding
me through my dreams." "You're inventing this." "Not at all! What if I

tell you that I learned to play the fiddle in my dreams, that I composed many, many songs where the ideas came from my dreams, that my ideas for my books came from my dreams, that I have ten very good inventions which came from dreams, that I found out the identity of the Antichrist from a dream and that I even learned to dance the cha cha from a dream. I woke up in the middle of a night once and I was all in tears. In this dream I was singing and living through a terrible nightmare." "What was this dream all about?" "I was singing my story and if you want to I'll sing it to you." "I would love this. It's called; I'm Always Upset and it goes like this.

I'm Always Upset

I'm always upset. I'll never forget what happened to me that night.
I took one more drink, one more than I can take, to keep eyes opened I had
    to fight.
When soon on my way, it's not easy to say, I hit somebody on the road.
I jumped out of my car and I could see this far, what happened was real and
    my fault
There was on the ground dying when I found a girl looking like my daughter.
When she looked at me, she said as you can see, I'm out of service forever.
She's sixteen years old and she was beautiful before she got hurt and fell down.
She said; 'It's not fair, I don't have to be there, not more than my brother or sister.
Go find my papa and tell my mama, I was on my way to back home.
I can remember when I told her mother what it was terrible to do.
I opened the door, she saw I was sore. She knew that I had a bad news.
And then she told me after hearing the story and I had to believe the truth.
When two years ago I left home to go, she could not stay and ran away too.
She went everywhere, she looked here and there . . . ."

"Stop this James! Stop, this is too sad and it could very well have been my own story. I just had better luck than this girl. I managed to bring my father home without any accident." "I'm so sorry sweetheart.

The last thing I would want to do is to make you cry." "It's not your fault, you had no way to know what happened in my childhood and this is not something I like to talk about." "Please sweetheart, stop crying, I just can't stand it. Tears in your eyes are just like darts to my heart. I was crying too when I woke up in the middle of that night and I went to sit at the table to write the whole song, the same song I was singing in the dream. This was a story I have never heard before and one that was never on my mind either. It's not easy to understand all this." "It's no wonder why you're so full of wisdom. You say that you found the identity of the Antichrist, the name of the beast?" "The name of my second book is; The True Face of The Antichrist, written following up a five thousand hours study of the Bible. The Antichrist himself challenged the world for the last two thousand years to discover his name, or the name of the beast he created. He said its number is 666." "But James, what is its name?" "Forgive me Janene, but I'm not ready to reveal it to the world just yet. The time is not come yet and don't forget, the day it will be known, the beast will roar with rage and many disciples like us will be murdered. The day I will reveal it is the day I'll sign my death certificate, unless I have a lot of money to hide. I'm not really in a hurry for this. This beast has always been cruel and murderous." "All this is very scary." "But Jesus gave us a real good message on this subject in Matthew 10, 28. 'Don't fear the one who can kill the body but cannot kill the soul, but fear the one who can destroy the body and the soul in hell.'

I love the word of God, it is instructive, it is comforting and it is full of life. I don't understand why so many people read it without following it." "No one can say that you don't follow it." "I love walking with God." "Talking about God's will, when do you think you're going to start making babies with me?" "As soon as you want to my dear love." "What if we start this right away?" "You mean put it in right away?" "I worked a lot of hours today, better take a bath first." "Don't forget that I have to pick up Danielle at eleven thirty." "That's true; better go at it right away, there is not this much time left." "We have two hours in front of us; this should be enough to make you happy and a nice looking baby." "You always make me happy James; it's so good to be with you. Sex must be the best thing God has made." "His will to fill up the earth would have never been fulfilled if He didn't make sex this good."

I think it was this particular night according to my calculations that my second son, Jonathan was conceived. I was on time to pick Danielle up after work anyway. Among many others, this day was quite special in our lives.

A week later I was just beginning to get use to my new machine, my new backhoe. I managed to get three feet deep before I was stop by the frost again. In a couple of days I'll be most likely under the frost and be ready to start the foundation. It's very important the frost don't reach under otherwise it can break everything. Yes, frost is stronger than concrete.

One night taking Danielle after work like I did for the last ten days, she was in tears. I don't think there is anything else that breaks my heart like this.

"But what is the matter with you for goodness sake?" "I made a mistake with the medicine and one of my patients is very sick because of me. She is so swollen, she's basically unrecognizable." "But you can't let this get to you like this; otherwise you won't be able to do your work anymore." "This is the first time it happened to me." "One mistake in eight or nine years, I don't think this is exaggerated." "In our position there is no room for mistakes, people could die from them." "You are too hard on yourself, even doctors make mistakes. Which doctor was on calls tonight?" "It was Raymond, fortunately he knew the antidote. He said she should be okay. I don't know if he reported me or not." "He won't miss such an opportunity for revenge." "It's true that it would be a great opportunity for him." "Let's go to bed anyway, there is no point pulling your hair off and yours is way too pretty anyway."

It took me a couple of hours, but I managed to comfort her. The next morning she asked me to take her with me to work insisting to know the basic of my trade.

"I don't go to the property today, because the ground is still frozen, although tomorrow if you still want to, I will go finish the excavation. Go back to bed and rest well; I'll wake you up tomorrow morning."

She went back to bed and I went to my jobs site. Raoul had everything under control and within ten days all the work in progress would be finished. There were three houses, but two of them were bringing me good profit when the third one barely brought me any. I thought I will have to check this out to see what didn't work for that one. I just knew there was something wrong somewhere.

"If you don't mind Raoul I would like you to finish the 222 and the 228 first." "I don't see any problem with this and you surely have a particular reason for asking." "Yes man, those two bring me a profit and the other one for some reasons I don't know yet don't bring me any." "This is very strange, isn't it? You made the estimations and the calculations of all three, didn't you?" "Yes, and this is why I'm concerned, but I will find the cause, don't you worry. Alright, in ten days I want you all at my farm. You know the directions, don't you?" "Yes, you gave them to me the other day." "That's all I had to say, do you have any questions?" "No, I think we have everything we need for now." "That's good then and call me if you need anything."

I then went home to find Danielle setting up the table and the meal was ready to be served. I don't think there is anything more enjoyable than to see the woman you love pregnant serving you a meal. I felt so much love for her at this precise moment that I had a hard time holding back my tears. I thank God every day He brings me for my two loves of my life and for the joy they give me.

"Hi you, how are you doing?" "I'm fine, thanks to you." "I'm fine too because of you. We're even." "You've received a few letters and I put them on your desk." "Thank you, I'll look at them after diner. Did I have any phone calls?" "No, they let me sleep like an angel." "But you are an angel, my angel." "Only for you!" "Then I don't mind to be a bit selfish and keep all of you for myself." "Don't worry, I'm yours and I belong to you only." "You're such a charming lady, no wonder I love you so much. Give me a kiss, that's all I want for dessert." "That's all I want too; I don't want to gain too much weight." "Same here, I don't want you to suffer too much giving birth to our first baby."

After diner I went to open my mail. There was a letter from the provincial court and another one confirming the registration of our new property in the name of Janene, Danielle and myself. The letter from the court kind of forced me to show up in the court of Her Majesty the Queen at the indicated address on March the thirty-first at ten o'clock a.m., to testify at the trial of M. Bernard Sinclair. I wondered who could have cited me as a witness. I certainly don't think it is one of the Sinclairs. It's got to be one of the doormen who wanted to prove he had a good reason to throw Sinclair out of the building. But why me? There were dozen of people who could testify of that. Finally I told myself there was no point questioning, that I will find out soon enough. Janene could have been called as a witness too, but neither I nor she was there when Sinclair went back to the club armed with a loaded pistol. In fact there was no reason for neither of us to be called as a witness for a crime we didn't witness. I had to show up in court anyway if I didn't want to be charged for a crime against Her Majesty the Queen though. In the mean time life goes on.

The next morning Danielle came with me to the property and I got her to join me inside the backhoe. So I continued digging while she was with me. I was happy to find out the ground was rather dry. The necessary building material was delivered the day before. I spread out a good layer of crushed rocks, which is good to avoid ground movements under the foundation. Everything we needed was there, the re-bar, the concrete forms, the draining pipe, which is very important to get rid of the overflow waters, the sticky blue sealant, which makes the foundation as waterproof as a swimming pool, the Styrofoam that keeps the cement from freezing. Of course Danielle wanted to learn and to know everything on her first day. She certainly wasn't made for this kind of work, her who is so delicate and feminine. Tomorrow I will have to bring a helper who is capable to pound nails where I need and wood stakes in the ground. Then I had to bring Danielle back so she could get ready for work. I certainly didn't like her situation at the hospital these days, but it was another week since we had another problem. The next day I finished the first part of the foundation with my transit and my new helper and at the end of the day we were ready to receive the cement. I got to say that I found a new way to pour the cement all in one shot, meaning footings and walls. When it's done all in one shot, it's way more waterproof this way. I make the foundation four and a half feet high to bring it two inches higher than the ground level, which is cheaper and gives me a house a lot more heat efficient. I build up the rest of the foundation with two by eight so this way I can put in a good quantity of insulation and big size windows in which I can slide full sheets of plywood and drywall. Believe me it's worth it. It's also a good advantage if you ever want to rent out the basement.

The next day we had a very nice eight degrees, which was perfect for pouring the cement. Most of the foundation workers line up the outside of the building, but I do it inside, so this way I almost have a finished basement, meaning that I only have to put the Styrofoam on the walls and strap it with one by three every sixteen inches before the cement gets really hard. The spikes get into the cement then like it would in the soft wood and when the cement is hard, there is no way you could pull those nails out. There you are, with this trade trick you just can save quite a few thousands dollars and a lot of space and all of this very easily. We were done pouring by noon, which set me free for the rest of the day. I will have to come back in a couple of days to take off the forms. I brought my helper to the other site and then I went home.

I was anxious to find out if my neighbours were for sale as well and of course I wanted to buy before those two properties gain to much value. There was a lot of wood on them that I was interested in.

"Hi, is this M. Fillion?" "Yes, it's me. What can I do for you?" "It's me James. How are you M. Fillion?" "James who?" "James Prince of course! Have you already forgotten me?" "No, I didn't forget you, but I have a hard time recognizing voices on the phone." "It's understandable at your age." "Is there any problems?" "Not at all, but I can use some information from you." "If I can help you, I will." "I would like to know the names of my two neighbours, is this possible?" "Of course it is. The name of the one on the right side is Jean St Amant and the one on the left is Maurice Doiron." "Do you know where they live by any chance?" "Yes, they both live in Trois-Rivières." "Did you spend all of your money already?" "No, but I have a hell of a nice forty-eight inches TV though." "That's good, take advantage of it. You know very well that we can't bring our money to the ground with us. Well, that's it for me, you've been very helpful and I thank you very much." "I'm glad to be able to help you James." "Take good care of yourself and see you soon."

It was almost time to take Danielle to work, but to free me some time she suggested to travel by herself from now on.

"Don't even mention it, for as long as Bernard Sinclair is not behind bars. There are only a few days before the trial, so be patient, would you?" "But you could accomplish so much more if you didn't have to watch over me." "But I love to spend those extra twenty minutes with you."

This put an end to the discussion. Four days later it was the Sinclair's trial finally. I was there on time at the address of the invitation. Bernard Sinclair was already in the prisoner's box and the procedures had already started when my eyes stop on a face that was not unknown to me but was intriguing me a lot. The buyer of the condo agent was there present. I wondered about what would concern him enough to come and spend time in the court house, knowing how busy and always in a hurry he is. Then came the time where I was called to sit on the witness seat and an officer came close and asked me to put my hand on the Bible.

"I don't swear sir." "You have to swear M. Prince." "No sir, I can not be forced to swear."

"M. Prince, would you tell the court why you don't want to swear?" "Yes your honour, I can tell you, but better yet if you allow it, I would like your officer to read the reason there in the Bible. If he wants to open this same Bible in Matthew 5 from 34 to 37 and read what is written." "Go ahead officer."

"'But I tell you not to swear at all, not by heaven, because it's God's throne, not by the earth, because it's his footstool, neither by Jerusalem, because it is the city of the great king, neither should you swear by your head, because you cannot make you hair black or white. Let your word be yes, yes and no be no, for what so ever is beyond that is coming from <u>evil</u>.'"

"Officer, ask the man to promise instead of swearing, would you please?"

"You understand M. Prince that you could be charged for perjury the same way if you get caught lying to the court, don't you?" "I'm aware of this your honour."

"M. Prince, do you promise to tell the truth, the whole truth and nothing but the truth? Lift the right hand and say; I promise." "I promise."

"Who said all this in the Bible?" "This was the Christ himself, your honour. As far as I am concerned, the courts and all the governments are antichrists your honour." "Keep quiet M. Prince." "But your honour, he made me promise to tell the whole truth." "If you don't keep quiet M. Prince, you will be charged with contempt of court."

"Can you tell the court M. Prince what happen at or around twelve thirty in the morning the night of the thirteen of March of the year of two thousand and eight at the dance club; Le Tourbillon?"

"Answer the question M. Prince. Answer the question M. Prince."
"But now I don't understand anymore, you made me promise to tell the whole truth and after I barely started to do so I'm told to shut up. I decided then to shut up and you're forcing me to speak for an answer. At twelve thirty that night I was with my fiancée at her apartment having the best snack of my life for my birthday."

"I've heard enough of this, please officer set this man free to go and call in the next witness."

I then stepped down the swearing box and a woman came to take the seat I was on. The same process continued and the woman on the stage told the court she was confused and didn't know if she should swear or not. The judge then asked her to make up her mind and to decide one way or the other. She and more than fifty per cent of the witnesses decided to promise instead of swearing. I couldn't help thinking about another message from Jesus in Matthew 10, 18. 'You will be brought before governors and kings to be witnesses to them and to the gentiles, because of me.'

Me here could mean; the word of God.

The judge declared the defendant guilty as charged and sentenced him to two years less one day to a minimal security facility, mainly because he had no record of violence prior to this crime. It was at that moment I found out what M. Charron's agent was doing at the court house when he said to Sinclair he was lucky the justice found him before he did. I found out later on that Bernard forced the door of the condo thinking it still belonged to my women. What Bernard didn't know is the new owner had installed some cameras inside and outside.

But to me the biggest surprise came when the judge stood up and said this was his last trial, that he would never be accused to be an antichrist again. He then asked for a replacement judge on the spot. He gave me a very sad look and he left the room. Another thing which surprised me a bit is the fact the doctor wasn't there for his brother's trial. He must have known his brother was in deep shit because of him.

Three days later Danielle made the same mistake again, but this time she was reprimanded by the director who didn't think it was funny at all. There is always the risk to be sued by the patient. One more time Danielle was devastated and didn't know what was going on. She even asked herself if it was because she was pregnant.

"If this happens to me again I will be suspended." "Of course not, they are too short of nurses in Quebec for this to happen, even temporally. They're going to put you on surveillance before anything else. Right now they're asking retired nurses to come back to work. Why don't you ask to be on the same shift than Janene?" "This is a brilliant of a good idea. I have the impression I'm going to need her. I'll see what they say about it. It's a good thing I've got you."

I don't know exactly why, but for some reasons I had doubts about her guilt in this whole affair as if all of the sudden Danielle was not a responsible person anymore. It just didn't make any senses. There is when I made a plan to discover the real guilty party. Of course I had my doubts when it comes to Doctor Sinclair, but I needed some proofs and there was no time to waste. I couldn't talk to Danielle about it either, because she could give me away with only one word at the wrong time. I found it hard to keep the secret from her, but I knew it was necessary. I called a friend of mine, a P.I., private investigator. The doctor didn't have too many friends, but he was going to make one he won't forget too soon.

"Roger, I need you for a special and urgent cause that concerns me a lot." "You sound very concerned." "Yes, I am very disparate right now. I need you for a week or two. Are you busy?" "No, this is a good timing, it's pretty quiet right now and I'll be able to give you a good deal. What's the problem? What can I do for you?" "I need you to make yourself a new friend." "You know me James and you know I choose my friends very carefully." "This one would be an exception and I chose him for you." "Who is he?" "It's Doctor Raymond Sinclair." "What do you think he's done?" "I think he has manipulated the medicine and he let Danielle take the blame for it." "Why would he do such a thing?" "It could be by jalousie or for revenge, this is what you need to find out and bring me proof of it. You cannot let him have a clue the investigation is going on, otherwise it would be a complete failure, that's why I need your help. He eats every day at the restaurant a cross the street from the hospital." "What do you want me to do?" "I want you to become his friend and make him talk about it. I don't want to accuse him or anything like that, I just want him to leave and give his resignation if he's guilty of course. You can choose your own methods, but I need a recorded confession." "Leave that with me, I'll take care of it as soon as tomorrow." "Roger, it's urgent." "Don't worry, I understood."

Now that Bernard Sinclair was behind bars, there was one less threat to us and I could perform full days work again. The work was going pretty fast since I create a sort of competition among the workers. There were two teams, one on the left of my quarters and the other one on the right. I put the foreman on one side with two carpenters and one apprentice and I took the other side with one carpenter and one apprentice. Both teams were equipped with the same tools. I gave the instructions to everybody in a fair way, specifying the strategic points.

"Where it takes two nails I want two nails and where it takes three I want three. I don't want any mistake anywhere and if you make one, you'll have to repair it before you go any farther. It won't pay to cheat to save time. I will inspect the work each day after five. When one team is ready to lift one wall, the other team will come to help right away. Any question? Every one is ready? Now, let's go to work then."

I could tell right from the beginning that every one of them wanted to win. Raoul with his men went on to Danielle side and I took Janene side with my two helpers. I also told Raoul not to hesitate to contact me if he needs to. In one single day all the walls were standing up. At four thirty I went on the other side to measure the openings just to make sure they were right. I was quite please, because only one of them was too small. After verification on the blue print, we concluded the mistake was a reading one, so we fix the problem without any cost to the other team. These things happen, but Raoul was concerned anyway.

"How come you did just as much as we did with a man less? You didn't even seem to rush." "You just try to pound nails down while rushing. You would miss more often than if you take your time to do it right. The whole trick is in the way to proceed. First I have to tell you that two men working together at the end of the day have accomplished one and one half day and that two men working separately have accomplished two days work. I'm talking about two good workers in both cases, of course." "How can you explain this?" "There are different reasons. Sometimes one guy is in the other one's way, sometimes there is too much discussion between the two of them and sometimes one is waiting for the other one to move before he can do anything. I was just a young boy of thirteen years old when I learned about this. We were six teams working in the wood and I was teaming with my dad. Father was the foreman and he was gone out of our road a full day every week to measure all the other teams' wood from Friday noon to Saturday noon and yet, none of the other teams could beat us. Every one knew that my dad wasn't the hardest worker also. We didn't work any harder than the others, but kind of smarter. This is the reason why one house didn't bring me any profit. I was not there as much as I was in the other two. The difference is in the cost of labour. I don't want men to work harder, but only smarter." "You should teach me how." "It's simple Raoul; you just have to diversify the work. You pick the best man with measurement, who knows the reading of the plan right and he will supply all the others who will keep installing. What you did today is one guy picked up a 2 x 6 measured it, cut it and went to install it. Every one of you did the same thing. I saw you going, but I wanted to prove my point before I talk to you about this. Many times I saw one of your men waiting for another one to finish cutting his piece before he could cut his. On my side the saw didn't stop for almost five hours. The carpenter and I installed all day without worrying about the measurements and without touching the saw and a measuring tape.

The difference is we save one man salary without working any harder than you guys. You know as well as I do that three hundred dollars a day is a lot of money at the end of the month." "I'm forced to admit that you're right, the result is there."

After supper that day I went to show Janene what we had done and she couldn't believe her own eyes.

"But all this is incredible, how do you do it? You must have a dozen workers at least?" "No, we are seven guys, but we work efficiently and also the erection of the walls is what is the most impressive. Nothing shows in the morning and at the end of the day you have a whole building to show up." "Danielle and I have to talk to you this weekend about the house. We want to be together and talk with cool head." "This sounds very serious." "It's nothing bad, don't worry, but we both think it's important." "The least I can say is you can be intriguing." "This house is going to be magnificent James, I can't wait to live in it, but it's going to feel strange to live without Danielle, you know that we live together for more than ten years." "Yes I know, but it's not very far from one place to the other and you can visit as much as you wish." "I don't understand what's happening with her at work. This never happened before." "Is Doctor Sinclair has been there long?" "About a year and a half!" "You have worked with him too, haven't you? How was he with you?" "He was rather gentle, but as you already know, he was after me." "Did he ever show any sign of violence or impatience?" "Not really, I made a mistake once with the medicine too, but he never said a word about it and there was no consequence." "Do you know if this happened to other nurses?" "Not that I heard of!" "It is kind of strange this happened only to the most conscientious nurses of the hospital, isn't it?" "Well, we are two women deeply in love, anything can happen." "This could be one reason yes, but let's hope nobody dies in the process." "There is nothing we can do to change the way we feel about you anymore." "This is not what I want to change Janene; I love you both way too much for this." "And what about going home now and make love my favourite carpenter?" "I want you too sweetie." "Take your time and make it fast, would you?"

There are things and words we never forget and some of the moments and memories that remain precious the whole life time and I have a lot of them. Eight days after my conversation with Roger I had a phone call from Him.

"Do you want to come and meet me at my place; I think I have what you need." "Are you sure your place is the best place for us to meet? If the doctor ever sees you and me together or if he sees me near your place, the whole thing would be compromised." "You're right, it's risky." "You just wait till he's at work and you come to my place. The girls here know nothing about this and it has to stay this way until we got him." "Can you tell me why?" "Yes, he is a very intelligent man and he could pick up a clue in one of their conversation and I cannot take the risk." "If I ever need someone to help me investigate, I'll think of you." "Nevermind, I have enough to do with my flock."

The next day just before supper time Roger was at my house and I invited him to the basement after I introduced him to Janene who was preparing supper. I told Janene that we couldn't be disturbed under any circumstances for the next half hour and this was very important. I listened very carefully to the tape and I understood it wasn't quite enough to charge the doctor. The indisputable proof I was looking for was not on this tape.

"You've got to make him talk about the medicine more than this. He's got to say he's the one who changed the prescription without telling Danielle. We know now that he did it, but I need a solid proof." "You realize this will take more time and Danielle is at risk to lose her job?" "Yes, but if we don't have a solid proof we are still a step behind and she could lose her job even more. Without a solid proof he's the winner. So you keep going, would you? You are on the right track and you did well, but I need more." "It's hard to believe he can do such a thing, he's so gentle."

"This only proves one thing and this is bad guys too can be gentle, but we still have to stop him. You going to stay with us for supper, otherwise Janene would be insulted." "I wouldn't want to insult such a beautiful woman." "You can look, but you can't touch. For the details, you want to get a house built." "Understood!" "One more thing before we go upstairs, you make it quick, invite him, make him drink, but make him talk and the sooner the better." "I think he's got the next weekend off." "This is the right time then. Let's go."

We had a good supper and Roger had a very hard time to keep his eyes away from Janene, but I couldn't blame him, because I told him he could look. It's also true that she is the prettiest women I ever had the chance to meet. It took him three more days, but Roger came back with the necessary proof to put the doctor Sinclair ambitions away for a long time. This solid proof was directly from Raymond Sinclair's mouth recorded on tape as clean as a whistle.

"I had a hard time to believe my own ears James, he's such a kind man and so intelligent, but I don't think he wanted to do wrong." "Do you call this doing right; to let someone else being accused for the thing you've done wrong?" "But I think in the bottom of his heart he wanted to protect Danielle." "No matter what his motives are and no matter what he thinks, he caused us a lot of grief and his brother took two years in jail because of his ambitions, this too is not right." "Even so, I don't think he deserves jail time." "But I don't want to send him in jail, I only want him to stop causing us trouble and I wouldn't object if you want to be his friend. He really needs good friends, but I sincerely doubt he could ever be in my circle of friends." "Can you leave me out of this from now on?" "No problem, if this is what you want. How much do I owe you?" "With all of the expenses, you owe me two thousands dollars. Do you think it was worth the cost?" "He was ruining Danielle's career and health; of course it's worth it. All I need to know now is where I can meet to discuss with him without causing too much commotion." "At the restaurant where he goes for supper every night is a fairly quiet place at the time he goes. I have to tell you that he believes you're cheating on Danielle with Janene and frankly, I don't think he's completely wrong." "I will inform you maybe one day, in the mean time I thank you very much, see you." "I wish I could say that I am proud to be any help to you, but I can't, sorry and good bye."

He was a friend, but not one whom I could confide to at this time, especially not as far as my two women were concerned. The next day at seven thirty I was waiting at the restaurant where Doctor Sinclair usually takes his supper. I had with me a little tape recorder and the tape with the doctor's complete confession. I waited until he was almost finished and let me tell you that I didn't worry about him having indigestion either. Then I got up and I walked to his table allowing myself to sit down across the table in front of him.

"May I join you M. Sinclair?" "Go ahead, don't be shy M. Prince. You will understand that I don't have anything to say to you, but you certainly have a good reason to be here." "Good, because I need you to listen and to listen very carefully." "Ho, this sounds very, very serious M. Prince." "This will only depend on you Doctor." "So what can I help you with?" "On the contrary Doctor, you will need to help yourself." "Me, but I don't need anything." "This is what you think, but I have in my pocket the proof that you need to find another job." "I don't want to go anywhere else M. Prince. I'm just so happy here surrounded by very capable nurses and gorgeous on top of all." "I've got something that you need to listen to Doctor." "What is it?" "Listen carefully; it's a short message that tells a long story." "Where did you get this?" "Where it's coming from is not important. What is important for you me and mainly for Danielle is that it is in my possession and I won't hesitate at all to use it if necessary." "But this is blackmailing." "Call it the way you want it, but I have to protect the one I love and what you did to her is absolutely disgusting." "What do you want me to do?" "I want you to give your notice immediately and clear Danielle of any wrong doing. In return I promise to never use this proof against you unless you force me to. Nobody else than you, me and the P.I. I hired to make you talk knows any of this. By the way, the private investigator is devastated about the whole thing and he thinks you were doing this to help Danielle. Tell me why you changed the medicine?" "I was hoping she beg me to help her." "Contrary to what you seem to think, Danielle and Janene are both very happy and satisfied with me. What you have done to your brother is also very disgusting and I'm sure he needs you now. I saw him at his trial and he seemed to be lost." "Is there anything else?" "No, that's all, but I expect you to move on this as soon as tomorrow." "It would have been easy for you to send me to jail. I could be with my brother." "I couldn't do anymore for your brother and I'm sorry, because I don't think he deserves this and the province of Quebec needs too many doctors now days, even one like you is needed. You don't have to fear anything from me for as long as you stick to our agreement. I got to go now, Janene is expecting me."

I took off and I was sure he would move away, because he had no choice, it was this or justice and his career. I went home to find Janene lonely, because she's not used to spend her evenings by herself anymore.

"How come you so late?" "I had to discuss with a client who had special restrictions." "I hope it doesn't happen too often, I missed you." "No, these cases are pretty rare; maybe one in a life time, at least I hope so. I'm tired, this guy has exasperated me." "I'm going to run you a hot bath, this will do you good." "You're a sweetheart, just be sure I appreciate it." "If you want to I'll soap you, rinse you, dry you and after you'll see." "Anything you want darling."

I let her do everything she wanted, but the next day I wondered if I was drugged or not, because I could hardly remember what happen after that. Everything I had at the restaurant was before the doctor came in. Janene had to go get Danielle because she just couldn't wake me up. So I concluded then it was only some accumulated fatigue. For the last couple of weeks I was going to bed late and getting up early, so I didn't look any farther.

The time to shingle the house has come and if is there a place where you have to be awake among others is on the roof. My two loved nurses understood it was time for them to give me a little break. They decided to give me a complete weekend off and did I sleep. At supper time the following Monday Danielle came up with the great news.

"James, I'm clean." "What do you mean, you're clean? You're always clean." "I mean the director of the hospital apologized to me, because it was not my fault with the medicine, but Doctor Sinclair's mistake. He admitted it and gave his resignation. He's no longer one of our staff." "Ho what a great news darling, though I confess to you that I didn't think you were guilty. You are so conscientious with everything you do. We have to celebrate this. What would you say if I open a bottle of champagne?" "Champagne? You're always ready for everything, aren't you?" "This is a great day, we have to celebrate." "I'll be able to travel alone again now that Sinclair is no longer around. He said having a job at the other end of the country." "I'll go to the basement and get a bottle and then we'll put some music on and dance until my legs give up. What do you think of that?" "It's magnificent my love."

Yes, it was a nice day and yes we have celebrated and yes we danced and yes we made love until we fell asleep. It was nice to come back to a peaceful and normal life again.

One day I received a strange letter from the penitentiary. It was from Bernard Sinclair who was asking me to pay him a visit. At first I thought of ignoring him completely and then I asked myself; what if it was me who was behind bars, wouldn't I want someone to pay me a visit from time to time? I knew my answer the day I went.

"I was not expecting you anymore." "I wondered for a long time what possible business I could have with you and I told myself that I didn't need you and I didn't want to have anything to do with you.

Then I told myself that your brother was far away and you might have nobody at all to pay you a visit. So here I am. What do you want from me?" "First I want to thank you for saving my idiot brother's buts. He probably didn't deserve your compassion. Then I finally realized you could very easily demolish me the night at the club, but you didn't do it. I was at your mercy, but you didn't hit me even though I deserved it. And I also reflected at what you did at my trial where you have chosen not to testify against me, which could have been a lot more incriminating. And finally I've been wondering since then how you could convert a provincial court judge and more than half of the attendance like you did. There is something in your ways that is not natural, at least not very normal. I would like you to tell me what it is." "If there is something special, I would say that it's because I walk with God and God is with me." "This is exactly what I thought. You know when someone is in a place like this here; he's got a lot of time to think and to reflect about his life. I would like to walk with God too and when I'm out of here I would love you to show me how." "Why wait till you out of here?" "But there is nobody but criminals in here and most of them are pretty much set in." "There is no better place in the world to start a ministry than here." "You're joking?" "Not at all!" "But what can I do over here?" "Just be a blessing for everyone around you and you will receive a multitude of blessings from God, but don't expect anything. Look at yourself, you're a criminal too and you want to walk with God. This might be someone else's case as well. I will come back to see you and I will bring you a book I like very much and it is called: The True Face of The Antichrist. You can learn just about everything you need to know from it." "The visiting time is almost over and I had so many more questions for you." "Don't worry, I'll be back."

'Over, visits are over.'

"I'll be back." "Thanks for coming."

Far is away from my mind the thought of such a thing to happen. It's true it is written the thoughts of God are precious. I went back a week later and I brought him a Bible and the book I mentioned to him. There was enough in this book to cause him death for the knowledge he will acquire, but I warned him about it.

The work in process with our house was going pretty good and one evening after supper I brought in this next question just to make sure everything was alright with all of us.

CHAPTER 5

"If one of us had a reproach to make to another one, either small or big, what would it be?" "Do you really think this is necessary?" "Yes, I think it would be better to talk about it than repressing the feelings even unconsciously. I had a girlfriend who kept things to herself for six months and when she finally let it out, I was totally stunned. I could not believe a person could have such a grudge against you and keep kissing you. I'm telling you that my arms drop down and so did my hope for a happy life too, with her anyway. I could not accept the fact she pretended to be happy while she wasn't. It was a lie, treason and this just can't be good for the relationship. I could never put my trust in her anymore and I left her, so yes, I think it is very important. I only have a small reproach for both of you, but I think it could have some very serious consequences." "Ho yeah and what is it?" "It's your lack of cautiousness!" "It's your turn now." "We both think you were too hard on M. Tremblai. After all it was our decision to ask him to keep our contract in his office." "Ho, this is what you believe my dear ladies. Here is what I'm going to do for you. I will change the scenario to help you understand my point of view. I hope you would allow me." "Go ahead, we're listening."

"Here we are. You just sold your condo and your furniture for three hundred thousand dollars and you go to M. Tremblai to complete the transaction. Here how it goes."

"Hi, can we speak to M. Tremblai please?" "I'm sorry, but M. Tremblai passed away and this is a bit more than two months ago now. Is there anything I can do for you? My name is Alphonse Gagnon and I'm the one who took over M. Tremblai's practice.

More than half of his files will be destroyed by the crown very shortly. Can you tell me your names?" "I'm Janene St Louis and this is my friend Danielle Brière." "Ho, this is you. I was just getting ready to contact you for an eviction notice.

The condo was sold lately and the new owner wants to take possession of the apartment right away. Normally you can get thirty days notice, but in a case of a sale you would have to leave immediately. You only have two days to get out of there. So here is your notice and a list of the things you cannot take with you. You are allowed to take all of your personal belongings, but nothing else if you don't want any trouble with the justice." "But all of this is ours." "Do you have your contract?" "You know very well where our contract is, bastard." "Ho, here come the big words. Yes, I have here the contract of this condo in the name of barrister Alfonse Gagnon and it was acquired in 1999 for the amount of one hundred and forty-nine thousand dollars. It's written black on white right here. If you need any references I can supply them to you, since you always paid you rent on time and no one can blame you for anything, except big words. I like to thank you personally." "It wouldn't end here you dribbler, son o.a.b." "Big words again, but I think you are the ones who are dribbling right now."

"Your next appointment is with a different lawyer and one you don't know, because the one you had so much trust in just passed away unfortunately. So you tell him all the facts to the best of your knowledge and here is his reaction."

'This is going to be a very long and expensive process. It's always the way when a lawman is involved. I will need ten thousands dollars to start with and there is no guarantee I will succeed to recover your money.'

"Now, this lawyer already knows it's a lost cause, but he's got in front of him two young women completely ignorant of the legal process and he's got to make a living anyway, the poor man. Six months later you spent fifty thousands dollars and you're still at the same point, meaning a dead point. In the mean time the work on our beautiful house was suspended, because of a shortage of money. Your lover, the poor man did everything he could, but he ran out of money anyway. It was not a project he could handle by himself. He mortgaged his house to the maximum possible, because he has to supply a shelter to his two loves of his life. Now he's facing bankruptcy and the risk of loosing everything is quite high. He put a lot of trust in his two partners, but they can't do anything to help him anymore. They are very desperate, but this doesn't change the facts. Now their beautiful dream is shattered. James was so confident that he invested everything he had in his new projects. He has already bought the two neighbours' properties, because he's got a great vision and he has at heart the privacy, the tranquillity and the peace for his family." "Stop right there James, that's enough. Stop this scenario before you leave us." "Do you still think I was too hard on M. Tremblai?" "No, but you're too hard on us." "Don't cry. But I hope this is a lesson you will remember for the rest of your live, because I might not always be there for you." "Do you think of leaving us one day?" "Certainly not voluntarily, but anything can happen.

Jesus was only thirty-three when God called him on the other side." "Stop, you scaring us." "This said; I must leave you for a few days." "Can't we come with you?" "No, I have to be alone a little bit to collect myself." "Where are you going?" "I'm going to Winnipeg." "What are you going to do over there? You don't know anyone." "No, but they are exposing Louis Riel's poems and I want to see if I can find the proof of what I think, that he was a prophet. I wanted to clear the matter up for a long time. Those poems are a hundred and twenty-five years old and more." "I would love to come with you so much." "I'm sorry Danielle, but not now, maybe some other time." "Why do I have the impression you're leaving us?" "Don't be stupid, I will never leave, but you must understand that I could use a break, if it's not too much to ask." "You're right James and you deserve every bit of it. I'm going to use this time to visit my parents."

"And I'm going to be left here all by myself like a cold turkey." "Poor Janene, you just have to come with me, my parents will be glad to welcome you and we have so much to tell them." "We should take pictures of the house, otherwise they won't believe us."

"When are you leaving James?" "I'm leaving Friday morning and I'll be back on Sunday night." "Then we have to take advantage of the time we have left." "Now I recognize you, we always have to take advantage of the time we spent together. Sorry for being a bit rough on you earlier, but I want you to know there are two legs rats with short tails in this world and they cause a lot more damages than the four legs ones with long tails." "We understood now James." "Do you have anything else to blame me for?" "Nevermind, we'll let you know as we go, if you don't mind." "That's my girl. Well, what about a few dances now to change our minds?" "This is a very good idea. It's a Samba."

"No, it's a meringue." "You're right James."

"Hey, I want to dance too." "Come Janene, I love to do the mambo with you." "I'm so glad you have invested in your legs." "It's a good investment, because we're going to benefit it for the rest of our lives. Did you think about a dance floor in your new place?" "You can bet that if we have enough money left, we both going to have one." "I save you more money with the finishing of your basement that it will cost for the dance floor, besides allowing you to get one hundred square feet more." "How did you do this?" "Simply by avoiding building an extra wall inside the foundation." "I noticed that you left a foot with no Styrofoam at one foot from the floor, can you tell me why?" "Sure I can, this is necessary for the cement not to crack and besides, it gives me the space I need to run the plugs and the electric wires. Also at this particular place we don't really need insulation." "This is genial." "It only comes with experience." "To change the subject, you're not going to Winnipeg with your car, are you?" "Of course I'm going with my vehicle; I like it too much to leave it behind." "But you don't mind leaving us behind?" "Yes, but it's not the same thing." "No it's not; your car would miss you too much. You didn't want me to take my car to travel at four hundred miles from here in four days and you want to travel three thousand miles in three days." "Yes, but for me it's not the same, I'm a man." "If you go with your car, I'm going with you; you will need an extra driver."

"I'm going too, because you'll need two extra drivers." "Don't you realize that I'm pulling off your legs?" "You're pulling our legs and you think you're funny." "No, I'm taking the plane Friday morning and I already have a rented car waiting for me at the airport." "But this is really expensive, isn't it?" "No, not for me." "Stop pulling our legs, would you? It's getting to be annoying." "I'm not pulling anything, did you feel something? I have accumulated enough air miles for the trip, that's all." "Ho, that's what it is. Janene and I are going to enrich the poor gas companies and the poor government by travelling by car to visit my family." "Be careful travelling on this road, there are some storms even in May sometimes. Check with the forecast before you hit the road too." "We will, don't worry. You be careful too and be good." "Me being good, but girls, you already know that I'm full of wisdom, don't you?" "Yea, yea, we know."

"No but seriously, this is the first time you're going away and frankly we don't like it this much." "This is only for a few days and we will come out of this stronger." "Ho, you must be right again." "Ho yea, this is not very funny, isn't it? I know, I hate to always be right, but I cannot be wrong just to please you, can I? There is no way out. Alright, I'm going to bed, which one is taking me tonight?" "It's mine turn."

"No, it's mine." "I'm telling you that it is my turn." "I'm telling you too that it's my turn."

"Come on, who did I sleep with last?" "We can't remember." "Come on, you cannot forget something like that."

"About you Janene, do you remember?" "Give me a second here to think about it." "Nevermind, you're pulling my leg. Ha, ha, ha! Let's go Danielle."

"Good night any way Janene." "Good night James and let me kiss and hug you."

"Good night Danielle." "Good night Janene and sleep well to be in good shape, because tomorrow night it will really be your turn." "Don't worry, I'll give him enough for the three days he'll be gone." "So I should leave him enough for you." "That's nice, thank you."

When Friday morning came I was like I should at the airport an hour earlier than my departure. I didn't have too much luggage, because I was only going for a few days. All I took with me is a shaving kit and a bag with underpants, socks and a few shirts plus my briefcase. I had a problem going through the metal detector, because of a little negligence from my part. I passed through once and I was told to take off my belt, because of the buckle. When I passed through the second time they asked me to put my arms up.

"What's going on?" "Keep your arms up sir." "What is going on? I'm not a criminal." "Do you have a weapon sir?" "A weapon, of course not!" "Keep your arms up sir; don't force us to shoot you."

Then I remembered that now days the police officers seem to have a light trigger finger and they don't mind using their laser gun which have killed many people so far. So I calm down and I let these people do their job, which was to my advantage anyway. Then a woman police officer approached me carefully pointing a gun towards me like many other ones and she put her hand in my right side pocket and pulled out three spikes.

"You must follow us sir." "Listen, this is an innocent mistake, I'm a carpenter." "What do you want to build in the plane sir?" "I took my wife to be to our new house in construction last Sunday morning and I picked those three nails up to save tires and I totally forget about them, that's all."

Then another policeman entered the room with document in hands.

"You are M. James Prince, president of Fiab Construction Enterprises of Trois-Rivières?" "Yes sir!" "You have no criminal record." "My record is clean sir." "Alright, you can go, but just be more careful next time." "I'll try to never forget what happened here today sir."

Of course it was an innocent mistake, but it was one that could have turned to a tragedy. The rest of the trip was fine, but this was a rather sour start. Once in Winnipeg I managed to read many poems, but I didn't really find what I was looking for except the fact that Louis Riel said he wasn't scared to die, him who was still young and had a wife and young children. This in itself demonstrated that he was in peace with God and with himself a bit like the Jews when they were facing death during the holocaust. I also took advantage of this trip to visit Louis Riel own house he had in St Vital and I have to admit that it felt strange. Vital was my grandfather's first name. I felt a sort of uneasy feeling and a sort of wellbeing feeling at the same time. I couldn't really explain it, maybe his spirit is still around, who knows?

On Sunday night at eight in the evening I was back home. I found the house quite empty, because my dear ladies weren't back from their trip yet. Danielle's parents are living only a couple of hundred miles away, but I know that anything can happen on the road. Nevertheless, it was still too early to start worrying about it. It was a bit different though when they weren't in pass midnight. So I decided to call M. Brière, even if it was late in the night to find out if he knew about where they may be. He reassured me when he said they left late and they should be in by one thirty. I thanked him and I apologized for calling so late in the night.

Alright, I told myself, it is time to prepare their return properly. I set up the table and I got the candles out. I also prepared a little snack and I put in front of their plates a little present I bought for them in Winnipeg. I then turn off the lights and I went to lie down on the couch while waiting for them to come in. As soon as I heard their car come in I got up and I light up the candles and I went back to lie down again.

"Don't make any noise Janene, he must be sleeping and you know how much he needs his sleep." "He works so hard and it's true that we take a lot of sleep away from him." "Hay look, he brought us something."

I got up making sure they couldn't hear me to watch them from a distance hiding behind a corner.

"Do you think we should open them?" "Yes, he put our name on them." "He's not sleeping for long the candles are hardly melted." "You go first Janene, this looks like a diamond ring's box."

"Do you really think so?" "Come on, open it up, aren't you curious? Here, take this knife to cut the tape." "It's crazy, but I'm a little scared." "Don't be foolish Janene; there is nothing bad coming from him." "Ho, ho, ho!"

Janene busted into tears and I quickly came out of my hiding.

"I didn't really and officially ask you to become my wife and I thought it was over due time to do it. What is your answer?" "Yes, yes, yes, yes, yes, yes! I love you so much; I'll be for you the perfect wife." "But you already are sweetheart." "It must have cost you a fortune? It looks like real diamonds." "It's not polite to ask the price of a gift, but they look good on you, so don't question anymore."

"What is the matter with you Danielle, you're not curious?" "I just want to congratulate Janene before I open mine."

"Come here you, I'm so glad you are my friend."

"And you James, you will never stop surprising us, will you?" "Come on, open yours now; I can't wait to see your reaction." "It's a blouse; gosh, it's the nicest I ever see. Thank you darling, it is wonderful. Let me kiss you." "Danielle, I would like you to try it on now." "Ho, this can wait until tomorrow." "Please Danielle, try it on okay?" "It is late James, it was a long day and I'm tired and it can wait until tomorrow." "I'll help you; just take your sweater off." "James, please?" "This wouldn't even take a minute. I'm just curious to see how it fits you." "Alright, gees you can be a bugger when you want to." "It fits you wonderfully." "Something is scratching me in there though."

123

"I wonder what this can be. Take it off and take a look." "This must be some needles to hold the pleat together." "James, why are you doing things like that?" "Because I love you with all of my heart my love."

This is what I told her getting on my knees at her feet. I had hidden the diamond necklace with the ring and the bracelet in the shoulders of the blouse.

"Would you marry me the sooner the better my love?" "I'll marry you tonight, tomorrow and every time when it is my turn, my love."

"Hey, me too!"

"I hope you didn't think I was going to ask one to marry me and not the other." "No, you basically asked me to marry you the first night we met." "Ho yea!" "Don't you ever do something like this again." "There is no chance; I don't plan to ask you another time. Take me to bed and marry me."

"Good night Janene." "Good night both of you."

"How did the trip go?" "Good, but if you allow me Danielle, will talk about it tomorrow, because tonight I need an affectionate lover not a questioning one." "Come here and let me love you then."

It was one thirty in the afternoon before I felt like going to work. Raoul already knew I could be late. The roof was almost ready to receive the shingles and then it will be time to install the windows also. My little lesson at the beginning worked well, because we were two weeks ahead on our predictions. There were two or three more projects I couldn't wait to start also at that time. The main one was my marriage with Danielle and for this all we were waiting for was for the house to be completed. Then I couldn't wait to get on my backhoe to clear the road all around the property. The third but not the least was the stock breeding, a dear project of mine. I didn't really have to, but I preferred to talk and discuss the matter with my two beautiful spouses.

"Sweethearts, I need to talk to you about my new project tonight." "Tell us, what is it?" "To start with I have to tell you that the house will be ready on time and maybe a bit sooner." "Does it mean we're going to have enough money?" "It means more than that, it means you wouldn't have to use the money you borrowed from the bank, so you can go pick your furniture as soon as you feel like it." "Are you sure of this?" "Of course I'm sure of this. Now I would like to talk to you about my breeding project that I mentioned to you once." "You never said you wanted to breed animals. You're talking about animals, don't you?"

"Of course I want to raise a family or two also, but here right now I'm talking about breeding and training dogs." "Dogs? But what kind of dogs?" "I want some Mutesheps." "What kind of dogs are they, I never heard of them, in fact I never heard even this name." "This is because they don't exist for very long. It's a mix of Malamute and German shepherd. I have a friend in the West end of the country who created this new breed. I met him a few years ago. He had his problems with the Kelowna S.P.C.A in British Colombia. I was quite impressed with a phrase he told one journalist that I was lucky to read." "What was this phrase which touched you so much?" "He said; 'when we are persecuted in one town we have to flee to another, but because I am persecuted by the province, I have to flee to another." "It's normal to flee somewhere else when we are persecuted; there is nothing so strange about this. What made you want to meet him?" "This phrase is from Jesus and to my knowledge there are not this many people who follow his instructions. I knew then this man was a Jesus' disciple. I learn a lot of things from this man. I can even tell you that this man put me on the trail of the Antichrist. He also made a song on the S.P.C.A. about his dogs. Every once in a while I go on his Website to listen to it and it touches me every time." "What is his Website address?" "It's; www.hubcap.bc.ca. He also owns what is believed to be the largest hubcap collection in Canada." "Interesting, but why his dogs?" "They got something special. You can also see them on his Website. You can read a part of his book too. In fact he looks a lot like me in many ways and this is probably why I'm interested in this man. But let's come back to our business here, that's not all I want to raise, I want to raise pigs and rabbits also." "Pigs?

Don't you realize it will stink awfully?" "Not if I put them where I'm thinking of." "But why pigs, you don't even eat pork." "But you know why I don't eat it, don't you?" "Yes, you told us that you think pork causes cancer." "And why I told you this?" "Because God has forbidden it to his children." "You cannot deny that there are a lot of cancer cases in the world now days." "So why do you want to raise them then?" "I need to prove to the whole world that God had a good reason to forbid it." "Don't tell us you're going to give us cancer to prove your point." "Are you nuts? I want to feed my dogs with pork and rabbit's meat. Yes, I'm going to raise rabbit too and make a dogfood and catfood with pork and rabbits. Both of them are forbidden meat from God and I strongly believe God has a real good reason to do this. You see, we know for sure that cancer is caused by parasites and we also know that pigs are full of them. I don't really know if rabbit is full of parasites too, but I know that God has forbidden it and this is enough for me. Parasites, do you know what they are?" "Yes, they are little worms, aren't they?" "You're right and either you cook the worms or not, it is still vermin. Do you know what the pig's surname is?" "Not really!" "It's called a boar, which is verrat in French and it means ver for worm and rat for rat. Now we know that pork is extra fat and rabbit is extra lean, which will give me a very well balanced dogfood and besides, it will be all natural. If I'm mistaking it will be okay, because I will have a good business and dogs and cats will be well fed and if I'm right, then I'll have the necessary proof I need to alert the world population." "Where in the Bible did you find this?" "It is in Isaiah 65, 4 and Isaiah 66, 17. The whole warning is also in Leviticus 11, 6-8. 'The rabbit also, for though it chews cud, it does not divide the hoof, it is unclean to you, and the pig, for though it divides the hoof, thus making a split hoof, it does not chew cud, it is unclean to you. You shall not eat of their flesh nor touch their carcasses; they are unclean to you.'

God's children, the ones who know their Father in heaven and do His will won't eat nor touch either meat.

Do you know that I can't find beef sausages in the stores that are not wrapped in pork skin? I also have to go to many restaurants before I can find beef sausages or turkey bacon to eat with my eggs. This is not to inviting for the children of God and for the Jews for breakfast in the restaurants. This got to be very antisemitism. I'm glad I finally found turkey bacon in the grocery store. I often gave my pork bacon to my dog." "The only thing that bothers me is the smell of the pig's shit." "You will smell nothing at all or next to nothing unless you come directly in the pigsty." "How would you do this?" "As you know now, I bought both of our neighbours and as you know too the wind almost always blows from North to South and from West to East and besides, I will have a very well kept pigsty. And if I can't eliminate the smell completely, I'll move the pigs somewhere else." "So we are not at risk at all." "This might not be completely true." "What do you mean?" "Well, all this is a very huge project and I was hoping you would lend me the money you have borrowed from the bank. I could pay you a ten per cent interest." "I think I have a better idea than this." "If it's better I will certainly consider it." "What would you say if I invest this money in your enterprise?" "I'd say this would be splendid, awesome, but are you sure you want to do this?" "If you want to invest in this business it's because you think it's good, so yes, I want to invest with you."

"Me too, take me with you and I don't care if I lose everything." "Well, I didn't really expect this outcome. Don't worry Janene, you won't lose anything. I've been giving this project some careful considerations for quite some time now. How much do you want to put in?" "I will put in the whole loan amount, the one hundred thousand dollars."

"Me too!" "Then I will give you both twenty-four per cent of the shares." "If you think this is fair we agree." "This is not all, with the rabbit fur I will make some jackets, some coats, some slippers, some mitts, some bedspreads and mainly some sleeping bags. The rabbit fur is one of the most thermal of all. Of course we'll have a tannery too. I need money to start with to build the slaughterhouse, the pigsty and the tannery and also for the fence. This fence has to be put two feet deep in the ground and stand up eight feet high, so we don't lose our rabbits even in the winter. We will need approximately sixteen thousand lineal feet of fence to cover the three miles around the property. The brushwood is very important to protect the newborns from the daddies who don't want any competition. All the branches piles are good for this reason as well. They will have the water they need in the summer and in winter they can eat the snow like every other wild animal in the country. If I start with two bucks and twenty females now, we will have one hundred thousands rabbits in eighteen months, which will be worth around one million dollars." "Come on now James, you are pulling our legs again." "No, I'm taking you for a ride and it's quite a ride, you'll see. The rabbits will attract the wolves, the coyotes and the fox from everywhere around and I intend to ask for a trapping license for my properties, which shouldn't be too hard to obtain. This should bring another twenty to forty thousands a year. I actually invented a big cage to trap them." "Don't you think those wolves will be dangerous for us and the kids?" "No, they won't be able to come in because of the fence and they will die trying. But first I will find out if there is a market for their fur and also find out if their meat is eatable. I don't see why not, since the Japanese eat dogs, I don't see why dogs cannot eat wolves' meat. Although, I'll have to go get the rabbits in Alberta." "Why so far? It's got to be a lot of rabbits around here." "Yes there are a lot of rabbits around here, but they are small like four to five pounds. I saw some in Alberta that are from eight to twenty pounds and they are the ones I want to breed." "What do you want to do beside all this?"

"Come on Danielle, don't you think this is enough now? We'll never see him." "There is a lot more I want to do, but don't you worry, I love working, but I'm not workaholic." "But what else do you plan to do?" "I would like to make a plantation on each of the two farms I bought on both sides of this property. If I plant a pine tree or a cedar tree now, in twenty years from now it will be worth twenty dollars at least, so if I plant one hundred thousands of them I'll get two millions dollars and in the mean time we can use the wood. This would certainly be a nice gift to leave to our children." "The least we can say about you is that you think ahead and see far away. When in the world did you get the time to think about all this?" "I didn't have to rack my brains about all this; it simply comes in my dreams. If my father would listen to my mom, he wouldn't have to wait for his pension cheque to eat when he's retired. I just don't know if this is still possible, but it was a time when the government actually gave the trees and loan the tree planting machine. Mom bugged my dad to do it, but my dad never consented. They really had a nice place for this as well." "Did you ever think of becoming a politician?" "I thought of it, but I love my freedom way too much for this and besides, I would be impossible to be a politician and also make your happiness. Another thing too, I cannot be a politician without being antichrist, because they all have to swear on the Bible and this is antichrist. See Matthew 5, 34-37.

I don't see why not an individual could just make a solemn promise with the same rules and the same consequences could do the same.

"This is true too. Forget about politics then. I rather have the pigs and keep you at home with us."

"It doesn't mean I cannot have an opinion on the matters." "What do you think of Obama?" "I think he's very intelligent and a real diplomat." "What make you say this?" "When he came to Canada he took it by the tail of a . . . . beaver." "What do you think of the <u>Bloc</u> Quebecois and the péquistes?" "The name says it all, they will end up causing a lot of quarrels in the province, it's unavoidable, because it is one half of the population which wants to remove the other half. This is what the separation would do. It cannot happen without any hitches. These couple of last sentences will make me a lot of enemies, but I already have more than half of the world population as enemy, because of the word of God. If things go the way I see them we'll have one store or more in every large and medium city in Canada. We will do like most of the big store chains do, meaning rather than to pay income taxes, we will open more and more stores. The world is big, but this is enough talking for tonight, we got to sleep too, because tomorrow we got to start working on all this." "When do you plan to begin all this?" "As soon as our house is completed."

As usual I put both of them to sleep my own way and the next day I was on the roof of our house with the other workers. There again I divided the work in even parts for everybody. I was completely done on my side when Raoul was hardly half way done on his side.

"You didn't already finish your side, did you?" "Yes, we did." "How could you? Are you a sort of magician or something like that?" "A magician wouldn't have half of what you've done, but you are travelling from left to right while I install shingles. Come with me on the other side of your roof and I'll show you how. You make four lines from the top to the bottom right in the middle at one shingle distance then you shingle from the bottom to the top following these lines and all the rest will be straight. Then you put one guy on each side and if you have a lefthanded and a right-handed this will be better yet. Don't forget to put the bundle of shingles near you, so this way you will stop travelling. Now if you do this you're going to save me money without working any harder or faster. I easily install seven bundles an hour. You install three and you're costing money when you supposed to make me money." "I have to admit that we learn a lot with you." "Yea, you will probably be my competition before long." "It's not really my intention, you know when a man is treated well and he's happy, he doesn't look anywhere else." "That's good then; let's cover this roof before we get rained on."

From one thing to another we were already close to the summer vacation near the last two weeks of July and the house was almost completed. There were just a few minor things left to do. In the mean time I had paid Bernard Sinclair a few visits as well. This man became a devoted Jesus' disciple inside the jail. I couldn't believe my own ears when he told me that more than half of the prisoners became his fans and the guardians could for the first time of their history take an afternoon coffee break. The most rebellious among them didn't like this as much though, but they didn't dare intervene. Another one who didn't like it at all was the penitentiary chaplain who couldn't understand what was going on. The result was a good saving for the government, because many prisoners were released sooner for their good behaviour. I was laughing to myself thinking that maybe I should send a bill to the government. I was quite happy to hear this news and I was glad to see Bernard happy as well. I reminded him not to forget his brother in this race for the conquests, that he might be his only chance. He made a funny face, but admitted I might be right. He might have known by then that a prophet or a disciple is not welcome in his own family.

Then the big, big day finally arrived. Danielle's flat was completed and it was there we celebrated our marriage. We only had our close family and sure friends as guests. A magistrate for a decent price came to our place to celebrate the ceremony. Janene and Danielle synchronized their holidays with the construction holidays to allow us to leave all together for a well deserved vacation. Danielle tried to but couldn't really hide her pregnancy. It is true that she carries one part of me, but God do I find her extra pretty when she's pregnant.

My last employee, this young apprentice was not too enthusiastic about the forced vacations, because he didn't work for too long and he didn't have enough money to enjoy them. I offered him to work those two weeks on the road around the property consisting in cutting the good for nothing little trees and to replant the good ones in the field. I spent enough time with this young man to know I could trust him. He also had to keep an eye on our house for the time we were gone. I also told him he could swim and fish as much as he wanted, but he has to save us a few trout and also I was not paying him for the time he was entertaining himself.

Danielle had already bought bran new and complete furniture that caught people eyes and made many of them envious. Janene bought hers too, but it wasn't home yet for the simple reason that her side wasn't quite finished yet. On Danielle side even the basement was all finished and we had the reception right there on a super nice hard wood floor. We had a lot of congratulations not only about the marriage but also about the house and it was quite flattering to hear them.

I made a little scenario for Janene to be included and be part of the ceremony. Here is how it went:

"Repeat after me. I Janene St Louis, I mean Danielle Brière." "I Danielle Brière." "Take you for my husband." "Take you for my husband." "James Prince here present." "James Prince here present." "To love and cherish." "To love and cherish." "For all the eternity!" "For all the eternity!" "I James Prince!" "I James Prince!" "Take you Janene St Louis, I mean Danielle Brière." "Take you Janene St Louis, I mean Danielle Brière." "To love and cherish." "To love and cherish." "For all the eternity!" "For all the eternity!"

"I declare you husband and wife, you can kiss now and may God be with you."

There we were all married to one another almost without causing any suspicion. Only my sister Céline noticed the artfulness of the ceremony. The judge himself declared us married without making too many faces. Each one of us had pronounced the necessary words to be united forever. Both my wives knew about the sincerity of my feelings and in the bottom of my heart I knew I will be their husband for the rest of my life and beyond. I kissed Danielle the way I should and I also kissed Janene and I thanked her for her artful work.

I had rented out a full size motor home and we head towards Niagara Falls. I had also rented out a nice covered boat that contains everything a person could possibly need on Lake Erie. There is where we spent most of our holiday. After many calculations the difference between this and hotels wasn't this much. This way everything was handy and there was nobody to question the fact I had two wives, but we had to help ourselves.

We did just about everything; some fishing, some sun bathing, some swimming, some walking, some dancing, some boating of course, some movie watching, some sex and to tell you the truth, those were two weeks gone way too fast. Both of my wives were extremely happy just like me and wouldn't want to have it any other way. Everything was perfect. The whole trip was way too short and we promise ourselves to do it again every year. As far as work was concerned though, it was more than time for me to come back. I had men to put back to work and some customers to satisfy. It was time too to start the breeding business, which I had at heart. To start with I rented out a trencher to make a trench two feet deep by three inches wide all around the property. Then I slid some insulated boards, which are twenty by sixty-four inches into the trench. Those boards are two inches thick and made out of insulation covered with galvanized sheet metal on both sides. They actually came out of your metal entrance door, those pieces that were replaced by your door window. I can get them cheap, because they end up at the dump otherwise. But because they are solid and strong they are ideal for my needs. I put them in the ground at twenty-four inches deep to stop the rabbits and the dogs to cross over the other side through a tunnel they could dig. This way they will get discouraged long before they could get through. This will also stop predators from coming in as well except in the places where I want them to come in.

Some times ago I offered to one of the Harper government's deputy to build with these panels shacks the size of a single or double garage for the Haitians who have to sleep under the stars and some times under the rain and bad storms.

These panels are of a nice color, pure white, they are waterproof, they are of good insulation against cold and eat, they are also as safe against fire and thieves as our solid houses and the material is practically free. What more can we ask for?

No one ever got back to me about this and yet, I think they would be cheaper than the unsafe tents they have put up over there for these people.

We could also show these people how to build them for themselves.

My two ladies were following me every day, because they both had another week off. There is nothing like seniority. There is nothing either like questions to be informed except answers maybe and they had a lot of questions for me. We had sixteen hundred posts to put in the ground, which is one at every ten feet, but that was quite easy, because I pound them down with the backhoe. Since we don't have a rocky ground it went very well. The whole place is also pretty well level which is a very good thing also. Of course, we had to clear the road first and the brushwood and the branches didn't look to nice, but they were going to save a lot of little rabbits. I had spent enough time with Raoul by then too to let him take care of my construction sites, which gave me a lot of free time. Everything went well and pretty soon I had the two ends and the West side completely done. I would need a lot more hands to do the East side. When all the posts were in the ground and all the boards were installed and the whole fence was ready to install, I invited in twenty-five additional people to make a battue to bring in as many dear as possible and then lift up the whole fence all in one shot. I was hoping to get at least one buck and one doe. I knew we could possibly bring some predators too, but I knew too I could take care of them. The nearest any wild animal could get to the house was four hundred feet. All along that fence I installed a thousand of six inches solid plastic circles to trap the predators. I put some at two feet from the ground for the summer and some at four feet for the winter. Of course I put something there also inside the fence to stop the rabbits from going out. Everything was finally ready to receive the rabbits and my dogs and I invited everybody in for a good snack that was appreciated by every one.

Danielle was ready to deliver our baby any time now. She was already on maternity leave for the last month and this was what hold me back for my trip to Alberta, because I wanted to be with her for the birth of our first child. I wish I could have taken a paternity leave too, but I couldn't afford it time wise. Then Samuel came to this world crying like most babies who no doubt was just fine inside her mother. I sure can understand that.

It was a real great day for all three of us, but I couldn't help thinking that we should have our babies at the retirement age when we have all the time in the world to take care of the mother and the baby. Even though I'm a busy man I spent every moment I could with Danielle and Janene did just that too. Danielle was well surrounded, but I wish I could have done a lot more. Janene's delivery was not this far away also; luckily Danielle will have time to get back on her feet to assist her when the time comes.

It was now time to go get in Alberta the rabbits we need and this too was quite a challenge. I didn't worry too much about the way to catch them, but rather about the way to bring them back home alive and healthy. I also anticipated seeing my friend, the dog's breeder with the intention to get a few of his dogs. I was glad the trip was a success. I only lost one rabbit out of thirty. The harvest was rather good. I heard one day that there were more rabbits in Calgary than people and this is a town of around eight hundred thousand people. I took the plane to go and I came back with a rented moving truck. I bought the thirty cages in Calgary and everything else I needed to bring them home safely. I also brought back six little Mutesheps puppies from different parents and a couple of adults. I already knew they were sled dogs. If my children like dogs like I do, they will have a happy childhood. I never forgot the fun I had with mine when I was a kid. In fact, if it wasn't for the dogs I had, I simply wouldn't have had a childhood, because my father was putting me to work constantly. I still wonder why when my father was playing the fiddle we had to put our dog outside, because he wouldn't stop howling. I had a few years back, a female dog, my passed away little Princess who lay on my foot and let herself be rock to the sound of my fiddle. It's certainly not because I play better than my dad, because I don't, I call my dad the fiddler with the magic bow.

One day when I was walking my new property, the one on the East side I discovered something quite special.

There were, it seems like thousands of little trees which seems not to have enough space to grow properly. It is then that I got the idea to rescue them all from the three farms and to replant them in a straight line and in a proper space on the East farm. It became a very nice plantation. We now have some pine, some spruce, some fir and some birch, which will be very good for our firewood, besides hockey sticks, some cedar and also a nice row of maple trees. I also planted a good number of apple trees behind our house. I just love the McIntosh. No need to tell you that I will keep an eye on the little ones and make sure to make them fruitful.

We did not too bad with the dear as well. I got two bucks, three does and two fawns. It was worth our troubles. I was thinking also about making the rabbit field bigger just to make sure they have enough food. It was then I decided to plant a large quantity of clover, which I thought will save a lot of trees. My young apprentice carpenter became a very good agriculturist and there is no way I could change his mind now. He is now my handyman and this is why when he suggested staying on our property I didn't hesitate one bit. I told him; 'Michel Larivière, if you're very serious you will help me at no cost to me for labour and we will build you a cottage by the river. It cannot be to close to the beach, because I still would like my privacy when I'm swimming with my two women. In fact I plan to build one for us also near the beach. He agreed and he promised me complete discretion.

Then came the time to recruit the seamstresses we needed to put our articles together and the workers for the slaughterhouse. I was looking for a tanning expert, a taxidermist, a good cook, an expert in canning, a publicist and a commercial traveller who would be busy finding business premises all across Canada. After many discussions with my partners I came to the conclusion the best formula would be cookies for dogs that would be very nutritious and canned food for cats. Both can be a long time on shelves and still be good. This is very important, especially when you start the business, because it's not known and it might not sell for a long time even if it's the best in the world. On the containers it will be posted; 'This food is especially made for dogs and cats, but is not improper for human consumption. Warning, it could cause cancer.' The chapter 11 of Leviticus verse 6-8 from the Old Testament of the Bible will also be posted.

My wives thought this could scare most people away from buying our product, but I argued differently. The same warning is on cigarette parks for many years already and people continue to smoke anyway, besides, cancer is always rising. When you're stock, you're stock. They admitted I might just be right and besides, this way our company, Rabbitech is protected.

"By the way girls, I caught on the news there were a lot less of cancer cases in India than there are in North America. I just wondered if they eat less pork, less vermin than we do." "I mainly worry about those dogs and cats that you might make sick." "And I worry about the world population of people, which I think is dying with a little deadly bite at the time. I think cancer is a little bug inside us which is feeding on what ever it needs to grow. For example, the lungs cancer is feeding on smoke and keeps growing for as long as these people are smoking. I knew a man who only had six months to live according to his doctor, but added seven years to his life by quitting smoking. The worst in all this is that children inherit the disease from their parents. This is not really the kind of inheritance I want to leave to my children. If all the smokers knew that not only they are killing themselves when they smoke, but they're also killing their offspring, maybe a lot of them would quit. Researchers are spending billions of dollars for a cure of this lazy disease and I believe the answer is in the Bible, I guess they have looked everywhere but there."

We also needed about one thousand pigs to make sure we had a balanced nutritious food from both meat and this is why I made a large portion of the East farm a pasture for them. Pigs are going to cultivate and enrich the soil for us at the same time. This is why I planted fruits and vegetables in great quantity and get them delivered directly to the poor people who needed them. Everything grows quite good with pigs shit as a fertilizer.

We cannot if we are God's children get the money by millions of dollars and ignore the poor at the same time. I knew very well that I needed to have a good bunch of it save for the day I will be attacked either by the governments or by the churches. It was not only important for me to give food to the poor, but also to supply them with what ever it takes for them to start their own gardening. In one of my trip I showed them how to witch for water. The ground is like a human body, it's full of veins and when you pierce one it gives you what ever it holds. There is water almost everywhere, but you need to know how to find it. I looked around to find someone who could learn from me, someone with this gift. Let me tell you that they were in demand after this and became quite rich for their region. Where ever I went there is water now even in some place I was told I would never find any. Generally we can find water in less than twenty feet deep. Nevertheless, I got those gift people to promise me to never abuse their new power if they want to keep it forever. Is there a need to tell you that in a lot of these places now a lot of them think I'm a kind of a god? I got to tell you too that where I went the word of Jesus, the real truth is also seeded. I put a lot of efforts to explain to them the difference between God and a person who walks with God.

CHAPTER 6

*T*alking about money, I would have needed a lot just to register my inventions and this is why I got the idea to post a little ad in the papers and on the internet which goes like this: 'Men who owns many important inventions seeks financial help from honest and serious people interested in sharing the profit at fifty per cent. If interested join me at James Prince . . . .' It didn't take very long for me to get over twenty answers, but the most interesting came by Email. Many of them asked me to tell them what I had over the phone and on the internet. Come on people, get serious would you.

Danielle, would you come to see this please?" "What is it?" "Look for yourself."

'I am very interested in your ideas. Please don't make any deals before I have a chance to see what you have. If still available I will take a plane tonight and be there tomorrow by noon. I'm waiting for an answer, Laurent.'

"Could this be the same man?" "This would explain why he's so much in a hurry all the time. He travels the whole world looking for other people's ideas and getting rich with them at the same time." "You have nothing to lose by listening to what he has to offer. We got a real good deal the last time we answered him." "I'm afraid he wouldn't give me much time to think things over." "Then think about it before you meet him, that's all." "You're right and it's all considered, I'll meet him and see what he's got to offer." "So don't waste any time and answer him."

'Hi Laurent, I am interested to meet you before any one else if you are very serious and if I can trust you with this, James.'

"If he is just as quick with this as he was with your condo, I wouldn't have to wait too long. There is already an answer, let's see what it is."

'Give me the name and address of your bank and your full name with your birth date and I'll send you ten thousands dollars to the desk for you. If I meet my appointment with you this money will go towards our agreement, if not the money will be yours with no question asked. Answer me if you agree and if not forget about me, Laurent.'

"Agreed, meet me tomorrow at noon at the Grandma restaurant in Trois-Rivières Quebec. Here is my name and . . . . James."

Laurent met me at the said time and address the next day.

"Good day M. Charron." "How do you know my name? I don't remember giving you my last name." "You gave it to me two years ago." "I don't remember you and yet I think I got a good memory."

I quickly understood he was getting nervous probably thinking he was trapped. His bodyguard also straightened up all of the sudden.

"Don't you worry; I met you two years ago when you bought my wives' condominium." "Ho yea, it was you who took the decision for one of them. Now I remember you. The least I can say is you can take a quick decision." "Some decisions are easy to make."

"I brought some non disclosure forms, which are essential in this kind of transactions and when they are signed by you and me I will ask you to tell me one of your ideas. This would be enough for me to make you an offer." "Your bodyguard here is not deaf, is he?" "I don't think I have anything to fear from you. Go Jos; go wait for me in the car, would you?"

It was obvious he wasn't only a chauffeur. There was no doubt in my mind that he was also a bodyguard.

"You already know that I have a dozen of these inventions, don't you?" "What do you mean by a dozen, is that ten, eleven, twelve or thirteen?" "I have thirteen of them." "Then describe me one of them, not the best one and not the least either, would you?" "Then I'll pick this one here." "And you say you have better than this?" "Yes sir!" "Then I'm giving you ten millions for all of them." "You kidding me sir, just one of them is worth more than ten times this amount." "I know but the cost of registering the patent and the cost of the marketing are also millions of dollars." "I know all about this sir and this is why I called for someone like you." "How much do you want then?" "I don't want anything sir, I mean, I don't want money." "You do want something for all of this." "I want a fifty fifty association sir." "Sixty forty!" "No fifty fifty!" "Sixty forty and this is my last offer." "Sixty forty is alright if you take the forty per cent sir." "You're not too easy to negotiate with, but I like your style, you've got a head on your shoulders. Fifty fifty is alright for me too. Would you show me another one of your inventions?" "I will the day this one here is on its way to success." "You're not too easy to deal with, but like I said, I like your style. I was just like you when I started. For what I saw, we're not done doing business together just yet." "What about the ten thousands you sent me?" "It should rightfully come back to me, but keep it as a proof of good faith from my part. You're going to hear about it soon, because with me things don't drag too long and I have what it takes to get things moving. And you are right, what you just showed me will figure out about the one hundred millions." "I thank you very much sir, because I too appreciate honesty. Good, I wouldn't retain you any longer because I know that by nature you're not wasting your time. Just one more little thing I want to tell you before you go and this is about the man who forced your door just after you bought the condo. He has totally changed since." "What is he doing now?" "He's spreading the word of God mainly to the prisoners and you couldn't pay him enough to do something wrong anymore." "This means he will succeed. If you see him, just tell him I have forgiven him." "I'll take care of the restaurant's bill." "It's already taken care of. Did you see anybody come in since we're here?" "No and it is rather strange at diner time, isn't it?" "I don't let any one disturb me when I discuss business." "I see and I'll try to always remember this. See you soon. It was a pleasure to discuss with you." "For me too and I'll give you some news very soon James. Bye for now!"

It's not always easy to hide our emotions, but I felt a huge need to scream out with the whole strength of my lungs and this is exactly what I did as soon as I turned the little road which leads to our property. I stopped my vehicle, I stepped outside of it and I screamed as loud as I could for about five minutes. When I got home I didn't have anymore voice. Danielle tried to get something out of me, but I couldn't push out a single word. I took my pen and I wrote on a piece of paper, fifty millions dollars.

"Don't give me this shit James, you're not funny at all."

I pointed out to her the piece of paper I just gave her.

"This is not something to joke about James, I will not lose my voice over this; I will lose my whole head."

Then I wrote again.

"No point losing your head, it's only money." "Just a minute, I will put a warm sock around your throat. What did you do to lose your voice like this? Come and lie down, you can talk later."

A half an hour later my voice started to come back and I asked her if she had something to calm me down.

"What are you going to do with all this money?" "I will certainly spend the first million getting a letter circulating around the world and if this is not enough; then I'll spend the second one too. You know there are so many things we can do with this money and that's not all, this is only for one invention." "And how many do you have now?" "I have another twelve and this one I'm sure is not the best one." "You are a real genius." "It's not me who is a genius darling, it's God. He's the One who gave me all those ideas." "Nobody will believe you." "But you believe me, don't you?" "Of course I believe you, you only tell the truth." "Then others will believe me too. I will write our story if you allow me to and publish it, surely someone will believe the power of God. They wouldn't be able to do otherwise when they see what God have done for me and my family." "You want to write our story. Do you really think it could interest a lot of people?" "But sweetie, there are a lot of men who are dreaming to have more than one wife, but to do so they have to divorce and remarry. Many have to do it many times. It ends up costing a lot of money. Some men go as far as killing their wives thinking to be free this way. But I have to admit it; it's not easy to find two women who are not the least jealous. I know that for me it would have been impossible to be in our relationship if one of you would have been jealous." "What would you have done if one of us was?" "I don't want to think about it, but certainly it would have been very difficult. I would have had to pick the one who was not jealous or forget about both of you. It would have been very hard almost impossible I think." "You said you want to make a letter circulate around the world?" "Yes, I wrote it a little while ago and it's now time the whole world take notice of it. This is what God is asking me to do and I must obey Him. This will infuriate the beast, but I don't care, I'll do it anyway." "You're going to get killed." "I'm going to write anonymously, this way it's not going to be easy for anyone to find me. Maybe this is why the money seems to come from heaven, some of it will be use to defend myself and even to hide if necessary. I might even have to change my name one day, who knows? Here is the letter. Do you want to read it?

This letter is from a Jesus' disciple to the entire world.

If you knew?

It is not easy to decide where to begin, for there are so many lies and contradictions in the Bible for the ones who want to see them of course. I will do my very best to expose a few that are susceptible to touch you or to open your eyes This is something Jesus really like to do. He said in Matthew 13, 25: 'But while everyone was sleeping, his enemy (and he said it was the devil) came and sowed the lies among the truth.' The truth Jesus himself was seeding.

They are there those lies and I am sure you will see them too, if only you make an effort to look. No matter what I say, but him, Jesus, listen to him as God Himself asked you to do. See Matthew 17, 5.

There are some big lies and some of them are very obvious. Take for example John 3, 16, it is written: 'For God so loved the world.' But God asked his disciples to withdraw from the world, not to live in the world. He basically said the world is the way to hell. I personally know that the world is the kingdom of the devil and you have the proof in Matthew 4, 8-9.

It is said in the same verse John 3, 16 that God gave his one and only son, which means that Jesus would be his first born. It is written in Luke 3, 38 that Adam is also the son of God. It is written that Jesus is the only son, and not me, but the Bible proves otherwise. This is a lot in only one verse, but there is more.

Now it is written in Genesis 6, 1-2. 'When men began to increase in number on the earth, and daughters were born to them, the sons of God saw that the daughters of men were beautiful, and they married any of them they choose.'

So according to this, there were more sons of God. Take a look also in Deuteronomy 32, 19. 'The Lord saw this and rejected them because He was angered by his sons and daughters.'

"So according to these words from the Bible, it is not true that Jesus is God's only son.

In fact, I think I am the son of God too, because I do his will. According to the Christian believes I am God's brother, because they say that Jesus is God became man and the same Jesus said that the one who does the will of his Father in heaven is his brother, his sister and his mother. Look in Matthew 12, 50.

But let's go back to John 3, 16. According to this, God sacrificed is first born, because it is said that he is the only one. Go read now 2 Kings 16, 3. 'He walked in the ways of the kings of Israel and even sacrificed his son in the fire, following the <u>detestable ways</u> of the nations the Lord had driven out before the Israelites.'

God would have chased some nations in front of the people of Israel, because they were offering their sons in sacrifice and He would have done the same thing????????? Please. What for? To save the children of the devil, the sinners. Look in 1 John 3, 6-10.

I will tell you what is the truth and you can reed it in Deuteronomy 18, 18. 'I will raise up from them a prophet like you (Moses) from among their brothers, I will put my words in his mouth, and he will tell them everything I command him.'

This is what Jesus was sent for, to preach to us, to tell us what to do to be saved. Then, what Jesus told us? Look in Matthew 4, 17. 'Repent for the kingdom of heaven is near.'

This is the truth either you want to believe it or not. Turn to God, not to anyone else. When did you hear Jesus say pray Marie or Joseph or any mortal? He didn't even say to pray Jesus, but he said to pray the Father who is in heaven. See Matthew 6, 9-14.

When you pray anyone else, you pray the dead and it is an insult to God. It is impossible to men to live without sin, but with God everything is possible. When Jesus said to the adulteress, 'I don't condemn you,' he also said something else very important and this was; 'Go now and leave your life of sin.'

"This is the way to be saved and if you do sin, God will forgive you as long as you truly repent. See John 8, 11 and 5, 14.

There is a very important message in Matthew 24, 15. 'So when you see in the holy place (in the Holy Bible) the abomination that causes desolation, may the reader be careful when he reads.' This is what I'm asking you to do too, not only to be careful about what you read, but to be careful to whom you talk to, because the beast is still killing the Jesus' disciples.

There is another abomination I would like to talk to you about. You can find it in Matthew 1, 18. 'She was found to be with child through the Holy Spirit.'

Was this the same Holy Spirit that was not yet in the world? According to John 14, 26, John 15, 26 and John 16, 7 Jesus was to send the Holy Spirit down as soon as he was going to be with his Father in heaven. When we know that God was so mad when the angels took the pretty girls in the time of Noah, that He almost destroyed the whole earth and all the people on it, and He would have done the same thing to get Marie, mother of Jesus pregnant. It is simply a total none sense. Look again at Genesis 6, 1-2. If I understand well here, the sons of God, (the spirits or angels if you like it better) had sexual desires. It is possible to talk about these things today, because the knowledge has increased. See Daniel 12, 4. 'Many will go here and there to increase knowledge.'

This is what I'm doing. We don't need to be a genius or a scientist to know now days and to witness this phenomenal truth.

My dad and his cousin were looking in the stumps to find babies at age twelve, because this is what they were told. Today a child under two knows better. Yes, knowledge has increased.

It is true there are some things which are hard to understand and this mainly because of the lies and contradictions, but there are other things that are very simple and easy.

Take for example the Paul's rapture. See 1 Thessalonians 4, 16-17. 'For the Lord himself will come down from heaven, with a loud command, with the voice of the archangel and with the trumpet call of God, <u>and the dead in Christ</u> will rise first. After that, <u>we</u> who are still alive and are left will be caught up together <u>with them</u> in the clouds to meet the lord in the air. And so we will be with the lord forever.'

The lord of the dead in Christ is the devil.

"There he is, the bird will be caught in the air. For one thing, we are not dead in Christ, but we are alive. It is though up to you to be caught in the air with him and his followers.

See what I found while I was looking for some guys in the Bible who had very little respect for the name of Jesus. The ones who say; Christ, in Christ, for Christ, by Christ, etc. This is when I found Paul in 1 Corinthians 15, 18. 'Then those who have fallen asleep in Christ have perished."

Lost in the Bible means condemned. To condemn oneself is quite an accomplishment, but I believe the devil can do this, since he condemns everybody.

Let me tell you what Jesus said now. See Matthew 13, 41-43. 'The son of men (means prophet) will send out his angels, and they will weed out of his Kingdom (means on earth) everything that causes sin and all who do evil. They will throw them into the fiery furnace, where there will be weeping and gnashing of teeth. Then the righteous will shine like the sun in the kingdom of their Father. He, who has ears, let him hear.'

Do you want to shine like the sun in the kingdom of God with me or to be caught up in the air and be thrown in the fiery furnace with Paul and his gang to join his lord?

It was said that Jesus died for our sins. Personally I think that if someone who would give his life for our sins it would have to be the devil, he likes them. When it comes to Jesus, he said that if we follow him (the word of God) we would never die, that we will have eternal life. This also means he is still alive. He told us also what he would do with the one who keeps sinning. See Matthew 7, 23. 'Then I will tell them plainly, I never knew you. Away from me you evildoers!' (sinners) Jesus repeats the same message when he talks about the judgement of the nations. Matthew 25, 31-46.

This is what he said also in the explanation of the parable of the weeds. Do you still feel like saying that we all have sins? See Matthew 13, 41.

I will end with two different messages, one from Jesus and the other one from Paul.

Jesus told us in Matthew 5, 17-18. 'Do not think that I have come to abolish the Law or the prophets, I have not come to abolish them but to fulfil them, I tell you the truth, until heaven and earth disappear, not the smallest letter, not the least stroke of a pen, will by any means disappear from the Law.'

"God said, see Jeremiah 31, 36. 'Only if these decrees (the law, the commandments) vanish from my sight declares the Lord will the descendants of Israel ever cease to be a nation before me.'

Now, I don't know if you are blind enough not to see the earth and heaven or yet not to see that the nation of Israel still exists, but the truth is they're all still there.

On the other hand there is Paul who said that the Law is gone, disappeared. See Galatians 3, 25. 'We are no longer under the supervision of the Law.' See also Ephesians 2, 15. 'By abolishing in his flesh the Law with its commandments and regulations.'

There is another one I call a terrible if not the worst abomination in the Bible. We all know that the goal of the devil is to condemn everybody. Go read Paul in Hebrews 6, 4. 'It is impossible for those who have once been enlightened, (like the apostles) who have tasted the heavenly gift, (like the Jesus' apostles) who have shared in the Holy Spirit, (like the apostles) who have tasted the goodness of the word of God and the power of the coming age, (like the apostles) if they fall away, (like the apostles) to be brought back to repentance, because, to their lost they are crucifying the son of God all over again.'

There will always be room for repentance for everyone who looks for it before they die, even for the last comer, just as the parable of Jesus said in Matthew 20. The parable of the Workers in the Vineyard.

Now, if it is impossible for the Jesus' disciples to be saved, no one can be, but here what Jesus said to his apostles. Matthew 19, 27. 'Jesus said to them, I tell you the truth, at the renewal of all things, when the son of man sits on his glorious throne, you who have followed me will also sit on twelve thrones, judging the twelve tribes of Israel.'

Check it out yourself and see Jesus in Matthew 5, 17-18. 'Do not think that I have come to abolish the Law or the prophets, I have not come to abolish them but to fulfil them, I tell you the truth, until heaven and earth disappear, not the smallest letter, not the least stroke of a pen, will by any means disappear from the Law.'

Now, can you compare this to Paul in Romans 10, 4? 'Christ is the end of the Law, so that there may be righteousness for everyone who believes.'

There is a liar, but this is not Jesus.

Here is a bit of homework for you

Jesus in Matthew 11, 19 versus Paul in Galatians 2, 16.

Jesus in Matthew 10, 42.

Jesus in Matthew 16, 27.

James 2, 14-24 and many more.

I'm going to let you digest all this, because I know this is not going to be easy for everybody. On the other hand, if you want to get some more, just know that I got another five hundred and more.

Remember that I warned you to be careful to whom you talk to. Louis Riel confided in his so called friends, a bishop and many priests and he died young, but not before being locked up for three years in St-Jean de Dieu, an asylum in East Montreal on a pretext to protect and hide him from persecution. They accused him of treason against the state, but in reality it was against the Catholic Church. This was not the church of Jesus Christ. The church of Jesus would not have him killed or condemned him to death. If you talk to someone who have a business like a church to protect or to defend, don't expect to be welcome, neither you or the word of God. Jesus too warned us. Look in Matthew 10, 16. 'I am sending you out like sheep among wolves.'

It is serious, be careful. Remember though that the work for God is never lost.

To be shrewd as snakes is certainly not to be dumb enough to go yell what you know on the roofs, so be innocent as doves, lower the tone and tell carefully.

The last time I had a message from God; it was in a dream as most of the time. The message was to let you know my knowledge about these things.

The dream.

I was crying and I told God there was no point telling anyone about all this, because nobody, but nobody listen to what I have to say and everybody argues the truth. He told me then: 'You don't have to worry about this at all. All I ask you is to tell them either they listen to you or not or what they think or say, this way no one will be able to blame me. They will know that I sent them someone to wake them up.'

End of the dream! It was for me the most peaceful message I have ever received from Him, but it was also a message which told me to do it. If you're ever afraid to lose your mind or anyone accuses you of that, you can answer this, it is better to lose an eye or a hand than to lose the whole body. See Matthew 5, 29-30. I would like to add to this; It is better to lose you're mind than to lose your soul.

My Goal is to get this letter circulating around the world and this in all possible languages. This is also the goal of Jesus and the goal of God.

See Matthew 28, 19-20. 'Therefore go and make disciples of all nations, and teaching them to obey everything I have commanded you, and surely I am with you always, to the very end of the age.'

Now, if you want to be part of Jesus' gang, you can make as many copies as you can and send them to as many people as you can. It is possible also to do everything you can to stop it and to get me executed. The decision is totally yours and so will be your judgement in front of Jesus (the word of God).

Good luck! James Prince.

"But darling, this letter is out of this world. It looks like it was written by an ancient time prophet." "I'm only a Jesus' disciple sweetie and nothing more. It seems at times we're the only ones in the world so much everybody is surprised to hear that disciples exist still today, someone who really knows the word of God. Don't you think this is terrible?" "What you're saying is true, even my parents seem to be stunned by your teaching and they're not school kids. Everyone whom I know and who went to talk to their priest or their pastor could see this was bothering them when they heard about these things. The pastor of the church where I was going in Westside BC strictly warned his congregation not come near me or to talk to me.

The word of God, the real truth is very dangerous for the churches anyway and it could be contagious as well. It is a very good Baptist Evangelical Church. Why do you think the scribes and the Pharisees were looking everywhere for Jesus and tried to kill him? They also accused him of breaking the law by healing someone on a Sabbath day. They said he had a demon and more yet, they accused him of being the devil. Look in Matthew 10, 25. 'If they have called the master of the house Beelzebub, how much more will they call his disciples?'

We have to know that in those days the Pharisees would cut off the head of someone who was caught picking up a piece of wood on the Sabbath day (Saturday), especially if he didn't have any money to pay the fine. Jesus said he (the devil) was a murderer from the beginning.

A few years back I made a small garden where I planted some potatoes, but I was too busy to take care of it for the rest of the summer. When I went back to see what happened at the time of the harvesting I only found a few potatoes, because the weeds had completely invaded the garden. They were up to four and a half feet tall. The same way the potatoes weren't easy to find among the weeds, the truth is not easy to find among the lies in the Bible. Although, Jesus said that both of them (the truth and the lies) will be together until the end time. Look in Matthew 13, 39-40.

If the beast could have got rid of the truth completely it would have done it by now, but luckily for us the beast had to use the word of God as well to attract a clientele. Unfortunately it is true too that there are a lot of lies and not this much of truth. The truth is the truth was hidden by the weeds (the lies) just as Jesus said it two thousand years ago. I got the indisputable proof that we are at the end time, because the harvesting has started. The truth is coming out and the beast will not be happy at all about it. If you read up till now, you probably already understand who or what is this beast which Jesus talked to us about. Just in case you are scared, just remember the end time of this devilish world will be the beginning of the one thousand years of the word of God reign. Jesus is the word of God, so it's the word of God that will reign for one thousand years. I can't wait for this to happen. This reign should be easy though, because the devil will be tied up for one thousand years and all the sinners will be locked up as well just like Jesus said it in Matthew 13, 39-43. Think about it for two seconds, nobody to hurt us anymore. This in itself would be hell for the demons and heaven for us. This would make them gnashing their teeth. God created the world in six days (six thousand years) and He rested on the seventh day (one thousand years. Look at 2 Peter 3, 8.

It is clear to me that God couldn't rest for as long as the devil is roving around the earth and deceiving billions of people.

According to all the prophets men is on earth for as long as six thousand years and God largely deserve his rest. All the nations are on the verge to find out about the truth and I'm very glad to be part of this gigantic challenge. I got to say that I asked God to use me the way He sees me fit for it. I'm happy for the trust He puts in me.

"But when will He come darling?" "According to what Jesus said, only God the Father knows the day and the hour. Jesus himself doesn't know and it's just as well, otherwise men would have tortured him until his death trying to find out. This is why he asked us to stay on guard days and nights and be ready all the time. I know I am." "I am too." "I know you are and this is why I told you at our marriage that we'll be together for the eternity. You see, this is the kingdom of heaven Jesus has talked about. We can read about it only in Matthew. This is why I doubt very much that the writers of the other three gospels ever saw or met Jesus." "The greatest thing you have ever done for me is to show me the truth." "This is the greatest thing you have ever told me, my love. I love you almost as much as the word of God." "This means you love me extremely and I know it. Jesus is the word of God and when he said that who ever loves is mother or father or anyone more than he (the word of God) is not worthy of the word of

God. This was wrongly interpreted. It's the same thing when it comes to the little children when he said let the little children come to me, which means let the little children come to the word of God." "This was never presented to me this way. James, you are a real prophet." "Danielle, I told you before, I'm only a Jesus' disciple.

There are a lot of things which were wrongly interpreted and the next one I talk about is in Matthew 8, 21-22. 'One of Jesus' disciples asked Jesus to let him go bury his dad first and Jesus told him to let the dead bury the dead, you follow me.'

"How can the dead bury the dead? They are certainly not able to come out of their coffin to do this." "What if it meant: 'Let the sinners bury the cadavers?'

"Hey, this is powerful and it sure makes sense." "There is a more powerful message in those words; can you tell me what it is?" "This is a lot as it is, I don't see anything else." "Jesus just said about this disciple that he was sinless." "This is true too." "There is another one, do you see it?" "Come on, I'm not this blind after all, but I have to admit, I don't see anything else." "Alright then, let me heal you if you allow me to, which means to open your eyes on the subject. Jesus just told this disciple to follow him as well, what is this means?" "That's right too, you're right again. It means Jesus needed him, a sinless disciple and he was in a hurry to the point of not letting the disciple take the time to bury his dad." "Bravo! I don't want you to think I want to make you look stupid, but there is another one in there." "Ho, come on now James, stop it." "I'm serious." "What is it?" "Jesus is telling us that we cannot do anything anymore for the people who passed away, so everyone who prays for the dead is wasting his time and is also annoying God." "Anyone who cannot see and believe you were enlightened would have to be an incurable blind." "There will be a lot of them, unfortunately. You see, this is why I rarely go to funerals. It depresses me to see so many people praying the dead and for the dead. King David lamented for as long as his son was dying, but as soon as his son died, he started celebrating. See 2 Samuel 12, 15-24. King

David knew God and his word." "James, when I think about if I didn't meet you I would probably have never found out about the truth, this gives me shivers. God loves me." "God loves and blesses you mainly because you love Him and you are always ready to receive his word and turn around and make it known to others. That is what is called the good seed which fell in good soil. This is what is called; the light that shines in the darkness. When you receive and accept the word of God, you receive Jesus in your life and this is something that pleases God.

Well, all this is good, but we also have to talk business if we want to keep feeding the poor in the world. I cannot see to everything and keep making you both happy. I got to find a supervisor, someone honest who can manage and is good delegating. Do you know anyone who could do this job?" "No, I don't, but I think you do." "I don't see. Who do you have in mind?" "You have nothing but good things to say about Bernard Sinclair." "I will have to talk to him, but first, I need to talk to Janene about it, because for nothing in the world I would want her to be unease concerning him. For sure, I don't want her to get her nails out against him again. When I think that his brother had nothing to do with his behaviour, I still blame myself for this." "We have to learn to forgive even ourselves." "You're right sweetie. I will talk to Janene tonight and if it's alright with her, then I'll talk to Bernard and the sooner the better. I'm pretty sure he needs a good job with a good salary."

"Bernard, how are you doing my friend? Tell me what are you doing for work, for a living these days?" "Ho, I work here and there, what ever I can get. It's not this easy to find a job when you're just out of jail." "Tell me, are you bilingual?" "Not at one hundred per cent, but I can help myself quite well. But James, why are you asking me all of these questions?" "I'm looking for a man on whom I can count to ease my duties. I got too much to look after." "Not that it matters very much, but what would I have to do?" "You would have to travel across the country and give assistance to some employees in some locations where things are not going too well. First of all, tell me if you are interested or not and if you think you can do it." "I think I can do it, but it also depends on the salary which comes with it." "The salary will be good, trust me on that, but are you interested?" "Of course I am, keep talking." "Would you be interested in taking flying lessons to become a pilot?" "This yes, I already have two years to my credit. I quit because I couldn't afford it anymore, but this was always one of my dreams to become a pilot."

"Don't tell me you wanted to fly from the sixth floor?" "Don't tell me you're going to come back on that, I thought it was far behind us?" "No, the only reason I talk about it is not to blame you or anything like that, but to warn you that I don't want Janene to feel angry at you ever again. She has forgiven you, but she didn't forget it and neither have I." "Neither one of you has anything to fear from me." "I believe you, otherwise I wouldn't be here." "When can you start?" "What kind of salary am I getting?" "Would two hundred thousands dollars a year be enough for you?" "Dammit James, don't mock me please?" "What, this is not enough?" "I don't believe it." "If you can do the job I'm offering you and do it well, it's not going to be too much." "You're serious, two hundred thousands a year?" "You should know me enough to know I never joke when I talk business." "Tell me what to do and I'll start tomorrow, no right away boss." "Do you have a suit and a few clean shirts?" "I'm not dressed very well and I don't have much money either." "Nevermind dresses; I want a man who wears pants." "You said you weren't joking in business." "Business is over, now it's time to talk about the pleasures in life. I'm giving you five thousands dollars to go buy clothes you need to do the work." "You would do this?" "No, I'm doing it, here is the cheque. You always have to look like a real gentleman. I want you to represent me everywhere you work for me. You'll have to have an iron hand in a soft glove. Did you hear about the new sowing shop on Chemin des Sables?" "Do you mean the rabbit skin shop? Everybody is talking about it." "It's mine, so be there at nine o'clock tomorrow morning and stay there until I get there even if it's five o'clock in the afternoon." "I'll be there, see you tomorrow boss." "I prefer you call me James." "Alright James, as you wish."

The next day I went to meet with Bernard at four thirty in the afternoon. I had arranged everything with the forewoman to show him the site and everything we were fabricating with the rabbit fur. I knew very well the whole process should have taken only a couple of hours, but this man had to go through his first test. If he couldn't obey an order from one day to the next, he was not the man I needed for this job.

"Hi Bernard!" "Hi James, is everything alright? I was just wondering if I should wait any longer." "You did the right thing by waiting, because your new position was at stake. I like your suit, it fits you nicely." "But I didn't do anything all day." "You've met with our staff and you've learn about our products." "Yes, but this only took a couple of hours. I'm not the kind of guy who likes to get paid for doing nothing, you know." "Well, I'm glad to hear this, because you'll have a lot to do. I paid you eight hundred dollars today because I wanted to be sure you can follow an order even if it's not pleasant. Now I want you to learn from my ways, because you'll have to do the same thing with a lot of my employees who need to be tested. The best way to find out if a man will be true to you is to talk with him about women, because if he can cheat on his wife who is supposed to be his number one in life, don't expect him to be faithful to you. This individual is cheating on himself. If he can steal a nickel from you, he can also steal five thousands and more. Tomorrow you'll have another easy thing to do." "What would this be?" "I want you to go register yourself to finish your pilot course." "It should be no problem, especially if I have the money to pay for it. The courses are very expensive, do you know this?" "I want all the details, the days you'll be taking the courses, the time and the price, I pay for everything. I want to know how long it will normally take you." "I need to know what I will have to fly and if I'll need to fly outside of Canada." "This will be a fifty passengers company jet and you will have to fly everywhere in the world. I must be able to count on you at anytime. I will build you a house on one of my farm near the landing strip." "All this is very intriguing and knowing you, I know you don't do anything illegal.

I have to admit though that I still have a problem believing in all of this." "Count all the cities in Canada which hold more than fifty thousand people and those are the places you will have to land for now. Until you get your pilot license you will have to fly quite often with commercial companies. I hope you're not afraid to fly." "Very funny!"

"You are allowed to talk about the word of God to anyone who wants to hear it, but not on your working hours and you should never impose yourself. You will never work for me on the Sabbath day (Saturday) unless it is absolutely necessary and I don't talk about money here. This goes for all of my employees too and everywhere. You already know that God's blessing come with the obedience in his laws and in his statutes." "Yes I know, but I forgot where it is written. Just give me a minute here so I can remember. It's in Genesis 26, 4-5. 'I will make your descendents multiply like the stars of heaven, and I will give all these countries to your posterity and all the nations of the world will be blessed through your posterity, because that Abraham obeyed my voice and kept my charge, my commandments, my statutes and my laws.'

This is a nice promise Bernard. I can tell you one thing and this is I cannot count all of my blessings anymore. God gave me a bunch of books I wrote until now, hundred of songs, inventions, beautiful music and a wonderful family. I cannot count all my enterprises and I also have the opportunity to feed thousands of people around the world. I cannot forget also the opportunity to spiritually heal people. I'm also predicting having more than one hundred thousand employees in the world within five years. God gave me the opportunity to become the richest man in the world, me, a man who never looked for wealth. In the last three years nine of my enemies died and I wished no harm to any of them. Any point telling you that I find this a bit odd?" "I got to agree with you, it is strange." "It's just as if God wanted to show me that I shouldn't fear anyone anymore; that my enemies will fall before me." "Don't look anywhere else, this is surely the reason." "I wanted to ask you if you heard from your brother." "Not much, he doesn't write very often, but as far as I could understand, he's not very happy." "I would like you to send him a letter I wrote lately, one which I hope will go around the world." "Just a minute now, are you talking about the disciple's letter to the whole world? You're the one who wrote this letter? I received it and I sent it to at least one hundred people." "Did you send it to your brother?" "No, I'm sorry, but he never wanted to talk about those things." "You have to send him this letter even if all it does is giving you a piece of mind. He can always do what ever he wants with it." "You're right; I'll send it to him tomorrow." "Why not today? By the same occasion could you ask him if he would be interested in a job in the underdeveloped countries, but without mentioning me, would you?" "Can you tell me what you have in mind?" "I'll tell you later if you don't mind. You can tell him the salary will be good, but it will be a very hard work in a very difficult environment." "You don't want me to tell him where the offer is coming from?" "You'll tell him later, because if you do now he wouldn't even have a chance to consider it, because it would be from me, one of his enemies from his point of view. I don't want to influence his decision. Let me know as soon as he asks more information. I'll leave you with this and keep me posted, would you? Here is a cell phone. It's yours for all is concerning your work, but you're not to abuse it, because just remember that a dollar saved in this country could save the life of one person in an undeveloped country." "I never thought of it this way." "See you soon."

In the mean time Laurent was working on my third invention and he was more and more excited about it. He told me that if this one was just as successful as the other two he would spend all of his time working on the rest of my inventions. It's promising. Wood grows just like mushrooms, which means very fast on my farms because of one of my last inventions. There is a reason why in British Columbia, in the Vancouver region wood grows almost all year round. It's because it doesn't freeze. We can sell our wood at a low price or yet use it in a more efficient way. I build a shop to make trim boards like casing and base boards and all. This way a twenty years old tree is worth more than two hundred dollars, which is ten times more than for regular lumber. It's worth putting a warm sock on the tree foot for the winter.

In all of this I knew too that one day the beast would want to put a price on my head and this is why I also built a replica of our house on one of the Caribbean Islands. Right now it is rented out to a rich industrial company president for a reasonable price.

We have now four children who are of a docility model, a boy and a girl from each mother and it's not over yet. I had to adopt Janene's children to give them a legal status, this way everybody is happy. Any point to say they've started asking a lot of questions?

Bernard has been flying a lot of hours and once a month he brings back his brother from Africa or from somewhere else. Raymond's duties are always where the needs are the most urgent. I showed him how to build some shacks with the insulated boards and in turn he shows these poor people how to do it. Those shacks are giving good shade in the summer and good shelters in the winter and besides, they are absolutely waterproof.

The letter is still working its way around the world and the governments pressed by the churches are looking for the people who have initiated it. There is a lot less people who give their money to those churches today and they have to sell their gold to pay their bills. When gold was worth thirty-nine dollars an ounce the chalice was worth sixty thousand dollars and the ciborium was worth one hundred thousand dollars in gold. Yet there are many Christian children and none Christian who walk bare feet everywhere in the world, because they are too poor to buy some shoes. Today gold is worth around fourteen hundred dollars an ounce, which is twenty-six times more. This is a good enough reason for the churches to keep their solid door locked. The leaders of those churches will soon or later face the one who inspired me this letter, Jesus Christ, my master. This one man from God, who said not to accumulate treasures on earth. See Matthew 6, 19-20.

This is from James Prince, a Jesus' disciple who is hoping you have appreciated those few commentaries. I wish you the best of luck and may God inspire you too.

Always and Forever;
Ten Years Later

CHAPTER 7

I am now the happy father of nine and not only are they making me happy, they are also very happy themselves. Ho, it's not very easy every day and far from it, especially when one of them is questioning my decision. I try not to let them see my frustration most of the time and on the other hand I want them to feel free to express themselves. I love to know their opinions on a lot of subjects. Samuel the oldest, son of Danielle has a very bright spirit and he likes to challenge me with the dogs races. He trained himself his team and I have to admit that he did a very good job with his dogs.

To have an even load size we had to add one hundred pounds on his sleigh. The distance of the race is a tour around the main property, the one where the house is located. The road that goes around it always gave us a lot of good times.

Samuel defeated me a few times, but he was never far behind. He doesn't like me to trap foxes, coyotes and wolves though, mainly he said because they look so much like dogs. It was not easy, but he finally understood it was not a question of money, but one of security. I challenged him to find a better solution himself.

"We could erect a tall fence all around our properties." "This would only push the problem a bit farther without fixing it and you would endanger the lives of other people not counting the cats and dogs, the hens and turkeys, the rabbits and all of our neighbours' animals. If I didn't do what I did, nobody could walk on our roads without risking their live. The authorities, either the army or the police

JAMES PRINCE

would have come to eliminate them all and they would have sent me the bill on top of all." "It's got to be a way around it." "Wolves, foxes and coyotes can smell the rabbits from miles away. To stop them from coming here you will have to block their noses or eliminate the smell of the rabbits." "Wow, that's quite a challenge." "Yes my young man, you better get things moving up there, because I couldn't find a solution to this problem. It's the rule of the strongest down here on earth; some have to die to allow others to live." "But dad, you are so rich with billions now, we don't need those rabbits anymore." "I don't need them, but the rest of the world does. I think it's time for me to inform you about the reason we raise rabbits and pigs and the reason the dogs are involve in all of this. I'm warning you though, it's going to be a shock to you, but you are a young man now and I know you can take a good punch. I'm not talking about one of my fighting trick here that I've been teaching you. I hope I'm wrong, but I believe the dogfood and the catfood we're making can really cause cancer." "You're telling me that my adorable dogs are going to die from a disease you gave them?" "Not necessarily yours, because it could take many years before the disease shows up. Although, there is a big risk that the next generations of our dogs die younger hit by cancer. Right now according to the last report from our laboratory, half of our dogs have developed a benign tumour. Half of our dogs eat our food and the other half eats regular food." "This is not fair." "What is fair Samuel? To let people like your brothers and sisters, like your mother and aunty Janene die from cancer? Come on boy, don't cry, it's not sure your dogs are going to die from this anyway. Only one of yours is fed from our products." "But why didn't you just tell the whole word that pork could cause cancer?" "But I told the world and the world mocked me. 'It remains to be proven.' I was told. It's one of those things you have to prove to be believed. I thought the life of so many people depends on this experience and it was worth it." "I know dad that all you do is to do good, but this one hurts." "I could have done this experience with my dogs only, but it would have taken fifteen years longer at least and think about how many more people who would have had the disease. Every day I turn the TV on, I hear about the story of another one who died from cancer. Yesterday again the parents of a two year old child affected with the disease were asking for financial help to send the kid to New York for treatments. They need four hundred thousand dollars. What do you think it does to me when I hear something like this?" "It hurts you, I know." "We're not talking about dogs here; we're talking about a young child who didn't do anything to get this bloody bug. I love my dogs very much too, but I would give them all to save this child if I could." "Nevermind dad, give them four hundred thousand dollars instead." "It's a real good idea my son, do you want to give half as well?" "Alright, let's go make a transfer of founds."

"We have to stay anonymous with this kind of donation; otherwise people would go after you like vampires. We'll have to keep an eye on this too, because there are a lot of crooks out there who take advantage of people with good heart." "Tell me dad, which one of my dogs had this damned food?" "Watch your language my son, it might be like you said for some animals, but it will be a blessing for millions of people it might save. If it wasn't for the stupidity and the stubbornness of people, this experience wouldn't be necessary. This is also a word I don't want to hear from your mouth again, because only God really have the power to damn.

What would you say if we get some firewood in now? It's always nice to use the fireplace, but the wood always goes down." "This is one of my favourite chores dad, you know this, don't you? I love everything I can do with my dogs and it helps me get my muscles stronger." "Let's make a trip and then, we'll take your brother and your cousin Andre along with us." "Hey, this is fun, I like that."

The dogs can pull five hundred pounds like nothing. We only have to help them to get going and they are happy to pull the load until they get home and then they can't wait to get going again. They go from the pile of wood straight to where it has to be pile in the garage in the summer. I made some sleighs especially for the wood with wheels which leaves the skis one inch and one half off the floor when we get into the garage for the winter. Kids thought it was very smart, especially because it's a lot easier on the dogs from the driveway to the end of the garage. I also made nice wagons with bicycle's wheels to bring the wood in at summer time.

I think the day Samuel will lose one of his dogs will be a very sad one. The other eight kids love dogs too, but they're not attached as much, at least this is what I think. Another thing Samuel loves a lot, not to say that he's crazy about it, it's flying an airplane. He never misses an opportunity to get on with us every time he's got the offer. He knows now all the mechanisms and I'm pretty sure if he had to, he could fly us out of troubles. So much that I asked Bernard to never let the keys out of site. I certainly don't want that if he ever has the idea to run away to do it with a fifty millions dollars unit. I bought him books on flying and I offer him to take some courses as soon as he is old enough to be admitted. When the time comes, he sure would have the theory and a bit of practice, because Bernard let him take over the controls quite often.

My second oldest son, Janene's oldest is quite a different character and he also has totally different ambitions. He loves dogs too, but he has adopted only one and it's his dogs and no one else. Do not touch his dog. He is passionate with wood and everything that can be done or built with wood. I can see him becoming a cabinet maker and a very talented architect. He wanted to build a doghouse for every one of our dogs, but I had to say no. I only allowed him to build one for his own dog. His doghouse is a palace, but the main reason I didn't want him to build one for all the dogs is the fact the dogs pee on them and the smell never goes away on a wood unit. The smell stays impregnated in the wood. This is why I built with his help the doghouses with insulated boards and we built them without a floor. The dogs, just like the pig knows how to build its own bed better than anyone else. The hard and flat floor is simply not good for their hips.

The doghouses built with this kind of material are easily washable and with a bit of rain the smell goes away. But to Jonathan, my doghouses are too plain and he preferred to build for his dog a house like ours. He also designed many different wood moldings and said that one day he likes to change all the moldings in our house with our permission of course.

He spends most of his spare time in the wood shop designing and experiencing new techniques. This is why I let him run this part of the business, because he does a better job than I could do myself even at his young age. He is also the one who does all the finishing of our new houses for Fiab Enterprises.

We have founded our own private school and every child of a Jesus' disciple is welcome. We have among us qualified teachers who lead our children to their graduation safe from the lies of this world.

When they'll be ready for university, they'll know enough about the truth not to let others stuff them up like turkeys. Any point telling you that they are like their parents always thirsty for the truth and that they love God with all of their heart knowing the repentance is the only way to be in peace with our Creator.

Raymond Sinclair is the doctor in charge of our laboratory, besides travelling still to the poor countries. He does it now by pleasure for he became a millionaire longtime ago. He started to work for me at three hundred thousand dollars a year and I believe this was the reason he took the job in the first place. I'm very happy today that he took this challenge seriously and I have to thank Bernard for that, he who is still of an extraordinary help and most faithful assistant.

Right from the beginning of breeding dogs and rabbits we have tested our dogs for cancer and there was nothing to report. We have also tested dogs from strangers and neither there was anything to report, but all the dogs that have been fed with pork and rabbit for more that ten years have developed a benign cancer to their intestines and to the liver for now. All of the other partners who are involved in this enterprise believe too now the disease will be transmitted to the dog's offspring. We have the convincing proof now, because the puppies born from a sick mother also has the disease which was not the case before. Keep in mind too that this food is the most natural.

Now all I'll have to do is to create a real panic among the population. I'm sure of one thing though and this is people instead of congratulate me will sue me for the lost of their animal. So again, I'll have to remain anonymous. It was obvious the main cause of the disease was pork and I told myself God had a good reason enough to forbid people from eating it. It was clear in my mind too that the people responsible for what ever is written in the Bible kind of put a lid on this one and the leaders of Christian churches never to my knowledge preached against eating this pork meat, at least not in my time.

'He was a murderer from the beginning.' Jesus said. To most people I talked to about this, they argued that Jesus said it's not what goes in the mouth that defiles men, but what comes out of it. I asked them then what was Jesus talking about and they don't really know. I asked them too to be careful when they read Matthew 15, 1-20. Jesus is not talking about unfit food but about unclean hands.

Jesus, as far as I know said in Matthew 5, 17 that he didn't come to abolish the Law or the prophets. This means then he didn't abolish what the prophets said either. Many prophets said that God doesn't want his children to eat pork. Jesus knew also what each and every prophet have said before him since he spent many years studying.

We changed the food diet of some of the sick dogs completely to feed them with beef stew only. There is only one problem with this one, the dogs always want more and they are getting too fat, so we have to make them run a lot more. One good thing about it is they're getting stronger and more energetic. Samuel is the happiest about this one and for a good reason too; he wins almost all the races now. He was also happy to hear that his little Princess' condition was stabilized. Unfortunately we had to keep the experience going on and what we have been doing is to feed half of the sick dogs with pork and rabbit and the other half with the beef stew. Again the results are astonishing, because all the dogs we kept feeding on pork and rabbit got worst while the others were stabilized.

We had a special meeting to discuss the best way to alert the population. My main argument is always the same and I say that most people and organizations would want us to supply them with proofs and it's basically impossible to do it without giving ourselves up. It was then I decided the best way to do this was to become an anonymous columnist. It was not for the money, because I have more of it at this time than I will ever need. So I looked for a newspaper that could publish my chronicles, not only in our province but in many other papers around the world and this in as many languages as possible. I introduced myself as someone who knows the Bible more than anyone else. The biggest problem was to keep my anonymity and because I wanted to sign my chronicles with a pseudonym, which is; from a Jesus' disciple, not everyone at the assembly was in favour of it. One of the members let out:

"Hey, have the courage to face the music and be responsible for your actions." "You want to be the first one to pierce me?" "I answered him with this question. To my surprise the majority of them voted in my favour anyway. Only the director knew my real identity and he promised me to keep the secret. He also told me he would be the first one to read my chronicles.

"Why not be the first one to ask me a question?" "Alright, here it is. Does God really exist?" "What would you say about eight published books, fourteen patented inventions, two hundred and sixty beautiful songs, besides divine music, fifteen successful enterprises across the world, one of them is operating in the whole world bringing me a billion dollars a week, two beautiful wives and a wonderful family. All of this came to me with dreams where I spent time with God." "I would say this is impossible." "My friend, nothing is impossible to God, except doing something wrong." "Why do you want to write chronicles for our newspaper when you could buy our business like a piece of bread?" "Don't tell me you're thinking I don't have enough enterprises." "I guess you're right." "I got to admit though that it crossed my mind and I didn't completely excluded the idea either. I'll see how it goes under your directions." "Did you say you have two wives?" "Yes I do have two charming and beautiful wives and nine adorable children." "Are you Moslem?" "I belong to no religion." "Many would say that you are an atheist." "An atheist is someone who doesn't believe in God, not someone who doesn't believe in religions. If you're going to read all of my chronicles, you'll understand a lot of things." "I must know about everything that is written in my papers." "I understand and I must warn you that it's going to be some protestations from time to time, mainly from churches." "Why would the churches protest against the word of God being preached?" "The fact you're asking should be your answer. It's my intention too to buy some TV stations" "Tqs is almost always in trouble maybe you can afford it." "Yes and the government will probably dictate to me what to say on the air." "You're not far from the truth. Well, the direction has voted for you, you just have to start and we'll see how it goes." "Would you object if I publish our conversation, I mean your first question and my answer?" "No, go right ahead, I approve. It's just a proof of your integrity." "Can you give me the name of the fiercest opponent of this meeting?" "I don't blame you, his name is Charles Dumas." "Thank you M. Courrois, I appreciate it and see you soon."

"Darling, you got to be careful and not take over more than you can do. You know that your physical and mental health is very important to us." "Don't worry Danielle, I will not do what I cannot do, but as you know, it takes what it takes. I obtained a column's space in the newspaper, but there was quite a bit of oppositions. A man called Charles Dumas is one to keep an eye on." "What was his argument?" "He absolutely wanted to know my name. He smells like trouble that we shouldn't neglect at any time." "Alright, I'll warn the others and get a picture of him." "How is it at work? Did you think about my proposition?" "I discussed it a little bit with Janene, but we didn't take any decision yet." "You realize that the risk of being kidnapped is getting higher every day, don't you? The day someone finds out I'm the author of this famous letter; we will all be in danger." "I know James, but maybe we are over reacting. Maybe the world is not as bad as we say it is." "The danger is permanent Danielle and I hope you're not waiting until it's upon us to believe in it. This is why I have to inform you about our run away plan in case of an invasion. Our alarm system is good, but it might not be enough. If something seems very unusual to you, you gather all the kids and go to the cottage and put the seadoo in front of the rowboat and pull all the kids up the river to Bernard's house. He then will take you all to a safe place." "Yes, but you're forgetting there is a fence that blocks the river." "Five feet of it is just a mirage. It just looks like it's there, but it's not. It's just a mirror trick, that's all. I'll show you this on Saturday. We cannot tell the others for security reasons. It's not good to show all of our trumps and if ever Samuel knew about it, he would be in the plane every day. This would jeopardize our secret that has to stay secret." "Let's talk about our job in the hospital, what do you have in mind exactly?" "I thought about either buying or building a bran new private hospital, a hospital where you could share the direction with Janene. I don't know if you know about this, but hospitals will be the best places to kill the Jesus' disciples when the beast is infuriated. In those days all it would take to be sentenced to death is for a person to say in court that he doesn't want to swear. There was a real good reason for Jesus to tell us to reconcile with the one who wants to take our coat. See Matthew 5, 40: 'If someone wants to sue you for your coat give him also your tunic.'

Your life is worth more than your coat and your job, don't you ever forget this. In the new hospital we could put in place an appropriate alarm system, which the government will never do for the hospital where you're working now." "Well, all I can say is that your arguments are rather convincing. I will talk to Janene again on Saturday about it and we'll let you know what we have decided." "Don't forget we have billions that are sleeping in the world, we should do something important with some of it, especially if it's for a good cause." "We already have more than thirty good causes in the world as we speak." "This gives thousands of jobs to people and it never impoverished us the least, on the contrary." "You're right, we are richer and richer every day." "A lot more than necessary, except maybe, to help others and to make things better, like your work situation. It's true that you don't need to work anymore except to keep you busy and maybe help the health department. Although with your own hospital you could do all the same things, plus, you would be more secure. We could also form new doctors and new nurses and finance them without choking them for repayments." "You will never quit, will you? I hope all of our children have inherited your sense of generosity." "I hope they will be more like you, a bit more balanced."

The chronicles in the papers are more and more popular and all of them but one were approved by the direction of the journal. The only one that was refused was quite a bit spicy towards the government, but to my surprise even the spicy ones towards the clergy were accepted. There are still some people who love the truth even if it is not always good to tell, I mean it is sometime risky to tell. Critics towards me are often very harsh, which makes debates quite hot. I got to say that I'm never out of subjects when it comes to writing. I receive thousands of letters through the newspaper and I only have to choose the subject on which I want to debate. Most of the time, my interlocutors have to argue with the Bible of their choice. I'm not responsible for what it contains and neither the interpretation the churches made of it. There was very bad news in the paper one day though. The director, M. Jean Courrois didn't show up at work as usual, which is not at all one of his habits. I called my friend Roger, the P.I, because I wanted to know more about the whole thing.

"Why do you thing it concerns you?" "I got the feeling it has something to do with my chronicles in the paper." "Ho, this is you too, the controversial chronicles in the paper?" "It's secret, but yes Roger, it's me the controversial." "What can I do for you?" "I need to know if someone missed work in the last few days. I think that if we find out who missed work, we're going to find who is behind M. Courrois' troubles. I also received a suspension notice for my chronicles written in the paper and this is exactly where my chronicles usually are. I know for sure the director wouldn't have done this without talking to me first." "If he's not there, he cannot tell you." "I agree with you on this one, but just the day after his disappearance, I find this a bit odd, mainly because there are five more days before my new article should be published." "You might be right." "I also need to know who the interim director is and who the director in waiting is. This too could lead us to the right suspect. Don't forget the cops are probably already investigating." "I don't think I can help you with this one James, I'm sorry." "Can you tell me why? You're the only one I can trust with this?" "Everyone knows me at the paper and they will be suspicious as soon as I show up there, especially if the person responsible is present." "You say everyone knows you, but would you know someone in there who could do something to hurt M. Courrois?" "Frankly I don't." "Do you know someone we can trust and can get in there and try to find out for me? Maybe a pretty girl who is looking for a job as a journalist? We need someone who can write without making too many mistakes." "There is my secretary, but I would have to talk to her." "We have to find her some references other than the ones from you. We also have to make sure that nothing is tying her to you." "You seem to be suspicious of someone?" "I don't have something very solid and even if I had it would be best I don't talk about it." "Why is that?" "Because, the only fact she's suspicious of someone in particular she would be distrustful and this would give her away, which could then be very risky."

"You're absolutely right. It shouldn't be too long, because all you want to know is if someone is out of there more often than he should and who replaces M. Courrois, is that it?" "That's all I need for now. When she got this information will get her a doctor notice and she can stay out until the next assignment if it's necessary. Then we'll need somebody to follow the absentee loafer. Do you know someone who is dependable and could do this secretly?" "There is a P.I. I hire from time to time and he is very competent. I can introduce him to you if you want?" "No, it's best I keep a low profile in this and I'm sure you can take care of it yourself. I trust your judgement. Send me an Email as soon as you got something new, there is no time to waste. The life of the director might be at risk. Don't mention my name to anyone at any time, would you?" "Can you tell me why?" "Yes, my life too depends on it." "It's quite serious then?" "You said it Roger, but I trust you can do the job. I got to go now, there is another mission awaiting me, see you."

"Raymond, can you come to my place the sooner the better, I got something to discuss with you." "Of course I can come James, you're still the boss as far as I know. I'll come right away. I should be there in fifteen minutes." "Alright, I'll watch the gate and let you in when I see your car. Can you pick Bernard up on your way in? I got to speak to both of you." "Something's wrong James? You sound worried." "It's very serious and pressing Raymond, please hurry up, I'm waiting for you."

It was not very long before they were both at my door and I invited them to come in.

"You sound so worried James; tell me what the heck happened." "I have good reasons to believe someone wants to know who I am and this would be the reason why M. Courrois, the paper director is missing." "What does he have to do with this?" "He knows the identity of the writer who pisses off the churches leaders and I think they will go as far as torture him to find out who he is. This is why I think we have to act very fast. The one behind all this knows it and he wants my head." "What do you have in mind?" "I want to create a special swat team to deliver this man and keep this team ready to intervene in other similar situations in the future. I want a secret team that can act very quickly and efficiently." "You know James that at the laboratory we make all kind of experiences and there are a couple of them I was going to talk to you about this week anyway. Maybe it's the time now?" "What it is Raymond?" "It's a solution that can put everybody to sleep inside a room for up to three hours." "Do you know if there are any consequences in using it?" "All the animals that were in contact with it seem to be normal when they wake up." "This is very interesting. In what form does it come?" "So far we only have it in a form of powder." "Would you dare using it on yourself?"

"Just a minute here James, you're not going to risk my brother's life just to make an experience, are you?" "I don't want to risk Raymond's life Bernard; I just want to know if it works on people."

"Don't worry brother, it's not dangerous at all, except maybe for getting caught sleeping on the job and I'm sure the boss would be understanding in this case. I was on the verge to experiment it any day anyway. If you want to, I'll go get some of it and come right back for the experience." "Do you know if there is a way to wake up the person?" "We tried to wake up the rats and there was no way we could. They only woke up when the effect was over, but they were in good shape then." "How they absorbed the solution?" "We simply threw the powder in the air and walked out of the room to keep an eye on them. When the powder was down we returned with our gas mask of course and tried to wake them up, but like I said there was no way." "This is very, very interesting and it could be very useful as well."

"I don't like the idea of seeing you out of control, it's scary." "I told you Bernard, there is no danger."

"There is another experience you wanted to talk to me about." "Yes, I can paralyse a person with only one touch and bring it back to normal with another touch." "This is a bit more disturbing, don't touch me please? We'll talk about this one later, if you don't mind. Go get this powder now, you need some rest."

"What about you Bernard, do you think you can follow someone without being caught?" "No chance, I would be caught in less than five minutes." "Would you like to be part of a swat team?" "This yes, I would like to use my karate from time to time too." "You could keep in shape by teaching my kids, boys and girls. I'm sure they would like it and this would keep you busy in your spare time and besides, this way you could keep an eye on them. I only have one restriction." "What is it?" "I want them to learn to hit someone only if it's absolutely necessary." "Always the same, you could kill a bear with your bare hands, but you wouldn't hurt a fly." "It's true that I can kill a fly if it's necessary, but in no time I want to hurt it and beware to anyone I see pulling one of its wings just to see it suffer. Bernard, among all the people you know by visiting prisoners, it must be someone qualified and trustworthy for a cause like this one? It's even possible that he could have some important tips for us considering where is coming from. When I was a kid I formed a gang to intimidate the bullies who were intimidating the smaller and helpless kids. We kind of gave them a treat of there own medicine and nine times out of ten it was enough for them to stop this little game. We didn't know much about the future, but I'm pretty sure that by doing so we have discouraged a lot of them from doing wrong. Here is Raymond coming back." "You can see everything that's happening around here." "Yes, and this for five miles around. I have forty cameras around the property. The one who would try to force the entrance's gate would get a pretty bad surprise even if this was a cop." "What would happen to him if you don't mind telling me?" "I can only tell you that they better have a lot of tomato juice." "No, is it what I think it is?" "It stinks a lot and lasts long enough for them to never forget about it. So if you ever hear about someone being sprayed, you can ask where exactly the beast was. Maybe you would find out who tried to break into my place." "I don't know how you do it, but I got to say that it's very tricky." "It would be hard for him to tell you where without incriminating himself. And if someone tries harder to come in my property uninvited something even worst would happen to him. Do you want to go down and open to your brother please?"

"Are you absolutely sure there is no risk about this formula?" "Yes Bernard, everything will be fine, you'll see." "You're my only family and I don't want something bad to happen to you." "I'm only going to sleep for a few hours, that's all. It's almost the same thing than a sleeping pill, nothing bad. The only difference is that it acts quicker because it's not watered from our saliva and neither by our body water. Also because the effect starts sooner it also ends sooner. So would you just stop worrying, I'm sure that you took some sleeping pills yourself without risking your life."

"We have to find a way to spray this powder without alarming anyone. We also have to be very careful with that product, if it ever falls into the hands of criminals, like banks robbers for instance, they could cause a lot of damage." "I think I have an idea that could work without anyone else to know about it." "Hold on to it Bernard, I want to hear the last minute news first."

'The percentage rate on bank loans are the lowest ever since their creation. And now here is a special news bulletin about the Courrois's affair. Police believes that we are facing a kidnapping and they expect hearing about a demand for ransom at anytime now. Police says it could also be for revenge about a publication that someone didn't like. The police commander in chef says that such a demand is usually formulated within twenty-four hours and he will be more able to answer our questions in a few hours.'

"I don't believe in a ransom and we too we'll be able to tell more in a few hours. In the mean time we're better keep working on our plan to save this man, because I would be very disappointed if we get there too late. So Raymond, you're going to rest for a couple of hours and don't sniff too hard, I don't want to lose you for the rest of the day."

"You and me Bernard, we are putting a gas mask on and watch how it goes." "This experience doesn't worry you?" "I learn to trust Raymond and I think that if he wanted to kill himself he wouldn't do it at my place and I also think that he has all kind of reasons to love life." "You're right and besides, if he wanted to kill himself, neither you nor me could stop him."

"You said you have a safe way to use this powder?" "Yes, what if we put it inside a cigarette which nobody would suspect anything, it could then been blown inside the room without alarming anyone." "This is a wonderful idea and we're going to experience it right away."

"You're forgetting something." "What is it?" "You don't smoke and none of us does, we don't have any cigarette." "No but, I have a pen and this is going to work for now. See, I'll take the bottom part of this pen, I'll put the powder in it and I'll blow it out when the time comes.'

"Raymond, you sit down on the bed, I want to experience it from ten feet away."

"Bernard, you keep your mask on, because one of us who sleeps on the job is enough and I'll need you for the next few hours. Are you ready? Bernard, you watch your brother and make sure he doesn't fall on the floor. You've got to measure the time it takes for him to go into his dreams also. Ready? I blow."

I blew the powder and I put my mask on as quickly as I could and then I felt immediately very dizzy to the point I had to sit down not to fall on the floor. I was half way gone, but I noticed when Bernard came and helped me to the bed. It was a good thing that we were three of us; otherwise we would have had to start all over again and maybe run out of time.

"What happened Bernard? How long did I sleep?" "You slept little over an hour and this even if I tried to wake you up. Raymond is still sleeping and there is nothing we can do to wake him up, he's totally passed out." "I wonder if my mask is damaged. We'll have to test it." "I think you were exposed to the powder long enough to be affected. Your nose was very close to the powder, you know?" "This is true, but I did it so quickly." "Raymond fell in twenty seconds." "This could be dangerous for us." "How's that?" "If the one who blows the powder falls asleep before the others, it's risky. We cannot blow this powder while someone else holds a gun, because he would have time to shoot before he falls asleep." "If he doesn't feel at risk, he wouldn't have a gun in his hand." "You're right; we have to make sure we don't look like a threat to them. It's got to be just like a surprise party. I can just imaging the surprise they will get when they wake up in jail. I hope I can get a picture of this and start a new collection. The cigarette idea is a very good one, because no one will suspect it and the one who will introduce himself could even offer them a cigarette after taking the one that is of interest to us. We need a cigarette rolling machine right away with which we'll practice with tobacco and flower, so we need tobacco and tubes also. We also need rope and duck tape to tie them up when they are asleep. Make sure to keep your cell phone with you. I would like the cops to pick them up while they are still sleeping. You can take pictures with your cell, don't forget. I already have someone who is working on following the trail that will lead us to M. Courrois and as soon as we got the information we'll have to act quickly. Please go get what we need, Raymond should sleep for another hour. Here is the list of items we need." "Are you sure we don't need anything else?" "Is your gun licensed up to date? We probably won't need to use it, but it's best that one of us got a weapon just in case. Go ahead now; I've got a lot of phone calls to make. You know your way out." "I'll be back as soon as I can, see you." "I'll keep an eye on Raymond."

I went down to the garage to pick up a drill and a drill bit even smaller than a needle. I quickly came back the same way in the small elevator, which I'm the only one to know about. Its door looks like the door of a huge safe similar to the ones they have in banks and no one ever asked any question about it. This elevator takes me to the cold room in the garage where there is in appearance another identical safe. On the door of this safe there is an inscription where it's written: 'Every attempt to open this safe without the proper combination would result in an intern explosion that will destroy all of its content, by James Prince. It's written in both official languages of this country. I couldn't wait any longer and I phoned Roger, because I was really getting impatient.

"Do you have something Roger, anything at all?" "No, I'm sorry, we have next to nothing. The only one who's taking a longer coffee break is a man by the name of Charles Dumas. He takes his break between two and four, which is a bit much and normal for a senior executive of this kind of enterprise." "Did she find out who replaced M. Courrois?" "She thinks it's either Dumas or a lady called Catherine Chouinard." "Don't lose any time and put your man on the trail of Dumas as soon as he gets out of the building, he is our man and find out everything you can on this guy. Phone me back as soon as you get something and I mean anything." "Why do you think it's him?" "What you just told me confirms my suspicions, don't waste any time, it's a question of life and death for Courrois. They cannot let him alive without risking jail time."

In the mean time Bernard was about to be back and Raymond showed signs of waking up. It was almost noon and we had so many things yet to adjust. I was afraid of one thing among others and this was our man falling asleep and the whole operation been a failure. We had to make sure this famous cigarette is just right. There was no room for mistakes. Then I had another idea which could help if the first one didn't work. I waited till Bernard was back and Raymond wide awake to talk to them about it. It was not too long, because ten minutes later we were all talking together again.

"How do you feel Raymond?" "Well, sleeping ten minutes doesn't change much in the life of a man." "You mean three hours and ten minutes?" "That's not true, I didn't sleep three hours?" "Ho yes you did sleep all of that time." "I feel really good and much rested."

"There was no way to wake you up brother. If I ever need to be knocked down, don't hesitate to use it on me." "I wonder if it could be damaging to use it twice in the row on the same individual." "There is only one way to find out." "We have no time to try it again today; we only have an hour to make this cigarette working well." "Do you mean that we already know who our man is?" "I know who he is, but we still need to know where they're holding M. Courrois and how many of them they are. Gentlemen, I think I believe knowing an alternative to the cigarette and I think it could be used in parallel to it." "What is it James?" "I little plastic bag of this powder that looks just like coke, one you'll put in the pocket of your jacket. If it is the way I think, they would want to search our man and when they'll find this little bag they will fall asleep very quick." "Let's hope they don't open it outside." "The one who will find it would probably want to share it with the others." "I think you're right." "Let's get on with the cigarette now. When I was a kid I rolled thousands of cigarettes for my parents. It was a conflict thing for us though, because my father didn't want me to smoke, but I had the smell of tobacco to my nose one hour every single day. Here, I'll put the tobacco and the flower in the bottom and only tobacco to finish. I'll then make a little hole in the filter to allow me to blow it out of the tube. The person who is blowing this has to retain his breeding until the whole tube is empty. Who wants to try it?" "I'm probably the one who will have to go, might as well get practising." "Here try it."

We all laughed our head off when this cigarette exploded instead of getting empty through the little hole. In one way it got empty, but not the way we had anticipated. Raymond had to blow too hard and this could alarm the others. We also had to consider the humidity in the air, which could affect the tobacco and the powder as well. We finally found the right recipe and is there any need to tell you the room needed a major cleanup? Three or four years old kids couldn't have done any worst than what we did with tobacco and flower.

"Raymond, when it's time to take the cigarette, you'll have to act like a real smoker. You'll have to take the cigarette case out of your packet. We forgot to get one and it's very important." "I'll go buy one on my way out of here." "So I was saying, you get your cigarette case out of your packet and keep coughing at the same time and then you take the interesting cigarette out and offer one to the others as well. This will create a diversion. Then you get your lighter out, the one we forgot to buy as well and you stay a step ahead of them by offering to light them up. If someone is ahead of you, then you blow strongly and quickly. Later on we'll make some sleeping cigarettes that will put the smokers to sleep, they might feel it's best to quit. Don't forget to buy the cigarette case and a lighter and go buy the best one you can find, which you will probably find in a jewelry store. The more you'll look like a rich man, the least they'll be suspicious of you.

Don't bring too much with you, especially not your cell phone unless you empty it completely, otherwise it could give us away. We won't be very far, but if they have guns, which is most likely, we won't be able to do much for you if they're not sleeping. This is our first mission of the kind and we absolutely have to succeed it."

CHAPTER 8

"*T*ralalalala . . . lala" "This is my cell phone. Hello! James here!" "James, it's me." "Roger, I'm glad to hear from you." "I got an address for you and it's the 888 Chemin des Sables." "I know where it is. This is my neighbour, a big white and blue garage." "That's exactly what it is James; I thought I would have to explain to you where it is." "You should know by now Roger that I know almost everything." "You're very funny." "Do you have anything on Dumas?" "There is nothing at all against him. He works at the paper for more than twenty years and he had many years of schooling and he even went to the seminary." "That's it. Don't look any farther, he is our man for sure." "Well then, I don't understand anything anymore and I hope you'll be able to explain it to me one day." "One day maybe, but not now, we are in a hurry. You can tell Diane to get sick now. You've done a real good job and I'll see you tonight, see you."

"Guys, we still have some work to do and we need to pay a surprise visit to our staff at the rabbit shop. The kidnappers are just across the street from it.

We are ready, let's go. Bernard, you have your artillery, if not go get it." "It's in my car." "Good, I'll get in with you. You Raymond, go buy what we're missing and join us at the shop. We have to be there before Dumas returns to the paper. I'm under the impression they need some sleep." "Tell me James, what put you on this guy's track?" "He opposed me very strongly about my chronicles in the paper and I knew from then on that it was just a matter of time before he causes me some troubles." "I was just wondering if you had one more of those revealing dreams." "You know Bernard that God guides us through our thoughts too." "Where did you get such information?" "In Matthew 16, 17. 'Jesus replied, 'Blessed are you, Simon, son of Jonah, for this was not revealed to you by man, but my Father in heaven.'

So there you are. This is very clear and with no ambiguity at all.

We went to my shop to find a forewoman absolutely disconcerted to see us there, because I never before showed up without announcing myself first.

"I'm sorry Pauline for not preventing you first, but I was concerned about a very bizarre event. Don't worry though, it has nothing to do with you or your staff, but I must nevertheless requisition your office for the moment." "My office belongs to you too M. Prince, don't be shy to feel at home."

Raymond joined us within a few minutes and we then put our plan to execution.

"Here is what you going to do Raymond. Take your first-aid kit with you and go knock on the neighbour's door and tell them that someone called for an emergency for this address. If they refuse to let you in, you tell them that you will have to call the police and you'll see how quick they'll let you in. After that you know what to do, good luck. We'll give you ten minutes and then we'll come after you. Did you find everything you needed?" "Yes it was twenty-two thousand dollars for the lighter and the cigarette case." "That's no shit; it is worth its weight in gold. Make sure you don't get stolen." "Do you think I look like a smoking millionaire?" "Go ahead comic."

Seven minutes later Raymond waved us to come to join him, which we did running towards him.

"What happened?" "They all are sleeping including M. Courrois who is doing well by the way. They are four men in there." "How come you're not sleeping?" "I do not understand this at all." "We'll talk about it later if you don't mind."

"Go Bernard in there, don't touch anything, but take a few pictures, will you?"

"Let's go back to the other side and let give the cops a gift on a gold salver. It would be best that we're not seen around here when the cops arrive. I will ask Pauline to call the cops for us."

"Bernard, do you want to go get her? I know you like her a lot?" "Is it this obvious?"

"You want to see me boss?" "Pauline, it's time that you call me by my name and you know that for you, it's James. Pauline, I need you to call the cops and tell them that there is something strange going on on the other side at the 888 Chemin des Sables, but don't mention any of us here, will you? Can we trust you to do this?" "Of course boss, I can do this." "I never saw so much going and coming out of there like today and this is bothering me. All three of us had to meet to discuss new Items for the rabbit blanket. I will keep you postpone of the new developments very soon. I'll see you soon bye." "Bye Pauline!" "Bye Bernard, come back to see us."

"I would love to let you talk longer, but you have to bring me back Bernard."

We took the road back home and I couldn't wait to get to my TV set to record the whole thing on a Cd.

"Bye Bernard, come back to see us. This woman is crazy about you, so what are you waiting for?" "It's not too easy to tell the one we love that we've been in jail." "This didn't stop you for finding a marvellous job. Most of the apostles have been in jail too, this didn't make them bad people. If you want to, I can try to get you the entire pardon from the government." "No, I don't want to lie to her anyway." "That is a good attitude. I can also talk to her if you prefer? I'm pretty sure she will understand." "No, I will probably jump in one day, but I'm so often on the road and in the air." "You'll always be able to find some excuses if you look for them. Maybe she would like the roads and the air, who knows? Don't deprive yourself on my account, as you know I have two wives and this doesn't stop me from accomplishing a lot of things." "All the things you do are nearly by miracles. James, you just said the magic word though and don't blame me if one day I'm not available to you." "Just a minute here, I'm not neglecting my responsibilities because I'm married to two women. What is the magic word like you said?" "When you said not to deprive myself on your account." "Do you want to celebrate this in our basement?" "Just a minute there, I have to ask her out for the first time first." "Make sure the automatic pilot is in good condition when you are in the air." "I don't want to scare her to death." "You're kidding me; thousands of women are dreaming of a situation like this, I mean making it in the air.

Here we are and I don't have my remote control. I hope Danielle is home. Pass me your cell phone, please."

"Danielle, it's me, would you open the gate please?" "I just wonder if I should listen to you. You scared me, do you know? Your car is down stairs and you never let home without it. You didn't even take your cell phone. You left the house without leaving a note and you know very well that there has been a kidnapping lately which we don't know anything about." "Danielle please, I'm in a hurry, open the gate and I'll explain everything to you later." "Are you smoking now? I went up there and your place is like a war zone. What do you want me to think?" "Let me tell you that you are lucky to be awake. Open this gate, you know that I don't like humiliation and right now you're embarrassing me."

"Women sometime!" "Well, this is not too encouraging." "We only have to understand them, Danielle has a good reason to be nervous, because of the circumstances and once we'll talk it over she will understand." "I'll leave you here James; you don't need me for what's awaiting you." "Good, go listen to the news too."

After Danielle had finally opened the nine foot high iron gate, Bernard drove his car to the front of the house where I saluted him and step down. I went directly up to my quarters where I put a Cd in the unit right away. I sat down comfortably to listen to the five o'clock news. Everything was there on the screen, five police cars, the prison van and two ambulances. The four people were taken out on stretchers to be taking to the hospital by police escort. We could see the three kidnappers were handcuffed and of course they were waiting for a declaration from M. Courrois to understand what happened. The journalists were on the ground trying to get as much information as possible, but all they could get is that every one of them was unconscious and that nobody understood anything about it. Finally the police chef came to meet the journalists to answer their questions.

"Are they all dead?"

"They seem to be all unconscious."

"Is M. Courrois one of them?"

"Is he alive or dead?" "Quiet, do you want answers or not? For one thing there are too many of you here. I will answer you only if you're not acting like wasps. I hate wasps.

You there, what do you want to know?" "Is M. Courrois still alive?" "He is among them, but we don't know yet in which condition he is. He doesn't seem to be hurt, but at this time we don't know the state of his health. He is presently at the hospital under our protection and under observation."

"Your turn now!" "How did you find out where he was?" "We got an anonymous phone call and it was impossible for us to track it down."

"You there, it's your turn now." "Do you know anything about the other three?" "We know that one of them is working at the newspaper." "Do you know his name?" "It's not something I can tell you at this time, because, we don't know if he was there to the defence of M. Courrois or if he's one of the kidnappers. They're all in our custody right now. This will be all. We'll have a press conference later on this evening when we know more about the whole thing. Thank you."

"Can you?" "This will be all I said, I'll talk to you later."

It looks like a complete success. My editor was in a safe place, the bad guys were in police custody and no one knew who could put them all to sleep. I couldn't wait for the trial to find out what was Dumas' reason for doing this. The phone ring and came to disturb my thoughts.

"James here!" "James, it's me. Did you listen to the news?" "Roger, you don't know anything about all this, understood? I'll see you at eight thirty tonight if it's alright with you or else tomorrow afternoon." "I would prefer tomorrow, if it's not inconvenient to you." "I'd like that better too Roger. See you tomorrow at two thirty then, bye for now."

"James, supper is ready, we are waiting for you." "I won't come down tonight Danielle. I have some cleanup to do and I'm not hungry. I will just take a cup of tea and a few biscuits and then I'll listen to the TV. Don't let the kids come up here either. I prefer to be alone anyway. I'll see you tomorrow. Like they say; sleep on it tonight, because tomorrow is another day." "You have never sulked even once in fifteen year; you're not going to start this tonight, are you?" "See you tomorrow Danielle."

The last think I wanted to do was to discuss with her while I was still angry. I knew too well that when I'm in this kind of mood words can come out pretty harshly. We don't touch a hot burner with bare hands and I was still boiling inside. Better say nothing at all than to say harsh things to someone, especially to someone you love and loves you back. So I cleaned up the room before taking my cup of tea with a few biscuits. Then I sat down in front of the TV to listen to the six o'clock news. There was nothing else about the Courrois's affair. News though retained my attention. The subject of my next article was there on the screen in front of me.

"In Brazil today, the mother of a nine year old little pregnant girl was excommunicated for letting doctors practising an abortion on her daughter and so were the doctors involved. They were excommunicated by their diocese bishop. The little girl was raped for three years time by her father-in-law. She was four months pregnant with twins and doctors said the girl and the babies had no chance to live if she was going through with it. The Cardinal approved the bishop's decision."

Dammit, I told myself, the series of murders is not over yet. This is noting to change my mood at all. With the pretension to be pro-life these churchmen with a prestigious influence would have killed three human beings with no remorse. He would have killed this little girl the same way they killed my grandmothers. And that's not all, in a few years from now these same men are going to be declared saints. Wake up people for Jesus' sake. Console yourself you excommunicated people, maybe you don't know yet, but what happened to you is most likely the greatest blessing from God you've ever received. Don't be foolish enough to go back to a religion, slavery. You are free now just turn to God and thank Him for saving you. Give Him all the glory that He deserves instead of lamenting. Amen!

"Janene it's me." "Danielle, how are you?" "I'm not too good tonight." "What is the matter? You're not sick, are you?" "It's not me, it's James and he didn't want to come down for supper tonight." "Do you know what's wrong with him?" "Could you come to see me when the children are in bed?

I also have to talk to you about another one of his projects." "Of course I can, it's eight thirty and I'll come in thirty minutes." "Alright, I'll be expecting you."

At the nine o'clock news there was on the screen the pictures of the four people involve in the kidnapping.

'Good evening ladies and gentlemen. There are some new developments in the Courrois' affair and we have a declaration from M. Courrois himself. Here's a report from our correspondent Rene Martel." "M. Courrois, can you tell us what happened since yesterday afternoon?" "Well, I was invited to meet with a member of parliament about a very important business deal. I thought because it was this important I should go to the meeting myself. I quickly understood it was a trap well set up." "Do you know your kidnappers M. Courrois?" "I only know one of them like I told the police, he works with me." "There was no request for ransom; do you know why you were kidnapped?" "It was not for money, he wanted to get a professional secret out of me." "Can you tell me what it is about?" "I just told you that it is a professional secret." "That's true too, where is my head? I'm sorry, forgive me please." "If I had betrayed this secret, I would be dead instead of being here talking to you." "Why do you think he wanted to know?" "I can only tell you that he's a man who doesn't like the word of God and he mainly doesn't want it to be spread out. He would have killed me without hesitation to get what he wants. I don't really know what happened this afternoon, but I know one thing, he had decided to kill me at four o'clock this afternoon with or without the secret. I really thought that today was my last day." "You really have no idea about what happened and how you were saved?" "I have no idea at all. I only know that a man came in and then it was a complete blackout. I woke up at the hospital and here I am. I have another life." "You don't know who this mysterious man is?" "I have no idea of who he is, but I would like to say thank you to him for saving my life. I'm not a strong believer, but now I think he might be my garden angel." "Well, I thank you very much M. Courrois. One last question if you allow me." "There is nothing else to say, but you can always ask." "How do you feel now?" "Beside my sore wrists, I have never been in such a good physical shape in a very long time. Before those few hours sleep I was so tired I was ready to die."

'Ladies and gentlemen, this was a report from Rene Martel directly from M. Courrois hospital room. And now we have the weather forecast for you.'

I was quite happy to have foreseen the problem even though I was still in a pretty bad mood. After earring the last two phrases of M. Courrois I was tempted to take a portion of this magic powder myself, considering how good him and Raymond felt when they woke up.

"Danielle, you seem to be very upset tell me what the heck happened." "Well, when I came home from work I saw that James' car was in the garage so I told myself he was up there and I was happy that he came in early. When I tried to call him, there was no answer and I got worried, so I went upstairs to see if he was okay and I found no husband, but a sitting room and a bed room absolutely messy like a war zone. I'm not kidding you there was tobacco and flower all over the place. There is a cigarette rolling machine, cigarette tubes, a bag of flower and a large quantity of cigarettes. There was nobody around and I thought the worst happened, because there was no note of any kind from him. As you know yesterday afternoon the director of the newspaper disappeared and I thought that maybe the same thing happened to James. I worried sick and when he came to the gate in Bernard's car he asked me through the phone to open the gate and I didn't open it right away. I was having a fit and for a long time I think I refused to open to him. I really felt his frustration and I think I ignored him for too long." "Did you think only for a moment how he must have felt to be locked out of his property by the one he loves, him who put his body and soul into it? He must still be raging up there and you're lucky he is who he is." "But I was not myself." "I know Danielle but still, it was you who did it. You both better to talk it over before it turns sour." "I would need to be able to talk to him for that, but I felt it in his voice, he doesn't want to talk to me anymore." "Come on now, don't cry; just let the storm go by." "He never ever acted like this before, Janene, I'm scared."

"Do you want me to go talk to him?" "I think you would be wasting your time, he didn't even want to say good night to the children." "I just wonder what in the world happened in his place. I'm sure he didn't start smoking. This is kind of strange anyway." "If I didn't act so stupidly, we would know by now." "You said that he's got another project, what is it all about?" "He wants to buy us a private hospital or else build one. He also said that we have a lot of money sleeping and it would be a lot more secure for us to work in our own hospital. He thinks we should form doctors and nurses and finance them at a low rate." "What do you think of it?" "I rally think it's a good idea. We know him good enough to know that we could have everything we need in there. Yes, I'm all for it." "He also wants us to be the administrators." "We might need some help for that, but I'm sure we can make it, what about you?" "We would finally be able to choose our working time. I'm sure it will feel funny not going to the center after twenty-four years." "This is true too, it's almost home now. What do we do? Do we try to talk to him about it or we should wait till the storm is over?" "We can always try, but I don't think we'll succeed to talk to him tonight. Call him, we'll see."

"James, how are you?" "So, so, Janene can you and Danielle come up here?" "You need two women tonight? You're in a great shape?" "I'm in good shape, but not for what you're thinking." "Can you tell me what's happening?" "Come up here, you'll see." "I will talk to Danielle and I'll call you back." "Good I'm waiting for you."

"He wants us to come up there." "Is he still mad?" "Let's go anyway, he's not the type of men to hit women and if he needs to let off steam so be it, it will be better for all of us after."

Knock, knock, knock!" "Come on in and make yourself at home." "I see that you cleaned up the place." "Ho, I'm sure I can afford a housemaid, but I didn't want to see anyone. Please sit down. I need to show you something. You're going to hear things that it cannot get out of these walls. Can I trust you for this?" "We cannot even talk to our children about it?" "To nobody!" "No point screaming, we're not deaf." "I just want to make myself understood, that's all." "You scream one more time and you'll be a long time before you see us up here again." "You are free to go if this is what you want, but I like to be listen to when I speak. You still didn't answer me; can I trust you with this?" "There is no point asking, you know you can." "What's so special that we have to see?" "It's only the last news of the day, but I'm asking you to pay special attention to what you're going to see." "Go ahead we're ready."

So I got the video rolling and I was watching for their reactions as the tape was rolling down. I saw tears coming down their cheeks and I knew then they just understood a lot of things.

"You're the one who save the life of this man." "If only I had taken the time to clean up the place here and written a note to you we would have been too late to save him. If these bandits were behind us with guns we could have died between them and the gate, because we couldn't get in. They went after this man and kidnapped him because of me. They want me and they're ready to kill to get what they want. The main reason why I want to get your own hospital is very simple, you could very well be the next target or yet one of our children. Do you really think I want to be blocked at the gate when it's a question of life and death? In our hospital I could install a proper surveillance system, which I cannot do where you're working now. The hunt for me is started, but it's far from being over. Either you're following my rules or I'll be out of here and I'll go where no one can find me, because I'm not going to risk the life of one of my people one more day. Crying wouldn't change anything." "I beg you pardon James." "For me Danielle forgiving is easy, to make myself understood is another thing. I'm not a fearful person, but I was very scared today that this man dies because of me. He only had ten minutes to live when we succeeded neutralizing his aggressors. I formed a swat team today; Bernard and Raymond are part of it. If this ever comes out in the open that we are the saviours, we would be finished. This will be all. I'm asking you to leave me alone now." "You don't want to take a hot bath with us?" "I'm sorry, but I don't feel like laughing. I'm rather real sad. Good night both of you. Tomorrow will be another day." "Good night James!" "Good night!"

They both left me very reluctant and I could feel it, but I thought it was the best thing to do according to the circumstances. I didn't want to explode like I knew I was capable of and say things I could spend the rest of my life been sorry for. I knew it was best to let the temperature come down completely.

"Do you think he can forgive me some day?" "He has already forgiven you Danielle, but he's still too upset and he wants to avoid the growling, that's why he wants to stay alone. I'm certain he will be alright tomorrow." "I wish I could be as certain as you are." "You should take a sleeping pill and go to bed; otherwise you won't be able to do anything good tomorrow. We have to understand him; he received a big shock today. I never saw him in such state of mind." "Me neither. I can even tell you that I was afraid of him for the first time. It's ironic isn't it, he's boiling with frustration and he's cold with us at the same time." "Too hot is too hot and as you know it could spill over." "We have to understand what he's been through today; you did shot the door to his nose and stop him from entering his home even if it's for a short time. If only he was alone, it wouldn't have been as humiliating. Think about it, he goes out of his way all the time to save the world, him who could pay the entire debt of our country and yet he can't get into his home when he wanted to. I suggest you go on your computer and send him an Email, telling him that you're sorry and to explain yourself. He will get your message either tonight or tomorrow. Certainly that couldn't hurt, then like I said, take a pill and go to bed." "That's a great idea, what would I do without you? I'm so happy to have you." "Good night, I'm going to bed now." "Good night you too and thanks so very much."

"Hi James. If only you knew how sorry I am to put you in this state of mind. I got to tell you though that you scared me for the first time tonight and this is something I never want to experience again. It feels like my whole world collapsed under my feet and there is no more reason to go on with my life. I can understand that you can be angry at me, but I cannot believe that you don't love me anymore and if this is the case, I cannot stay in this house where we have known so much happiness. I feel so completely lost and I have no one else to turn to. Can you tell me where your compassion is today, you who preached forgiveness for so many years? Do you really need to be so hard with me? Do you think it's the only way for me to understand?

Are you going to let me mope all night or come to put me to sleep like you know how to do so well, your Danielle?" "Lie down, I'm coming right away."

I came down very quickly and I found her lying on the bed ready to make love. I took my clothes off as fast as I could and I went to lie down beside her and then I let the magic powder that has been so good to us that particular day out in the room. She just received what she needed most in these circumstances and so did I. This was a very deep and beneficial sleep. The next morning it was a totally different story.

"What happened, I lost it completely?" "You seem to want to make love and you fell asleep leaving me on my appetite. I thought of doing it anyway, but it felt like a rape, so I fell asleep too." "You know very well that I belong to you even in my sleep. I think I would like it even then." "When I give you something I want you to be conscious of it." "I never felt so rested in my entire life. Do we have time for a quick one?" "It all depends if you're ready or not." "Why don't you check it yourself?" "Kids will be up at any minute." "Don't waste any time then. You seem to be bigger than usual, did you take anything?" "Not at all, but you too seem to be tighter. I came twice already and it's still hard as a bbb." "What's that?" "A baseball bat! This is not normal and I wonder what the heck is going on. Let's stop moving for a few minutes, would you?" "Not really!" "Ho, you think it's funny, but I'm rather worried. It's a good think that you are juicy as you are, otherwise I would be stock in there." "I could keep you there all day, you know?" "Where is you sense of responsibility? I cannot get out of here like this; the kids will laugh to death. Where is your phone?" "I left it in the kitchen." "Go get it please I cannot stay like this all day long." "I know what you need." "Is this a nurse's secret?" "No, you need another nurse." "I still need your phone." "Let me talk to Janene first."

"Janene, can you come right away please, we need you here?" "It sounds bad, what's going on? I'm still in my nightgown and the children didn't finish their breakfast yet." "Come right away, I'll take care of the children. Bring your cell phone with you too?" "Why, where is yours?" "It's too far away for now." "What is the matter Danielle?" "Come you'll see." "I'm coming."

"Hi kids, how are you this morning?" "We are fine, but something is going on in the master bedroom this morning and dad didn't even come to say good night to us last night and this is not normal at all coming from him." "Your dad wasn't well at all last night and your mom says he needs another nurse this morning. Don't you worry; I'll see what's going on." "Your mom will be here in a minute or two."

"What took you so long? What hold you back?" "Your kids are questioning a lot on what is going on and you should get some answers ready for them. What is going on here now?" "You better be in good shape for this, because I couldn't satisfy our man this morning no matter what I tried. I washed him with cold water, I washed him with hot water, there is nothing I can do. He's clean and still mounted like a stallion."

"Wow, did you take anything special?"

"Aright, I'll leave you now; the children need me more than you do."

"I didn't take anything else than a good night sleep."

"See you later Danielle. I'll get on this stallion and see how long I can stay on his saddle."

"You must have taken something that makes it bigger, it's as tight as the first time and this is not normal. As far as I know, I didn't take anything, but don't you think this is enough for you now; you've had at least twenty orgasms. You're going to kill us both. Keep some for the next time, would you?" "I got to call the hospital, I cannot work today." "Don't you think that I'm going to leave you do this all day." "This is not what I was thinking. I cannot stand on my legs." "Don't tell them why you cannot work or we're going to be the laugh of the world. Although, if we ever find the reason this is happening to us the demand would be endless. I'm beginning to think this could be dangerous, there is too much blood concentrated on the same spot. What if I couldn't get an erection anymore after this?" "Stop this, you're scaring me." "You still have to admit, it is not normal." "Do you want me to call a doctor?" "No, I'll call Raymond, I'm sure he will know what to do. Call the hospital right away, would you?"

"Hi, may I speak to the director please?" "Hi, Morin here!" "Hi M. Morin, this is Janene St Louis." "Hi Janene, what can I do for you?" "I won't be able to come in today, I don't feel good and neither is James." "Is it serious? What is it?" "I think it's temporary, but we are both to week to go to work and I will call you as soon as we are better." "Can you make it to the hospital? I can send you a doctor if you need to." "Thanks the same, but there is one already on his way here." "Alright then, take care of yourself and good day." "Good day sir!"

"Give me this phone, would you?"

"Raymond, it's me James." "James, I'm not in a position to talk to you very long." "What is the matter Raymond?" "Let just say that my girlfriend is happy, but I start to like it a bit less." "Don't tell me that you are erected like a pig?" "How do you know? Don't tell me that you can see from a long distance now. It's been on for more than five hours now and this is a bit more than I wished for." "No, I'm not presbyopic, I'm rather myopic, but I have the same problem on my side." "Ho no, ha, ha. This would be a secondary effect from this powder then." "This is exactly what I've been thinking, we have to find the antidote like yesterday and I hope it's not over for us." "It's not easy for me to get out of here." "Find yourself a hoop to put under your coat. Find also a solution to our problem, but do it soon. I will try to reach M. Courrois in the mean time to see how it is for him. Talk to you soon."

"May I speak to M. Courrois Please?" "I'm sorry, but he didn't come to work yet this morning."

"Was he supposed to come in?" "He said he would, but he didn't." "Thank you, I will call him at home." "You're welcome sir."

"Hi, may I speak to M. Courrois please and tell him this is James?" "Just wait a minute sir; I'll see if he wants to talk to you."

"There is a man on the phone called James. Do you want to talk to him?" "James, I wonder who this is. I don't want to talk to anybody except to a doctor."

"He only wants to talk to a doctor sir." "But this is why I'm calling Mrs Courrois, I am a doctor and I heal sick people." "He said he's a doctor." "Alright, let me talk to him then."

"Hello! How did you know I needed a doctor?" "M. Courrois, it's me James Prince, the writer of the chronicles in your paper. How do you feel this morning?" "Well, I'm well and even too well. My wife is very happy about this miracle, but I start to think it is a bit too long for me." "What are you talking about M. Courrois?" "It's rather delicate and an embarrassing subject James." "Are you talking about an erection a bit out of normal?" "How in the world do you know this?" "This is because I have the same problem sir. They are looking as I talk to you for a solution to our inconvenience. Don't you worry, they will find." "I couldn't do anything for three years now and the specialists assured me that I was incurable. I can tell you that it's a rather agreeable surprise, but it's nothing at all or too much. It would be nice to find a happy medium." "Take advantage of it while it lasts and in the mean time they will find a solution. I'll send you the antidote as soon as I got it. What about my chronicles, do I keep writing them?" "Of course you do and who ever don't like to read them just have to read something else. I'm just going to add a warning in the heading to protect the paper that's all." "I will call you as soon as I have news from the laboratory." "Thank you James for everything."

There were three more persons who most likely had the same problem in jail and it wouldn't be easy for us to do something for them. This will be a job for Bernard with his next visit to the prisoners. Maybe I should call him right away.

"Bernard how are you?" "I'm fine except worrying about you." "Why are you worrying about me for?" "I heard that when a woman is real mad it could cause some squabbles." "There was a little bit of it, but it's been almost fifteen years since Danielle was as smiling as this morning. Tell me, when is your next visit to the penitentiary?" "Just a minute there, I think it's tomorrow." "I just hope it won't be too late." "I think I'll have a mission for you." "What is the problem James?" "Try to reach your brother; he will explain it to you. I got to call him right away. Excuse me, we'll talk later."

"Raymond, could you make it to the laboratory?" "Yes, but my assistants find it rather funny." "Did you find a solution to our problem?" "Not yet, we're still looking." "I got an idea that might work." "Tell me, I started to feel weak on my legs." "Try a wake up pill to see if it works. I hope it works, here the rats are killing themselves jumping one another, males and females." "M. Courrois has the same problem. Do you have some of those pills?" "Yes, every once in a while I take one of those when I want to finish an experience even if I'm very tired. James it works, it's going down now, but slowly." "This is the antidote then; give some to the rats before they all die. Go also to M. Courrois' home to release him. I'll see that Janene help me out over here. Just a minute, he might recognize you, maybe he saw you yesterday. You send Bernard over, it will be safer. He's on his way to help you."

"Janene, can you come here for a minute?" "Yes James, do you want some more?" "Nevermind! This will be enough for today. Do you have some wake up pills?" "I didn't take any for years, but I'll look." "Go right away please." "I got some, but they are over dated and maybe there are no good anymore." "What is the date?" "They are two years passed due." "It won't hurt me to try it. Wack, it has a terrible taste. It works, look it works." "Shit, I was hoping for another round." "Darn, did you become a nymphomaniac now?" "It was absolutely wonderful James; we'll have to do it again some day." "You only think about yourself, gees it hurts. Give me something for the pain." "I'll be right back."

In the mean time Bernard went to M. Courrois' home with the antidote.

"Good day Mrs. Courrois! Is M. Courrois at home?" "He's home, but he's not in a good enough mood to talk to you." "That's alright madam, I brought some medicine for him to take from the doctor's office. This one is to release him and this one here is for the pain. Everything should be fine fairly quick." "Do you know what caused this reaction sir . . . . ?" "My name is Bernard Sinclair Madam! Our scientists are still looking into it madam. They're hoping to find out soon." "Can you let us know when they have something sir? We would be interested to repeat the experience from time to time." "Is M. Courrois thinking the same way madam?" "If it's up to me he will have no choice sir." "Should I understand this experience was good for you madam?" "It was just a dream come through sir." "Well, I'll tell who might be concerned madam. Tell M. Courrois that James says hi and wishes him good luck." "I will tell him M. Sinclair and thanks for coming. I'm sure that Jean will appreciate this very much."

Bernard walked out of the house and took the road to the laboratory.

"Jean, you must take one pill to release yourself and another one for the pain." "Yes Monique, but before I take them, I want you to take a picture of me like this; otherwise my doctor will never believe me. You make sure the date is on it too." "You're not afraid that we might be accused of carrying pornography?" "No, I'll be able to prove that it was for medical reason only. Don't forget to make an appointment with my doctor for me." "I won't forget."

"Are you better James?" "It's still painful, but I'm doing a lot better." "I had a good talk with Mrs. Courrois and I think this powder has a great potential for success on the market. She really did appreciate the experience." "I believe you, because Janene had the same reaction. I'll bet he didn't appreciate it as much though." "I'm on my way to the laboratory; do you have anything else for me?" "No, that will be all for now." "Just a minute James, there is something on the radio. Listen to this."

CHAPTER 9

"*W*e've learned that two of M. Courrois aggressors were taken to the hospital earlier today. Apparently one of them is charged with rape against his cell companion. According to the hospital staff doctors will have to practice an emergency operation on one of them."

"Well James, there is one of them who couldn't with until tomorrow." "I think we should bring the antidote to the police station before another one gets rape. I don't think our police chief would appreciate to find himself in such a position. I'm going to ask Danielle to go help this one at the hospital with the antidote. No one will ask any question about her, she will only be doing her job." "I'm sure the prisoners are well guarded." "This is why only a doctor or a nurse can get close to him. She might be able to find out a bit more about the whole thing. Make a stop at a pay phone, call the police station and tell someone just this here and hang up right away. Don't stick around there either. Try not to leave your fingerprints all over. Tell him to give them a wake up pill, they will understand. I got to let you go. I have an appointment at two thirty and I still have to talk with Raymond."

"Hey Raymond, on what scale can we produce this powder?" "As much as we can get the ingredients, no limit I think." "I think there is a market for this and for the antidote too." "I would like to make more experiences before getting too far with this James." "I understand, do what ever is necessary, I got to go now."

Then I went to see Roger to pay him for his precious services.

"Roger my friend, I'm in a hurry, but tell me how much I owe you?" "We did almost nothing. I don't think we worked more than three hours all together. I'll say that six hundred would be more than enough. Here's what I give you, but I don't want any receipt or register, you and your helpers don't know anything about the whole story. Twenty-five hundred dollars, this is way too much." "The life of a good man is worth more than this and we could save him because of your help. It's very possible that we get more of those cases in a near future and I want to be able to count on you at any time." "Any time James, any time!" "For the record, we're only friends." "That's understood James and the others don't know anything about you." "See you next time."

"May I speak to Danielle Prince Please?" "She's to busy right now, she's in the operating room." "Then ask her to call her husband as soon as she can please." "I'll tell her sir. It won't be easy sir; the hospital is full of journalists who want to know more about this phenomenal event. We had to call the police to control the situation and even they have a hard time with this. I think they are coming out of the operating room now. The surgeon will talk to the press anytime soon. Here is Danielle sir."

"Is this you James?" "Can you tell me what's going on for heaven sake?" "They brought us two prisoners who were connected in the lowest level. It was not easy, because the one behind is like a horse and the other one named Dumas was screaming like he was going to die. We couldn't put them to sleep, because the anaesthesia didn't work on them. We tried an injection to make the guy deflate and this didn't work either. So we had to freeze them both and cut Dumas at least two inches to get the other guy out of there. No one understands anything about this mysterious reaction and it remains a mystery to the medical scientists." "You couldn't give him what I ask you?" "I couldn't do it without risking to be caught." "I'm afraid they are going to start a no end investigation now. You should try to give this horse some medicine before he tries to kill himself." "There is no chance, he is on good police guard and handcuffed as well." "You should go in there before things get worst."

Well, I don't think they will feel like kidnapping anybody anymore. Maybe I should call Raymond.

"Raymond it's me, did you find something new?" "I have succeeded to calm down the rats, but most of them are exhausted. I also had to give them a pain killer and one of them ate most of his sexual parts. We didn't take anymore risk and we muzzled them all. What an adventure, I think this formula is especially good for women." "I don't know, maybe we should ask Charles Dumas and see what he thinks of it. He is the reason why I called, is Bernard still there?" "Yes, I'll let you talk to him."

"James, you want to talk to me?" "Yes, I would like you to go to the hospital meet the prisoners and try to find out a bit more about their intentions. You still have your pass for the penitentiary, don't you? Maybe you can give them a lecture about Sodomy and what lead to the destruction of Sodom and Gomorrah. They can't deny their calamity and their shame after such a scandal." "Can you remind me where it is written in the Bible?" "Yes, it's in Leviticus 20, 13." "What does it say?" "It says; 'If a man lies with a man like a man lies with a woman, they both have committed an abomination.'

Don't forget to tell them that it is better to lose an eye or a hand than to lose the whole body." "James, if we castrate everyone who sins because of their testicles, we would lose more than ninety per cent of the world population and maybe more." "No Bernard, this was Paul's idea, not mine and neither God's one; otherwise He would have created us without them. Let's concentrate on people who love God with all their heart, soul and mind, there wouldn't be too many anyways. It would have been a lot better for this man who is on trail right now for abusing his daughter during twenty-four years and making her seven children to be castrated before he commits all of those abominable actions. It would have been better not only for him, but also for his daughter. His testicles caused trouble to how many people? Think about his wife who is married to this monster for so many years. No matter, if she said for better or worst, yes I do and until death tears us apart, she never thought when she said these words that she was marrying a devil. I'm sure that death has installed itself between the two of them and this kind of death tears them apart. Anyways, it is best that you can talk to them and find out what their views about the whole event are." "I'll do the best I can James. I'm leaving right away."

Then I went to see how Janene was recovering from her performance of this morning.

"How are you feeling sexual maniac?" "Is it possible it was me who acted like this? I can't believe this." "You both told me one day you weren't nymphomaniac, allow me to doubt this now." "I sincerely tell you that I don't understand this." "This is fine as long as you don't expect me to perform every time like this morning." "What exactly caused such a reaction?" "I'm not quite sure yet, but I think it might have something to do with what we used to save M. Courrois' life yesterday. Every man who was exposed to it had the same reaction.

They got a huge inflation of the penis which lasted dangerously too long and this was followed by a terrible pain." "Is it still hurting?" "Keep resting, you had enough for today, besides the hospital had to compose without you and they are over loaded over there. I got to go and you try to concentrate on your supper, the children will be back from school pretty soon. The poor kids must be wondering what is going on this days. Either we like it or not, we'll have to give them some sort of explanation." "You're right James, they must feel abandoned. I'll do my best to come back on earth. You owe them an explanation about last night too. They had a real hard time to understand why you didn't want to talk to them. This was the first time it happened to them, you know?" "Yes, I know and I'll spend the evening with them, that's going to be good for me too. There are days when I wish I had only them to take care of, but my destiny ask me for more. As soon as they're back from school; I'll take then to a dogs race and if you're okay after supper, we'll give them a dance's lesson. They love it and I hope they can enjoy it as much as we do." "I don't know if my legs will hold me long enough, but I'll try. It will be nice to spend the evening all together." "I got to go; I got a few things to do to free myself for this evening. See you in a bit."

At the hospital things were a bit spicy.

"Good afternoon officer, I'm here to meet with the prisoners if it's possible, here's my pass." "I'm sorry, but I have orders to let no one near these guys." "You know as well as I do that they're allowed to speak to a legal adviser and spiritual also and this cannot be refused to them." "I'll have to talk to my commander-in-chief M. Sinclair, I need an official authorization first." "Go ahead officer, do what you have to do."

"Commander, there is a man here by the name of Bernard Sinclair who wants to talk to the prisoners; he also says this is their rightful rights. What do I do?" "I know this man, this cannot hurt anyone, but make sure he doesn't have a weapon with him when he goes in the room and if he's got one confiscate it for the time of the visit." "I'll do commander."

"Do you have any weapon with you sir?" "Yes I do and I also have a permit for it." "I got to take it away from you sir and you'll get it back when you're done." "I have no problem with this officer, here it is."

"Good afternoon gentlemen, are things a bit better for you now?" "Who the hell are you?" "My name is Bernard Sinclair and I've been visiting prisoners for more than fifteen years now and let me tell you that most of them do appreciate it. Most of them don't believe to the priests and neither in religion anymore, but they still need to talk to someone who can listen. Listen is what I do best. I see that you didn't wait to die to experience hell." "If hell is pain in the ass we sure spent the day in it." "You know that according to the word of God, two men who do what is allow to a man with a woman is an abomination, don't you?" "I didn't want this infamy sir, I was raped." "I didn't want it either and I don't know by what kind of curse I receive this uncontrollable erection, but I was only looking for a release and I never was homosexual." "You're telling me that it was stronger than yourself?" "This is what we're saying." "This is not going to be easy to believe by most people. A man is not this easy to undress, how can you explain the access from one to the other?" "He wanted to do me too, but I was just quicker than him, that's all. I'm glad too because, now he's the one with the pain in the ass." "And you're saying this was beyond your own will? Do you have any idea when this all started?" "Somebody put us to sleep by I don't know what kind of process and we woke up at the hospital. We don't know anything else. It's a total mystery. You were talking about the Bible earlier. Do you know who is writing the chronicles in the newspaper?" "I know he is someone who loves to make the truth known to people." "The truth like you said will cause the end of the world." "If you're afraid of the end time it's because you're not on the right side, I mean on God's side. If you were on the good side none of what happened to you would have. This is something that you should know. It is written it is necessary scandals happen, but woe to whom they happen by. It's the only way I can explain your problem.

I think the shame that is on you today is worst than the years of jail that are awaiting you for the crime you are responsible for. I can only tell you that if God is with you during those years ahead of you the time will be one hundred times less laborious and I speak with experience. I too made time for one of my stupidities. Remember that repentance is not only good before God it is also good before the judge you're going to face very soon. I can assure you too that your behaviour behind bars is directly link to the time you're going to spend in there. I'll do my best to explain to the population you were not willingly involve in this scandal, but for the crime you've committed, there is nothing I can do. What in the world went to your mind? What did you want to accomplish by kidnapping such an important man?" "I just wanted to know someone's name." "The writer of those chronicles? All of those troubles are not enough for you? You're still trying to find out who he is. I can tell you that if you don't change your attitude about this one you will experience more tribulations even worst than having your ass split and jail time. I got to go now, but remember that a warned man is worth two. Remembering what I told you will be beneficial to you and forgetting it will be disastrous, nevertheless it is your choice. Good luck!" "Where can we reach you if we want to talk to you again?" "Just remember my name, everyone knows me in jail."

"Thanks officer." "Here is what belongs to you sir." "Thanks again and good day."

In the hospital lobby it was still a big confusion and police started to evacuate everybody, this wasp nest as the police chief calls it and he could do without them also. The question was on everyone's lips; who could put all these men to sleep and with what? I found this very ironical; me who tries with so many different ways to wake up people about the word of God. Bernard could make his way out anyway and he went to his car to contact me on his cell phone.

"James, it's a real mad, mad world in there right now. A lot of people want to know who put these people to sleep and what was used in the process." "Go back to the laboratory and ask Raymond to get rid of everything for now that could be compromising. Tell him he can use my place until the dust is settled down." "Why don't you call him yourself?" "The phone line might be tapped as we speak, we cannot take any risk. I think all the laboratories will be search very soon. We have to operate clandestinely from now on, because we cannot stop now. Hurry up, you have to make it there before it's too late. Make sure he understand the seriousness of all this." "I'm sure he will understand. I'm there now and I don't see anything out of normal." "Take a good look all around you to make sure there is no surveillance and if there is, flush it down the drain. I'm ready to go in now, is there something else?" "No, you go ahead, we'll talk later. You take things over now Bernard, I have to spend time with the children. If it's urgent you call me, but if it can wait till ten o'clock you wait, Ok?" "Ok, bye now!" "Hey, pick me up a newspaper of the day please, see you."

"Hey kids, how are you?" "Dad, you're home, is there something wrong?" "There is nothing wrong; it's just that I miss all of you too much. What do you want to do until supper is ready?" "I want to take a dance lesson."

"No, I want to race with the dogs."

"Dad, I designed a new molding, I'd like to go to my shop and make some experiences with it."

"I want to play bowling at Auntie Danielle."

"Dad, you owe me revenge at the billiard table." "Well, I'm glad to have so many choices, but this is it, we have to choose. Here's what I propose. We're going to race the dogs until supper time, they need the exercises too. After, we'll have dance lessons for one hour. After this if you want to, we'll have a good bowling game and then it will be time for the youngest to go to bed. I'll be able then to give Samuel the revenge he's been waiting for. To finish I'll pay a visit to the shop with Jonathan if it's not too late. What do you think of my plan?" "It's perfect as usual dad. It was not so perfect last night though." "What, you didn't like a night off from your Dad?" "No, I didn't sleep well, it was terrible."

"It was terrible for me too." "I told myself dad had a very good reason not to come down." "Ho, you must be right Samuel. You're like daddy, you're almost always right." "I'd say like mom, that's very frustrating." "Nias, nias, nias!"

"That's enough both of you. Let's get the harnesses and the sleighs. Samuel, would you please get the dogs?" "Right away dad, I'm running to them."

"Jonathan, do you want to get yours ready too? I'm sure he needs some exercises." "I'll get him right away." "There come the dogs and they seem to be even happier than you guys. Now we have to split the weight as evenly as possible. The two youngest, you get on with me. How much weight is this? Let see yea, that's two hundred and fifteen pounds. Jonathan, Rene, and Jeremy you make two hundred and five and that's okay, because when I step off I got more weight off the sleigh."

"You Samuel and the two girls, you make the weight too. Is this seems fair to everyone?" "Yes, let's go." "I count till three and we leave at two. One, two, let's go."

There were a lot of go, go, go and faster, faster, faster and some, they're ahead. Nevertheless, it was a very nice race, but I was concerned with the performance of Jonathan's dog. They finished in the last place far behind, though they should have been in the race until the end. Samuel and the girls were very happy to win the race.

"Congratulation my boy for winning this race again, you've became a real champion now."

"Dad, is it because Samuel has better dogs that we win the race?" "Samuel has good dogs and he knows how to control them which is very important. There is also the fact that his dogs love him a lot and give everything they got to please their master, this is what we need most to win races." "Why is Jonathan so far behind?" "There could be a few reasons for this. There is only one dog who knows him and I believe he's not in a very good shape. Let just hope he's not sick. He seemed to slow down the other dogs too. I don't think Jonathan enjoyed this race. We still have to congratulate him for participating even though he doesn't like racing that much. I'm sure he will be smiling more when we play bowling."

"There you are, you finish the race no matter what. Do you know what happened?" "I think Rex is not well and he was slowing down the other dogs." "Do you think he's sick or just out of shape?" "I think he's not well." "I'll call the vet to check him up and if he needs more attention I'll refer him to the laboratory doctor.

Alright everybody, let's help Jonathan taking those harnesses off his dogs and put the sleighs away. Supper must be ready by now. Hurry up, the last one to arrive will be the last served."

I picked up the two youngest and I ran as fast as I could, but we were last anyway.

"I'm sorry kids, but I couldn't win this race either. I'll try to be better next time." "That was fun anyway dad."

"You would have to pick the youngsters up before you start to race dad and between me and Rene there is too much difference in size, he had no chance to win." "You're right Samuel; I'll try to divide chances better next time. Everyone puts its clothes and boots away; I'm not your slave nor is your mom."

"Dad, mom is not home yet and this is not like her." "I hope Janene made supper for everybody. Let's go see what is going on; maybe your mom knows something."

"Mom, do you know why Auntie Danielle is not home yet?" "Yes, don't you worry; they asked her to do some overtime. I made a fricassee for everyone and the table is already set."

"Yes."

"Yes."

"Yes."

"Yes, you're the one who makes the best." "I learned it from your dad, we cannot be mistaking when we listen to him." "Is this a message for us?"

"Did you make a lot of dumplings?" "There is enough for everybody, at least I hope so. It is best you don't eat too many of them anyway if you want to sleep well. You don't want to be blown up like a frog." "Who's turn to say grace?" "It is dad's; he jumped his turn too often." "Your dad is a very busy man, you're lucky to have him today. I'm sure there were many other things he could have been doing today."

"There is one person I absolutely have to talk to tonight and I'll have to call him right after supper. Well, if it's my turn I wouldn't want to jump it one more time. Shut your eyes and thank God everyone for himself. I will speak in one minute . . . . Please God bless the hands of the person who made this wonderful meal and the food we're about to eat. Thank you for this wonderful time we are spending together and make it so it can reverberate always. Protect every one of us, especially when we cannot do it ourselves Amen."

"Amen!"

"Amen!" "What reveeeerberate means dad?" "Reverberate? I would like you to look for it at school tomorrow and get back to me tomorrow night with the answer." "Do you mean you're going to be with us again tomorrow?" "I'll do my very best, I missed you a lot too, you know?"

"Is there any left mom, I want some more?" "Anybody else wants some? I will divide what ever is left between the three of you. You, you and you, you'll have a spoonful each. Here we are. Here, this is for you, for you and for . . . . you. That's all, I'll make more next time."

"Well, I got to go upstairs to make a few phone calls and you guys after helping mom doing the dishes go set the bowling game and I'll meet you there in about twenty minutes. Will you come to play with us Janene?" "Yes I will." "Thank you for this wonderful meal."

"Thanks mom."

"Thanks auntie Janene, that was real good." "Welcome everybody!"

"May I speak to M. Courrois please?" "Just a minute sir, I'll transfer you to his line."

"Hello, Jean Courrois here!" "M, Courrois, this is James Prince. I have a very important matter to discuss with you, but it's not something I can do on the phone. Is it possible I can meet you later on tonight?" "Of course you can James." "Something holds me back until nine thirty, will that be okay?" "There is no problem James, you come when you can." "See you later then."

"Bernard, I know that you must be tired, but I still have to ask you to do something for me. Will this be okay?" "There is no problem James, I'll do what ever is necessary. What is it?" "Danielle was asked to do some overtime tonight, but I'm worrying about her security. Make sure she doesn't notice you, but I would like you to keep an eye on her from the hospital to our home. She knows your car, so go rent one that she wouldn't recognize. I'll leave this in your hands and I got to go, bye."

I went down quickly, because I didn't want anyone of the kids to question if I was coming or not.

"Are all the pins up and ready to be put down?" "You kept your word Dad." "Yes, that's an important thing to do. Did you form the teams and who I'm playing with and who I'm playing against?" "It's the total of points that counts and you play against auntie Janene, myself, Jeremy, Claude and Rene. Jonathan, Isabelle, Louise and Mariange are on your side." "Do you guys feel strong enough for us?" "We're going to crush you like flees." "It's good to be ambitious Samuel, but you should not sell the skin of a wolf before you got it trapped and if you really think you are too strong for us, maybe it's because the two teams are not balanced good enough." "Auntie Janene thinks it's fair, we'll have to play and see." "I think so too. Let's go, we're on. Who's playing first?" "The youngest play first." "Then I'll play last. Alright, let's start this game. I can't wait to play my turn."

"Isabelle, it's yours to play go ahead sweetheart. Take your time and do what you can."

"Ha, ha, ha, she put it in the hole, that's a good start." "Don't laugh at her, I'll bet you anything that we will win because of the points she'll make." "How much do you want to bet Dad?" "Ho, you want to bet. Alright, if we win you're going to clean the poop from all the dogs for a week and if you win you're going to have to clean for the whole week and it has to be done right. What do you have to say about this?" "Han, han! I'm not a dummy dad; if we win you're going to clean the poop for a week. Fair is fair." "I see that you're awake. I always have to find a way to save some time some where. Fair then, the bet is on. Let it be as you said" "I'm going to have a nice week."

Samuel was praising himself and rubbing his hand with joy.

"The game is not over yet boy."

"It's your turn Isabelle darling; put some of those pins down. Alright, what a nice shot for six pins. Congratulation sweetie, we'll win." "There is no chance; we have twenty points more. There is no way you can reach us." "Just wait my boy, don't bet anymore." "Ha, I'll bet you anything." "Take my advice Samuel, don't bet on things you don't know and those you cannot control."

"You guys are putting too much pressure on the game." "It's alright Janene, it's just for fun and this makes the game a bit more interesting, but the bet is real."

"Go ahead auntie Janene, a big score and we win." "I'm going to get a big tenpins strike my boy, just watch this." "A hole! Go on the left side auntie, there is one more pin. Ho no, not in the same hole!"

"Dad, we can win with a big score of nine, go ahead I know you can do it." "Believe me sweetie; I'm going to do my best." "Seven pins, dad we need two more. We got to have them dad. I'm begging you; take your time and a deep breath." "It's alright Mariange, I'm ready." "He's got them, he's got them, we won, we won."

"Shit, I will spend the whole week in shit." "We won because of Isabelle; it's the first time she put some pins down. Can you sing with me my team? She won for us the game, she is a big winner, she won for us the game, she's the winner of the day, yoooowho!" "Congratulation, you really won it." "Better luck to you next time my boy."

"Alright, it is time for you to go to bed Isabelle, Mariange, Jeremy and Rene. I hope you had a good time?" "That was great dad; it's the nicest day of my life." "I'm glad you enjoyed it my little sweetheart."

"Me too daddy, It's the nicest day of my life."

"Me too!"

"Me too!" "I'm coming up with you and I'll cover you for the night."

"Jonathan and you Samuel, you guys can practice your shots in the mean time. I won't be very long.

Let's go now kids and I hope you have nice dreams. Do you know that everything I have here including you were in my dreams before you became reality?" "Dad, I think you're pulling my leg." "I didn't even touch you little brat." "Ha, ha, ha, hi, hi." "You can laugh, but you got to sleep now. Sleep well and I'll see you tomorrow if God is willing. Don't forget to thank Him for all the good things He does for us every day." "Good night dad, I love you very much. I'm sure you're the best dad in the world." "I'll do my best to always stay this way, but if I'm not up to it one day you would have to forgive me." "Do you mean like last night?" "I mean like last night sweetie." "You caught on with it today dad; good night, I love you very, very much." "Good night little treasure."

There is nothing like the word of a kid to make you reflect on things even if he scores a bull's-eye shot directly to the heart. We have to accept this as a blessing.

"James, do you have a minute for me?" "I always have time for you Darling. What is the matter?" "I only need you to hold me in your arms for a minute." "Would two minutes do you good too?" "This is going to be only twice better." "I would like to take you to bed too, but I promised the boys a pull game. I got to go." "Can you forgive me for this morning?" "I have nothing to forgive you my love, but just know that if this happened at the beginning of our relationship, you would've lost me in less time it takes to say it. I would have been afraid not to be able to satisfy you. That is exactly what goes to my mind right now." "Don't you worry, I'm not a sex slave; I just got caught by surprise, that's all." "I hope so Janene." "I just want you to know that I was not only turned on by your member. If that would have been someone else I would have walked out of that room quickly. I saw a lot of men in my nursing career and it never bothered me. I'm only attracted to you." "I'm happy about that, but I have to go now; otherwise I will receive complains that I'm not fond of." "I understand; you go ahead, I love you." "I love you too darling. Don't you think Danielle should be home by now?" "Yes, she's been gone for more than twelve hours." "Try to find out what is going on and I'll see you later."

I wished I could talk with her longer, knowing very well that she needed it for her peace of mind and heart, but I can't split myself in four parts even though it would be nice sometimes.

"Hey boys, did you have a good practice?" "We started to wonder if you were going to skip us like last night." "Yesterday was a rare exception as you already know and you shouldn't blame me for it more than necessary, but I nevertheless apologize for it. You didn't answer my question." "What is the question again?" "Did you have a good practice?" "Ho yea, dad, you know what, I would like to put this bet on again like double or nothing for cleaning the dogs poop, if you're not afraid to lose of course." "My son, there are a lot more things more scary than this, but do you feel ready to clean the dogs for two weeks with no break?" "I don't think I should worry about this one." "Well, I think you should think about it a bit longer before risking having to do something you hate to do. Two weeks is a rather long time." "It's all thought of dad, I also take the chance not to do it at all." "Don't say I didn't warn you." "Let's flip the coin for the break." "That's not necessary, you can break." "I don't want any favour." "Maybe this is another mistake that you're making my boy, I spent most of my spare time in a billiard room when I was a kid." "Do you want to intimidate me now?" "A lot of players use this tactic in games and in sports, but no, I just want you to be warned." "Head or tail dad?" "Okay then, I'll take tail." "It's the head, so it's mine to break." "Good luck my son. You didn't sink any ball" "No, but the number one ball is well behind the other balls. The rules are always the same; you have to call every shot." "Alright then, the number one two banks in the corner." "Wow, how did you do that?" "The number two directly in the side packet! The number three in this corner over there! The forth in this corner! The fifth in the center! The sixth in the same pocket! The number seven in the left corner! The eight in the right corner! And the ninth double cross side over there!" "Wow dad, you've cleaned the whole table." "It's easier to clean this table in five minutes than to clean the dog's shit for two weeks, that's for sure. It's the mark of a real champion and before you bet with someone you have to know exactly what your opponent can do, not only what you can do yourself. Now my son you're twice as much in shit than you were before the game and you didn't even have the pleasure to play. It was done to me one time and I never forgot it. I thought I was good enough and I loved to gamble, but my opponent came to get everything I had I my pocket.

Much later I went on holiday in Wildwood USA. I was with a friend and we entered a bar where a man was waiting for a victim at a billiard table. He asked me if I wanted to play and I accepted. 'Only one problem.' He said. 'It's ten dollars a game.' It's alright.'

I said and he won the break just like Samuel did and just like Samuel he didn't sink any ball. He paid me thirty dollars to watch me clean the table three times in a row. He made the same mistake than Samuel; he didn't know what his opponent could do." "You didn't know what he could do either." "No, but I was willing to pay thirty dollars to find out. After that I quit to play all games; especially because of the bets. I was gambling with cards, billiard, bowling, horseshoes even with knifes and nails throwing." "Can you teach us how to play pull like you do?" "Can you promise me to never take somebody else's money, except maybe to teach them a lesson?" "Will we have the right to participate in tournaments?" "This yes, I won three of them myself." "How many were you in?" "Three!" "What would be our first lesson?" "First thing to learn is to sink at least one ball on the break. The second is to learn your angles. The third one is to practice your across table shots. The fourth one is to control the cue ball after your shot. When you can tell me where the cue ball will end after your shot with precision, then only I'll show you something else." "Why didn't you show us before today how to play and what you were capable to do?" "Firstly, I wanted to have fun playing with you and you having fun playing with me and secondly, I was and I am still afraid that you become some impulsive players, which is very dangerous, especially when you become famous. It's already nine o'clock and I have a very important meeting at nine thirty. I'm sorry but I have to leave you now. Don't forget Samuel, all the dogs beginning tomorrow for fourteen days." "Yes, I know, this one is not so funny." "I hope you'll never forget it. You have to be in bed in thirty minutes, I got to go."

"Janene, did you find out what is going on with Danielle?" "She's still at the hospital. I talked to one of her co-worker and she said she's tired but otherwise she's well." "I got to go out for about an hour and you should take a good night sleep to give Danielle a chance to rest tomorrow."

I went to meet with M. Courrois, but for some strange reason I couldn't stop worrying about Danielle. I just had a bad omen concerning her.

"Good evening Mrs. Courrois, may I speak to your husband Please?" "He's expecting you M. Prince, he asked me to let you in and lead you to his office where you will be more comfortable to discuss." "Thank you Mrs. It's very nice of you."

"James, it's a pleasure to welcome you." "All the pleasure is for me M. Courrois." "What can I do for you James?" "I wish you can talk to me about your adventure, if it's not too painful for you." "This was not easy at all and I really thought I was going to die." "There was no demand for a ransom and this means they wanted something else." "I got the feeling that you already know what this was all about and this is the reason why you're here." "I remembered how Dumas reacted at our first meeting and as soon as I found out he got away from his office I set my suspicion on him. Also the fact that my chronicles were discontinued without a notice from you and that he opposed them so violently put me on his trail." "If you didn't acted as quick as you did I wouldn't be here talking about it with you. He had no other choice than eliminate me to avoid jail time. Dumas had already given orders to kill me when you intervened." "He probably thinks that it is his duty to save the Roman Empire of lies and murders and this is why he hates the truth so much. What did he want exactly?" "You probably have guessed it already that he wanted to know who you are." "Yes but why didn't you tell him who I am." "I knew too well that I would have died as soon as he knew. So tell me James, what can I do to pay you back?" "This is the main reason for me being here. I was wondering if you could with your influence try to stop this investigation on what was used to save your life." "Can you tell me what you used to manage such a successful coup?" "The reason we want to stop the investigation is exactly to keep this secret. The main reason why this is efficient is the fact it isn't known and keep it secret will allow us to save more people." "I understand, but I can assure you that my wife will do everything she can to get it." "What happened exactly M. Courrois?" "She got what she didn't have for more than three years and she thought she will never get it anymore." "And how was it for you?" "I would have preferred it doesn't last so long and hurt so bad. Fortunately someone brought us some medicine." "This came from my laboratory, but this too must stay secret." "What is it exactly?" "It's just a sleeping process which acts quickly." "How can you explain such a powerful erection?" "We don't know yet, but I think that it could be cause by the total absence of inhibition, doubt, fear, and stress which allow you for the first time to perform with one hundred per cent of your possibilities. We still have to make a lot of tests before we can market it and be able to control its side effects. One of my spouses almost kill herself mounting me this morning, so much she couldn't go to work and yes, it hurts too much for us men to appreciate it. For now we're afraid to be stolen either by the government or any other big outfit and this is why I came to ask you to intervene if you can." "I owe you this much. As soon as tomorrow I will ask the responsible minister to do something about it, he is a friend of mine. You'll have to get me this phenomenal prescription as soon as it is available and this preferably before my wife starts looking for it." "You will be the first, pardon me, the second one to experience it again M. Courrois." "Call me Jean would you please James, we have so many common interests now." "I should go home now before someone starts worrying about me. If you succeed stopping this investigation, maybe it would be a good idea telling the public in order to stop it asking questions." "I'll see to it James, good night." "Good night Jean and thank you." "It's me who says thank you James, I love my life."

Now this is another good thing accomplished tonight. I hope now that everything is alright with Danielle.

"Hi Janene, did you hear anything from Danielle at all?" "Yes, she left the hospital at ten and she will be here at any moment now." "Are the boys gone to bed?" "Yes, they went about fifteen minutes ago." "I'll be home in about twenty minutes myself, bye. Just a minute, I have to talk with Bernard, let's say that I'll be there in just a bit more than half hour."

"How things are going for you Bernard?" "Not too well, I'm afraid. I have the impression that I'm in the middle of something which doesn't concern me." "What is going on Bernard?" "Danielle stopped at a house on St-Euchetache Street, number 666." "This doesn't smell good at all and this is not one of her habits at all either." "She seems to go there on her own will and without any pressure." "Are you okay yourself? Do you want me to take your place?" "I'm alright, what do you want me to do next?" "Just keep an eye on the house and wait till she comes out. We'll give her until eleven thirty, the time she usually finish working. I'll call Roger tomorrow morning. I'm on my way home and you call me if it's necessary, if not I'll talk to you tomorrow morning. We'll take some arrangements then."

I got home and I found Janene all upset.

"But what in the world is going on with you?" "Danielle should have been here one and a half hour ago and she's not here yet. I tried to call her on her cell phone, but she left too quickly this morning and she didn't take it with her. She left it in her kitchen. I won't forgive myself ever if something bad happened to her. It's my fault if she had to go to work today." "Quit torturing yourself, it's not your fault if she stopped somewhere on her way home. I'm sure she has a good reason and she doesn't know that we are worrying about her. She'll be here soon, don't you worry." "How could you tell?" "I always have a bad omen when there is danger. It's going to be fine tonight, tomorrow will be something else." "I hope you're right. I know I couldn't sleep for as long as she's not in." "I'm going to wait for her in her bed. Good night Janene!"

"There she is; she's going to hear what I think of her. Danielle, can you come here? I have to talk to you." "What is the matter? You look completely chattered." "You left the hospital more than two hours ago and it only takes twenty minutes to get here. You left this house more than sixteen hours ago. Don't you think you could have phoned to tell us at least how you are?" "I forget my cell phone this morning." "This is no excuse; you could have used another phone." "I'm sorry, but I also thought you needed a lot of rest. You were exhausted this morning, don't you remember? You couldn't go to work." "That's true too, but I tried to talk to you twice, why didn't anyone let you know?" "At the time I received your message I thought you were sleeping and I didn't want to wake you up. You should go to sleep; you got to work tomorrow morning. I know I need to sleep in. Do you know where James is?" "I think he's in your bed." "Ho no, not tonight!" "What is the matter with you? You don't want him anymore?" "Don't be silly, I'm just too tired to answer any of his questions. Does he know that I quit working at ten?" "Yes he knows it and you should remember there is nothing like the truth, especially with him." "I'll remember, good night."

"There is no point being careful, I'm not sleeping yet. How are you?" "I'm exhausted." "That's understandable, you almost went around the clock. How come you are so late? Come here I'll give you a massage that will do you good." "I worked till ten and then I went to meet a very gentle couple who wants to know more about the life of a Jesus' disciple." "How did they know you were one?" "She came to the hospital for a stomach ache and then she asked me if I received the letter from the disciple which is circulating. She's a woman with an exceptional sweetness and I offer her my help to become a disciple. Her companion is very gentle too. I was a bit scared though, I had the impression I was followed." "The town of Trois-Rivières is not known to be dangerous for nurses, but this is not the case everywhere in Canada. In Saskatoon there is a tunnel built from the parking lot to the hospital, because there were too many attacks on nurses." "How come you know this?"

"It can't be bad to be informed, you know? Are you feeling better now? It's late and you should go to sheep now. I had a very long day too. Good night sweetheart." "Good night, you're an angel."

CHAPTER 10

*I*n the morning I was up for quite a while before Danielle woke up. I went to my place and I wrote a little note and then I called Raymond and Roger.

Roger, I have another few little jobs for you my friend." "What is it James?" "I need to know what the people who live at the 666 St-Euchetache Street want. I also sent a big amount of money for cancer treatments for the little two year old boy and I wonder if they have received it. You probably heard about the little two year old boy hit by cancer? There was no response to my gift and I don't think this is normal. If they are honest they should tell the public they reached their goal. In fact I sent the whole amount a few weeks ago. Check this out would you? Start with St-Euchetache though, it's more urgent."

"Have you got something new Raymond?" "We don't have much yet James. The only good news is it doesn't seem to be any side effect to the use of this product." "I don't think men would want to use it more than once a week, unless he is a real masochist." "There is also a very important fact about ejaculation, because the sperm won't come out until the swallow of the penis is down. A bit like it happens with dogs and some other animals." "This could be a way to control pregnancy in the way that men could choose to stay or get out before the ejaculation and this way he could decide for himself if he wants to be a father or not." "I didn't think of that, but yes this is true, although we cannot guarantee it." "There is also the risk that someone could get stock like what happened to Dumas and his partner yesterday afternoon." "There is very little risk this could happen to heterosexual couples though, but it could happen." "There are probably some risks with young girls who shouldn't play this game yet. We'll have to post the consequences for everyone. Did you manage a formula for wake up? I think we should try to get two birds with one stone. I mean make a tube where a man could inhale the soporific from one end and the wake up call from the other, this way men could decide themselves of the duration of the erection, unless the woman throw the tube away while he sleeps. I can see that millions of men would like to experience it thinking their penis is too small. We could set the price according to the number of puffs in each tube, let say fifteen dollars a puff. I would limit the tube to twelve puffs. It's the same price than viagree, but only many times more efficient." "You're really serious when you say you want to market it." "Raymond, dead men would come out of their tombs if they could to try this formula. Just think about all the impotent men too that would be temporary cured from one day to the next." "It's not sure yet this will cure the impotence." "It's already proven Raymond." "No, not you James?" "No Raymond, sorry to disappoint you, but he's someone who was impotent for more than three years and he was told he was incurable. Now we have to hurry and get it out before his wife goes looking for this. You have to go to Africa soon too for a short trip. We need to find another doctor to replace you for this, because you became indispensable at the laboratory. I thought you were coming to my place to continue on this safely." "I set it up in your place in one way; I'm at Bernard's place. I thought this way it would be secure too without disturbing your privacy, besides Bernard is a big help to me." "That's a very good idea Raymond. I'm afraid we're going to need this powder again before the experiences are all done. There is a suspicious couple who came too close to Danielle no later than last night." "Then I'll have to go to sleep to be immunized for the next twenty-four hours." "If it stays this way we going to need this powder more than anyone else. If what I think is right we might have to get away from here for a while and that's not going to be easy with the whole family." "I think we got rid of Dumas and his team rather easily." "Don't forget that a good man came close to death in the process." "Still you have to admit that we came out of it as winners and for as long that good luck in on our side it's a sign heaven is with us." "You're right, but still we cannot neglect the warning signals. Go to sleep, because for sure we have to put this couple to sleep before the end of the day. Don't forget the wake up pill. Call me as soon as you are awake for the next instructions." "I will James, talk to you later."

"Good morning madam. Allow me to introduce myself. My name is Roger Parenteau and I work for the town council. It's one of our rules here in this town to pay a visit to our new comers even if it's only to welcome them over." "Come on in sir and make yourself at home. My name is Sister Henri-Paul Toupin and this is father Charles Gregoire." "A nun and a priest who rent a house together? Excuse me but, isn't this a bit odd?" "We are just passing by sir; we are on a special mission." "Pardon me again but, if you just passing through; why not take a hotel room like everybody else?" "Well, we don't know how long this mission will take and here with an all furnished rent, we don't have to sign any register and it's three or four times cheaper." "The way you talk, it seems that you don't want to leave any tracks behind you. This too is a bit particular, don't you think?" "Just think for a minute, a priest and a nun in a hotel room and signing a register. We don't want to scandalize all the Christians of the world." "Can you talk to me about this mission of yours?" "Are you sure you're working for the town and not for the police?" "You know police too is working for the town and both want to know if a mafia person is in town and why. Police needs a search warrant and I don't. You have to admit that your situation is a bit ambiguous." "Listen to me M. Parenteau, we are not hurting anybody; we're only looking for some information for our personal and spiritual life, that's all." "Maybe I can help you find what you're looking for, I know a lot of people in this town." "Do you know the writer of the chronicles in the newspaper about Jesus' disciples?" "No, I don't, but let me tell you that the last one who tried to find out who he is he's in pain and in Jail." "Maybe it's where we should start looking." "I guess you can always ask him if he wants to confess his sins, but I would be very careful if I were you, it could be very slippery ground. Well, I wish you good luck with your search and a good stay inside our town's limits. I'll have to make a report, but I don't thing there will be any problem. Welcome sister, sir." "Thank you M. Parenteau, it was a pleasure meeting you, see you again."

"I think he might be a disciple." "What makes you say that?" "I think he should normally call me father and he called me sir." "That is a good observation."

"James, it's me. The people you asked me to check on are quite inoffensive I think. They are a priest and a nun looking for a Jesus' disciple, specifically for the writer of the chronicles in the paper." "I thank you very much Roger, you can take care of the other case now. That's all I need for this one here for now. Do you need any money for your expenses?" "No, I'm alright; I'll see you when it's all over. Thanks anyway."

"Sorry to wake you up Bernard, but we have on our hands another case of people who need to go in a deep sleep." "The last night couple?" "Yap, they are a priest and a nun who are looking for me." "Is it this obvious?" "Raymond knows it and he's already immunizing himself as we speak. I wrote a little note for them to read when they wake up. You'll have to come and get it." "What are we going to do with them?" "I didn't think about this yet." "Maybe we could bring them to your place while they're sleeping and question them when they wake up." "This would look too much like kidnapping and it's risky and illegal." "What about put them to sleep? That's not illegal?" "When have you heard it was illegal for a doctor to put someone to sleep?" "You're right, what do we do then?" "I still have a couple of hours to think about it and in the mean time you can return the rented car, we won't need it anymore. After that you should go see if everything is alright with Raymond. We cannot forget this is just experimental yet. When this is all over, you will have to make another trip to Africa." "When is it for exactly? I started making plans with Pauline." "So you finally moved on with this." "I think she will be a good partner for me." "I think so too. We'll talk about it later; you go see your brother now."

I went down to see if Danielle was still sleeping.

"Are you going to sleep all day or come to make breakfast for me? No wait, I got a better idea, you tell me what you would like and I'll go get it ready for you, what do you say about that?" "I say it's a wonderful idea. It's not over ten already, is it?" "Yes my dear, it's ten passed ten."

"And what happened with the children?" "The oldest gave something to eat to the youngest and they went to school and the youngest is gone to the nursery. Everyone is fine." "What about you, you didn't have breakfast yet?" "As far as I know, neither have you." "It's not the same for me, I'm still in bed." "What a disgrace, do you want to be served in bed?" "No, if you want to go make some of your granny's crepes with your pole syrup, I didn't have any for a long time." "Right away sweetheart, I'll call you when they're ready." "You're an angel." "See you in a bit."

It has been a long time since I had some myself. Too bad kids are not at home, they are crazy about them. If we listen to them we would make them every morning.

"Are you coming Danielle, I made a whole bunch of them; you only have to warm them up for the kids tomorrow morning." "They're going to be happy about it; you can bet they will be up early. Wow, look how nice they are, they are just right." "Well yea, there was no distraction around me." "It's true that this house is big and quiet when the kids are not around. How sweet this is; two of them will be enough for me." "You are still afraid to lose your young woman slim waist?" "Ho, I lost it long time ago." "Make me laugh, you only weigh ten pounds more than the night I met you." "The night we met, the time goes so fast, sixteen years already." "You didn't regret it yet?" "Regretting what? The perfect happiness? I can tell you James, there is only one thing I regret." "Ho yea, what is it?" "I only regret that no more people understand our friendship and our marital situation." "It's strange though that they can understand the fornication and the adultery that is going on everywhere in the world." "It's a funny world alright. These people you were talking to last night darling, did they tell you who they are?" "Not really, they only say they want to know the truth. I showed them a lot of verses in the Bible that they seem to be surprised to hear about." "You don't think you were not careful to go like this to some strangers in the night?" "This lady is so gentle and besides, with all the tricks you showed me, I'm sure I can defend myself." "I would like to be convinced of this. Are you in good enough shape to come down stairs on the mattress and show me what you can do against me?" "You know very well that I have no chance at all against you." "Come anyway, I won't use my arts. I'll just act like an ordinary man." "Alright, let's go."

"I want to know where this so called disciple who writes those chronicles in the newspaper is." "Is this gun loaded?" "No one will tell you it isn't." "You tell me where he is or I'll blow your head off." "Either I tell you or not it wouldn't change anything, might as well keep my mouth shut." "Yes but, before I kill you; I will rape you and than I will pull your eyes off slowly and you wouldn't even be able to scream, because I will seal your mouth with duck tape." "Where and when did you learn to be so mean?" "It takes what it takes, but you going to tell me before you die. Lie down there now; I want your ass before your face is unrecognizable." "Are you sure you don't want a striptease while you are at it?" "That is a very good idea; let me put the appropriate music on. You're good at it. Is that your secondary job or just a hobby of yours?" "My husband loves this." "Who could blame him, you are a beauty." "You like it?" "You're going to get it even worst than I thought. That's enough, lie down there now and don't try anything that would force me to shoot you in the head, because I don't like sex with a dead body even if she is the most beautiful woman in the world. Han, han, you're in a hurry to die? You try this one more time and you're dead." "I rather die than have sex with a shit like you." "This my dear I don't give a shit about it. Enough talking and lie down and don't forget that I'm a quick trigger. You are even prettier than I thought. You're going to ease my desire now, because you didn't succeed to disarm me. You seem to be pretty excited yourself. I can see some dripping in there." "My husband will make you pay dearly for this, you bastard." "For this he would have to find me before I find him. I win anyway, because I got his wife. Now you shut up, I run the show here and turn around and get on your knees, you will be less dangerous with my gun behind your head. You can scream all you want nobody can hear you down here." "This is so good, give me more. This is even better than yesterday.

Don't stop, don't stop just yet, it's too good." "I can't anymore; you just got raped for the first time." "That was extremely good James, there was something very exciting in all of this." "What, being rape by a stranger under the threat of a gun?" "Don't be ridicules, he would never get me alive and you can be sure of this." "I won't get you anymore either if you're dead. From now on you and Janene will always have a magic cigarette in your bag. This way you will be able to put your aggressor to sleep if necessary. That will give us three hours to find you and put the enemy away for a while. You will also carry a transmitter-receiver to tell me where you are at all times. No one will suspect this and I will feel better." "Poor you, you're always worrying about us, aren't you?" "Unfortunately darling the threat is always present. The demons always want to destroy the truth in every way they can and they're getting closer and closer every day. We might even have to get out of here for a while." "This is not going to be easy for the children and neither for me; our house is a paradise for all of us." "I built its twin in the Caribbean." "You're not serious?" "I sure am, I rent it out to M. Charron who loves it a lot, but he's willing to trade anytime we need to. He's been there for twelve years already." "I was wondering what happen to him." "We always kept close ties and he didn't forget the billions he made out of my inventions. I could have done without him after the third one, but I didn't and he always was grateful to me for that." "You always share everything with everyone, don't you? Everyone who deals with you is doing well. When I think of Bernard and Raymond, it's incredible who they became because of you." "They paid me back many times and even today they are devoted loyal friends even though they don't need work or money anymore." "What about Samuel who is many times millionaires at the age of fourteen?" "He earned it as you know yourself, this is the result of his ideas and it's not over yet for him, because the Samuel's hats and boots are selling better than hot cakes." "I only hope he will be as generous as you are." "He is sweetie." "What make you say this?" "I sent four hundred thousand a few weeks ago for a two year old child to receive cancer treatments and he gave half of that himself and besides, this was his own idea. I must get this investigated though, because there was no response to it. I'm afraid it could be a fraud. I should find out soon. It's almost noon and I have to speak to the two brothers. Did you recover from this rape?" "This was not a rape, because I was completely willing." "You right for that, but when it comes to defend yourself, it was a total failure, so I suggest you be more careful in the future before this scenario becomes a reality." "Are you coming with me, I'm going to jump in the tub?" "Run the water and I'll be right with you."

"Ho my God! Bernard you phoned me?" "Why don't you answer the phone?" "I was town stairs with Danielle and the phone was left in the kitchen." "I've been trying to reach you for more than an hour." "I'm sorry Bernard, but showing Danielle how to get out of a bad situation was important too. She needs to understand that she cannot be unwise like last night." "What do we do with this couple now, our time is running out?" "Send Raymond to their place to blow the powder and you go meet them three and a half hour later." "Why's that?" "I think by then they will be interlaced in a shameful way if you know what I mean. In the mean time you hide yourself not too far from this house. Instead of coming to get this note for them you type it yourself. Here what I want you to write; 'You were looking for me, I found you.' And nothing else and then put this note near the phone and make sure not to leave your finger prints in there. You do understand that Raymond has to leave the note when he goes in?" "Yes, I understood." "Tell Raymond to contact me when he's done and you keep me informed of all the facts." "Alright James, I'll talk to you later."

"How come you were so long, I thought earring you were joining me in the tub." "I'm sorry, but I had to make an important phone call." "Come in, I'll soap you up." "You would do that for me after what I did to you with a gun." "This might mean I want some more." "I really loved you strip-tease too with the appropriate music." "You sounded like a real criminal; if I didn't know you I would have been real scared." "Just remember this before entering a stranger's house again. I wouldn't want to pick you up with your eyes pulled out." "I think you are making too much of a deal for something insignificant." "No darling, anything you want, but not this. You should take my warnings and my advices very seriously. I spent more than a billion for our security and you think that it's insignificant?" "Are you serious?" "It seems sometimes you wouldn't understand or believe in it until a disaster hits you. Up until now I made more than twenty attacks on us fall through and it doesn't mean there is no danger because I didn't talk about them. Even your family and Janene family are under my protection continually." "Why didn't you talk to us about this?" "I always wanted you both to be happy and not to leave in fear all the time, but because of your attitude now I'm forced to do differently. It's too bad, because I wanted to avoid this." "I beg you pardon, I had no idea it was like that." "If we didn't have the money we have we would be dead and buried at least twelve years ago. God allowed us to have all this. I thought you understood all of this in the first year, but I see that it's not the case. To build you a bran new hospital with all the modern facilities will cost less money for us than to continue as we are and a lot less scary for me. It cost more in security than both of you make in a year. I would have preferred a lot more that you stay at home with the kids, but I wanted you to decide for yourselves." "But at what cost though?" "The hospital needed you too." "We caused you a lot of worries, didn't we?" "Let me tell you that you both worth it." "I don't think it's necessary for us to cause you so many worries. You go ahead and build this new hospital." "It is already started and you'll get the very best in the world, but I count on you to scrutinize every single individual who comes to work for you. I especially count on you to encourage Janene and all the children to the carefulness, because I'm very tired to be seen as a paranoiac. We should get out of here before kids come back from school. Janene was real good yesterday and she made supper for everybody." "She's wonderful, isn't she?" "You both are wonderful and I don't love you more than her nor her more than you. This is what you wanted and this is what you got. This is the truth." "I believe you my love." "Get out, I'll dry you up." "How can you stay such a charming man in every circumstance?" "I try to be myself as natural as possible. Ho there are some days I could throw a fit like everybody, but the presence of God is calming me down. I'm very grateful to Him for this." "You really love Him with all of your heart, don't you?" "He loves me even more, think of all the good things He does for us." "He is the Almighty." "That's true Danielle. Do you want me to help you with supper?" "As you wish, but if you have something better to do I will understand." "I sure could make a few phone calls, but it could wait till after supper too." "What are you making?" "I'll make a spaghetti meat sauce, kids like that and you too." "What about you? What would you like to eat?" "I'll tell you tomorrow night on the pillow." "This is true too; it is Janene turn to have me tonight." "I'm serious; I want to know what do you want to eat?" "There is no point talking about it, there is none in the house." "And what is that?" "Shrimps!" "You're mistaking, I have some upstairs. I'll finish peeling the potatoes and I'll go get you some. There we are; you only have to put them on the stove." "This is your phone at least take the time to answer it."

"Hello!" "James there is a problem." "Bernard, what is it?" "The ambulance just left here for the hospital with our couple. Do you have any idea of what could have happened?" "Maybe they got stock and they don't know how to handle it. Shit, too bad we couldn't get a picture of this; we would have had what it takes to keep them quiet for a long time." "You must be right; they are both on the same stretcher." "We're going to have a scandal every time we're going to use this powder." "We could call it; the scandalous." "The name is good, just don't forget it." "What do we do now?" "Go see in this house if there is anything that could give us away, but make sure you don't touch anything if you can. If the note is still there, pick it up, it already served its purpose, for the rest, we have to wait and see. How is Raymond?" "He said he feel real good like the first time he used it, only this time he didn't wait too long before taking the wake up pill." "So his partner didn't take advantage of it this time."

"He didn't say anything about that." "Don't stay around there and wait for my call. Call me if you have something new."

"Danielle, there is a couple here in a very bad position who claims you urgently and they say they won't talk to anyone but you. They say you're the only one they know and in whom they can trust." "But Janene, we are just in the middle of our supper." "I can assure you that they need someone more than anybody else right now. They don't even have identifications, not even a health card. I'm telling you, they are claiming your immediate help." "Give me a minute; I'll talk to James about this."

"James, someone is claiming me urgently at the hospital, what do you think I should do?" "This has never happened to you before, isn't it? That's a first. This is kind of strange, isn't it? Try to find out who this is; otherwise you don't move from here."

"Janene, you tell them that I won't move from here for as long as I don't know who they are." "Alright, just wait on the line; I'll be back . . . . Are you there Danielle?" "I'm here." "They won't tell me their names, but they say they are the people you met last night at 666 St-Euchetache Street. This is the number of the beast, isn't it?" "Is she very gentle and very pretty?" "She looks more like a crazy woman right now." "What is wrong with them?" "He's locked up in her and the usual injection didn't do anything to release them." "Tell them that I'll be there, but I won't be alone. I'll be there in about thirty minutes and if they are suffering too much give them a pain killer and put it on my account."

"They are the people I met last night James, do you have anything to do with this?" "My security program is always at work no matter what. What happened to them anyway?" "They are locked in like dogs and I don't like it one bit." "Me neither, but I'm not responsible for their actions. If you want to go I'll ask Bernard to go with you. He will wait for you in the lobby and if you need assistance he will do what ever is necessary. I'm telling you though that he needs to talk to them even before you release them and I want you to introduce him to them. Can you do this? If I made a mistake concerning them I'll do everything in my power to repair the damage, but if I'm right, they'll remember their misfortune for a long time." "I'll do what ever is necessary, but let me tell you that I trust them." "I hope you're right, because I never wish to meet with the enemy." "I know that, but even then, you've been a bit harsh on them." "We'll see. Enough talking, I think they're waiting for you very impatiently. Do you have what it takes to release them?" "Yes, I got it." "Be very discreet alright? Don't you worry; I'll take care of the children and all the rest. Go ahead now."

"Keep eating kids, I'll be back right away."

"Where are you now Bernard?" "I'm in a second class restaurant near St-Euchetache Street with Raymond waiting for your instructions." "What did you find in the house?" "Just the note we left there." "Was there any clothes?" "Of course, there were all the man clothes and the woman pink panties on the floor." "We'll have to make a few recommendations to the ambulance's people." "As far as I can tell, they covered them with a bed-spread." "Then don't waste anytime and go back there, pick up all the clothes and put them in a bag and go wait for Danielle in the lobby at the hospital. Keep talking and go to your car. Leave the restaurant bill to Raymond. Danielle will introduce you to these people even before she releases them. If you can, try to discreetly take a picture of them, it might be very useful. Give them their clothes back and at the same time offer them your help." "I'm at the house now." "That's good, but don't interrupt me anymore, we don't have time. With Danielle's help and her recommendations you will gain their trust, then you'll take them for a long turning around ride before you bring them over here with their eyes blindfold. Explain to them that it is necessary for security reasons. I will watch for your arrival and open the gate and the garage for you. I don't even want Danielle to know they're here, not now anyway. From there you will guide them up to my place. In any case they cannot see me. Then we'll proceed to the interrogation when they are well locked up in the guess room. I will keep them under observation for a couple of days and after that we'll see.

You've got to be in the hospital before Danielle; otherwise she might just proceed without you and this won't be good at all. You have all the instructions and I have to leave you now. Phone me if you have any problem. Any question?" "No, I'm at the hospital now." "I'll talk to you later."

"Are you at the hospital yet Danielle?" "No, I'm stock in the traffic; it's the rush hour right now. Those two must be living a Calvary." "It's almost over now for them. Bernard is already in there." "I should be there in five minutes." "Bernard has their clothes with him and he'll do everything in his power to make their lives easier. I count on you to make them trust in him." "I'll do my best." "You call me if you need, I'll keep my phone close by. One more thing, get me their hospital bill please? I love you, so be very careful." "I love you too, see you later."

"Hey both of you, you have a funny kind of activities."

"Who is this? We don't want to see anybody but you." "Calm down, this man has a job to do and believe me, this is much better than having the police over here with whom come all the journalists."

"She's right Henri-Paul; don't make things any worst than they already are."

"I brought your clothes over that the stupid ambulance men left at your place. You refused to give your names to the admission; you know they could have turned you away, don't you? You don't have any identification either. Consider yourself lucky, because you could very well be in police custody right now. I'll come back to get you when Danielle is done with you."

"Consider yourself very lucky he's the one who takes care of you; otherwise you would be on the first page of the newspaper." "Ho my God, we would be excommunicated on the spot." "So you are catholics?" "I'd say more than that, I'm Sister Henri-Paul Toupin and this is father Charles Gregoire." "How do you explain your actual situation then?" "We don't understand it at all. We slept and when we woke up he was like a demon and in less time it takes to say it he was inside me. I'm a virgin Danielle." "Let me see this for a minute." "Maybe you were, but not anymore my dear lady." "We prayed none stop for the last two hours and nothing has changed." "Who are you praying to?" "To the good holy virgin, of course." "Do you think God will grant you what you're asking for when you pray someone else then He? This is idolatry pure and simple. Didn't you ever read the Bible?" "We read it every day." "Can you show me one place where Jesus prays his mother? He was praying his Father who is in heaven. Although, his mother was still in this world and I believe we have more power alive than dead. Dead is powerless." "Jesus too is dead." "Can you show me one place in the Bible where Jesus says pray Jesus? No, he said: 'If you ask my Father something in my name, my Father will give it to you.'

"How many years did you study?" "I've never stop studying since I'm five years old." "Jesus is right when he says they are blinds who lead blinds. Now pray the Father who is in heaven and take this pill, I'm sure you will see a difference. Now, remember that the best medical science in the world couldn't do anything for you, but a Jesus' disciple freed you from this shameful situation. Why didn't you tell me you were members of the catholic clergy?" "If our religious authorities ever find out we're looking for the holy man who writes the chronicles in the newspaper to whom we're writing since the beginning, we would be in real danger. Just remember the priest who got married a few years back; our authorities cancelled this marriage and this was not done with prayers, believe me." "What do you want from this writer?" "We want to kiss his hands and feet and get his benediction." "I don't think this would please him at all, but when it comes to educate you about the word of God, this you need it a lot. You should be able to come out of there pretty soon, here's a towel to wipe yourselves. It is possible if you get out fast enough that you won't drip inside there. Try to avoid the worst if you can. Although, it is the will of God for us to be fruitful."

"That's it, I'm finally free." "I leave two pain killers on the table if you think you need them. I'll give you five minutes to get dressed and the man will come to pick you up. Trust him, he will take you to a safe place and thank God for your luck."

"They're yours Bernard, give them two more minutes to get dressed and I'm not sure of their intentions anymore."

"Are you ready? Follow me; we're going for a little ride." "Where are we going?" "I'm sorry, but I can't tell you this. All I can tell you is you are safe with me and you have nothing to fear." "What is it going to happen to us?" "You'll have to answer our questions and as soon as we don't have anymore reason to retain you, you'll be set free." "Why are you doing this?" "Because you were looking and we found you first." "Why can't you tell us where you're taking us?" "I can't even tell you that you'll see, because I have to blindfold you and if you try to take it off, I'll know then that you are the enemy. We don't hurt anybody; we only and simply try to protect ourselves. Another ten minutes and we'll be there. You must be getting hungry by now?" "It would be good to get something to eat, but we can wait too." "Here we are, keep your headband on, I'll guide you up there. Walk now, following me. Make a half turn on the right and stop. We are in front of stairs where there are eight steps. Now you walk three steps forward and there are fourteen more stairs. Are you alright?" "That makes me a bit dizzy, but I should be okay." "One more stair and we'll be on the main floor. I'm going to guide you now to your bedroom. Would you like a bedroom for two or separate bedrooms?" "How long you think we'll be here?" "For what ever it takes and it depends mostly on both of you." "Are we in a hotel? This looks quite a bit like kidnapping." "Not at all, I asked you to follow me and you did it without being forced. I'm I mistaking?" "That's right sister, he's telling the truth." "You were cooperative up till now, keep it this way and everything will be fine, you'll see." "Right now we don't see anything." "You'll see as soon as I take this headband off." "You didn't answered me, are we in a hotel? What choice do we have?" "You have a choice between a bedroom for two with two beds, two communicating bedrooms and two bedrooms completely separated." "I let you decide Sister Henri-Paul." "Can we be together for the evening and separated for the night?" "Of course you can, but I thought you were united for a life time. I don't think the big boss will tolerate any fornication in his building." "Who is the big boss?" "Do you think I'm an idiot? Do you think we're going through all of this trouble just for fun?" "Don't get mad and just put yourself in our shoes." "If I were you I wouldn't have put my foot in it and in nothing else. We arrived now just wait a sec, I'll open the door. One little step on the left and then straight ahead. You are in now wait here and I'll help your companion too and I'll shut the door behind us. Alright, I'll free your hands and your eyes now. Each bedroom has its own bathroom and everything you need it it, but before you go I would like you to look at the menu and choose and tell me what you would like for supper. Everything should be ready in about thirty minutes." "This is not our last meal, isn't it?"

"I said that you were safe with me." "Do we have all of those choices?" "It would still be nice if you both choose the same thing. We're not in a restaurant here. Did you choose?" "Anything would be good to me, you choose father." "I sure would like a good beef stew." "Alright then, beef stew for two. White or brown bread?" "White bread please!" "Tea, coffee or milk?" "A tea and a glass of milk!" "What would you like for dessert?" "Apple pie à la mode please?"

"Me too, please! It's been a long time since I was treated and spoil this way." "Don't be too greedy Sister, this can be a sin."

"It's not a sin to satisfy you hunger sir at least not in this house." "You can choose to clean yourselves either now or after the questioning period, it's up to you as long as you are available between seven and ten. I will be back in thirty minutes with your meal." "Can you tell us if we're going to see the writer sir?" "You might be able to hear him, to see him; I'm not so sure, he will have to decide, see you in a bit."

"What took you so long?" "They just don't stop questioning. They are worried and puzzled at the same time. They seem to be very gentle and harmless, but one can never tell, I know.

I videotaped the whole scene at the hospital including Danielle's meeting with them." "This is wonderful, but how did you managed this?" "If you want me to I can download it on your computer?" "Go ahead; I'm very curious to see this." "She's very messy right now, but she's still very pretty. This won't be long, about ten minutes. You want to come and take a look at this?"

"There are a few things that bother me a lot in all of this." "What is it James?" "You don't see anything abnormal in this scenario?" "Not really!" "Listen, she's a nun and he is a priest, they called an ambulance instead of calling for a doctor to come home, which I would certainly have preferred in those circumstances and do you think she really looks like a woman who just got raped and had sex for the first time in her life and with a man she didn't want in the first place on top of everything? Would you have left your clothes behind? Why didn't she want to talk to anyone but Danielle? Why they don't even have their health card with them?" "I have to agree with you, there is something very odd in all of this." "Are you sure there was nothing at all in their clothes?" "Absolutely nothing!" "Do you thing this is normal?" "Actually no, not even for a priest!" "There is something very suspicious in this story and we'll have to get to the bottom of it. I'll have to keep the cameras on them days and nights. Take note that we'll have to get an x-rays machine as soon as possible to search parts of the body that we're not allowed to. With all of the technology that exists today we have to be more careful. They could have a time bomb inside their stomach and this would explain her careless behaviour about being raped. As soon as they have finished eating, you will go search their place a bit more, it's got to be something in there which could help us understand. Just a minute this is a job for Roger if he's in town."

"Hi Roger, are you in town?" "No James, I'm in Montreal trying to track down your money. Why?" "I was hoping you could search deeply the house on St-Euchetache." "When do you need that done by?" "Immediately!" "This will cost you double at this time of the day, but I have the man you need for this, trust me." "You don't have anything to fear, the renters are in my house right now and I think the door is not even locked." "This should be very easy then." "He cannot let any part of the house unlooked." "Don't you worry; there is no one better than this guy for this job. Leave this into my hands." "I trust you, but do it quick."

"You know my kitchen Bernard and it's already all cooked. Nine minutes in the microwave and everything will be ready for our guests. In the mean time, I'll go down stairs to see my family."

"How are you kids?" "We would like to play another game like yesterday." "I am very, very sorry, but I won't be able to play tonight. Maybe your mothers can. Did you ask them? I'm lucky to have these few minutes right now. I have a very important matter to solve and I can't help it and again, I'm very sorry. Believe me I would like far more spend the next few hours with you if I could. This will keep me the whole evening and maybe all night too." "This seems very serious darling?" "This is in fact a bit more complicated than I anticipated and that I wished for. So I got to say good night and have nice dreams."

"I wanted to tell you about the dream I had last night dad." "You should write it down, so you don't forget it sweetie and you can tell me another time." "That's a good idea daddy." "That's all the time I've got and I have to see my other family too." "Do you have a hug for me James?" "Always Darling!" "I'll see you tomorrow; I should be off this time for real." "You might be useful for us in this interrogation. Excuse me now I have to go, I'm out of time."

"Hello kids, how are you?" "We are fine dad; we're having a card game. Can you join us?" "I wish I could, but I can't. I have a very important mission and I just can't postpone it. I hope with all of my heart it will be done by tomorrow." "Ha, ha, ha, always the same story." "No, I'm sorry to contradict you, but this one is different and all new. Good night sweethearts. I love you all." "Good night dad and have nice dreams."

"Can I speak to you for a minute in private Janene?" "Of course I can darling. Do you have a problem?" "I won't be able to join you tonight sweetie, I'll have to watch a few people maybe all night long, but if you care to join me around ten you'll be more than welcome. I will explain to you then." "I would like to, but I don't like to leave the kids alone." "We can watch them better from up stairs than you can from your bedroom." "That's true too. I'll come around ten then. Mmmm I love you, see you later."

"Is there something new Bernard?" "Not really, they're almost done eating. We can start questioning them in about ten minutes."

"Tralalalala . . . lala." "James, I got something for you. We found their identifications papers. He is a priest named father Charles, Joseph Gregoire and she is Sister Henri-Paul Toupin. He is thirty-nine born on January eight nineteen seventy. She's twenty-nine born on June the fourteen in nineteen eighty. Strangely they have both register a new will seven days ago in the town of Richelieu at the notary public name Caron. Their respective beneficiaries are their own families. Beside the papers they have two thousand five hundred dollars in one hundred dollar bills. There is nothing else but a bran new park of paper matches but no sign of cigarettes. Everything was hidden very carefully such that no one could find anything." "The whole thing is a bit contradictory. In one way they seem to be ready to die and on the other hand they have money to move around." "Maybe they have found what they were looking for sooner than they anticipated it." "I am certain they were looking for me." "My man left everything in place as if nothing was touch." "That's good Roger, I'll see you later."

"Did you bring me the newspaper like I asked you Bernard?" "Yes, but I left it in my car." "After you picked up all the dishes in the room, please bring it to me." "Sure, they are done now, I'll go pick up the trays."

"How are you guys doing? Did you have enough to eat?" "Thank you, this was excellent. You must have a super cook in here? I didn't eat such a good beef stew since I left my mother."

"Me, I never had as good a stew in my whole life." "I will tell him your appreciation, he will be happy to hear this. It's the same stew we feed our dogs with. Let me free you from these dishes if you allow me to. We're going to ask you questions in about five minutes. You won't be able to see anyone, but you will hear clearly and we'll hear you too. Be relaxed as possible, that will make it easier for everybody." "We are ready when you are. Thanks again for this wonderful meal." "I hope you are welcome. I got to go, be frank."

"Are you going to start without me? I'll go get your newspaper now. Maybe we should ask Raymond to join us?" "I don't think it will be necessary tonight, but tomorrow when I have enough of it myself. I'll have to keep an eye on them all night. We cannot afford to let them without surveillance until we know exactly who they're looking for and mainly why. Go ahead, I'll wait for you. They already know your voice, so you will ask the questions, this way I won't have to disguise mine."

"Danielle, can you come up here and help us with the interrogation?" "I'm afraid I won't be any help to you. You know that women think more with their heart than with their head." "I think you handled things pretty good at the hospital today." "How do you know that, you weren't even there?" "No but, I have all this on the video." "How could you manage that? Are you spying on me now?" "Not at all, I'm spying on this couple and you were in the same room." "I think that if they hear me tonight they could make the connection between you and me and this could be risky." "You're right about that, but on the other hand, you could just listen to them and write down your questions. Bernard will ask the questions because I don't want to risk they could recognize my voice at any time. The priest is a very educated and an intelligent man, he could put one and two together just with the phrasing of the sentences. Remember this is how I tracked down Paul's writing in what was supposed to be Peter's gospel." "The weeds among the wheat!" "Exactly!" "Alright, I'll come up for a little while, but I want to go to bed early."

CHAPTER 11

"*H*ere's your paper James." "I'm going to write you a bunch of questions for them. Take your time and above all don't show any sign of frustration, this way we'll wear them down. I'll shut down the microphone every time we need to discuss." "Go ahead you can start."

"Why don't you keep your identification papers with you?" "If we had them with us today we would have been caught in a terrible scandal. As it is our reputation is still untouched, so far so good."

"The world doesn't know it, but don't you teach that God sees everything?" "You also know that God forgives everything too." "Can you tell us exactly why you came to this town?" "We are looking for the writer who writes the chronicles about the word of God in the newspaper." "What do you want from him exactly?" "He inspires us a lot and this is the real reason we want to meet him or her, who ever this person is." "Don't you have Bishops, Cardinals and the Pope to inspire you?" "None of them speak like this writer." "What makes you think it's not a bishop who writes this chronicles?" "There is no chance." "What makes you say that?" "No people from the clergy can speak against the clergy without risking his life. What makes you think that we're not members of the clergy?" "There is no chance." "On which base can you say that?" "The clergy is pitiless against its enemy." "Give us your name address and date of birth please?" "I am father

Charles Joseph Gregoire born on January eight nineteen seventy in Ste-Agathe des Laurentides."

"I am Sister Marie Henri-Paul Toupin born on June fourteen nineteen eighty at ten pass five in the morning in the town of Rivière-du-Loup."

"No wonder she is so pretty, this town is known to shelter the prettiest women of the country." "When I first met her I thought she would make you a wonderful third wife if you ever want another one. I also found her very gentle, but I changed my mind this afternoon." "You're better be forgetting about this idea, I'm quite happy with what I've got now. You don't think I am King Solomon, do you? You're right, women talk with their hearts sometimes. For this to happen, one of you would have to sleep on the clothes line twice a week at least and alone of top of all."

"Here Bernard are a few more questions." "What makes you believe this writer is living in this town?" "We think he is the one who freed the newspaper director. We believe he is more efficient than the police force." "Why did you want to talk only to Danielle this afternoon?" "Because we knew we could trust her. She is a very good person and we believe she can lead us to the person we are looking for. She knows the word of God more than anyone we know and we won't be surprises if she is the writer." "You're giving me the impression that you did everything in your power to get yourselves in the situation you are in now, I'm I wrong?"

"If we are questioned by the one we are looking for, which I think it's the case, then we have succeeded. Only I never anticipated an uncontrollable erection." "I understand you're not homosexual like most of your co-fathers, otherwise you would have chosen the other hole." "I'm not for anyone of what you're talking about, I gave my life to the Lord." "No one could say that this afternoon." "What happened this afternoon was completely out of my control sir."

"Sister Henri-Paul, you pretended to be a virgin before this incident this afternoon, allow me to doubt this, you certainly don't look like a virgin who was raped lately." "We have to accept our destiny sir and who knows, maybe I unconsciously wanted this to happen to me, I mean having sex. May God forgive me! I would have preferred to choose my own partner though." "Both of you have chosen the celibate life, why?" "To better serve God sir." "Do you really believe that our patriarchs Adam, Noah, Abraham, Isaiah, Jacob, Joseph, Moses, David, Solomon, and all the others including Jesus' father and Jesus himself didn't know how to serve God because they were married? Don't you know that God said it was not good for a man to be alone and this is why He gave him a wife named Eve not Steve. Don't you know that God asked us to be fruitful, to multiply and fill up the earth?" "Don't you see that this is the reason why we are looking for this famous Jesus' disciple? Inside our church there is no one to turn to, to talk about those things that we know about for some of them. It would even be dangerous for us to talk about these things. You talked earlier about Jesus being married, but there is no proof of that." "There is a Bible beside your bed in the drawer of the night table; you want to pick it up please? Do you know what it takes to become a Rabbi?" "I think I do, yea. A man has to be thirty years of age, been married and have at least ten followers." "Then Jesus was qualified." "I don't think so, he wasn't married." "Please read to me out loud what you see in Mark 11, 21." "'And Peter said to Jesus, Rabbi the tree you <u>cursed</u> has died.'"

"Now, if you don't mind, go read Matthew 26, 25." "'Then Judas, which betrayed him answered and said Rabbi is it I?'" "I would like you to read one more for your own information in John 1, 38." "'They answered Rabbi (which means Master) where do you live?'

Jesus told his disciples not to call anyone Rabbi." "This is true, he doesn't want his disciples to call themselves rabbi and he doesn't want his disciples to call anyone father. Do you know where it is written?" "It's in Matthew if I remember well." "I hope you like to read, because I would like you to read one more time for you own benefit, it's in Matthew 23, 8-9 exactly." "'But you my disciples, don't let yourselves be called Rabbi, for only one is your Master, the Christ and you are all brothers and don't call anyone on earth father, because only one is your Father the One in heaven.'" "Jesus doesn't want anyone to call us master and he doesn't want us to call men father and this is a formal proof that you priests are not Jesus' disciples at least you don't listen to Jesus. You prefer listening to Paul, your master, Jesus' mortal enemy, like you can read about in the parable of the weeds. On the night table there is also a note pad and a pen so you can write notes of references that I'm going to tell you about Rabbi. It's John 1, 49, John 3, 2, John 3, 26, John 4, 21, John 6, 25, John 9, 2, John 11, 28, Matthew 23, 7-8, Matthew 26, 49, Mark 9, 5, Mark 14, 45, No one can tell that Jesus wasn't a Rabbi." "On the other hand we know for sure now that the person who is talking to us is really a disciple of Jesus. Can you lead us to the writer whom we are looking for?" "Certainly not before we are sure that you don't want to hurt this person or even kill it." "What if I tell you that Sister Henri-Paul and I are here specifically to make sure this doesn't happen?"

All three of us straighten up on our seats being surprised from this last statement.

"What are you guys thinking about this one? Is he just saying this to get favours? Or else to get closer to me yet? He wouldn't do any better if he wanted to kill me." "I personally think they are sincere. I personally think if they wanted to hurt me they could have done it last night." "Not if they wanted to use you to get to me." "You really think they are going through all this shit to achieve their goal?" "I think that if they act for their superiors they have no choice and their lives are worth less than mine right now. I mean they might be in danger if they don't obey the orders." "This is true too; remember he said the clergy is pitiless against its enemies." "This means if they're on our side, we'll have to give them a complete and ceaseless protection. We didn't reach this point yet, I'm not yet sure of his innocence. I think he is very crafty and this worries me. Now we all know what Paul succeeded to do with craftiness and the devil is the craftiest of all." "I remember seeing that, where is it written?" "In Genesis 3, 1 it is written that the serpent is the most subtil of all the animals and in 2 Corrinthians 12, 16 you can read what Paul said: 'Nevertheless, being crafty, I caught you with guile.' There are quite a few references in Matthew too. Here is one, Matthew 26, 4; 'And consulted that they might take Jesus by subtility, and kill him.' Things didn't change that much except ways to do it maybe. Luckily, ways of defence did progress too." "I'm going to bed, I need some sleep and I'm tired of all this." "Lucky for you to be able to do it, I wish I could say as much."

"You too can go Bernard, but I would like you to come back early tomorrow to replace me. That will allow me to get a bit of sleep. A few hours should be enough." "Would you have a wife with you?" "Don't worry, I took measures beforehand. Janene will join me in about twenty minutes. Before you go I would like you to tell them to go to bed when they feel like it and we'll continue this interrogation tomorrow morning. Wish them good night and good night you too." "Are you sure you're going to be alright?" "Inside this room they cannot harm anything else but themselves and the furniture anyways."

"Hi James!" "Janene are you going to spend the whole night with me?" "If it's what you want, I'm willing." "Do you know them?" "Yes, this is the couple who were stock at the hospital this afternoon. She looks much better now than she did then." "She's probably not as stressed out as she was then. She's a nun and he is a priest." "No wonder she acted so disparately like she did." "According to her saying she was a virgin this morning, but for some reasons I have my doubts on that." "Her, being a nun? She looks more like a top model from either New York or Paris." "You and Danielle seem to think she's gorges, but let me tell you that I think you are prettier than she is." "Come on James, don't you find her attractive?" "I agree with you to say she's pretty, but not to the point to fall on my ass." "How old is she? She looks like she's only twenty or so." "What ever, I am happy as I am. Are you coming in the tub?" "Yes dear, this is always good for relaxation." "I know something else that is also good for relaxation.

246

Would you like a good glass of wine too?" "No thanks, not tonight!" "Relax, I'll run the water in the tub." "This is nice of you, I just feel like being spoil tonight." "You had a hard day too, haven't you?" "One of the craziest day in a long time." "Mine was not any better and it's not over yet, I'll have to watch them all night." "Why is that? What can they really do locked in this room?" "They can only hurt themselves I think. Come Janene, it's ready." "Mmmm, this is going to be good." "There is still something that is bothering me in their story." "And you don't know what it is?" "It's clear they did everything they could to get our attention. I don't think they know about you, but I know they know for sure that Danielle has something to do with me. Danielle will never be safe in the hospital anymore and I will need your help to convince her unless these people give us the proof. They know a lot more than they told us thus far. Come here, I will dry you." "It's so good to let someone coaxing you, especially by the one you love and loves you back." "There is nothing like holding the one you love in your arms knowing you're going to make love to her, especially if she's the most gorges woman on earth." "It's nice of you to tell me this, but I'm not forgetting I doubled my twenties already." "I find you just as attractive as the day I met you. I never told you this, but when I met you that evening, I desired you like I never had before and I felt a bit ashamed of myself, because I had just fell in love with Danielle. Did you ever ask yourselves in which position you girls put me in that night?" "No, I was just thinking for a way to share you with Danielle and if she hasn't been my friend I would have done everything in my power to pull you away from her." "For me too it was love at first sight and to me it was just breathtaking. I had heard about it, but until then I never believed in it. It never has been a moment of doubt in my heart since that night and I never ceased to love you even for an instant." "Same here!" "On the other hand I often asked myself how it could be possible to love two women so completely and equally. I had my answer the day my second child was born and with the birth of every other one after that." "I would have loved to give you many more

247

children if my gynaecologist didn't stop me for heath reasons." "In no time at all I would have want you to risk your life for any reason. If something bad happen to you I think I would lose my will of living." "What if we make love before you lose anything?" "Lose what?" "Lose anything, you know getting tired." "Maybe I should take a wake up pill?" "Later darling, I know what this does to men." "Everybody is sleeping now darling, so you can surrender to the pleasures that I love."

Janene fell asleep in my arms while I was watching all the screens that cover one complete wall of my conferences room. I thought I was sheltered from worries for the night, but this was not the case.

"What the heck are you looking in the toilet for?" "I don't look for anything, I'm just trying to retrieve a little battery that I was forced to swallow before I left home and believe me I don't search through my poop with joy in my heart." "Why somebody forced you to do this?" "Because they want me to blow myself up and everybody with me in the building where I am with the writer of these chronicles in the newspaper. I'm holding now in my hand a two megaton bomb. I was given a suicidal mission a bit like the Moslem extremists." "Why did you accept such a mission?" "To do what I'm doing right now, meaning to make it fail. This is the reason Henri-Paul and I volunteered for. You are the writer we're looking for, aren't you?" "Even if this bomb explodes, it would only destroy what ever is inside your room. Every wall, the floor and the ceiling are made of reinforced concrete and covered with one inch thick of solid steel. We would hardly feel anything like a far away earthquake aftershock. Your room could resist a five megatons bomb and it was tested with a four megaton. How are you supposed to alight it?" "It could explode being exposed to the sun for five minutes or on top of a flame for twenty seconds." "Does Henri-Paul have one too?" "I'm not sure, but I don't think so." "Is she really a nun?" "Not anymore, she would have to confess her crime against the church and they would send her out naked like a worm if she is lucky, but I think they would rather lock her up and keep her prisoner for the rest of her life without being able to talk to anyone until she dies." "What do you plan to do from now on?" "We have a bit of money and we're going to try to get lost in the nature. I know this won't be easy, because the church has bases in every country in the world." "It is possible that both of you died in an explosion for the rest of the world." "This is an idea, but neither one of us is really suicidal." "I would call this a necessary lie for the newspapers. The power of this bomb will only leave ashes. In less than six months I could supply you with a secret plastic surgery. I could get you some new ids too. Do you have complete trust in Henri-Paul?" "The idea of saving your life is from her, she just love your chronicles in the paper." "You should put this little battery in a glass of water and go to sleep for a bit now, we'll continue this conversation tomorrow morning."

"Good morning darling, could you sleep a bit?" "I slept very well my love, thank you." "One mystery is solved and another one came up." "Tell me about it." "There's no more mystery concerning our guests, but one came up in one of our children's bedroom." "How serious do you think it is?" "It's too early to tell, but we'll have to do something about it and the sooner the better." "What happened exactly?" "I'm going to show you on the screen. Just give me a second; I'll back up the video. There it is, look?" "This is Jeremy, what is he doing?" "Just a sec, you'll see." "He goes to lie down with the girls. He's only eleven, why is he doing this for?" "I don't know exactly why yet, but when I was his age I was getting up at night to go lie with one of my sisters' girlfriend in the next bedroom. I was attracted to the opposite sex in an uncontrollable way. My sisters told her that I was a sleepwalker and that it was dangerous to wake me up. The result was that I could do what I liked without having her to say anything either she liked it or not, but I think she liked that." "And you were only eleven?" "When I got to be fifteen I became very timid. That's a good thing in a way; otherwise I could have been the father of fifty kids or more. I would have been worst than my dad." "God loved you and He protected you this way." "Not only He protected me, but He protected many young girls too." "What happened to your sisters' friend?" "She got caught by one of my cousins." "Nice family!" "We were a family like thousands of others." "What are we going to do with Jeremy?" "It's best not to scare him, but to try to find out why he doesn't stay in his room. You'll ask him to come to see me later on and I will confront him with these images. We'll have a talk between men, this way I'm sure he'll be more comfortable. In the mean time, would you take your breakfast with me? We also have a couple of guests." "I'm going to help you get everything ready."

"M. Gregoire and Miss Toupin, would you care to have your breakfast at my table this morning?" "Yes, it will be an honour sir." "I'll come to get you when you're ready."

"What happened? What is this change of attitude?" "I told him what was going on, he knows about the whole thing or almost." "Are you sure he is the writer we're looking for?" "I am absolutely sure." "Don't tell me that I'm going to sit at the same table of the man who inspire me the most in this world. This is great. This is an answer to our prayers. It's a sign that we're getting close to our goal. I told you he is a God sent man." "I wanted to be convinced of that too. You should dress a bit more decently." "I have nothing else but what I have on in here."

"Hey Janene, you are almost the same size as her, would you give her a few dresses of your collection?" "Of course I would, I'll go get some right away." "Where are you going, you have some right here in my bedroom." "That's true too. I will give her a couple of them.

There are many of them I don't wear anymore, but they are still like new. I hope she will like them." "Don't you worry about that, she is rather the humble kind." "I'm going to take them to her right away. Are you really sure there is no danger for me to go in there?" "I am sure darling, you can go without fear. You can enter, it's unlocked." "This door is so heavy." "It's built to resist explosions, just let the automatic system open it for you."

"Good morning both of you. How are you today?" "You are the nurse I didn't want to talk to yesterday?" "I hope you changed your mind this morning."

"Do you mind leaving us alone for few minutes abbot, we're going to try those few dresses to see if they fit her or not." "There is no problem, but please don't call me abbot anymore, I'm no longer a member of this club. From now on my name is Charles for my friends. Nice to meet you madam!" "Same here Charles!"

"Mrs. Toupin, do you want to try this?" "I am a Miss Madam. How gorges are those dresses. I have never worn such a luxurious dress in my entire life and never a decent dress in the last ten years." "Do you really believe that God forbids his children to wear nice things on earth? Don't you know this declaration from God in Hosea 6, 6? 'For I desired mercy, and not sacrifice; and the knowledge of God more than burnt offerings. Also in Matthew 12, 7. 'I am please with mercy, but not with sacrifices.'

It's evident that God doesn't like sacrifices." "So I would have sacrificed ten years of my life for nothing?" "If it was for nothing it wouldn't be so bad, but that must have pleased God's enemy, the devil a lot. Every disobedience to God has to please his enemy without a doubt. This dress is good enough for this breakfast and I'll give it a few adjustments later on to make it fit like a glove on you." "Do you mean madam that you give it to me?" "It's yours if you like it and you can address me with more familiar terms." "Thank you very much! What is your name?" "My name is Janene and James, my husband is waiting for us." "It's just like I died and went to heaven." "Heaven will be much nicer than this, just say that this is the kingdom of heaven." "Do you mean it's not the same thing?" "My goodness you have a lot of things to learn. Is there anything you're good at?" "M. Gregoire and I are pretty good with music and singing." "Let's go eat, are you coming Charles?"

"Hi Danielle, what would you say about coming to take your breakfast with us?" "Who do you mean us?" "This mean, Janene and our guests and Bernard should join us pretty soon." "What happened for you to let our guests out of their rooms?" "I just found out they are on the good side, our side." "You know, I'm not really interested in meeting with them." "I think you should come up darling, there will be some discussions that concern you personally." "I don't see what could be interesting for me with this people." "Just start with your security and your job and I don't know what else yet. You were the first one to be interested in them, so what happened to you to change your attitude towards them like this now?" "I finally understood that they used me and I don't like to be used, that's all." "That could have been to hurt us, but it happens that they did it to save my life. I think it's important for you to come to this breakfast." "If you insist, I'll come up, but don't you expect me to came up with a smile on my face." "If someone, who ever it is goes out of his way to save my life, I think you should run to them and say thank you, that of course if you like to keep me alive. This is what I think, bye."

"You look upset James, what's wrong?" "It's Danielle who is making a fuss this morning. Sometimes I have a hard time to understand her." "What is she doing this time?" "She refuses to come to this breakfast that concerns her particularly." "Do you want me to go talk to her?" "No, let her do what she wants to do, her head belongs to her. Bernard should be here any minute now. Did you make enough for everybody?" "I would think so; there are a lot of other things anyways."

"Bernard, you're in? How did you do that?" "Danielle let me in, she knew you were expecting me and she said she'll be up in about five minutes. What a surprise here this morning. What happened?" "You have in front of you two people who risked their life to save mine." "Is that true? This is great."

"I'll leave Henri-Paul and Charles tell you all about it, but first we'll wait for Danielle to arrive. It shouldn't be long now. Here she is."

"If it's not my favourite nurse." "It's true that you owe her a lot. Henri-Paul and Charles, I like to introduce you my wife Danielle." "Just a minute here, I though I heard you say that Janene is your wife." "Janene is my wife and so is Danielle." "But this is not allowed, is it?" "Who said that? Is it David, Solomon, Abraham, Jacob, or any king of Israel? Both of my wives think Henri-Paul would make me a nice third wife, but I told them I was not interested. I don't mean to offend you Henri-Paul when I say this." "Ho I'm not offended, but I know I couldn't play the second violin. I like the music too much for that."

"James, Henri-Paul was telling me that Charles and she are professional in music and in singing." "That's interesting; I am a musician myself, but mainly a composer. We'll have to talk about this another time, not this morning. This morning we have to talk about how to get out of this mess we are in. We have to find a way to get rid of Henri-Paul and Charles for good."

"I though earring you say they were on our side?" "Yes Danielle, this is why they have to disappear for the rest of the world."

"Would you explain to them what brought you here Charles?" "Well first I have to tell you that thanks to Henri-Paul who heard that someone intended to assassinate the writer of the chronicles in the newspaper. I thank God that she had the courage to come to talk to me about it. After that I wanted to know more about the whole story and I did everything I could to find out who wanted to kill this person and why, but I was not getting anywhere. Then I got the marvellous idea to make a very arch sermon on Sunday morning against my will and against this writer telling my congregation that we have to stop this person before our church is completely destroyed. No later than the next day I received a visitor, my bishop who came to ask me what went through my head to talk this way in church on Sunday morning. I told him then that this writer will destroy the church if we don't do anything to stop him. At that moment he told me that there was a plan in place conceived by the Holy Spirit to settle the situation and its success will determine that it was the will of God. He left me with that and I decided to let Henri-Paul know the intentions of our superiors. Then Henri-Paul said we should volunteer to execute this horrible crime in the name of God. I contacted my bishop the next day to tell him that Henri-Paul and I were willing to sacrifice our lives to safe the Holy Catholic church. He told me then what he had on you and that the main contact was a nurse name Danielle Prince working at the Trois-Rivières hospital and that soon or later she will lead us to the writer of these chronicles whom they want to see disappear from the face of the earth before the sky unleash itself against our church. I don't know what you think about this, but I personally think they have declared a pitiless war against this writer who makes them tremble in their black and purple long dresses. They already have all the information about Danielle and her where about. I'm certain she's the next target and maybe they think she is the writer." "That means she'll have to disappear too. So it was a real good idea to have sold our house in principal a couple of years ago." "This is why we couldn't find her address then, which forced us to use the hospital to get to her."

"I'm sorry to have to tell you this Danielle, but you're not working another day in this hospital. You became a too easy target to our enemies and this time you cannot say it's because I have too much imagination. So you can call your director right away and tell him to find you a replacement."

"You're wrong James, Danielle is irreplaceable." "I agree with you Janene, but it's not our problem anymore. I'll have to push the workers on our hospital project in a way we can start operating in four to six months." "So I'm forced to be on vacation." "The situation is more serious than when you were on pregnancy leave and they had to operate without you."

"James is perfectly right to be concerned, the situation is critical." "Thanks Bernard! We have to find a way to make Danielle, myself and our guests disappear and get rid of this bomb at the same time. We're going to blow up this bomb with the pretension that we are blown up with it.

This will quiet down the game for a while." "How could you talk about playing games when someone is planning to kill us?" "Don't you think they are playing the cat and the mouse game with us?" "Maybe, but I would prefer to be the cat." "This is exactly the role I'm getting ready to play." "Alright tom cat, what are we doing now?" "We have to find a place where some sure witnesses could see us getting in without seeing us getting out."

"I think I know the perfect place James." "Where is this Bernard?" "What would you think about the garage where they hold M. Courrois?" "Maybe it is far enough not to damage anything around it."

"Do you know Charles how much damage this bomb could cause?" "I was told it will destroy everything in a radius of one hundred and fifty feet." "It's very limit, but I think this is the place we need. We cannot find better witnesses than our own employees, because they know us personally. This way they will cry sincerely. I count on you Bernard to console the forewoman and the other employees. We have to make sure they are not in danger. This will be your duty Bernard, to make sure they see us inter this building and get them to go back to work right after. You could always run back in front after you've heard the explosion. You could also testify if it's necessary. We might get some broken glass and some damage to our building. Once you got Pauline to calm down, try to get her to call 911 and then the glass maker or the glass repair.

Here is the scenario. Henri-Paul and Charles, you both are real estate agents and you will come to meet us at the Hair Blanket shop. You got to be there at exactly two forty-five for the coffee break. Pauline, Bernard and a few others well chosen employees are discussing with us about the garage across the street that we need to buy for a warehouse. Danielle, you're good in making business cards well designed and you make about twenty of them with the complete names of Henri-Paul and Charles. We'll put a few of them where they live, a few more in the rented car they will be driving and one from each of them on Pauline's desk. We have to be inside this garage before the coffee break is over, so the witnesses see us entering and I count on you Bernard to encourage them to do the same thing as you, meaning looking through the window."

"If I should die in a few days or even today there is no point giving my notice to the hospital." "You might just be right, but I'm not too sure you're not at risk until you disappear."

"What about me, I don't have anything to do in all of this?" "Janene, you'll have the hardest thing to do of all of us." "Wow, if I knew it I would have kept my mouth shut. What will I have to do?" "You'll have to cry bitterly for the lost of your friends and show some madness against the people responsible for this horrible crime and make sure they understand they might be able to kill the body of this movement, (the word of God, the truth) but they'll never be able to kill its soul. You cannot go back to work either."

"We were due for long holidays anyway."

"But in this whole scenario I think you're forgetting something important James." "What is this Charles?" "How you're going to explain your coming back to all your friends and relatives?"

"Your mother James, she won't take it at all." "The least they know for a time the better it is. This way they will have a genuine sadness. Only Janene will have to act and this is enough. You have to remember the journalists will be on the watch and on top of things. We'll send them a consoler before our resurrection. I have the impression the people responsible for this crime will be shaking in their shoes when they'll hear of the coming back of the disciples and even more when they'll receive a little note refreshing their memories. I got the feeling the bishop who planned this crime might have some remorse."

"The big question is, when are we going from words to actions?" "What ever time it takes to enter this garage and rent a car for Henri-Paul and Charles."

"Bernard, you we'll have to fulfil many of my duties for a few days including paying what I owe to Roger."

"Danielle, I need you to drive Henri-Paul and Charles to their place and it's even better if you are seen with them. Try to get the cards ready before you leave in case we can execute our plan today."

"Henri-Paul and Charles, you have to write a very convincing suicidal letter and leave it at your place. I have the feeling this house will be burned down the same day anyway, so don't leave any money over there."

"Bernard, on the pretension to get some information on this garage you check if there is a way out in the back and a get away road on that side of the building." "I think there is a lane behind the garage."

"Janene, you'll be the one parked there and waiting for us. Any questions?" "Where are we going from there?" "We'll come back here for a few days then Bernard will take us to the Caribbean for a three weeks holiday, this will give us time to make more plans for later. I will contact M. Courrois, because I want him to use the space of my article for a week in the paper and to prepare a funeral like nobody has ever seen before and televised on top of that."

"Did you think about a lot of people requiring about your will?" "There are some instructions already in place to open it only a year after my death. I will leave instructions also for all members of our family and close friends who come to the funeral to receive five thousand dollars in cash for compensation." "You're not afraid this could cause some suspicions among the population?" "On the contrary, everyone who knows me will say that I died like I lived."

"What are you going to do with the children?" "We'll bring all the children with us and all the teachers too. Michael is very capable to take care of all the animals. Bernard won't be too far either and I'm sure they can find help if they need it. I got a couple of days to contact and inform all the employees who are directly concerned. I like to see everybody go now to your duties, except Bernard, we have a lot to discuss yet, but you got to leave as soon as this meeting is over, because we'll have a bunch more things to discuss later on."

"Janene and Danielle, I count on you both to inform the children about our departure. They cannot have access to the television sets in the next few hours and days. It is not necessary to expose them to our drama. We'll do our very best to be ready to execute this plan for two forty-five this afternoon if everything goes well."

"Why so soon?" "Because our new friends are under continuous surveillance and this is everywhere out of this property." "Where did you get this information?" "No where!" "But why then?" "Because, I wouldn't give anybody such an important task without making sure these people are on my side and without constant supervision." "I hope you thought of everything, I wouldn't want to blow up with this bomb." "There is only one thing I can't tell for sure and this is the speed in which this bomb could explode. Charles was told it will explode in five minutes when exposed to the sun, but was he told the truth? No matter what, I will deposit this little battery on a sunny spot when you guys are all safely sat down in Janene's car waiting for me. You pray for the rest of this day to stay sunny."

"If you allow me James, I will deposit this battery in the garage. I'm the one who volunteer to do this job." "If I was absolutely sure of your salvation Charles, I would let you do it without any hesitation, but I want to save you from hell at all cost so, I'll be the last one to get out of this garage. Alright, we have to execute everything without neglecting any detail and we only have four hours in front of us, so let's go.

Bernard, you'll have to talk to your brother and don't forget you have to make a trip to Africa as soon as you're back from the Caribbean. You'll be the one to distribute the five thousand dollars too." "Why giving them this kind of money?" "Some of them will come from far away and some of them don't have much money, besides, I like to do things differently than everybody else and at the same time I put hot coals on the heads of the people who want my death. You'll ask Raymond to help with the work on our hospital when he can without neglecting the formula at the laboratory. We are taking holidays this time, but I thing before long we'll have to consider staying away for good. I count on you to collect all the news you can from papers, television, radio, reports from police and churches.

Every, even small details could be useful in the future. You'll be able to recognize our enemies who will be at the funeral too.

Make sure you don't give anything to the bishop who planned my death, but be good to Henry-Paul and Charles' relatives. Now you should go see what we can do at this garage and tell Pauline that we'll be there at two forty-five exactly. I got to go talk to M. Courrois now." "Do I wait for you in town or come back here when I'm done?" "You come back here to pick Danielle and me up and to tell me what you found out about this garage. When you leave here, take Henri-Paul and Charles with you to the car renting company. You will use Danielle credit card to pay for it, this way police will think they stole it from Danielle or else they used her good heart to get what they wanted. You could help the investigation to go this way. I will ask M. Courrois to get in touch with Raymond about experiences on impotence; this will be useful to us in the future, besides helping him with his marriage. This is all Bernard, just make sure their suicidal notes are very convincing and they meanly involve their superiors. They have no idea in what sort of hot water they got themselves in, I would say it's a bath of boiling water. You go now before it's too late."

"I would like to speak with M. Courrois please?" "Just wait a second; I'll see if he is busy."

"M. Courrois M. Prince would like to talk to you." "Switch him to my private line right away Rolande."

"James, what can I do for you my friend?" "Jean, I got to see you as soon as possible and it's very important." "Ho, I don't like the way this sounds. There is a big problem, isn't it?" "Not only it's big, but it's also urgent. Where can I meet you in a safe place in the next hour?" "I think my place will be the safest." "Alright, I'm leaving right away and I should be there within a half hour."

I got in my armoured limousine without telling anyone and I went to meet with my friend Jean. I never thought before it could be so hard to prepare our death the best way as possible. I sure didn't have time to prepare everyone I would like to. I could just imagine important people who die suddenly, how their love ones are caught by surprise. I told myself laughing that if this exercise was not good for anything else it would at least be a good practice. I don't think it's very important for the person who dies when it happens as long as we live fully our live and for the good reasons. Life is only a loan from God and the honest person will pay back his debt soon or later, but then he has to know this. When I think of all my dogs and pigs that are so grateful and I see so many people who don't worry about the needs of our Creator, I scratch my head like them (my dogs). Here I am.

"Good day Mrs. Courrois, is your husband home?" "He's waiting for you in his office sir. Would you have something to drink and a few biscuits of my own?" "This will be with pleasure Mrs. Courrois." "Tea, coffee or something else?" "I will take a black tea with one sugar, please?" "You already know your way and I'll bring this to you in a few minutes."

"James, come in and take a seat old guy." "Hey old guy, you should say young man instead." "You're right, you must be twenty years younger than me. What brings you in James?" "Do you have a strong heart Jean?" "This is what my doctor tells me all the time and that my wife found out it was true lately. It's that bad, isn't it?"

"Nock, nock, nock!" "Come in darling, it's opened." "Here is your tea and a few jewels sir." "Thanks madam, this is very nice of you." "This is nothing, but welcome anyway. This must be very important, I'll leave you alone."

"Jean, at around three this afternoon my wife Danielle and I will be assassinated." "What? If this is a joke, it's not funny at all." "Unfortunately it's not a joke, but we won't die and in a few days we will be in the Caribbean. Some high rank people in the church's hierarchy, whom I won't name, ordered our death to happen in a way no one could even find our ashes. They want us to disappear, so we will." "This is quite a bomb you dropped on me." "They are using a two megatons bomb." "I hope it won't blow up at the newspaper." "Don't you worry; you're not the target this time. In fact they don't really know who the target is, except the target is the writer of the disciple's chronicles in the newspaper. They found me and I want to let them know or think they have succeeded in getting rid of me. This is why we'll blow up the garage across from my shop (The Hair Blanket) this afternoon with the bomb they've supplied." "But what do I have to do with all of this?" "I would like you to replace me in the next article and use my space to blame the people responsible for this horrible crime and for the lost of your best seller. Make them understand that when one is gone two more will come in. I think that might help to get them discouraged." "What if it does the exact opposite and they want to attack our business?" "There are two things I can do. First I could supply you with an efficient and steady protection or else I can buy the business and let you in place with my protection." "There are always some controversies with the newspaper business, but this is a serious threat. A third solution would be to stop these chronicles completely, but I would get thousands of people on my back and they will call me a coward. Can I mention that all the profits of your chronicles were given to the charities?" "You write what ever you want, I trust you entirely with this." "All I have left to do is to wish you some nice and peaceful hilidays." "Thank you and don't forget to go to my funeral." "I won't miss this for all the money in the world." "It won't be that much, but I have to go now or I'll run out of time. I'll send you my next chronicles from over there and let me know what you have decided about the business. So long Jean!"

"Have a nice day madam and thanks again for the special treat."

"James for heaven sake, where are you?" "I'm on my way home. I'm sorry, but I had to leave quickly. I had to speak with M. Courrois without any delay and I'll be there in ten minutes. Is everyone ready?" "Everything is ready; you're the only one missing." "Did you talk to Bernard? What did he find?" "Everything is set and we're all ready. Janene will be parked behind the garage at two forty-five. Henri-Paul and Charles have the rented car paid with my Visa and they left a suicidal letter explaining their action and asking their families to forgive them. They also have their business cards in their pockets. The sun is more shining than ever. We should have an exceptional death. I'm telling you that the eternal rest will be welcome after all this." "The sun of the south will be good for us. I'm almost there. I'm turning on the little road now. Did you talk to the teachers for them to hold the children until we come back and forbid them to watch the television?" "Let me go, I'll call them right away."

The first thing I did when I enter the house is to go unhook a transistor in every television set in the house except the one in my bedroom. I also asked Janene and Bernard to help me pick up all the radio units we have. This might cause a bit of confusion, but we had no choice.

"Would you Bernard take the squad and go inform Michel about everything is going on around here? I don't want him to panic either and I'll talk to him later. Janene, go reset your voice mail and say you don't want to talk to anybody until after the funeral. Danielle and I cannot answer the phone anymore and we should disconnect the phone lines this afternoon. We have to leave as soon as Bernard is back." "He's here now." "So let's go down right away."

"How did it go with him?" "He's sorry that we have to go through so much trouble, but he said not to worry, that he will take care of everything like nothing happened. He's happy we told him what's going on." "We have to hurry without getting the attention of the police force, this will come soon enough, but I don't want to see any of them right now."

"All this makes me nervous James." "Don't worry, all this will be over shortly." "Why do they want to hurt us so bad?" "For the same reasons they wanted to get rid of Jesus. The truth is a double edge charp sword. As much as we like it as much God's enemies hate it." "We're almost there now. You park in front of the shop Bernard. You'll probably have to get your car repaired and even replace it maybe." "You're not serious; this is a one hundred and twenty thousands dollar car." "It's important that everything looks as natural as possible;

otherwise it could be some suspicions in someone's mind and we don't want this." "You know James; I think you're a genius to think about all this like you did. I knew you were intelligent, but this is beyond me."

"I can't believe this either." "Let's get to the next level before starting celebrating, would you?"

All three of us got down from the car and entered Pauline's office where she was awaiting us with a smile. A few minutes later our real estate agents were coming in also, just like previously planned.

"Good afternoon ladies and gentlemen. I am Charles Gregoire and my partner here with me is Miss Henri-Paul Toupin and we're here to meet with M. James Prince. Here is my business card and if you are happy with our services, don't forget to tell people around you, times are tough." "Nice meeting you Charles, I'm James Prince." "Here's my card too." "There are pretty women in this field too, nice meeting you. This is my wife Danielle and this tall man there is Bernard Sinclair, my right arm and this is his fiancée Pauline, next to her is Monique and Helene." "Nice meeting you all! I know your time is precious, so what if we go take a look at this building now? It's just the other side of the road; we can walk this much, can't we?" "Of course this will be good for us."

"Are you coming Danielle?" "I don't think I would make any difference, but I'll come with you anyway." "You like making people laugh like always, don't you? Let's go."

All four of us walked to the garage. I was very surprised and almost shocked to see that Charles had the key for the service door. For a moment I was scared and I felt like taking Danielle by the hand and run away as fast as we could far away from the other two, but I recaptured myself.

"Where does this key come from?" "It was giving to me by the new owner of this garage. We have no time to discuss now. We have to act right away." "Give me this little battery and all of you go wait for me in the car." "Why don't you let me do it James?" "I told you why and don't dispute this with me, you wouldn't win anyway, so go wait with them in the car. Your work is done and you have done a good job, both of you."

So all three of them went out and I started looking for a sunbeam right away. There was not much of it, in fact there was only one little spot let in by a missing screw in the roof. It seemed that it was stronger because of its smallness. Then I put this little battery on the sunny spot and I walked towards the back door with no hesitation what so ever. Blessed be the One who inspired me this way, because I was not at the car yet parked at two hundred feet from the garage when this bomb exploded with a devilish noise. I thought I became totally deaf on the spot. I was thrown thirty feet away from where I was standing. I was not hurt, but I was in a state of semi unconsciousness when I felt someone grab me to take me farther.

"Are you alright James? Are you hurt?"

I could hear, but I couldn't answer. I felt I was searched by Danielle and Janene and I couldn't react to their pangs. They laid me down on Henri-Paul's and Charles' laps who were sitting on the back seat of the car and I heard Charles say; 'Quick, let's get to the house.' I could feel the super soft hands of Henri-Paul on my face, but I couldn't react to that either. The least I can say is I was really groggy. I got the feeling I just went through what many boxers experienced. I was conscious, but yet like paralysed. I was there but not there.

"You must know a doctor on whom we can trust for total confidentiality?" "Raymond, we have to call Raymond immediately Danielle."

"I don't know is phone number." "Phone Bernard, he will give it to you." "I cannot use my cell phone, I'm dead. Give me yours Janene." "Here!" "I can't dial, I'm too shaky."

"Give me this phone. What is the number?" "It's 866-7788." "There is no answer." "Let it ring, he will end up answering. He must be busy with the employees panicking, the police and the journalists."

"Bernard?" "Yes, it's me. Is this you Charles? Something is bad, isn't it?" "We don't know yet, but we need a doctor as soon as possible." "What happened exactly?" "This bomb exploded a lot sooner than it was supposed to." "Is he going to be alright? He is hurt?" "We don't know; you have to ask Raymond to come to James' house at the lightning speed." "I'll take care of it immediately."

"Raymond, thanks God you're there. You got to go to James' house right away, he's not well." "Do you know what he's got?" "He doesn't react to anything. I think he's in a state of shock to his nervous system."

"If this is all he's got, it's not too bad." "What happened?" "I think he saw death at a close range." "I'm going right away." "Hey brother, you will understand later, but don't say a word to anyone about this and trust me." "Explain!" "Later Raymond!"

"Charles, Raymond is on his way to the domain; he'll be just behind you. Keep James under observation at all time, he cannot feel abandoned at all. Tell one of the women to hold his hand continually. He must be like a child who is scared to death right now. This must be terrible for him who is always in control of everything." "I got to leave you, we just arrived. Is there a lot of damage?" "There is not a single glass left and my car will need a lot of repair, but no one is hurt. The garage is completely destroyed and instead there is a big hole four feet deep. I'll get there as soon as I can."

"We have to bring him to a bed as gently as possible." "Help me a little and I'll carry him on my shoulder." "Come this way Charles, follow me. I wonder what happened to him. We never had such a case in more than twenty-four years. We cannot leave him alone, not even for a second." "This man saved my life today. For sure I would have taken my time knowing I had five minutes to get out. This guy has more instinct than an animal. I'm sure this bomb blew up in less than one minute. He is lucky despite everything to be alive." "Are you alright Charles? You're talking like you're in shock too." "I'll be alright. This was a hard hit for me too."

"Janene, would you watch the gate for Raymond's arrival?" "Someone has to stay with James all the time. Do you want to do this

Henri-Paul? I'll have to be there when the children arrive. I hope he's going to be fine. I don't know what we'll do without him."

"Danielle, stop this, don't even think about that and stop crying. This doesn't fix anything and you're going to create a panic among the children. He's going to be fine. Nobody is touching the phone in the house and the voice mail will take over. What takes him so long? What is he doing?" "Here he is, open the gate Janene, we'll know more in a few minutes. Open the garage door too and don't forget to close everything after."

"Where is he?" "This way Raymond; he is in my bedroom." "What happened?" "An explosion!" "This is what they're talking about on the radio, but they didn't name anybody. According to some witnesses, there should be four victims. They say it was a very powerful bomb and it's a miracle there are no more deaths than this. He is in shock, but doesn't seem to be hurt otherwise. He seems to be lost. This is not too bad, it is just a bring blockage as if he needed to stop thinking. I'm going to give him a tranquillizer and he'll be back to normal in less than twenty minutes." "Are you sure of what you're saying?" "Yes Danielle, I am." "Who are these people?" "This is Marie and Joseph." "Ho, I see, the Holy family? Where is Jesus?" "Very funny!" "I don't know your reasons, but I know you're hiding things from me." "Just wait till James is alright; he will tell you what he wants to, but we cannot tell you anything except that we need your discretion." "He closed his eyes now, this is a good sign."

"Anyone wants a cup of coffee or tea?" "I would like a good cup of black tea myself."

"For me too!"

"About you Marie, do you want anything?" "Any kind of fruit juice will be good for me."

Danielle was wondering if this was her magic secret to keep her skin so young. I was wondering myself if this was Charles or the bishop who lied about the timing of this awful bomb. I didn't understand my mental state of mind either. I could hear everything around me without being able to react to anything. I could feel deep love in Henri-Paul's hands as if she was evaluating her luck to be able to hold me like this on her laps and caressing my face and my hair." "I don't think she knew I was conscious of everything that was going on. She reminded me of a nun I have known when I was a young child at the Magog hospital who ironically was named Sister Paul Henri. She dressed me completely from head to toes with bran new clothes, something I had never known before. I got everything, a suit, a white shirt, necktie, socks, underpants and beautiful shoes. Everything I needed really. It was enough for me to want to go back to the hospital just to live this happiness again.

I hope to have the chance to go back there to see her again as soon as I can. She was one of the nicest people I ever met in my life, a woman of an exceptional goodness. I hope she's still alive to give me a chance to say thank you again one more time. I'd say this is one of my best souvenirs of my childhood. I'm not talking about the clothes I got from her, but about the love of this woman for others.

Henri-Paul stayed with me the whole time of me agony and I had the impression I was held by the reassuring hands of an angel. It was very comforting.

"Charles, go tell the others he's waking up."

When Charles was out of the room, Henri-Paul leaned on me and kissed me on the mouth and I let her do as she wished.

"You are conscious?" "Yes; you too!" "You scared us to death." "I think I got scared more than anyone of you. I thought hearing you say you wanted to kiss my hands and feet." "I prefer and by far the mouth and besides, I have never foreseen holding you on my laps, besides, Danielle said that you wouldn't like to have your feet kissed."

"James, are you alright? My God I was so scared." "Did you get the news?" "How do you think we can do this?" "I got to go up stairs. Oups, oups!"

"Take your time James; I just gave you a tranquillizer, so you're going to have soft legs for a while." "Help me someone to get up there;

I need to get to the news." "Come Joseph, give me a hand, we're going to take him up there; otherwise he won't make it and we don't want him to get a relapse."

"Don't let the kids coming up there under any circumstances." "Is anybody will let me know what is going on?" "Some people tried to kill me Raymond, but obviously they missed and I want to let them think they have succeeded, which we'll give us a precious time to fight back." "Couldn't you tell me about it?" "Everything went so fast, we didn't have time."

"Would you turn the TV on Danielle please? Where is Janene?" "She's with the children."

"We have to tell her not to answer the phone and she should be up here with us." "I can go tell her if you want." "This is nice of you Henri-Paul, thank you."

"Henri-Paul?" "Marie Henri-Paul Toupin and Charles Joseph Gregoire. They both died in the explosion with Danielle and me this afternoon."

"Here I am. Is there something on TV?" "We'll have the news in five minutes." "You're alright James, nothing is broken?" "I'm fine Janene, how are the kids?" "They are fine, all of them are playing bowling right now except Jonathan; he's gone to his molding shop." "Ho my God, there is a radio over there. If he ever hears that we are dead from the news he'll go crazy. I would like to, but I can't, someone got to go get him right away."

"Raymond, you're the only one who knows where this is and can do it fast enough to avoid the worst. Would you run over there please?"

'We have to interrupt the current program for last minute news. There are not two words to describe what happened in our town this afternoon. The only word is horror. There was an explosion like we usually only see in the Middle East. It was blown up, thanks to God at the town limit in a garage on an isolated street. Authorities believe it was a two to three megatons bomb. According to the ex owner's declaration the building was sold earlier today. He is sure there was no explosive material in the building before the transaction. He was ordered to stay around for future interrogation. Specialists in explosive say this bomb was made of different material known to them, because it destroyed everything it touched. They say it destroyed even steel beams which would have normally been twisted, but stayed near by anyway. Police is questioning if it has something to do with last week kidnapping of M. Courrois, because we are talking about the same building that was at the 888 Chemin des Sables. There are a lot of crying witnesses just across the road from it who seem to be still in shock. They are questioned by police officers still on the ground. They would have seen four people entered the garage just a minute or two before the explosion. Police have withheld the names of the presumed victims, because next of kin is not informed yet, which should be done in the next hour or so. We just have received a last report. We are told that a rich industrial man and his wife and two real estate agents would have died in this building."

In the following few seconds following this last information all the phones in the house start ringing." "I knew then that panic will install itself in our families in an uncontrollable way.

CHAPTER 12

"Hurry up Janene, Danielle you go down there and make sure that no one can take one of those calls. They don't need to be confused."

"Charles, do you know anything about phone wiring?" "I can disconnect a wire, if this is what you want to know?" "Go down to the basement, you'll find the electrical box. You will find also all kind of tools near by. Go quick, hurry up."

I don't know if he knew it or not that he was under observation in this last task. There were three cameras pointed on him and spying the least of his movements. He was filmed in three dimensions.

"You're still mistrusting him, don't you James?" "I'm not doing this with joy in my heart Henri-Paul. There are a few details that make me wonder." "Are you mistrusting me too?" "It's always intriguing to be kissed by a pretty woman who is not your wife." "You didn't like it?" "I wouldn't say that, but it's intriguing to say the least and right now I wonder if you're not simply trying to keep my attention away from Charles. You wouldn't do any better if this was the case." "What makes you mistrust us after everything we went through?" "The fact that he had the key of this building and also the fact this bomb exploded five times sooner than it was supposed to." "Charles is the most honest man I know and I know for sure he didn't try to mislead you in any way." "The protection of my whole family is my main responsibility and I cannot make any mistake." "I understand and I admire you for all you do and if I knew men like you existed, I would have never entered a convent." "I see you as a woman who has to fight back her desires for love." "I have never felt before what I feel today and I got to say that I'm a bit ashamed of my feelings right now." "What do you mean?" "I mean that I would like you to take me in your arms, hold me very tight against your body, that you lay me on your bed and make love to me for hours, but there is no point telling you all this, because I know you are too honest to fulfil my desire and besides, I wouldn't want to betray Danielle's and Janene's trust. I wouldn't want to take something that belongs to them, especially not without their permission." "You're right, I never did and I will never cheat on them even though I would love another woman, so your destiny is in the hands of my two wives whom I love more than myself. Nevertheless, I know for sure that it is possible to love more than one person at the time, because I am in this position. I sympathize with men who are stock with this dilemma and don't have the luck I have." "I wish there were millions of men like you." "It is written in Isaiah 4, 1 that some day seven women will ask the same man to marry them just to get his name and something else I presume." "I don't think there is anyone else in this world who knows the word of God like you do." "I don't know about this, but I know for sure that God spoke to me and he does it every so often. I had another example this afternoon. There was this voice that told me to get out of this garage as fast as I can; even though I was supposed to have a lot of time to do it. It's certainly not the devil who wanted to save my life, he who wants my death by any means. This same voice which is telling me now that; Henri-Paul is one of the prettiest and the most desirable woman on earth, she loves you more than you can imagine, you find her very attractive and you would take her if this was allowed. I sure could lock this door and get in bed with you, which would be I'm sure very pleasant and nobody would ever know about it except you, me, God and all the angels in heaven and also the devil who would like to come to my judgement and say: han, han, han, this man is no better than anybody else. We all have the power to choose and believe me, God helps the ones who help themselves." "Thousands of people were declared saints, but none of them measure up to you. There is only one you could be compared to and this is Jesus himself and he was never called a saint. We say St Peter, St John and every other imaginable saints but I never heard St Jesus." "Is this telling you something?" "If one person deserved to be called saint it's got to be Jesus." "Charles is on his way back now, I'm glad you could express yourself like you wished to. We might have a chance to talk about this again one day, who knows? PS, it was nice to be on your knees."

Raymond couldn't bring back Jonathan from his moldings shop, but he managed to do the job in his own way anyway.

"How come he didn't want to come back with you?" "He said he's got new important designs in mind and he didn't want to lose the inspiration. Then I got mad and I broke the radio. I kept insisting and he even challenged me, so I got mad again and I broke the phone. Then I left leaving him behind knowing very well he couldn't hear the news anymore." "Good thinking man, but I'll have a few words for him anyway."

"I think I disconnected all the phone lines in the house." "Thank you Charles, good work."

"Are you feeling better James? Would you like me to give you a stimulating tonic? You know that if you're doing too much you can have a relapse and this wouldn't be good at all for your brains." "This might be a good idea Raymond, but we still have a lot of things to get ready. Call Bernard please and ask him if he can free himself over there. I would like to leave as soon as possible." "To go where?" "That's true too, you don't know about this. I gave Bernard a lot of information and a lot of it concerns you. I'm very sorry, but I couldn't do differently, we're running out of time." "Here swallow this." "Thanks, what is it?" "It's a bit like a Red Bull, an energetic drink." "Bernard knows it; you have to leave for Africa as soon as he is back from the Caribbean."

"What is there for you in Africa?" "I'm a doctor without borders. James pays me and all the medicine necessary for thousands of helpless people in every poor country in the world."

"Would you like to travel Charles?" "I went to Florida for a week about ten years ago, but I went in a car."

"This is something that Charles and I could do and this way we could be hiding from the people who want to hurt us." "You're forgetting one thing Henri-Paul and this is you will never see me get on a plane alive."

"About you Henri-Paul, are you afraid to fly too?" "I can't tell; I have never been on a plane."

"You do realize Charles that I cannot protect you if you stay around here?" "Why can't I just stay over here for a while? It's a nice place to live." "Because somebody else is coming here and this house will be scrutinized shortly. Excuse me for a minute."

"Danielle, would you get the children ready for the trip, we'll leave tonight if it's possible." "Are you serious?" "Very!"

"Janene, I would like you to get the children ready for the trip, if it's possible we'll leave tonight." "What do we take with us?" "What ever is strictly necessary, we have everything we need where we're going. Can you talk to the teachers too and tell them to only bring their personal needs and I bring them to the sun of the South for three weeks." "What do I tell them if they ask me what to bring?" "Tell them to bring their bikinis and their toothbrushes. Do it quick though."

"Henri-Paul and you too Charles you should go lie down for a couple of hours, this is going to be a fairly long trip and we'll need you a bit later."

"Did you reach Bernard?" "Here, I got him on the line."

"Bernard, could you avoid the questions?" "You're doing better James? You gave us quite a scare time. Just a minute James, I can't talk just now, I got to go a bit farther. It's good now, I can speak. What were you saying?" "I asked you if you could avoid the questions." "Yes, but I'm having a hard time consoling Pauline and many others." "I want to leave tonight if it's possible." "It's not the very best timing." "If I stay here one more day I'll go crazy." "This is got to be a real mess aver there?" "If we don't leave pretty soon we'll be in a complete chaos? We'll take only what is necessary to us for now and you can always bring what ever is missing when you bring Janene over after the funeral. Just wait a second Bernard."

"Raymond, do you have anything to put Charles to sleep? I would hate to have to force him to get on the plane." "I could put a couple of sleeping pills in a glass of water that should be enough to knock him off quickly." "Do this and bring it to me and a glass of water for Henri-Paul as well. Hey Raymond, after this please, go tell Jonathan that we are leaving shortly on a trip and he has to come home right away and if he refuses force him. I have no time to discuss anymore."

"Excuse me Bernard, but I got a real mess over here. How are things over there?" "The firemen are still here, but all the ambulances are gone since they were no customers for them." "When you can, you pick up all the documentation and I want everybody at the funeral on tape, this is very important, because our killers we'll be there too. That's all for now, do as quickly as possible, see you in a bit."

"Laurent, how are you my friend?" "I'm fine James and I see that they couldn't get you as they planned." "What do you mean by that?" "You should know that news travel at the same speed than light today. I saw images of the explosion. This is strangely looking a lot like nuclear." "Do you think you know what they used to make this bomb?" "But you didn't call me just to say hi, did you?" "No, I need to talk to you about trading as we talked before." "I thought so James as soon as I heard the news." "Are you a seer too?" "Nobody would spend many thousands dollars just to blow up an empty garage or some not too important people." "Good deduction and I understand your astuteness. Would you be ready to come back with Bernard?" "When are you planning to be here?" "A seven hours flight with the time difference, we should be there by noon tomorrow, but I want Bernard to take a good day off to rest before he comes back here. How is fishing?" "Fishing is very good and your boat is a marvellous jewel." "Water is good with not too many sharks?" "I got a wire mesh fence built at three hundred feet from shore to stop them from coming too close. The biggest ones could always break it, but we would have time to get out of the water before they could reach us." "That's a very good idea." "It happens to me sometimes by dint of using somebody else ideas." "We really don't have time to get everything ready or cleaned up for you over here, so you'll have to put up with it. How is it over there?" "I guest you will have to put up with it too; I don't have maids to help me with this." "I myself have a few wives to help me with the cleaning." "Don't turn the knife in the wound, would you?" "Alright, I have to go. I just wanted to let you know we're coming and we can talk a little more tomorrow."

"Charles it's me, I thought a good glass of cool water would do you good. Would you like to eat something too?" "No thanks, a glass of water should do." "I'll take one to Henri-Paul as well, see you later."

Nock, nock, nock!" "Come in Charles, it's open." "It's not Charles, it's me. Would this be good enough for you?" "That's even better James. Would you like to lie down with me for a little while?" "I would like you to stop talking to me like this Henri-Paul; you know very well this is not what will attract me to you." "I thought you like challenges." "I love challenges alright, but if it wasn't for the fact I have to protect both of you, you would be very far right now." "You will send us very far from here, won't you?" "I'll do everything in my power to save your lives. You rest Henri-Paul; we'll have a lot to do in the next few hours. I'll see you later."

"Did you see if Charles took his glass of water?" "He swallowed everything and I expect him to fall in a deep sleep any minute." "When he is sleeping you bring him on the plane with the help of Bernard who should be here anytime now."

"Janene, would you send Jeremy over, please?" "Can he finish his game first? It's only a matter of about ten minutes?" "Of course he can, this is not fire. How did it go with the teachers?" "They seem to be happy to get premature and paid holidays. A few of them asked me what the occasion was, but I didn't say anything knowing you will talk to them on the plane." "Tell me if all the suitcases are ready." "They are and so is everybody." "Is Jonathan in too?" "This was against his will, but yes, he's here." "I'll have a few words for him too as soon as Jeremy is back down there." "Alright, I'll tell him."

"We should be aboard the aircraft within the hour. About you, are you going to be alright?" "I got to darling; I don't really have any choice, do I?" "My mom would probably want to be with you and maybe a few of my sisters too. It is imperious that you join us as soon as the funeral is over." "I wish I could spend a few hours with you before you go." "Me too sweetheart, but we'll catch on to it in a few days on our yacht, that's a promise. It bothers me to leave you behind and I'm sure the children will miss you too, but I'm also sure this is the best thing to do." "Here is Jeremy now; I'll send him to you right away. Don't be too hard on him." "Don't you worry; I just want to know his motive."

"You want to see me dad? This sounds very official." "I just want to show you a little movie and get your opinion on what you're going to see." "What is this?" "This is an abomination exposed in the newspaper." "What are these two men doing?" "They are in a position that shouldn't be exposed like this. It's called homosexuality." "That exist?" "That exist, but it is not the nicest thing to see and I wish you have never seen this. This is not the reason I called you up here for. Come to sit down here my boy and watch this on the screen. I want you to know that I wasn't spying on you, but your mom was out and I wanted to keep an eye on all of you while she was away. Why did you leave your room to go lie down with your sisters?" "It's not my room that I left dad, it's my brother." "Has he done something you don't like?" "No, Rene doesn't know anything about it, it's me." "What is the matter with you Jeremy?" "It bothers me to be with him at night." "What is bothering you exactly my boy?" "I don't know how to explain it dad, all I know is it bothers me." "And it doesn't bother you to be with your sisters?" "No, I can sleep well with them." "You don't feel the need to touch them?" "No, never, I love them too much for that and I love my God too much too." "Do you think it's because your brother is a boy that you are bothered?" "I'm not sure, but I think this is why. I found the word in the dictionary and it's; impulse. I have some impulses when I sleep with Rene and I don't like to feel like that, this is why I go sleep with the girls." "Well, I thank you my son for your honesty and I'll see what I can do to help you. How would you like to have a bedroom for yourself?" "Ho yes daddy, this is a very good idea." "I'm going to make a bedroom in the basement just for you." "Which colour would you like to have your walls painted?" "I would like to have the walls painted pink." "I don't mind this colour myself boy, but I think if you do this, you're going to be laughed at and I would like to spare you this. What about a very nice light blue?" "It's not as nice, but it's more normal for a boy's room and the others too will think it's more normal for a boy." "Let's go for the blue walls and we'll talk about all this another time, when we're not so much in a hurry. Is that alright with you?" "It's always fun to be able to talk with you dad." "To me too my son, go now and tell Jonathan to come to see me right away this time, otherwise I'll come to get him." "Thanks for the bedroom dad." "You're welcome my boy."

"I have the feeling you're mad with me dad." "It's true that I am very disappointed with you today, but I'm not mad and I'll tell you why and this is because I know you're old enough to hear what I got to tell you. We did everything in our power to spare you a big shock today, but you didn't help us to help you at all." "Why this sounds so darn serious?" "It sounds serious, because it's very serious. Your aunt Danielle and I got killed today for the rest of the world and for a bit it could have been for you too. When Raymond smashed your radio and your phone earlier this was to spare you from learning our death from the news and that you in return come to cause the panic here in the house. In the future when I ask you to come to see me you obey without any question. Is that understood?" "Yes, but why this entire masquerade?" "Because someone tried to assassinate me this afternoon and we play their game to avoid them to try again." "Why would someone try to kill someone like you dad? It doesn't make sense at all." "Because I am who I am and it's obvious it makes sense to somebody. They spent a huge amount of money doing this, the least we can do is to give them their money's worth. I don't have time to talk to you about this any longer right now, but we'll talk later. You're the only child to know about this so far and we don't need to have a panic on board, so you keep this to yourself for now.

We'll have a familial meeting later on. We're leaving tonight and I'm not sure of the day we'll be able to come back, maybe never." "Ho no, my moldings, I have two new designs." "Just remember they'll never be worth as much as your life. You'll have to show me that you have attitudes to lead men, because I want to eventually pass on to you the Fiab Enterprises, if you are interested of course, but to give orders you have to be able to take some as well." "Are you serious dad? You would pass on to me those big projects?" "When I talk business my boy, I'm always serious and when I give orders too." "I beg you pardon dad, I never wanted to offend you." "I just want you to remember son, that's all. Vacations won't necessarily hurt your moldings one bit, you will be able to come fishing with me or else playing with your designs, this is going to be your choice." "That sounds good." "You go now; I have a few more things to discuss with Raymond."

"Did Bernard give signs of showing up?" "He should be here in less than five minutes. Tell him to make sure the plane is ready to go, especially the fuel. Get everything and everybody on the plane; I'll go spend an hour with Janene before I go. This is not fun for her at all to stay behind like this for a funeral which is not one and see all the relatives and friends crying without being able to say anything." "This is quite a challenge, that's for sure." "I leave everything into your hands for you and Bernard. I'll join everybody in one hour and then we'll leave right away. Do you have a few cigarettes for me?" "I made a full box for you, do you want it now." "We never know it could be useful."

"I got it in my bag there, here take it." "Do you have the antidote too?" "That's in the box too." "I hope I won't get stolen." "That would be funny to catch the thief sleeping on a golden tray." "Well, talk, talk, talk, time goes by, I got to go." "Have a good trip and we'll keep in touch."

I went down quickly to see Janene who was getting disparate to see me before our departure.

"What took you so long? What were you doing all this time?" "A thousand things as usual, but I never ceased thinking of you for a minute and don't waste the little time we have left complaining, come and make love to me." "I'm not really in the mood for this right now." "Alright, let's just take a hot bath and lie down for a bit and if you only want to talk, that's what we'll do." "I don't like to see you all go and leave me behind." "I don't like it either and I would like so much to find you a substitute, but as you know you're one of a kind and unique in this world. If only I could find you a stunt woman it would be great and I wouldn't hesitate at all to pay a million to be able to bring you with me." "Just a million, but that's only a drop in a barrel." "It is still a million." "I know, but I find it very difficult." "Do you know I find you just as pretty as the night I first met you?" "Do you know you are even better than the night I fell in love with you and we are talking about the same night." "Do you know that I'm dying to make love to you just like that first night?" "Do you know that I feel the same way?" "What are we waiting for?" "Nevermind the towel, come."

That was a quick one, but also one we never forget. I got dressed very quickly, I held her very tight in my arms and I left without looking behind, because I couldn't stand seeing her distress and her tears. I went because I had to. Everyone was waiting for me to get on our way towards the Caribbean that was awaiting us with open arms.

This was a very smooth trip and Charles wondered why he was so scared of the plane. Bernard turned around our Island a couple of times before going down and most of the kids had only one question to ask;

"How could you move our house over here so quickly dad?" "Come on youngsters, we don't move a house like this one, we build another one just like it somewhere else."

"It's not easy for them to understand all this Samuel. They don't visualize things like you do." "They have to learn some day." "It would be nice for them if they could learn as gently as you did, don't you think?" "Excuse me, but I miss my dogs already."

"I understand your love for the dogs, I experienced that too, but your love for your family should come first, don't you think?" "I know and I'm going to get over it."

"Did you sleep well Danielle?" "I slept like an angel." "My angel, my angel, my sweet angel! Did you dream of your vacations and what you would like to do with them?" "I didn't dream, but now I'm dreaming about a little cruise of a couple of days alone with you." "Your desire is an order to me my darling; we'll do it as soon as everybody is settled in our new home. I only need twenty-four hours to organize everything and believe me I need a good rest too."

"Are you alright Charles or should we put you to sleep before we go down?" "No thanks, I'm fine. This is just as smooth as a couch at home." "We might get some turbulence from time to time, but Bernard has an extraordinary scent to avoid them."

"I'll have to let you all help yourselves with moving in, because I myself have important things to discuss with Laurent as soon as we touch ground. Is everything fine Bernard? It seems to me that you're turning around more often than usual." "I just want to make sure everything is fine down there. There should be a vehicle waiting for us and I don't see any, which is a bit strange to me." "I'm calling Laurent and he'll tell me if everything is fine."

"Laurent, is everything alright over there?" "Yes James! I thought for a moment this wasn't you up there, come down, I'll send you someone to get you right away with the bus. We are leaving right away, don't we?" "Thank you, we are coming down."

"Go ahead Bernard; he thought this was somebody else plane." "This doesn't make sense James; he knows this plane like the bottom of his packet." "Do you think there is something going on down there?" "I'm sure of it, if everything was normal, he would be there waiting for us." "You're right, he also mentioned leaving immediately to return home, but he knows that I want you to rest a full day before you return." "What do we do?" "Let's go down anyway, Laurent might be in danger. Everybody stays in the plane, it's bullet-proof and you are safe in here. We'll just react to their action; for now we don't know what this is all about. I'm sure this has got something to do with me and I'll go see what it is. Get ready to take off just in case. If something goes bad, don't hesitate to call the authorities." "You should wear your bullet-proof jacket, it would be safer." "I'll simply go offer them a cigarette. I'm sure this has nothing to do with the word of God; they have no way to know about it. This is a complete different story. Can you see how many they are inside this bus?" "It looks like they are only two, but they are big men." "Open this door and shut it behind me, I think it's only a kidnapping. We are used to that now and I'm going to solve this problem in five minutes."

I stepped down the plane and I walked to the bus where they invited me in pointing a gun.

"What are you looking for?" "We just want you to open your safe for us and if you do what we ask there will be no problem." "But there is nothing at all in that safe." "Go tell this to some bosos, but not to us, a many thousand dollars safe and nothing in it?" "That's true Gilles; this guy thinks we are stupid, isn't he? Ha, ha, ha!" "Would you guys like to have a smoke?" "Yea, especially if you have a Cuban cigar. Ho, look at the nice box. Give me this, this is pure gold."

"You don't know anything about gold. I'll bet you this is only plated with gold." "Let me see this. I'd say this is lead plated with gold." "There is only one way to find out, let me have your knife for a minute."

"Can't you guys just have a cigarette now and argue later?" "That's a good idea do you have a light?" "Here, come on, pull. Don't you know how to smoke? About you do you know how to smoke or not? Sleep well shit heads and let me drive this bus now, would you?"

"Let me speak with Laurent now, I'll give him the combination of my safe."

"Laurent, is someone listening to this?" "Yes!" "Tell them I won't give you the combination if they listen." "They understood and they went farther." "Tell me how many they are?" "Two!"

"Do they have weapons?" "One has." "Try to open the garage door and then do any kind of combinations and if it doesn't open try again saying you made a mistake." "I got it."

So I entered the house with no problem and I ran to the elevator, then I went up to the second floor and wait for someone to simply open the door for me.

"It's open guys, you take what you want."

They both ran to the safe with a bag one of the two guys was holding and the other one after putting his gun away in his belt came to open the door hoping to load everything they could, but surprise, surprise, there was something else waiting for them. It has been a long time since I've used my marshal arts, but I couldn't remember went I had so much fun doing it.

"You must be gifted with all the talents in the world." "Not quite Laurent. Have they been here long?" "Since last night! I told them I was only the tenant and I didn't know the safe's combination. They told me they will cut me to pieces if I don't give it to them. It was then I told them you were coming today. I thought I will gain some time this way. This worked, because they decided to wait for you before acting on me. I would have preferred a better welcome for all of you." "Don't blame yourself; it's not your fault. Which way did they come in?" "I think they came through the beach and they probably have a boat not too far out there." "We'll have to reinforce the security on that side. Do you want to help me clean this shit before the others

come in?" "What are you going to do with them and what happened
to the other two?" "I put them to sleep. I'll explain to you a little bit
later. We have to tie up these two before taking them to the bus. We'll
take them on the beach and I'll come back later with Bernard to take
them to their boat, but first I want to get my people over here. Do you
mind keeping an eye on them in the mean time?" "This will be my
pleasure." "We'll be back as soon as possible. See you in a bit."

"Everything is fine Bernard. Get everybody ready to come down
and help you with the luggages, I'll be there in a few minutes."
"What happened?" "I'll tell you later if you don't mind, we have to
concentrate on getting everyone in right now." "I understand."

"We'll never find peace no matter where we go." "Ho come on
Danielle, waiting five to ten minutes is not the end of the world."
"These were five to ten minutes of worrying and this is not funny at
all. Who are those trouble makers?" "They are trespassers who thought
getting richer by taking from someone who is well off, that's all. They
are now worst off then they were before and it's not over yet for them.
They're not yet at the end of their sorrows. But what is important
right now is to get you in that house the sooner the better. Jesus was
right when he said not to pile up treasures on earth where thieves want
to steal, but he never said what could happen to the thieves when
they do. I can tell you that those thieves here weren't too lucky when
they opened the wrong door. Here we are. Now everybody gets busy
putting all things away, Bernard and I have a little job to do." "This is
the exact same house than we have in Quebec." "Yes, there are a very
few changes, because I wanted you to feel at home here too. We got to
go; I'll see you all in a few minutes."

"Are you going to kill us?" "Maybe you deserve it, but this might
be your lucky day, we are not killers. This might be good for you."
"What happened to those two?" "They are sleeping very well for now.
How did you guys come in?" "We have a little boat not very far from
here." "Who does it belong to?" "It's mine. Where are your papers?"
"On the boat!" "How much did it cost you?" "Ten thousands!" "Did

283

you pay it with stolen money?" "No, I work in construction and I paid it with honest money." "What went through your head to do such a criminal offence like you did today?" "One of the sleeping guys planned everything and he said it was a sure thing and I went for it." "Is your gun registered?" "No, it was bought on the black market. We didn't want to hurt anyone; the gun is not even loaded." "This is a good point for you." "I want the first and the last name of every one of you."

"Would you write this down Bernard please?"

"I also want your address and your phone numbers." "Are you from the police?" "What makes you think that?" "You're asking a lot of questions." "I'm always interested in my guests and this even if they weren't invited." "What are you going to do with us?" "Well, I could put you all on your boat and send you to the see after I pierced it, but I already told you that we're no killers. What do you think I should do with you?" "The normal thing to do would be to call the police." "Yes, but I hate courts even if it was only to testify. Is there one among you guys who has a criminal record?" "I'm not sure about every one, but I don't have one."

"I don't have one either." "I'm going to let you go and I make you a promise that I always keep by the way, no matter what. I promise you that if I see you around here one more time or if I hear you have committed another crime, I'll come to get you myself and make you pay for this crime here also. You are the chief and you are responsible for the other three. What would you think of that?" "I'd say we don't deserve this much." "Do you know how to swim?" "We swim like fish sir." "So, I'm going to set you free and you take your friends with you, but I keep your gun, because in theory you won't need it anymore." "I appreciate what you're doing for us sir and I thank you and I speak for every one of us." "Here, take this; you will give to your friends when they wake up. One more thing before you go, I think you owe my friend an apology for what you did to him."

"We're very sorry sir and you'll never see us again."

"Let's go men, those guys will never come here again, you can bet on that." "Why are you doing this James?" "There are some guys in life Bernard who only need one chance to turn their life around and I hope they are some of them."

"I was expecting anything but something like this. It must be because you are what you are that someone wants to kill you James, it's beyond me." "If there was only one chance those guys turn away from sins, they might just have got it today and if I'm mistaking, I'll get them another time. I gave them the opportunity to like me instead of hating me and like I said it before, I hate courts and trials."

"When you came to my trial it paid off and now there are thousands of people who don't swear anymore." "You said it Bernard, this message is already passed, now I have to concentrate on other messages and there are hundreds of them. 'There are so many things to say and so little time to do it!'

"You've never told me who you really were James." "I'm only a Jesus' disciple Laurent and so are Bernard, Danielle and Janene."

"Ho no, not me, I'm only an apprentice." "What are you saying? You're the first one to find out there was something wrong down here." "It's my job to know it's safe to touch ground before I go down." "This is what I'm saying, you're a disciple too."

"I always thought you have to be poor to be a disciple." "You mainly have to follow Jesus' recommendations, know how to recognize his messages and then pass them over to others who hopefully will become disciples too. A poor man even with the best will in the world can't give much physically and financially, because he's got nothing, but spiritually he can do the same thing I do. On the other hand the rich man can do a lot of harm or a lot of good around him. There is a terrible stupid story in Luke 16, 19-31 where it is said that a rich man is in hell because he was wealthy in his life. This story says there is a great chasm fixed between hell and heaven and no one can cross over, but they are communicating from one place to the other with no apperent problem. I don't think they had internet back then. Worst yet, the rich man in hell calls Abraham father and worst than worst, Abraham calls the man in hell son. That's not all, the rich man in hell asked Abraham to go save his five brothers, which is totally against the devil's policy. Besides, Jesus said that a kingdom cannot stand if it is divided. Look in Matthew 12, 26. 'If Satan casts out Satan he is divided against himself; how then will his kingdom stand?'

"I don't think the writer of this stupid story ever met Jesus. We all know that to this day the bad is still in the world, in fact we got another proof of this here today." "I'm going to follow your writing from now on James." "I would like you to follow the news closely too if you don't mind and keep me informed." "You can count on me; I'll keep my eyes opened."

"You should bring Pauline for a couple of days off Bernard when you bring Janene over on your next trip. You have to excuse me now; I got to have a serious talk with Laurent."

"You were saying the nature of this bomb came from somewhere else?" "Yes, I was telling you that we cannot find this substance on earth and it's unknown to the authorities. It cost many millions to the new owners." "I can tell you that it doesn't take a big quantity to make big damages. A battery the size of a quarter almost took my life from a distance of forty-five meters away and I know who tried to use it against me." "You do? I thought I was going to tell you who has it. The patent is registered in the name of a church in Rome. The Italian government tried everything it could without success to get it. I think they want to make people believe after the explosion that it was the arm of God that hit. Just like many other events, they'll try to make people believe it is an act of God, just like thunder and lightning." "That sounds like them and this won't be the first time they lie to their people this way. We should get the confirmation of what you're saying in the next few days. You're going to have visitors in Trois-Rivières shortly and it would be good that you let them see the foreground. I'm sure they'll want to know if I was around for sometimes before my death. That would be a good lie if you tell them you didn't see me for a long time, that you were in vacations and you came back for the funeral." "I think I can do this much for you. We have to gather everybody for a meeting on security now. We're all going to meet down in Danielle's basement."

"I need everybody attention without exception now. I want everybody in the bowling room in less than five minutes and this is very important." "What is so special James?" "Well, the thing is there is danger here too and I want everybody to be aware of it."

"Alright kids, we have here a very beautiful beach, but it is absolutely forbidden to go swimming." "What?"

"What?"

"What?"

"What?" "We have many ducks in here today. It is absolutely forbidden to swim alone or without the presence of an adult. It is also forbidden to go farther than the fence that is there to stop sharks from coming in. I'm going to let M. Charron speak to you now, he knows this place more than anyone and don't be shy to ask him any questions you like."

"Do you also believe there is danger swimming at the beach M. Charron?" "All I can say about this is that I lost my best friend to the mouth of a shark and this is why I got a wire mesh fence built at three hundred feet from shore. It hurts pretty bad to see our favourite animal being killed and eaten and I'm sure it would be a lot worst if this was a brother or a sister or a child and not be able to do anything to help" "Do you mind telling us what happened here with these strangers who stop us from coming down the plane?"

"May I James?" "Go ahead Laurent, they might take you seriously."

"Well, there were four bandits who kept me as a hostage since eight o'clock last night at the point of a gun and they asked me to open the safe, but because I didn't know the combination they threaten to cut me to pieces. I was quite happy to know that your father was coming today, which I'm sure is the reason I'm still alive and I'm here talking to you now." "What do you mean by that, he saved your life?" "Well, I told them that your father was coming today, which allowed me to gain some time, but I didn't expect your father to put them out of combat in less than ten minutes. I rather thought this would end up with some kind of negotiations."

Samuel as usual was more curious than any others and he wanted to know everything and every detail and he was asking all kind of questions.

"What did he do to get rid of them?"

"That's enough questions for this particular matter. Let's talk about more serious things now.

Is there anything else we should know about for our security over here Laurent?" "Yes, the sun is very hot and we have to be aware of it, because it could cause skin cancer beside burns. We also have to be aware of the sea pirates who are prowling around fairly frequently. It's possible that some of them try to kidnap someone in the hope to obtain a ransom, especially because your parents have money. There is not much risk they can come in by the way of ground, but we know better now that they could come in from way of water." "This is why that right this afternoon I'll give orders to reinforce the security on this side. You can be sure that I'll do everything in my power for you all to be safe on this Island."

"You can trust your dad for this; we're almost prisoners of his security." "I think this is better than weeping and gnashing your teeth."

"That's a good one James, where did you get it?" "I got it in Matthew 13, 42 of the Bible, Jesus said it."

"Do you think we should arm ourselves James?" "I don't think so Charles, we just have to help ourselves and God will do the rest."

I didn't want to get into the details about defence equipment in front of everybody, but the whole island is equipped to defend us properly. We only had one weak spot and we discovered it this afternoon. We even have an anti-missile cover up in the ground on this island. We also have many garages hiding rocket launchers and tanks. I also have anti-aircraft guns, anti-tank guns pointing in every direction and mainly we have some radar that can tell us what is going on thirty miles around. I can see the coming of the big boats that they're not allowed to come any closer than ten miles away from our island. I also plan either to arm our plane with machine guns like they have on the f-18 and on the f-35 or else trade it for one already equipped with them. I obtained from this government with a big pay off the permission to shoot any uninvited guest even if it was from the police or the army. Everything has a price if we have the money to pay, but nothing is too expensive when it comes to the protection of my family and friends.

"Do you see anything else that we should know Laurent?" "Not for now James!"

"Do you have anymore questions?" "I would love to have the chance to speak with M. Charron about a few ideas I have that could become good inventions I think." "And what is your name?" "Samuel!"

"This is another one who has a fertile imagination Laurent and it would be good if you introduce him to your son."

"M. Charron, can we patent moldings?" "Sure we can my boy, but chances are good that everybody cheats and you get nothing for your ideas. What needs to be done is to register the design of the rotor bit that you want people to use to make those moldings and then you can get one part of every bit sold, but absolutely nothing on your bit imitations." "Is it very expensive to register an idea like that?" "It depends a lot on who you talk to and which organization that does it for you. Some lawyers are worst than the sharks of the sea. One of them could take ten thousands for a job and another one could take one hundred thousands for the same thing. Myself I increased my fortune at least one hundred times with your father's inventions and this is why I can take it easy today."

"Now every one here knows every one and if any of you ever sees someone else on this island; you don't even talk to this person; you run to the house as fast as you can and you tell the others, because if someone else is here, there is a huge chance he or she is there to harm you, no matter how gentle he looks like and what he's talking about and this even if he walks with his head under his arm. Is that understood from every one? I don't need to have anybody to play hero over here. This will be all unless someone has more questions on security."

"When are we going on the boat?"

"Ho yes, I want to go too."

"Me too!" "I'm going to go first with Danielle to make sure everything is fine around here, but first I have to call someone to get the beach more secured."

"I'm telling you that if I had all of my dogs here we wouldn't need anything else for our security." "It's true that we have good dogs, but I don't think this would be enough to secure us all and they would be at risk to be killed, which I wouldn't like that at all and neither would you."

"How do you feel Bernard?" "I feel a bit sleepy, but I rather stay awake now and have a good night sleep before going back tomorrow." "Do you mind taking care of the work at the beach?" "What do you want over there?" "I want the same thing we have on our little river in Quebec." "Do you know if we can find it around here?" "I'll see to it and if not I'll order it over there and you can bring it when you return. Keep your eyes opened on everything is going on around here and I'll go for a little cruise with Danielle."

"Can you tell me Laurent if the boat is filled up with gas?" "I fill it up every time I go out for an outing." "Alright then, we'll be back in a few hours."

The sun was beautiful, the see was quite calm and Danielle as beautiful and as attractive as the first night we met. We went around our island and around a few others too. I was happy to realize we were still insulated from other people. It would have been very easy to believe that we were in paradise. It is comforting to know that we are under our Creator's protection.

"Do you feel for it as much as I do darling?" "Sweetheart you should know that I feel for it every time I see you, I just have to restrain myself, because I want to have enough for the rest of my life." "Are you afraid to run out of energy and power?" "What would you say if a man had a limit just like a pen? Let's just say for fun ten thousands words for a pen and ten thousand ejaculations for a man. It takes a good pump for that, don't you think?" "Would that mean every time a person do it alone is missing a good session with a partner?" "This would mean too that men would have four sessions a week for fifty years with two weeks off every year." "Hey, at one hundred dollars a shot you would get a million dollars." "Gees, you're quite good with numbers too. Let's see if you're just as good in bed. We have to hurry though, because we don't want to worry the others. Maybe next time we won't give them a time for our return. Go down and I'll reach you in a few minutes. I'll leave the yacht on neutral and let us rock with the little waves. You didn't want to wait for me to get undressed?" "You don't want the others to worry, so get at it, don't waste your time." "I was just wondering if you really knew how much I love you." "Yes my darling and if you miss telling me one day, then I'll be worried." "This was wonderful again, let's get dress and go before they send a search signal." "What are those three men doing here?" "They seem to be sleeping well; I wonder what they were looking for. Search this one over there and see if he's got some identification." "This looks like a gold cigarette case. He also has a knife and a gun." "This box is mine, this means they are thieves and maybe some sea pirates. Look over there, this must be their boat. I'm going to go look to see what it is." "Are you sure you should go on this boat, it looks pretty creepy to me. Those guys stink like hell. They must have been months without taking a bath." "I'm just going to take a quick look."

Danielle was right; it was very pernicious on that boat. There are some dead bodies that began to smell terrible. It was obvious they were pirates, because there were all kinds of different things that a group of persons cannot gather together with the best imagination in the world. We were very lucky not to be caught with our pans down. I grabbed three life jackets and I came out with them pinching my nose.

"Watch out a bit Danielle, I'm going to throw this on the yacht."
"Did you become a thief too?" "Do you really think this, clown? Help
me a bit, I'll put this on them and throw them in the water." "You're
not afraid they get eating by sharks?" "Frankly darling, I don't give a
damn. Thieves and murderers like them do they really deserve to live?"
"This is the first time I hear you talk like that." "Do you really think
God will be full of compassion for people like these? They stink so bad
I think even sharks will reject them. In the case over there are wake up
pills; I'm going to shove one in every one of theme's throat." "You are
too generous, why waste those pills on them?"

"I'm not generous at all, with them anyway, it's just that I don't
want the authorities to follow their trail up to me. They're ready now;
please help me throw them over board. No, just wait a bit, we better
get a bit farther so they don't get back to their boat too quick, then I'll
call the marine. That should be enough now. Help me would you?"
"No, I don't want to, but I'll help you anyway. This big pig is heavy."
"It's worst because, he's a dead weight. Just wait, I'll pull him over
there and just roll him over."

"Here's JP to the marine! I repeat; here's JP to the marine." "Here's
the marine, what can we do to help you?" "There are three men
overboard near a pirate boat. They seem unconscious near an island."
"What is your position? I repeat what is your position?" "Our position
is four miles North, North East from White Point Island." "Received,
we'll send a petrol boat right away, but you can count at least an hour
before the marine gets there." "I'm sorry, but I cannot wait for you,
I got to go right away, because the security of my family is at stake."
"Received, thank for your help, we appreciate."

"I pushed my machine to its full potential and we went home in a
hurry. Bernard welcomed us with a worried look on his face.

"Something went wrong, isn't it James?" "Nothing that is really
bad Bernard, it was just a pirate boat. They were three men, but they
are sleeping right now while taking a salted water bath." "You will
never find peace, will you?" "I guess no one wants me to get bored,

but it's the other way around Bernard, it's my enemies who cannot find peace. I wouldn't want to be in the shoes of the people who attacked me lately." "You're right with this one too, your position is much better than theirs." "Don't you go think that Jesus' work for the thousand years reign will be one of rest, might as well get used to it if I want to reign with him. We have to understand that when Jesus said this, he meant the word of God will reign. Same thing with the judgement, the word of God will judge the generations. Jesus is the word of God." "By watching you go we can almost say it's already started, the bad guys experience hell and the good ones are treated well." "I think I might be a bit responsible for this." "How could you be responsible for this?" "When I prayed one time I asked God to use me the way He wanted. I often had the impression while I was growing up to hold the world on my shoulders." "No one can say that you are a very big man." "Do you know the expression about the little jars?" "Yes I know; the best ointment." "What about going out for a boat ride with everybody now?" "Let's go get them." "Go fill the boat, I'll get them."

"Hi every one, are you ready for a couple of hours boat ride?" "Ho yes!"

"Yes!"

"Yes!"

"Yes!"

"Yes!" "I think we have unanimity here." "Where are we going?" "We'll just go around the islands just in case one of you eventually wants to become my neighbour some day. I would like to buy a few more for myself." "Yes dad, this is something I would be very interested in." "Mm, it's funny, but I kind of thought this would be something that would excite you Sam. Maybe you don't have enough money just yet, but it shouldn't be too long before you have it. If this is interesting for somebody else I might be able to loan you the money for a deposit. Lift up your hand if you are interested."

"I want the one that got the most wood." "That might be hard to find Jon, but we can always look for it."

"What about you Bernard? We'll talk about it a bit later if you want to, but you can look and see which one would interest you. When you can, talk it over with Raymond, you might be able to share one between the two of you." "This is a good idea James, I will talk to him and I will talk to Pauline too about it." "Let's go see how many they are around here. If I remember well from looking from up in the air, I think there are about twenty of them and all fairly close to one another. Some are smaller, but there are also some pretty big ones too. I would like to have a smaller one myself for a question of resting when things settle down a little bit and get a family life too. I have to admit I miss that."

"It's very true that you weren't spoiled this way. You better start soon to train someone to replace you one day." "Ho, I'm not ready to give my place up just yet, I like it too much for that, but it would be nice to have a helper to take over from time to time." "Samuel should be ready in three years time and he should apply for the pilot course as soon as possible. He's got all the proper attitudes for this kind of work."

"Look at this one dad, it's so beautiful." "That is true, let's measure it to see how big it is. It measures three quarters of a mile by half a mile. It's very beautiful and only a mile from our home. Who wants that one?" "Me!"

"Me!"

"Me! Too." "I thought this would be the case, ten takers for one islands. We'll have to spin the bottle to determine the winner. Here's what we're going to do, we're going to fly above the islands and take pictures of them. I will probably buy them all and distribute them later. I want the ones on both ends to be armed and owned by the most alert and responsible among all of you. We'll discuss this later on at home."

"So, do you mean every one of us will have one dad?" "You would like to have yours too Isabelle?" "Of course I want to, not only boys can do great things, girls too if we get the opportunity." "You're right about this my girl and yes you will get yours too and I would like you to be as close to me as possible. What do you say about that?" "You are a golden dad, I love you so much." "Did you think about what you want to do later on in life?" "Yes dad, I have and this for a long time now. I want to be a doctor and have my own hospital." "And you have never said anything to me about this." "You know dad, we don't have this many opportunities to talk to you about a lot of things." "Yes, I know and I'm so sorry about it sweetheart, luckily we have these vacations. But you're talking about very big ambitions here." "I know and I know too that I will be able to." "Would you be willing to spend your summer holiday on stages learning at the hospital?" "I don't ask for anymore than this dad." "But you're only twelve. I know how old I am dad, but this is what I want to do." "Alright then, as soon as we get home you ask your mom for an application form."

"Can I do the same thing dad?" "If you still thinking about it in one year time Mariange, you remind me, would you?" "Don't you worry, I won't forget."

"What about you Rene, do you know what you want to do?" "For sure I do, I want to do just like you." "You don't think I do too much?" "Maybe so, but I want to do just like you." "Then you must be the most ambitious of all."

And you Jeremy, do you know what you want to do?" "I want to teach everything we need to know." "What do you mean everything?" "I want to teach everything you know dad." "You don't think this is a bit too much?" "That's what I want to do with my entire life dad."

Then I started asking myself a lot of questions, like how long would his life be with so many who want to end mine? How many more times will I escape from those attacks that come one after another? How long will it be before someone finds out where I'm hiding? Which weapon will they use next time? Who will be my next attacker? Who will be the first one to betray me?" "Which one of my people will they attack to get to me? Only You my Lord Almighty knows the answers to all of those questions. I leave my life into your hands and may your will be done.

"Are you looking where you're going dad?"

"What is the matter James? Are you alright?" "Yes, yes, I'm fine." "We could almost tell you were unconscious." "I was lost in my thoughts, that all." "We have to be careful when we're at the wheel and we hold so many lives in our hands." "You're right Bernard; would you take the wheel please?" "Where do you want to go?" "I would like to measure from outside of the last island to the outside of the first one and then go home for supper before the children start being too hungry."

"When I come back from Quebec I would like to try my luck fishing." "That's a done deal Bernard, I would like this too." "Alright then, see that all the kids are securely buckled up, I'm going to accelerate a little bit." "That's good Bernard, go ahead."

The kids found the speed very exciting on water and we were at home in a reasonable time for supper. Henri-Paul and Charles preferred to wait a little bit later in the week to give the kids a chance to be all together for the first outing.

"There are about twenty-two miles long and fifteen miles wide to include all of the island James." "That is almost the size of Ville Marie Island." "You mean Montreal?" "We can stack a lot of people in there." "Are you thinking about populating them?" "That's an eventual possibility. We have to be careful not to let a word slip out about this; otherwise this would be a very big lost and we would have to start all over again somewhere else." "This wouldn't be very easy." "While I think about it, you find out if we can arm the plane and this boat properly for our defence, we should make it bullet-proof or get another one bullet-proof. Always make sure that you're not followed. Don't mention it to the children, but see to bring Samuel favourite and Jonathan's dogs back here. This will make it easier for them to be away from home. I got to spend a bit of time with Laurent, because he'll have a lot to do over there."

"How are you Charles?" "I'm fine James, thank you. How was the ride?" "It went well and the kids appreciated it a lot. You are fine in the air now; don't tell me you are scared of water." "No James, you won't have to put me to sleep to bring me fishing." "Are you coming to have supper with us?" "This will be a pleasure, just give me five minutes to clean up a bit." "We'll eat at Danielle's dining room."

Nock, nock, nock! "Are you awake Henri-Paul?" "No, I'm in a deep sleep and I'm dreaming of you, so please don't wake me up?" "No one can stop you from dreaming and I won't even try, but we don't survive only on clear water and love and this is why I came to invite you to come down and have supper with us. Danielle is waiting for us, so please don't make her wait to long, alright?" "Just the time to get dressed and I'll be down there."

Then I went to invite Laurent whom I didn't have to twist his arm very long to get him to accept the invitation.

"Are you coming to have supper with us Laurent?" "For once that there is a woman who cooks in this house, I won't miss this, not even for all my fortune." "Let's just talk about your fortune for a minute. Can't you afford to have a cook for yourself?" "To find one that would be happy to cook only would be great, but she could cook for six months and then ask for half of my fortune and the judge who would listen to her would be happy to clean me out. You just have to make her sign a premarital agreement and you'll be safe." "Some of them know how to manipulate the justice system. It seems sometime they sleep with the judge to get what they want." "You mean like the one who got three millions dollars for a hot cup of coffee she spelt herself on her laps?" "Exactly!" "I think you have been too often near inventors and you invent stories to yourself. I don't think you should be this scared. They're not all bad, you know? I got two gorges ones myself and a third pretty one who is after me right now." "Are you living on viagra?" "Ha, ha. No, at least not yet. For as long there is love there is desire and this seems to be enough up till now anyway. Come down for supper, we'll talk later." "I think you are very lucky and I'm not jealous of you, but sometimes I envy your situation." "There is no need for you to be envious. You just have to do the same thing and you can afford it. Having a fortune and nobody to share it with is kind of a none sense. If you are afraid of our Canadian women just go to China or to the Philippines and you will find women that will serve you as if you were a god." "I would have to cut off with the pass completely before I can think about a life with another one." "This is true; you cannot drag the pass in a new relationship; this is not good at all. On the other hand having a good partner is happiness, but being alone like you are, that's not good at all. I only have one advice to give you." "I'm listening, shoot." "You keep you eyes open, you shut your mouth, you open wide your ears, you shut the door to the pass and you open your heart very wide when you have found the right one." "This makes five." "Five what?" "This makes five advices." "Yes, but they're all in the same phrase." "What all of this means?" "It means for you to go where you can find some women and you will always find one who is interested in you. You don't say much, but you listen to what they have to say, that's the only way to know them. You especially listen to the ones who you are attracted to; otherwise you wasting your time. You put your pass behind you, because you're looking for a new relationship and not for one like the one you were unhappy with. When you'll find the one you like physically and you also like her intellectually and she showed you a genuine interest, then you make her laugh, you make her enjoy life and give her what she expects from life and from you. You'll win her heart and she will believe she won yours. She'll be happy and you too." "I got to say this is a good plan, but one has still to believe in it." "I dreamed and I believed in my plane before I got one." "Is there anything you didn't dream of and you got anyway?" "I never dreamed and I never believed living with two women before I was thrown in head first and I never thought possible to live through such a wonderful happiness." "Even though you went through a lot of unfortunate situations I don't know anyone on earth who has got as many blessings as you and I went around the world many times and I met more people than anyone I know." "All the great patriarchs who walked with God experienced the same blessings." "So this is the secret of your success." "God is my supplier and my shield, He works for me and I work for Him, we are a team and I would be absolutely nothing without Him. I just know that if He ever forsakes me I would be poorer than Job, a human wreck. But Laurent we are expected at the table, we have to go." "Thanks James. This was short but very useful to me." "You are very welcome every time you feel like it Laurent. Don't you ever be shy with me."

CHAPTER 13

"*H*ere you are now. Too bad, but the meal started to cool off."
"Business is business and we have to do what we have to do. Excuse us,
but what ever is more important comes first."

"Just grab a seat M. Charron. I hope you will like this modest
meal." "This modest, you should see what I've been eating in the last
few months." "You don't spoil yourself M. Charron and yet you can
afford it." "Yes, but you know when we were burnt, we become a bit
chilly."

"I cannot understand that someone could be chilly in a place as
hot as here." "Ha, ha, ha, ha!"

Everyone around the table burst laughing.

My son Rene to be chilly also means in a figurative meaning, being
a bit scared."

"Auntie Danielle, we didn't learn this in school yet." "There are
a lot of things you would have to learn yet Rene and this is the main
reason you have to study more."

"Listen to your teachers and you'll learn a lot more by listening
than by talking."

"A big and tall man like him to be scared, this is beyond me." "I
don't know about that, all I can say is that I'm scared almost all the
time." "You dad, being scared?"

"This really means being afraid, doesn't it Miss Dion?" "Yes Jeremy, that's what it means." "I believe that my dad is afraid of nothing at all."

"Jeremy, if we are here today it's because I'm terribly afraid that something bad happen to some of you. It doesn't look like it, but we are here on this island because I'm afraid someone wants to hurt you. Besides, I'll always be afraid that something bad happens to one of you. I also think that whoever is afraid of nothing is either inhuman or unconscious."

"This is extremely good, what is it?" "This is a fricassee that my dear husband showed me how to do a long time ago." "You'll have to show me how to make this, I adore it."

"We can only adore God." "I told you before not to reprimand adults Mariange even if you think you are right. You got to apologize now."

"I beg you pardon M. Charron."

"You are right about adoring only God, but adore also means to love a lot in a figurative way. So M. Charron has the right to love our meal a lot. To adore God only means mainly to adore nobody else than the Creator, but also not to adore some object. You didn't see M. Charron getting on his knee and beg it to bring him the moon, did you? To adore also means to love more than oneself.

I am sure that even if M. Charron loves this meal a lot, he would not give his life to get it. Now this subject is closed for today. I'm sure no one would want to embarrass our guess, would you?"

"I will be pleased to write you the recipe M. Charron."

"I would love to get it too, please." "I will make many copies of it, this way everyone can get one, but don't go to adore it, especially not in front of the children."

"They are all so charming; you are extremely lucky James."

"Thank you very much for this delicious meal Mrs. Prince" "You are more than welcome M. Charron." "Please, call me Laurent." "And I'm Danielle."

"Did you have enough to eat Charles, Henri-Paul?" "This was plenty Danielle, thank you."

"Me too, but I wouldn't want to have this every day; I would gain too many pounds. I ate way too much, this was too good."

"Who want some desert" "Me!"

"Me!"

"Me!" "Only the children? What is the problem adults? Are you all afraid to gain too much weight?"

"I will take a piece of your nice pie sweetheart, with a bit of ice cream." "Anyone else?" "I want some too."

"Me too."

"And me too. Mmmmm, it's so good"

"It is so delicious."

"If you ever look for a cooking job, you just let me know."

"No, I'm sorry Laurent, but this one I keep to myself." "Ho, I didn't want to still her from you James, I just wanted to show her my appreciation."

Henri-Paul gave me a nasty look, but I told myself that she has a long way to go if she thinks she could replace Danielle one day. In fact, I know for sure that no one will ever be able to replace Danielle or Janene in my heart and no where else, this I was certain of.

"M. Charron, would you mind coming to sit in the livingroom with us; we would have quite a few questions for you, if this doesn't bother you." "This would be my pleasure my boys, let's go. What do you want to know?" "I personally would like to know how my dad managed to get rid of the two men who were keeping you captive." "This, my boy I won't be able to tell you, because everything just happened to quick. I was pushed out of the way because they wanted to enter the safe and ten seconds later they were on the floor begging your dad not to break their wrist. I couldn't understand a thing, but I was quite relieved to be freed from these gangsters. I always thought we only see these things in movies. Your father is a very special man, do you know this?" "Yes we know, but all this kind of put the bar pretty high for us." "I myself accomplished a lot more than my father and your father accomplished a lot more than his dad. You can accomplish a lot too if you put your mind to it. You have the luck to have a father from whom you can learn a lot just by watching him operate every day. You just can't do otherwise and your dad is right, we learn a lot more by listening than by speaking. You just have to give yourselves some time. For example, look at yourselves. I am pretty sure that you are doing a lot more than he was doing at your age." "I never saw it this way, but you are probably right. I'll have to ask him some day." "Put your trust in your dad and I'm sure you will accomplish great things as he does and who knows, maybe even better."

"Can you tell me how to proceed to get my ideas on my moldings patented?" "We cannot get ideas patented; we can only get tangible things patented. For example, if you design a tool which doesn't exist and you think that many people could use it, you might have something. But first we have to find out no one else got the idea before you and also make sure it is not registered. Only then we can begin the procedure and you have to be very careful not to talk to someone you can't trust. I'm sure your father could help you with this, he has many inventions which are making him richer every day. Don't you show your moldings to someone who could steal your ideas, because you will spend your time and your money for nothing. If you want to I could take a look at what you have and I will let you know your possibilities. It is very possible someone else already got the idea and registered it. We never know until an expensive search is done. You can ask your dad to see if you can trust me, in fact this is my advice to you."

"Henri-Paul and Charles, would you mind to come up stairs with me please? I have an important subject I would like to talk to you about?" "Not at all James, we're following you." "Just feel at home and sit down please." "We don't have a home anymore James, we are just like hobos, worst we are fugitive hobos." "Well then, consider my home your home. You're not too bad here and if something is bothering you, you come to tell me and I'll see what I can do to help if it's reasonable of course." "Thank you very much James, this is very good of you." "You said before that you were good in music and in singing, is there a particular style you prefer or you can adapt to music in general? Charles, you go ahead first." "I like to listen to classic music myself, but when it comes to work I would do just about anything but heavy mental."

"What about you Henri-Paul, can you teach vocals, diction and singing in general?" "This is what I have always done." "What would be a fair salary for you if you were to do this for a living?" "I don't really know what would be fair. I don't know, three maybe four hundred a week."

"What about you Charles, how much?" "This would be good enough for me too." "I'm giving you four thousands a month each to work forty hours a week and we'll negotiate again in a year time. You'll have summer holidays paid for and two weeks at the Christmas break. I'll pay you with straight cash at the end of each month and you will be fed and board." "Are you serious?" "I'm always serious when I talk business. In one year time you will know better if you want to stay or to go. You will take your orders from me only and you will answer to me only, unless you choose differently. I will build you a cottage with all the modern facilities. Before Bernard leaves tomorrow he needs to get from you all the information that could help to bring to justice the people responsible for our change of life. Trust me, I will not expose you to anymore danger, so don't you worry about telling him everything you know." "All I want to do is torment them until they give themselves up." "What will we have to do?" "I want every one of my children to learn to write and read music. I want you to push a little more the one who's got a bit more talent. I want the same thing when it comes to singing. I want you to keep your ears wide open, because I was told I had no ears for music and I play five instruments myself and I composed more than two hundred songs. I would like to hear you sing to see if my style suits you." "What instruments do you play?" "I play the fiddle, the guitar, the mandolin, the banjo and the keyboard." "Would you sing one of your songs to us?" "Well, I'm out of practice and I don't sing very well either, this is why I like to have someone like you around." "That's not very important to us to know which is your style and what kind of songs you write." "Then I'll do this one here and it's called;

Tango For Mamma

We all need to learn as we grow, the things of life we need to know.
All the things they don't teach in school, I was lucky mom you're so cool
You always knew to advice me dealing out with integrity
Yes mom I learned all this from you, today I say big thanks to you

My opinion, there's not on earth a better mom
For all your life you have given to your children
That's the reason we are here to give you some
Of all those thanks that you deserved so often

Since I was just a little boy, I never met a better friend.
You gave all that you have with joy and you are there each time you can
Every time I needed a thing, you found a way to do something
As far as I can remember, you're the very best comforter

My opinion, there's not on earth a better mom
For all your life you have given to your children
That's the reason we're all here to give you some
Of all those thanks that you deserved so often

There are not too many like you, there is so much that you could do
And with so little things on hand you managed to be mother hen
No one can stay young forever my song will carry you over.
Your hair did turn to be silver; medal gold is for you the winner.

My opinion, there's not on earth a better mom
For all your life you have given to your children

That's the reason we're all here to give you some
Of all those thanks that you deserved so often

No one can stay young forever my song will carry you over
Your hair did turn to be silver, medal gold is for you the winner
No, you have never changed that much, you still manage to stay in touch.

They applauded me like I never was before, but I knew very well that it was for the song and not for the signing."

"This is the nicest song about mothers I ever heard in my whole life." "I often wished that Céline Dion could sing it to her mother, it seems to me that all the mothers of the world could hear it." "Do you have anymore of this type of songs?" "Let just say that I have many nice songs." "Would you sing another one for us please?" "Would you like to sing this kind of songs?" "I'm sure Charles would become a star in no time at all with songs like these."

"That is exactly where the problem is, I cannot afford to go public, because hundreds of people would recognize me." "With a good disguise and a different name, chances are good that no one recognizes you." "They could recognize my voice and there is nothing we can do about that one." "You can always work on the songs and we'll see what we can do later. People could say that your voice sounds like yours without thinking it's yours. One way or the other we'll have to resurrect some day." "Come on James sing another one for us." "this will be:

The Smell of Roses

Thank You my Lord, thank You my Lord, thank You my Lord.

1
Thank You my Lord for this wonderful smell of roses.
Thank You my Lord for giving me so many things.

Is it for You time of the apotheoses?
It's time for me to say thank You for your blessings.

I know You are the Almighty
And You have made beautiful flowers just for me.
They are faded, as You can see.
Only You can bring her back to what she used to be.

We are the seed, the garden of your kingdom.
Your creation made by your hands, your ambition.
Your enemy, yes the despicable phantom
He has faded my nice flower, my companion.

God You blessed us and You told us. Gen. 1, 28.
To be fruitful, to multiply, fill up the earth.
To rule over, birds in the sky,
Fish in the sea and everything upon the earth.

Thank You my Lord for this wonderful smell of roses.
Thank You my Lord for giving me so many things.
Is it for You time of the apotheoses?
It's time for me to say thank You for your blessings.
Thank You my Lord for making me as your likeness.

This is a very nice song James and quite a message for Charles and me. These are nice songs and I would like to add the music arrangement and the harmony to it."

"What about you Charles, what do you think of them?" "These are very nice songs alright, but I'm not so sure they are suitable for me."

"Ho I see, you still want to be a priest and keep preaching the lies? One thing is sure; you cannot remain catholic and preach the truth, because your life would be more at risk than now." "You're right James; I better put a cross on this one." "You know as well as I do that you cannot serve two masters." "I saw these words somewhere." "They are from Jesus and you can read them in Matthew 6, 24." "There is no doubt about it, you know the scriptures." "I know mainly the truth and we cannot find it in your church on the contrary." "I know we suppressed it and not just a little." "You just said a few minutes ago that you'd be better to put a cross on that one. I think you reached the cross road, now you have to decide if you are with or against us, but only you can decide for yourself."

"Charles, how could you hesitate between serving God and the devil?" "It's not who I want to serve Henri-Paul but how."

"If you don't know how Charles, go read Matthew 28, 20. 'Go therefore and make disciples of all the nations, teaching them to observe all that I commanded you and lo, I am with you always, even to the end of the age.'

This is what Jesus wants from us and what he has prescribed is the truth and the truth is, there is only one way to God and this is through repentance. Read now Matthew 4, 17." "'From that time Jesus began to preach and say: Repent for the kingdom of heaven is at hand.'

"Now, if I translate this in your language; it means to turn yourself to God and to ask Him forgiveness for your sins if you want access to the kingdom of heaven. It doesn't mean to turn to a man or a woman or anyone else." "So you don't believe in confession?" "I believe in the word of God which said in Jeremiah 17, 5: 'Thus says the Lord: 'Cursed is the man who trusts in mankind and make flesh his strength and whose heart turns away from the Lord.''" "How could I have been so blind?"

"We have to look for the truth to find it; otherwise Jesus wouldn't have had to say, Matthew 7, 8. 'He who seeks finds.'" "I often had suspicions about being on the right track or not and now I realize that I was completely lost and I was losing others." "Jesus translated this by saying: 'They are blinds who lead blinds.' I suppose you already know the result of that. This is why you found yourself in the hole." "How could I ever undo what I have done and bring back the ones I have lost on the right way?" "Most of the ones you have lost would condemn you for leaving the Catholic Church. This is what they have learned from you. If you decide to turn to God; you also let Him guide you for your future, so you put your life into his hands, your pass and your future. Remember too that when God has forgiven; He has also forgotten and you too should try to do the same. Believing in God or having faith, it's also knowing that once you repented for your sins you are forgiven and if you ask twice forgiveness for the same sin, it's because you didn't believe the first time. If someone apologizes a second time for something I already have forgave, he's insulting me and he's wasting my time." "I'll have to learn the truth before I can preach again." "Take it one day at the time Charles, one day at the time. God doesn't ask anymore from you and neither do I. I'll make myself available as often as I can for you or better yet, I'll let you read one of my books called; The True Face of The Antichrist. You'll find in this book a lot of information that will put you on the right track. Are you okay with this?" "We cannot ask for more, you're very generous." "God doesn't ask any less from me. You'll have to excuse me now, but I still have a lot to discuss with Bernard in whom by the way you can trust as much as you trust me. So can I count on you for one year?" "This is much more than we were hoping for."

"Dad, you finally came down. Do you want to come and play a game with us?" "I would like to my sweethearts, but." "Nevermind, we got the message." "I am very sorry and I can't help it. We have three weeks vacations, I'm sure I'll be able to catch up with you. You see, M. Charron and Bernard are leaving in the morning and I have many recommendations for them before they go." "We understand that this is more important than a game." "I appreciate your understanding and I love you all so much." "You are an extraordinary dad and I love you too dad." "You're a real sweetheart." "Do you know where M. Charron and Bernard went?" "They're gone for a walk on the island." "I'm going to look for them, because I'm running out of time."

"Are you alright James?" "Yes, it's just that we have so much to settle yet before you go. You have to go talk to Henri-Paul and Charles to get all the information we need to bring to justice the people who tried to kill me. It will be hard to get everyone of them, but if we can get a few, this might scare the others enough."

"Do you know Laurent if they have a lot of this substance and what is it called?" "This is kryptonite and it looks a lot like plutonium and as you already know it doesn't take much to make a lot of damages." "We'll have to find out who makes the little batteries and this should lead us to the owner of these bombs. I think they are made of stainless steel. I'm pretty sure also that they are totally illegal." "You got to be right and I'm going to ask my son if he can supply us with some information. I know he's bound by the professional secret, but when it comes to such a criminal weapon, it become a question of conscience too. If he knows anything he'll tell me. In fact if you allow me, I'll invite him and his family to come and spend time with me in Quebec." "You go right ahead; you know you're at home when you are at my place. You already know all of the security rules. It would be a good idea to let the police and the journalists know that you own this property." "I understand your point of view. I just wonder what all these people would do if you weren't there for them." "They've learned a lot from me and they will know what to do, believe me and besides, I'm not really dead yet. Do you mind to come and play a game with us? The kids would love to have you too." "What are they playing?" "I think it's their monopoly game." "Nobody will have a chance against you." "Are you kidding me; I never won even once at this game."

"Here we are kids, do you still want to play this game?" "Ho yea!"

"Ho yea! You are just in time; we were starting a new game." "Your mom didn't want to play?" "She said having a headache and she went to lie down." "The sun might have done that to her." "Here is your money dad, M. Charron, Jonathan, Mariange, Isabelle, Jeremy, Rene and I will be the banker." "Make sure not to go broke." "Don't you worry, I got good friends." "Your best friend in business is your savings and if you don't believe me just ask M. Charron."

"Your dad is right and I will add to this, the savings of your best friends." "Banks too can help, can they not?" "Banks will help you helping themselves. Credit is a double edge like a razor blade; it helps a lot of people getting out of the hole and also put a lot of people in the hole. A person has to know how to use his credit wisely. It's a smart idea not to use more than we can afford." "What would you think about borrowing the most you can when everything is lost? You would have nothing to lose anymore." "How could you borrow and being honest, if this is the case? He would have to be a complete idiot or someone who has money to lose to lend you the money in such a case." "It could be someone like me, a true friend dad who has a blind trust. I wouldn't hesitate two seconds to lend you my money dad even if I risk losing it all." "This is very nice of you son, but know that I won't risk your money or anyone else money unless I am absolutely sure to succeed with my project."

"I personally risked all of my relatives' money when I started." "Did they know about the risk?" "Most of them did, but still the risk was quite high." "Fortunately you succeeded. Many people ruined their family this way and even drove some of them to suicides." "Every one of those who helped me got one hundred times their shares," "They must be happy for keeping you on the saddle." "You can see it this way, because I was rather staggering, but everything turned out alright."

"I want a two hundred thousand dollar loan to buy the North Carolina." "I'll have to see if you have enough collateral dad. This is a risky loan and I'll have to take a ten per cent interest on it." "I will reimburse you everything, the interest included, but I'll remember your attitude when you need money." "North Carolina receives twenty thousands." "Thanks Laurent!" "It's your turn to play Mariange." "That's on North Carolina again." "Do you have enough money to pay?" "I'm short three thousands." "Keep it for now, I trust you to pay me later. It's your turn to play banker." "Not again on that bloody Carolina." "Come on banker shoot the money this way, it's twenty thousands." "Go ahead Rene. That's his, lucky boy. You have a lot of money Isabelle maybe you can stop at my place, it cost a lot, but beauty has a price. Go ahead you need five for that. A four and a . . . . one. Come on please twenty thousands. Hey banker do you still believe I was a risk?" "That sure was a good buy." "We'll have to stop at nine sharp at the first ring of the clock." "So we only have fifteen minutes more to play."

"Are you playing Jon or are you afraid to stop at my place? You can do it with nine." "Dad, there must be a wizard in you tonight, you just ask and you get it." "This one doesn't pay as much, but five thousands are nice to get anyway."

"The bank is almost dry someone will have to pay back." "I think I can pay you back now; here are the two hundred and twenty thousands."

"You still have many thousands dad." "Yes Jeremy, I got a few good shots today." "He's winning for sure today; he could lend money to everyone else including the bank." "Yes, and this at five per cent interests only!"

"Congratulation James; you sure have a good strategy." "It did work for me tonight for a change."

"That's true dad, this is the first time you won." "I felt like being aggressive in business tonight and it paid off. I couldn't win without the bank loan though. We have to pick this all up now; most of you are due for bed." "Jeremy, would you like to go sleep in your mom's bed?" "Ho yes dad, can I?" "If I tell you, it's because you can."

"Can I go sleep there too dad?" "No, this is a special for Jeremy. I have my reasons and they are not debatable for now.

Now, I know we are in vacations, but even in vacations we have to do something. Starting tomorrow morning and for two hours from ten till twelve and from Monday to Friday every one of you will take music and singing lessons, giving to you by M. Gregoire and Miss Toupin. You also get your regular class in the afternoon from two o'clock till four, because I don't want your schooling year to be compromised." "What kind of vacations are these?"

"Yea, I thought vacation was totally different than this." "What are you making of my vacations?" "For you it's not the same dad, you have res-pon-si-bi-li-ties." "And you are absolutely right at one hundred per cent, but it is time for you too now to take your responsibilities. At ten tomorrow morning in the basement for your first lesson, so you can sleep in a bit anyway. At two o'clock you will get your regular lesson. I will bring your teachers fishing in the morning and your music teachers in the afternoon, this way every one gets his turn. That will be all now, good night."

"Can I kiss you anyway dad, even if I'm responsible now?" "But Isabelle, this is one of your responsibilities." "Yes I know, honour your father and your mother." "That too, if you want a long life. Good night sweetheart!" "Good night dad, I love you very much." "I love you too pretty girl."

"Good night dad, I was very happy that you could play the game with us tonight, you know?" "I was happy too darling, sleep well."

"Good night Jeremy, I hope this will solve your problem temporarily, your bedroom will be done by the time we go back to Quebec." "How are you going to do that dad, you're not even there?" "I don't have much holidays my boy."

"What about you Rene, you don't mind too much to sleep by yourself?" "On the contrary dad, Jeremy often was disturbing me, but this was in his sleep and this is why I was not mad at him." "This is the main reason I let him sleep in your mom's bed. You are a very fine young man my boy and I appreciate what you've done; especially your discretion, good night." "Good night dad, this was a great day for me."

"Samuel and Jonathan, I have to talk to both of you about very important things, but I need you to use a lot of diplomacy towards your brothers and sisters." "Ho, I don't like it when you take this tone with us, but nevertheless, you can count on us, I'm sure." "I'm very proud of Jon; he had the strength to keep my secret. There are very serious reasons why were here right now Samuel." "My God, but what is it Dad?" "Someone tried to assassinate me yesterday and last week one of my friends was kidnapped, because someone wants to know who I am and where I am." "But who in the world would want to do this to you and why?" "They are enemies of the truth I teach, mainly through my chronicles in the paper. As it is right now, the whole world thinks that I died with your mom along with M. Gregoire and Miss Toupin in an explosion and that Henri-Paul and Charles are the murderers in a suicidal mission. For as long as every one believes I'm dead, no one will be looking for me. I don't think this will ever cease though." "This is why we don't have anymore television?" "Can you imagine the situation if all the kids would have learn our death without being prepared for it?" "But they must be looking for your children right now and so would be the police." "This is the main reason we're all here." "How our disappearance at the funeral will be explained?" "Ho, this is very simple, my principal agents had to assure your protection and they took care of it." "Are the men who were here earlier had anything to do with all this?" "No, those were just amateurs without any experience trying to rob the house of a rich man. I even think this was their first crime, for most of them anyway. I don't think they will try this again, at least not here. I already have given orders to reinforce the security on the beach side from where they came in." "But how could you avoid the catastrophe in Quebec?" "Charles and Henri-Paul volunteered for the mission to save my life. I have to protect them now and this is why I hired them to do what they do best and this is to teach music and singing. This is something I always wanted anyway." "What would you do if we don't have any talent?" "I would like both of you to take the lessons very seriously, even if it was only to influence the others in the right direction. And we never know you might be some virtuosos to come."

"Dad, we need to have at least some talent for this." "Do you know Jonathan that I was told I had no ears for music and that I was completely without any talent, but I play five instruments now and I composed more than two hundred songs and some of them are pretty darn good too? What do you think of that, han? Besides as you now,

I can teach dancing too. I'm sure that every one of you can do just as much. Each one of us is unique and receives ideas that others don't get, I can assure you that this is the truth." "We'll do our best dad, if this is enough for you." "I don't ask for more and neither for less from you my boys. I just know you have a huge influence on the others. They think you are genius and this is why I want to count on you. I'll see you tomorrow and good night to both of you." "Good night dad!"

"Good night dad."

"Did you write down all the information Bernard?" "This begins to be a lot of stock. I have a very good memory and I also wrote a lot of notes. This Henri-Paul is a very pretty woman and I have the impression she's very hungry. I got the feeling she likes you a lot." "Maybe so, but I'm very well served as I am." "No one will ever argue this, except her maybe." "She can argue all she wants, I'm not free and that's all." "Get your note pad out, I have more recommendations for you." "Go ahead, I'm ready." "Did you fill up the plane?" "Yes, that's done." "I would like you to take pictures of all the islands tomorrow morning and send them to me by Emails as soon as you get to Trois-Rivières." "That's no problem, it will be done." "I need you to talk to Raoul and inform him about our situation, but only after the funeral. Tell him about my new Email address, so we can communicate this way. You do the same thing for Roger. Did you get the name of my killer?" "Yes, he is a bishop by the name of Vladino Gomez and he is in the Sherbrooke area." "I need you to find a trustworthy person, Roger maybe, to go to the main mass of this bishop next Sunday to deposit an envelop with a little note that I'm going to send you by Email. We're going to force this man to make a serious conscience examination for himself. Jesus, the true prophet said one thing that comes to fulfilment more and more now days." "He said a lot of things, but what do you have in mind?" "He said; 'For it is inevitable that scandals happen, but woe to the man through whom the scandal comes.'"

"I'm sure it's not funny for anyone to be caught with his hand in the bag or with your pants down." "He's got the money to attack me and I'm fortunate to have enough to defend myself." "The last time you mentioned something about that you were at one billion every twelve days, how is it today, if you don't mind me asking?" "I'm up now to a billion every three days and it keeps increasing all the time. There are more than one hundred and fifty thousand people who work for me in the world and the worst the economy gets the better it gets for me. Many would say that I'm the one who runs all this, but they would be mistaking, the One who is running all this is up there, He's the One in control, I'm just a manager. You know Bernard no one could touch me for as long as God wouldn't allow it. You know don't you that death doesn't touch the children of God?" "Maybe so, but everybody dies." "No Bernard, Jesus said it, the ones who follow him will never die and they'll have the eternal life." "They still have to die first and he died himself on the cross." "Jesus never died either; remember he said I am with you until the end of ages." "Do you mean this was a hoax like many people seem to think?" "Not at all Bernard, but Jesus said it, that who ever follows him (the word of God) will never die and will have eternal life. He didn't lie. You're about to find out about this mystery. Jesus said in Matthew 13, 35 that he will reveal to his disciples things hidden since the beginning of the world. You see, as soon as my soul will leave my body it will be with God, which means there is no change at all, because it is already with God. For us humans, time could be short and could be long, but death has no time at all. So if there is no time between ten thousands years ago and now the answer is zero time. There is no time between your death (sort of speak) and your final judgement. So if you are with God on earth it means you're alive and you stay alive, but if you are dead meaning with sins on earth, you'll stay dead for ever and this is the word of God, which you can trust. Remember Jesus said that his Father was the God of the living and not the God of the sinners (the dead). Matthew 22, 32.

"I don't think anybody ever explained this mystery this way, not even Jesus." "I don't know about this Bernard, but I know for sure that

316

no one ever told me anything about this other than God Himself or one of his angels. I know it was revealed to me spiritually.

I know something else that Jesus said and I remember it is very important and I know it has something to do with me." "This would be something quite special, what is it?" "Jesus said in Matthew 13, 35: 'I will utter things hidden since the creation of the world.'

Jesus also said that others will come and do greater things he has done himself. See Matthew 17, 20. 'I tell you the truth, if you have faith as small as a mustard seed, you can say to this mountain, 'Move from here to there and it will move. Nothing will be impossible for you.'

See also John 14, 12. 'I tell you the truth, anyone who has faith in me will do what I have been doing. He will do even greater things than these.'

I don't pretend having done or doing greater things than Jesus has done, but I'm saying knowing things that I was never told by a human being or having read anywhere.

This last one is one of them and I got it from no one else than from God or from one of his angels."

"This is very special."

"I wrote a song that makes many people frowning.

I follow

Je suis in French which means I am.

Je suis also means; I follow.

It's called; I follow God which also means in French; I am God

I follow (am) Jesus of Nazareth, the one they have crucified.

I follow (am) the true prophet, who is telling us the truth.

I follow (am) the God of Israel the One Who created everything

I am one of his faithful sons; I follow all of his laws.

I will have to be careful, they going to put me in Jail.

For telling the truth I will be persecuted

Although Jesus predicted it to every one who follows him

We are like sheep in the field among wolves

I'll have to avoid like the pest the bad race of the devil
And to make it to the end I have to love with no end.
I won't never fear death, because I won't see death.
Because the One who has my soul already saved it from hell.
Be careful when you read, all the words that are written.
They can be deceitful the Lord said; 'don't be foul.'
Listen to Him, be ready his coming is very near
We don't know the time or the hour by Jesus we were told.

"It's true that it could be confusing, especially if one is not careful to what it is written." "It is true too that we have to be ready for the coming of the Lord, because it is written he would come like a thief. We sure need to understand the language and not be too quick to judge. I don't really like the fact the Lord is compared to a thief, I would have preferred something like; 'An unannounced boss who caught you with your pans down. I don't like Jesus to be compared to a thief at all, like you can read in Revelation. 3, 3, and Revelation 16, 15.

The one who is like a thief is no better than a thief and Jesus is too honest to be one of them.

"This is true; it is not the most flattering." "I think someone tried to discredit Jesus quite often. When he is undressed completely naked in front of his apostles at the last supper, see John 13, 4 and also when he was followed by a naked man in Mark 14, 52. Jesus is humble, but he is not a pervert. What a story like this has got to do in the Holy Bible anyway?

There is also the story about the disciple that Jesus loved as if he was the only one loved by Jesus or else make people believe Jesus had a man lover. See John 21, 7. What a shame to write such abomination in the Holy Book, but be sure of one thing, this was not written by Jesus' John. It was written by another John, a Jesus' enemy.

Peter didn't say that Jesus will come like a thief, but he said the day of the Lord will come like a thief, which is not quite the same thing. So yes, we have to be careful when we read, like Jesus said. See 2 Peter 3, 10 and Matthew 24, 15.

CHAPTER 14

$\mathcal{I}$ have to go Bernard and I'll see you before you leave tomorrow morning."

"Are you sleeping Danielle?" "Not anymore!" "Are you alright? You usually don't go to bed this early and leave your guests clean and dry in the lurch like you did tonight. You're not sick, are you?"

"I just have a huge headache, that all." "How come I'm under the impression you're hiding something from me?" "You know me, I don't like to complain, but it's just as if I lost all of my private life and I don't like what Janene has to go through now days either." "Things will never change between the two of you and I'm glad for it too. It will always be the same for both of you, isn't it? Always and forever, this is the story of your life." "She is more than a sister for me, you know this." "Don't you worry, she is strong and she will make it." "I know, but even so, it's not funny at all." "She'll be here in a few days and she'll be happy too. Do you want to talk to her too? I'll send her an Email right away." "We can't, the phone lines are cut off." "She can receive us on her laptop. Do you want to come up stairs and communicate with her by Email too and at the same time you can say good night to our protected guests." "It's true that I wasn't too courteous with them and I don't have any excuse." "I'm sure they can understand what we went through in the last few days. I got to tell you that I hired both of them to teach music and vocals to the children." "Do you want to form super stars among them now?" "No, I want to become a star myself, ha, ha. I want the children to develop their full potential and I also needed to find a way to keep these two busy." "That's a wonderful idea my love. You always develop the full potential of everything you undertake." "This could be one of my talents. Let's go wish them a good night first."

"How are things with you Charles?" "Everything is for the better Danielle and we cannot complain about anything. We had an excellent supper and we also have a sure job for at least a year. We cannot ask for more. It's almost as a secured job as priesthood and on top of everything, we have a ticket for the kingdom of heaven. All is well and ends well. Like I said we cannot ask for more."

"Do you know if Henri-Paul is sleeping or not Charles?" "I'm sure she's not, she just left me a few minutes ago." "Well, good night Charles and you give your first lesson tomorrow at ten and the children are anxious to start."

"Good night Charles and I hope you'll like your new job." "I will certainly give it my best shot."

Nock, nock, nock. "Come in, it's opened. James, it took you a long time." "Yes, but Danielle and I wanted to wish a good night to both of you. Did you prepare your course for tomorrow?" "I don't need to prepare anything; I've done this all my life." "The children will expect you for ten o'clock and don't forget they are very young for most of them." "I know, I'll start them slowly and I'll do it in a way it's going to be pleasant for them."

"Would this bother you to teach adults too?" "Not at all Danielle, but it would be best if it is separately from the kids. I don't want them to be disturbed or influenced by the adults." "I understand, so we'll make a course for adults too."

"Will you come too James?" "I'm not sure to always be able to attempt, but singing lessons couldn't hurt me." "You sing good enough, but you could use lessons on pronunciation."

"When did you hear him sing?" "Earlier this evening, when this job was offered to us. He sang a few of his compositions then, some very nice songs that gave me shivers all over." "I see; the room was quite cool." "Didn't you ever hear his songs Danielle?" "I did once, but I was not impressed at all."

"Must have been one of my first song or a song about a girl I met before her. Either way, I have never sung in front of her again and I choose my public since." "Bad critics can destroy great artists and some very good talents."

"I certainly didn't want to destroy his singing career." "He might not be a great singer, but I sincerely believe he's a great composer. We'll find out pretty soon, because Charles and I will put arrangements and harmony to his songs and record them and with his permission, we'll send them to recording companies, then we'll see what happens. I am sure we'll get good results." "What ever, I wish you good luck. Good night Henri-Paul!" "Good night Danielle!"

"Good night!" "Good night James!"

"She seems to think you are a Mozart." "She only thinks I'm a good song writer. Let her be and we'll see. I also think she knows a talent when she sees one. It must be day time at home now, let see if we can reach Janene."

"Hi beautiful, how are you managing in this shit over there? Here we had a very busy day, starting with some intruders who violated our property rights, but nothing very bad and we got rid of them fairly quick. The children enjoyed their ride on the boat and they too now would like to own an island. Every one of them can't wait to go fishing now. They will start music and singing lessons as early as tomorrow with Charles and Henri-Paul. Bernard and M. Charron will be there tomorrow night and if you get on right away with the funeral, you will be able to join us soon. We miss you terribly, so much that Danielle is not the same anymore. She is writing you too. Here she is. I love you with all my heart, James."

"Janene my true friend, this separation is breaking my heart and I feel sorry that you have to go through all this alone and without my help. I feel so useless over here. Please bury us very quickly and come here before I go crazy. Did you pick up a bit of our ashes? I think the public would appreciate it, but make sure the journalists and the police witness it. Be very careful and don't move alone among all of those wolves who are after us. James' mother must be totally devastated and so would be all her family. I hope we can bring them all over here one day on these islands which are very inviting. You know that there is always the risk to be betrayed by one of our family members. This is why we can only bring the ones who follow Jesus. All the others will have to face the tribulations, but this was their own choice. James, you and I have done everything we could to prevent them. Could you talk to my parents and my brother? I would like so much you were here with us right now. I'm leaving you with these words because I have too many tears in my eyes to keep writing and it's not the right time to sadden you with my sorrow. See you soon, Danielle."

This was something I didn't think of. I should have known those two were inseparable. One good thing is this is only for a few days; otherwise life would become unbearable. Although in moments like this I understand better their behaviour about the night we met and the following events. I could not separate them then no more than I can separate them today.

Janene's parents are still reluctant in receiving the word of God and so are a few of my sisters and my brother and yet the truth is so beautiful. My mom often says that a prophet is not welcome in his own family and neither is a Jesus' disciple. Some of them asked me to shake the dust off my feet and not to bother them anymore with my stories of the Bible and others simply asked me not to talk to them at all anymore. Others asked me to talk about anything but the word of God and about Jesus and this is why I had to turn to the chronicles in the paper to pass the messages which need to be passed.

It's pretty sad to have to risk my life and the lives of my close ones to do it. Fortunately, God gave me the means I need to protect most of them who help me with my ministry against my enemies.

I am aware that eight of my enemies died from heart attacks lately and one of them died assassinated. I know too that God is the Master of life and death. My greatest wish of course would be that all of my close ones would wake up in time. I must admit that it is very difficult to open the eyes of the ones who don't want to open them.

Jesus talked about it long before me and you can read it in Matthew 13, 15. 'For the heart of this people has become dull, with their ears they scarcely hear and they have close their eyes, otherwise they would see with their eyes and hear with their ears and understand with their heart and turn to God and I would heal them.'

This again is the word of God which says these things and the healing we talk about here is the healing of the lost soul, which allows me to say that I can heal the sick and I resurrect the dead. When a person listens to the word of God, this person receives the medicine and when it was accepted and it turns away from sins, that person is cured and resurrected from the dead and of course becomes a child of God. Jesus couldn't do it without risking his life and neither can I. It's really sad and strange that things are like that with all of the Christians and others who say they love God and yet they refuse to hear his word of God, the truth.

"Are you coming to bed sweetie? We'll probably get an answer when we get up in the morning. I think she's still in bed at this time." "I wish I could hear from her before going to bed." "It's only five o'clock over there, be reasonable and come to lie down for a while. Remember that the children too need you. They too have a hard time living without your smile and their mother." "Everything happened so fast, it's just like we were thrown in another world." "Be happy that we are in a better world for now, it's like paradise over here and this security is God's shield." "I know it, but I wish that all my family was here with us." "Do you want me to bring your parents here? I'm afraid we're going to run out of room for everybody." "It's so nice out here; they could even sleep outside under the skies in a tent or even on the boat." "This wouldn't be easy to wake them up when I want to take some of our guests out for fishing. What would you say if I get a hotel built near our airport for our guests in the future?" "You would do this for me?" "I would do anything that is honest for you sweetheart. A hotel is nothing at all if this could make you happy. We could never spend all of our money even if we try and neither could all of our next generations." "You are a love bug and you always find a solution for everything." "Good then, I'll get a hotel built, but it won't be easy to find some discreet workers." "I'm sure you'll find a way." "Are you coming to bed now? Let's go finish this discussion on the pillow."

The first thing the next morning I was at my computer and Danielle wasn't far behind me. There was no message from Janene yet. It was not easy for me to show a reassuring face at all, because I was quite worried myself.

"She must have left home without her laptop, there is no other explanation, I'm sure of this." "I hope you're right." "Bernard and Laurent will be there very soon and we'll find out what is going on, don't worry." "As long as nothing bad happened to her." "Don't say stupid things Danielle, nothing at all will happen to her." "How could you be so sure?" "Because, when I'm not there to take care of things myself, God does it for me, so there is nothing to fear." "I wish I could be as sure as you are." "What, don't you want to trust me anymore?" "Excuse me; I forgot that you know almost everything." "No problem darling, but believe me, everything will be fine. I'll bring the teachers fishing this morning, do you care joining us?" "I'll pass on this offer this time, I have nine hungry children who are demanding breakfast and four of them don't have their mother with them, remember?" "I better bring some cod and some mackerel for supper. Get me some fresh shrimps if you can." "I can't promise you anything, but l will certainly try." "You are a real gentleman, but don't you go risk your life to please me." "I got to get ready now and I want my breakfast before going out there. I go out again this afternoon with Charles and Henri-Paul; maybe you could join us then?" "Maybe, I'll see how things go. You don't need an answer right away, do you?" "No, there is no rush." "What do you want for breakfast?" "Just an egg and a couple of toasts!" "Have they been fishing before?" "I don't think so." "So you're going to have some training to do." "Certainly, but a person can catch quickly with that." "How far will you go?" "I don't think it will be necessary to go far away; I think there is all the fish we need near the islands just around here." "I'm sure the sea has a lot to give away." "The ground too, I will bring soon a big load of fruits and vegetables from our properties and all the material necessary to build a two hundred bedrooms hotel. I also plan to buy all the abandoned and fertile farms in Saskatchewan and make them produce to their full potential. This will give some work to hundreds of people and feed thousands others around the world." "Nobody could ever say you don't do your share." "Are you kidding me? People will say that I gave crumbs, scrap and bits for fiscal reasons." "I suppose it's natural for people to judge without really know what is going on." "It's mainly natural for people to cause trouble by any means they can. The opposition and the Bloc do everything they can to bring back to the country Omar Khadr I over heard on the news. They work like a devil in holy water for a presumed murderer and I just wonder if they would do as much for a presumed innocent man. People kind of forgot that Khadr is a member of Bin Laden clan who killed three thousand people in New York not this long ago. The opposition always like to contradict the government's actions and this is why I would give Harper one little piece of advice." "You are funny, what is that?" "He should propose the exact opposite of what he wants to pass, let the opposition oppose it and come back with what he wanted in the first place with the approval of all the opposition." "And you said you wouldn't be good in politics." "I've never said such a thing, but I wouldn't like to debate anything with a bunch of idiots who don't understand anything about the common sense, at least this is the impression I got from them. To tell you the truth, I think the opposition is useless and cost too much money now days with all the journalists who have their noses in everything and more aware of the loop holes than the opposition itself. Most of the time the opposition reacts to what the journalists found out anyway. Besides, they (the journalists) have the power to destroy any government. The country could save millions of dollars and probably get a better result. The government could work instead of arguing. I some times have questions about democracy.

Did you ever think what would happen if God Himself would run to be Prime Minister? I'm pretty sure He would be accused of being a dictator for one thing and that even if He wants the good of every one and He left the whole world free to do what he wants. I would be very surprised if He gets one per cent of the popular vote. The pope to me is a quack and he would have a better chance to win his seat. He's said to be God's representative on earth. My eye! Representatives of God on earth preach God's word and who could pretend to such a title anyway? I know I don't."

"Here come your fishermen, Marianna and Réal. I made you a little snack just in case you were slow coming back." "That's very nice of you darling and we should be back around noon."

"Are you guys ready for the big adventure? The sea is very calm and it should be very good for fishing." "We are ready alright, but we don't really know what to expect out of this. We trust you with our eyes closed, it worked out alright until now." "You have nothing to fear and besides, we're not going very far. Let's go, it's getting a bit late, but we should be able to catch a few of them anyway. Go ahead, get on board, I'm just behind you."

We tried around a few islands and there was nothing, but at the forth island it was completely different. We caught there two full wash tubs of cod and God knows this is not the nicest smell of all. These are no roses. Then, we went looking for another kind of fish. We caught a few of them that were unknown to me, but I anticipated finding out. Then we got on a bunch of mackerel that were biting like three of them on the same line. It was a bit too late though, it was already time to come back home. Although I took the time to set up a few lobster cages in the hope to catch a few shrimps for Danielle and Janene.

"Did you guys wonder why you are on early vacation?" "Yes and no, we know you don't do anything without a good reason."

"We know there must be a good reason to move us away like you did?" "You are right, someone tried to kill me and I had to move away with all my family and this very quickly. You're not bothered by it too much?" "On the contrary, it's rather pleasant, your problems put aside of course. There is no problem with your children either, they are ahead of the conventional classes anyway." "You will learn through the news soon or later that Danielle and I got killed the day before yesterday in an explosion and it is very important that this stays secret for some time anyway." "We understand the situation and you can count on us." "Just know that I appreciate your understanding and let me know if you miss anything while you're here with us." "Everything is fine for now." "You should write to your families and let them know that you had to go away with my children for their protection and that you are fine before they send a search call for you. Do they have a computer?" "Yes, we could just send them an Email." "We'll do that as soon as we get home. What do you think about fishing?" "I can understand that fishermen love it, but I prefer teaching and this far more." "Kids don't smell as bad as cod; luckily it doesn't taste as bad as it smells either.

I prefer pickerel and green bass myself. Perch is pretty good in the spring and in the winter also. Either way, I'll cook you a good fish supper that you yourselves caught today." "That sounds good."

Maybe I didn't let it see, but I was very anxious to see if there was an answer from Janene and the first thing I did when I got home is to go to my computer. Still no news!

Then I went down to see how the teachers and the children were doing with their music lessons.

"What a great idea this course is dad; there is nothing more fun than this in the world." "You love this, don't you Isabelle?" "Every

one of us loves it dad and Henri-Paul is so gentle, she's like an angel."
"I'm not too sure about that, not as much as you are anyway. How
is Charles with you?" "He's a little stricter, but he really knows his
stuff." "Anyone of you likes to sing?" "Only Jonathan doesn't like this
too much." "I'm pretty sure this is because he's the best one of all."
"What make you say this dad? He didn't even open his mouth." "This
is because he doesn't want to discourage all of you. I am sure he's got
a beautiful voice. He'll make a blast if he learns how to control it. So,
you're ready to continue tomorrow?" "Yes!"

"Yes!"

"Yes!"

"Yes!"

"Alright, then you have two hours to dine and relax and be ready
for your regular course at two o'clock."

"You have made a great impression on them, bravo. Henri-Paul,
I think you'll have to take Jonathan aside from the others to get any
results from him. He might be intimidated or else he's a bit afraid of
selfconscientiousness. I'll also need you to do me a favour." "Anything
you want boss." "My name is James." "What do you need James?" "I
need you to make a few phone calls for me to find Janene, she doesn't
answer my Emails." "Of course I can do this for you." "Let's go up
stairs in my office."

"Charles please, don't be shy and go have diner with the children,
would you? We'll be with you in a few minutes."

"Call at my mom first and tell her you want to talk to Janene,
saying you girls have been friends for a long time and you can't reach
her anymore."

"Hi, I'm I at Mrs. Prince of Trois-Rivières? May I speak to
Gertrude please?" "I'm Gertrude." "I'm looking for Janene, Danielle's
friend for a few days now and I can't find her; do you think you can
help me?" "Well, I don't know if I should give you any information."
"Alright, I understand, tell me only then if she's with you or not."
"She's not here."

"Here, this is the number for Janene's parents."

"Hi, may I speak to Janene please?" "Janene? Well, she's not here, she's busy preparing the funeral of her friends and we are leaving tonight for Trois-Rivières." "Thank you very much M. St-Louis. Have a good trip."

"She's not there either." "I'm pretty sure she is at my mom's place and the phone line must be tapped. Come on, let's go eat." "Yes, you make me hungry. If you let me do what I want, I'll make you happy." "Don't force me to be hard on you Henri-Paul, would you? I don't need to be tempted either little devil angel." "If only you could desire me as much as Samuel does. He's been eyeing me all morning." "Don't you dare, you would end up in an awkward situation, I promise you." "You can't blame me for desiring you, I love you." "If you weren't so selfish, you would understand and you wouldn't put me in such situation. I love my God and my wives way too much to let myself commit adultery and stop tormenting me." "But!" "There is no but and stop playing this comedy, I don't like it at all."

"Hey you guys, what took you so long?" "Yes, I had to ask Henri-Paul to make a few phone calls for me. I can't reach Janene." "Why are you so red?" "We had a little argument, that all." "What is the matter?" "This is between Henri-Paul and me, end of the discussion."

"There is no point getting mad; I have the right to know." "I know and I'm sorry, but if I have to tell you it is not a subject that is debatable in front of the children and our guests." "Forgive me; I had no way to know."

"How is the fish?" "This is very good and it's true, it doesn't taste what it smells."

"Is this you who fixed it Samuel? You made some very nice filets. You should teach the others how to do it." "But that's done dad, Jonathan and Rene helped me do it this time. Jeremy on the other hand preferred not to put dirt on his hands." "Well, I don't think we should force him to do things he hates to do and hopefully he'll never have to do it to survive."

"Next time you bring fish in I'll learn how and I'm sure I'll never forget." "Good for you my boy, I think you are courageous and you won't have to wait too long to learn it, because I'm going back fishing right after diner." "But dad, we already have a lot of fish." "And we are a lot of people around the table." "That is true too." "Come on kids now, you clear the table and you take care of the dishes. We are leaving right away."

"Come Charles, Henri-Paul and you too Danielle, I might have a surprise for you." "A surprise for me, I hope it's a good one." "Well, I hope you'll like it."

We got on board and I went right away to the cages I set up earlier.

"Let me bring that float up here." "What is it?" "Bring it up, you'll see." "Help me, it's too heavy. It's a cage and it's full of lobsters and shrimps. Was this the surprise you were talking about?" "What do you think? Not bad for a first catch, isn't it?" "There is enough for a few months in there." "Not if they all like it as much as you do. Just wait till Janene gets here and they'll disappear like ice under the sun. I got another cage a bit farther." "People could live out of fishing around here." "Certainly, I don't think this area was ever fish at all."

"Did you fish before Charles?" "I did a little bit when I was a kid, but that was while I was reading a book as well."

"What about you Henri-Paul, is this your first experience?" "It is my first experience, but I sure hope it is not the last one." "If you behave, you might have a chance to come back." "Ho, I see." "I hope you see right." "I think I understood."

"What are you guys talking about?" "Don't you worry Danielle, we understand each other."

"Here is the other cage. Do you want to bring it up Charles?" "I'll try, if you think I can do it James." "The ladies can help you if you need to. It will be easier if you put some gloves on." "I cannot move it." "What do you mean, that's only a cage?" "I'm telling you, I cannot move it." "What could that be? Let me try for minute. You're right, something is holding it." "But the boat is moving." "The boat is not moving. So there is something that is pulling on the cage." "I wonder what this could be, a shark maybe?" "If this is the case we're better say good bye to this cage. Help me Charles to tie up this rope to the hook; we'll see who is the strongest. Hold on to the bar; we're going to pull away from here a little bit." "If this is a shark I hope it's not as big as the one in Jaws." "Here Charles, take this knife and if he gives us trouble don't hesitate and cut this rope very quickly. I'm going towards this island. I think he let go now, I felt a release. Hurry up Charles, let's bring this cage up. There it is and the shark is just behind it. Ho the bad guy. No matter where I go there are thieves." "This cage is almost as full as the other one." "Don't you deprive yourselves from eating them; we know where to find them now. Let's go for the cod now, I don't like sharks this much."

"Yes, yes, I got a big one. Come and help me James, it's too heavy for me." "You go Charles, because I got one too." "You're right, that's a big one. I hope it's not a shark. What do I do if it's a shark James?" "Just wait to be sure and if this is one, you simply cut the line." "That's not a shark, but I don't know what it is." "Just hold it for now; I'll come to help you as soon as I got mine in.

Let me see that? Ho yes, that's a big cod. I was told that the smaller ones taste better, but I would like to find out for myself, so we'll try to get it out of there and inside this boat. Let me grab the tail grabber."

"Did you call me James?" "No Henri-Paul; unless you can bring this big fish out of the water by the tail."

"This is a very big one." "Elfish spirit! Come here you my big sucker; we'll have many plates out of you." "Hey, I'm the one who caught it." "You're absolutely right and if you keep it up, we'll fill this boat in no time at all. I would like to take a picture of you with your fish. This is at least a fifty ponds fish." "Hey, I got one too." "Can you handle it?" "No, I'm going to need help too." "Are you sure you're not just playing games?" "I'm not; this is a very heavy fish." "Can you go and help her Charles?" "I can't, I got one too." "Hold on, I'll come in a minute, because I want to take this picture first. There we are great fisherwoman."

"What do you have there Henri-Paul? Let me see this. Ha, ha, ha, ha, this is just a little minnow. Don't mock me; this one is just as big as the one Danielle caught, maybe even bigger. You guys are keeping me so busy that I cannot fish myself. Hold on, I'll get the tail grabber again."

"What about you Charles, can you take care of yours?" "I got a big one too." "We'll have to move away; it seems there are only big cod over here, and we'll have enough with those two. I'm the only one who doesn't have a big one; it's not really fair, is it?" "Come on James; you know the size is not very important." "I know, we're not really in competition, right?" "That's enough for me for today, do you want to come with me Henri-Paul. I'll show you around our cabin."

"Do you have it on top Charles?" "We're going to need your grabber here too. Hurry up my arms are getting sore." "Yes, that's a nice one too. Do you mind waiting a minutes girls, I would like to take a picture of the three of you with your big fish and my little one. Be careful down there; we're going to move away for a while."

"Did you ever get on a speed boat before Henri-Paul?" "No Danielle, I went directly from my poor family to the convent where I was promised to never go hungry. They kept their promise alright and I never lack food, but on the other hand I was thirsty for the truth and also my woman nature was in my way for saintliness. I spent a lot of time in the sin box to be reproved by my confessor." "That must have given him some ideas." "I don't know. I'll I know is that he knew how to make me feel real guilty." "Do you feel anything for Charles?" "Not at all, but I'm in love with another man who is unfortunately for me already married." "This is not right and you're bound to suffer and to make others suffer as well. The very first time I saw you I thought you would make James a good wife." "James already has a couple of good wives." "I just thought that if he ever wants another one you'd be the ideal wife for him." "I thank you for your appreciation. Too bad he doesn't think the same way." "The one you love must really be in love with his wife to refuse a pretty woman like you." "I don't think he's only faithful to his wife, he's also faithful to God." "Would you like to have some children?" "If my health allows me I would like to have at least half a dozen." "This is something that would please God." "Do you think it's wrong for me to desire the man I love?" "Not if this man is your husband." "I wish I could love without desiring, but this seems impossible to me." "Maybe you should talk to his wife; she might just be the sharing type. Janene and I are sharing James for more than seventeen years without any problem. In fact neither one of us would have wanted any other way." "You both are very lucky. This is almost a miracle, so much this is a rare thing." "What about you, do you think you could share your man?" "I don't know, maybe if this was the only way to get a part of him." "One thing I can tell you is that you cannot be possessive at all and neither jealous and you have to be happy for the other one when her turn to get him comes. This is something to think about, you know? You cannot be selfish to enter such a relationship. Don't forget also that loving someone is not enough, you have to be loved in return; otherwise you'd be much better to forget about him and the sooner the better." "That is easier said than done." "I know and I don't even want to think about it, because if I had to forget about James it would be impossible." "So we understand each other."

"I think we have enough Charles, what do you think?" "Ho, I'm ready to go home any time James." "Do you want to learn to make fillets too?" "I don't mind learning it, but I can't promise this would be my favourite activity." "One thing not to forget is to bury the waste parts to avoid predators to come around and the waste is very good for the garden also."

"Ho no, not all this fish to fix." "We'll help you Samuel if you bring us some pails and knifes." "That's impossible dad, they are almost as big as I am." "We were on top of a big cod bed and I wanted a few big ones to compare with the smaller ones. I was told before that the small ones taste better, but I wanted to find out for myself. I just know the taste is not the same for every one. I got to check my Emails first though."

"Are you coming with me Danielle?" "Yes I am. Go ahead, I'm following you." "There is nothing from Janene yet, but I got a message from Bernard."

"Hi James! We made it home just fine. Laurent is already set up in your place. Janene is not home and we don't know where she is. Raymond is fine and so is Pauline who can't wait to take her first flight. Everything goes well at the Hair blanket with a lot of large orders, especially for boots, hats and sleeping bags. There is a lot of work for me in the next few hours. Talk to you soon B."

"He wrote fifteen minutes ago. He might still be around."

"Hi Bernard, I'm happy you made a good trip, but I'm very worried for Janene. Please go look at her place for her laptop, because she doesn't answer my Emails. Take it with you and go at my mom to see if she's there or not. If she's not there send a search call right away. This is a priority J . . ." "You are worried too, aren't you?" "I'm sure she's fine. She might have got out of the house because of the journalists. She probably left in a hurry and forgot her laptop. The question is; where did she go?"

"Stay here, would you Danielle and let me know if you hear anything? I got to go help with the fish; otherwise they will never trust me again."

"I hope you kept some for me?" "Ho yes dad, you can have them all if you want; especially those three big ones." "We're going to fix them differently." "A fish is a fish dad, there are not hundreds ways to make filets." "We're going to make steaks, some filet mignons out of them." "You are funny. What is that?" "We're going to make steaks like we do with salmon. We have to clean them real good first and when the head is cut off, we'll cut the fish just like we cut slices in a loaf of bread. As far as the skin is concerned, we can take it off now or in our plate. Many people like it when it's well done. See, there is nothing to it." "It's so big we can almost feed three people with only one slice."

"Come James, we have news from Janene." "Are they good?" "Yes and no, Bernard found her in tears in the cabin by the river. There was a pack of journalists at the gate and she didn't even have a phone to call the police." "This bunch of wild beasts, we'll have to teach them some manners some day. They did the same thing to Princess Diana. I'm going to push things up to get a law passed against this sort of harassment. The right to the information should never supersede the right to privacy."

"Hold on sweetie, another two days and this nightmare will only be a bad memory. You didn't have a phone, but you could have used your laptop to ask for help." "I went out quickly thinking they could break the gate." "They all are on video and I'll bring them all to justice, this will teach them a lesson about private properties." "Is Bernard still close by?" "Yes he is."

"Bernard, I want you and Raymond to take charge of everything. Bring Janene back home, she'll be fine and safe there with Laurent in the house. Get the funerals organized for tomorrow and don't let Janene alone at all. If someone asks you questions, you tell them that you don't even have a bone to bury and you already have our ashes. Call all the news room you can and let them know about it, this way every one will know. Give a bed to everyone you can but not more. Janene had enough as it is.

Bring the video of those wild beasts to the cops and ask Laurent to file a formal complaint about them. They'll have all the proofs they need right there on this tape. Go see my mom and tell her not to worry about me; that God is always with me, but after the funerals. If this is not enough to calm her down, bring her here. Don't forget to put Raoul, Raymond and Michel in communication with me. Give them my Email address and tell them to be discreet about it. I would like you to have a private conversation with Danielle's parents as well. Find out at my notary public to see if someone in my family went there to request about my will. I'm curious to know who in my family can't wait for me to die. Pass me Janene again now."

"I'm here James." "I can't wait to hold you in my arms sweetie; if you knew just how much." "Me too my love, you know that you have never been so far from me." "I came here before, but this was to prepare for what we're going through right now and I wanted to do it without worrying you. It was just a short trip. Please don't dress in black tomorrow and smile to everybody you'll meet on your way telling them that I'm with God and God is with me and Danielle like He always has been. If they ask you to say something, don't forget to tell them that the chronicles will keep going around the world and only God could stop them. When you're at it tell them that we are always alive like Jesus told us and we have eternal life. I want to be informed of every detail. I'll stay near my computer until you're ready to leave. You might find that a bit odd, but I'm asking you to spy on my family, because I want to know who is on our side and who is not. The more we know about our enemy the stronger we get. I'll let you go now; you have a lot to do."

"Hi James, how are you? Here we are making great progress. First I need to know if it's safe for us to discuss our business on the Internet." "It's alright Raymond; I have a program which leaves no trail." "The formula is done now in one unit only for the public in general and I have the feeling you're going to get richer with this one too. Viagra will look pitiful beside our product." "Talking about getting richer, you better start making kids pretty soon, because you won't be able to spent all of your money yourself. You share on this formula will bring you a lot of money." "Don't you worry about my money, because just like you, I know a lot of poor people around the world. We cannot promote this formula in these part of the world; they have enough misery as it is." "How's work at the hospital?" "It's alright, but not fast enough to my liking." "I want to triple the manpower and if we have to, we'll call carpenters from France, because it's getting more and more urgent. Are you ready for your trip to Haiti?" "Yes, I'm scheduled to go in six days and I found a helper who would stay there ten days with my assistant. Everything is organized and he is very anxious to get on his first mission. This is what he wanted to do anyway and he never thought he would get paid for it. He's very happy and I think he will do a good job." "Did you warn him about corrupts?" "Yes, he is perfectly aware of the situation and besides, he won't be alone; my assistant has a lot of experiences now." "It is necessary that you meet with Raoul before you go, because I need two more cottages built at the teachers residence for Charles and Henri-Paul. They too are going to teach. I will send you the blue prints pretty soon. I also need to have a two hundred bedrooms hotel calculated by the usual architect firm. This is a four stories hotel I want to build on one of the islands here. I want it done within a year. I will check around here to see if I can get manpower. Everything will have to come by boat, so I'll have to get a wharf built first too. I got to let you go Raymond; Michel needs to talk to me." "Alright, I'll call you as soon as I have more news, Chow."

"How are you Boss?" "I'm fine my friend and how are you maintaining yourself?" "I'm fine and so are all the animals, although I wished I had your Email address to be able to help out Mrs. St Louis. I thought it would be best not to get the police involved in all of this and I knew she was alright in the cabin over here. I was ready to use the dogs if they had succeeded coming in." "If something like this happens again take with you the ones who look the most vicious to the gate, this will scare most of them away, I'm sure. I would like you to bath and shampoo Samuel's and Jonathan's favourite dogs to make the trip with Janene. I'm afraid they miss them a bit too much." "No problem boss, but I need to know when are they leaving?" "Today is Tuesday; get them ready for Thursday noon." "They will be ready boss and clean as a new penny dry and brushed." "This is all as far as I am concerned Michel; watch out for the journalists too when you go out." "Don't worry boss, I have everything I need here for at least a month anyway and I'm fine over here." "Go meet with M. Charron, he is a gentleman and offer him to play a chest game; he will enjoy this and he's a good friend for his friends." "I will do sir, nice talking to you."

"James, I'm I ever glad to know that you're doing well." "Raoul, hey champion, how are you doing with all this mess?" "I got to say that we are very busy and we are missing Jonathan a lot now." "I'm sure he misses his work a lot too. His moldings are a big part of his life. He's very passionate with them. How's work at the hospital?" "We are a bit slowed down by the electronics specialists. They seem to be a bit confused." "They will have to take their fingers off their noses, because I want to triple the personal right away. It's more in a rush now than I anticipated. If they can't do it we'll find another firm no matter what the cost is." "Alright, with this information I can go talk to them tomorrow morning." "Tomorrow it's the funerals too, were you told?" "I was wondering if I should go since, well you know." "It's very important that all of my friends are there to let my enemies think they got me." "I see." "A few hours of your time wouldn't change much on that project." "So you do want the whole crew to be there." "You got it. What would you say to go south for a whole year?" "Ho, I can't afford this James; I have a family, you know?" "Let's just say that you will bring your whole family too." "I think you have another big project ahead of us." "What about a two hundred bedrooms hotel? Would that interest you?" "I know you too well now not to think that you're really serious. I will have to discuss it with my wife and kids." "Think well and think quick, because this will be one year under the sun, room and board for you and all your family, free education for your children in a private school and one hundred thousands to come back home with and clear of all taxes." "You got my answer right now and this is yes. When are we leaving?" "As soon as the new hospital and the two cottages are done." "Which cottages?" "I need two more cottages built on my property near the other teacher's houses." "You're going to have a little village pretty soon over there." "From now on we'll call it the teachers' village." "This won't be easy, they already have made faces the last time." "I have the right to have as many residences as I have employees. This is the law and they cannot do anything against it. If they give you trouble, just tell them that my succession is ready to fight it in court if necessary. They'll understand that there is no point arguing this. If they ask you the names of the people who will live in them, you tell them they're teachers to come, but they need the housing first before they can be hired. We'll get their names to them as soon as possible. I'll send you the blue prints as soon as tomorrow maybe even today. I'll send you a design of the hotel I want as well. Retain the architect for this right away." "What are you going to do for the water?" "Same thing we did for the house, I'm sure to be able to find it and if not I'll find a way to change the salt water to drinking water." "Nothing stops you, is there?" "I think only God can." "I believe you and I think you became the most powerful man on the earth." "I only fulfil God's will and for the rest I'm powerless. I'm glad to be able to protect my brothers and sisters of the family of God. I got to let you go now; Bernard is trying to get in touch with me."

"I'm sending you the pictures you've asked me and I think this is the number eight wonder of the world. Take a look at this. Can you tell me approximately how much they worth?" "We're talking about many millions for each one of them and billions for the whole lot. The resorts builders make the prices go up and the government takes advantage of it. How many are there, did you count them?" "There are twenty-two." "We'll have to separate them in a strategic way to protect them all from intruders." "This is a good idea and I know you would do your best with this too." "Yes, I will make plans with it in the next few days. I just got a wonderful idea I think." "Ho, ho, this is another billion in spending. What is it James?"

"I was thinking about building a big cement wharf to receive all the material for the hotel, but now I think we should have a floating one, so we can move it from one island to another as we need to." "This is a great idea alright." "Get in touch with Bombardier as soon as you can, this is rush. If they cannot do it right away, we'll contact another builder. They might have a plant around here too, which would be a lot faster. It's got to be motorized and be three to five hundred feet long by eighty feet wide. Get some info about it and get back to me as soon as you can. It's got to have very solid guard's rails, because it will carry some ready-mix trucks, a crane and some other big machinery. The boat which will bring the construction material could maybe pull it all the way to here." "You could use this wharf to carry your material to the islands if you can buy it around there. This would be a lot faster." "You're right; this means I have to find someone to shop for me for the material around here. I got to go and I'll talk to you later, I need to talk to Raymond right away."

"Hi Raymond! I was wondering if you knew someone discreet who could perform a plastic surgery." "Of course I do, as long as he's got the right amount of money. What do you have in mind this time? Don't tell me that you want to change your pretty face. Your women might don't like this at all." "No Raymond, I was thinking more about Charles who needs to get busy. He will need this soon or later anyway. Get some information about it and get back to me, would you? We'll have to get those two some new identifications and this, the sooner the better." "I'll see what I can find." "If you can help Raoul about what concerns electronics at the hospital, do it, would you?" "Sure, I'll do my best." "You know that I want all doors to open with three different combinations, don't you? To open the doors one would need to have a card, a thump print and the right eye contact." "Are you sure you don't do too much?" "The lives of my spouses are more important than anything else Raymond." "Excuse me; this was a stupid question." "You're right, but I forgive you anyway. I got to go talk with Charles to see what he thinks of all this. Talk to you later." "Later James!"

"How are you Charles?" "I'm fine James, thank you." "I have a suggestion for you, but I want you to be free to decide what is best for you. You're old enough to decide for yourself. You know as well as I do that a picture of all four of us has circulated all around the world, don't you? You know too that if someone recognizes you this would be the end of us." "This is a sure thing." "What would say about a small plastic surgery to change the way you look?" "Do you mean I don't really look good?" "I didn't say you were looking bad, I said to change your look. That's not the same thing." "I know and I understood the first time." "If you would add to this a pair of no vision glasses, a moustache and new identifications you could even get priesthood somewhere." "Don't talk to me about priesthood anymore, would you? I accepted it, but this was the idea of my family at first." "I have known a bad priest when I was a child who lived through this too." "I don't mind, but this is something expensive." "Don't worry about that, I can afford it. I'll find out soon when we can go through with the operation and don't talk to anyone about this. It would be a very good test when you come back. Alright, you might have to go back with Bernard in a few days. If everything goes well you might be able to visit your family secretly. If your own mother doesn't recognize you no one will." "I'll see. This is not important to me." "You have to forgive your parents if you want to live a long life; you know this, don't you?" "Yes I know, but this is not easy." "Nobody says it is, but you ask God for help and you'll get it. You make me think of an important message from Jesus." "What is it?" "It's written in Matthew 23, 3. 'For they say things and don't do them." "You're right, Matthew 23 was always a burden to me and to tell you the truth I was ashamed of us priests, mainly when Jesus talked about the heavy burdens we lay on men's shoulders and that we don't touch with our finger. It's really true about what concerns the family. For years we forced men to procreate and us priest didn't get wet. At least this is what we say." "Do you know what Jesus did to a tree that was not producing?" "Yes, he cursed it." "This is not the version of Matthew. In Matthew 21, 20. 'The disciples asked: 'How did the fig tree whiter all at once?' In Mark 11, 21 it's totally different.

'Peter said to him; 'Rabbi, look; the fig tree which you <u>cursed</u> has withered.'

If you care about my opinion I would tell you that I doubt very much Jesus or Peter ever used the word curse." "It's true these are two very different versions of the same story." "Matthew was a Jesus' disciple, this I am sure of it." "Do you think Mark is an impostor?" "I just know he wasn't one of Jesus' apostles and I doubt very much he was one of his disciples as well. I should go back to my computer now, it's quite busy today. Bernard and Laurent had a good trip and Bernard and Janene should be here in a few days."

"You should take the time to come to eat anyway." "No darling, I'm sorry, but I have to be available to a lot of people over there. I'm sure you can find someone to bring it to me. I'm sorry and it's not because I don't want to eat with all of you, on the contrary." "I know; I saw for myself all the communications you have and I know how important it is. I hope it's not going to be like this all the time though." "If you don't mind I would like to take a day off with Janene and go out on the boat." "Why should this bother me? She's your wife just like me. Just don't leave the same day she gets here, that's all I ask." "You know very well I won't do something like that." "I just know you miss her a lot." "I miss you too when you're not by me." "I know darling, here you got another Email. It's Raymond."

"I found a surgeon James and he can operate as soon as Charles gets here and he will have nothing to fear. He can do the whole thing in two days and he only asks for ten thousands everything is included, but it will have to be straight cash. This is the only way to keep it secret." "I'm alright with this and so is Charles. He will return with Bernard and he will have to go directly from the plane to the clinic in the limousine, so no one can see him other than the surgeon. It's not the time to screw up our coverage." "I got you and I will advise him right away."

"James, the funerals are set for ten o'clock in the morning and the news is in every newspaper and on every radio station as well as all TV stations in the country. A formal complain is made against all the journalists involved at your gate and the police chief praised our action. How come the skunk didn't work? Do you have a limit for the five thousands you want to give away?" "I would say to limit you to the family and the closed and sincere friends." "What do you think of that?" "Does this include me?" "Yes, if you are a sincere friend." "It doesn't matter if this person is well off or not?" "You got it. It's going to be one of a kind funeral that people will talk about for a long time. The skunk didn't work because it was not activated." "I see. This could come up to many thousands dollars." "This is the key of its success. People will say that my inheritance was distributed to sincere people who love me for what I was instead of what I have. You will meet more liars that day than you will for the rest of your life and this includes your time inside. Did you install a large number of speakers? I expect a very large number of people. You will need many cameras too. I am extremely curious to see this mass of people. I'm going to try to get all this on satellite. Don't leave any priest or bishop pray on my coffin or I'll come to chase them away myself. Jesus told us to cast the demons, but he didn't tell us what kind of weapon to use against these animals, although, I think we can only chase them away with the word of God. Jesus himself had a hard time to get rid of the devil when he was tempted in the desert. Although, I have a hard time believing that Jesus let the devil carrying him around like the story tells. The word of God is really with you, isn't it? You talk about it every time you have an occasion." "When God is with you, his word is with you too. Keep me informed of every detail, I will stay available for you as much as I can. I'll even ask Danielle to replace me to give me a chance to sleep a bit. How is Janene doing?" "She went to bed, she is exhausted and she will need a lot of rest for tomorrow. I'm sure this is going to be a very hard day for her." "I would like you to ask for police protection for her and if they refuse you hire some bodyguards. I fear someone might try to kill her or harm her in some way. You can tell the chief too that you are sure the murderers will be at the ceremony tomorrow. Tell him to watch for the ones who want to talk without being invited to do so." "It is written in Matthew 23, 6: 'They love the place of honour at banquets and the chief seats in the assembly.'"

"I start believing you are more than a disciples, I think you are a seer." "This is the way they called the prophets in ancient times, but I tell you one more time, I'm only a Jesus' disciple. Could you find the fence we need here for the beach?" "It's already on the plane." "What about the weapons for the boat and for the plane?" "I was told it would be best to trade them for some already equipped." "Are you aware your work will become more and more dangerous?" "It is also more and more exciting." "Don't forget that among all of my staff you're the one who would be the most difficult to replace. You don't say anything." "I think everybody is replaceable, although I just wonder who could ever replace you." "I think you are handling things pretty good without me over there and all of you know my line of thoughts and I think you could continue my work." "We would be shortly out of ideas." "There are a few who are growing up behind me and they are not short of imagination." "You're taking about the young millionaire?" "Him and the master of the moldings! The others are pretty smart too. They're still young, but I'm sure Isabelle will do great things. I'll leave you now; I got to sleep a few hours, because I want to be awake when you'll need me the most."

"Did I sleep all of that time?" "Yes, you slept a whole five hours. I watched your Emails and there is nothing very important so far." "I'll turn the TV on to see if we have a good reception. The children are missing you, especially because you told them we were in vacation. They don't understand why you are isolating yourself like this. I tried to explain to them the best I could, but it's not the same thing as if you do it yourself." "I know and I hope everything will settle down after this bloody funeral. There is CBK; we should be able to see everything from here even better than if we were there in person." "What are you saying darling, we are there in person. After all we went through don't tell me we did all this for nothing." "I'm warning you sweetie; we're going to see some close ones cry out over us and this is not going to be easy. Raymond and Bernard will talk to them as soon as they can." "I know we had to do this even if it's very painful." "I should go eat something; there are two hours in waiting before the ceremony." "Do you want me to make you some crepes?" "This would be wonderful darling." "Are you coming down or you want me to bring them here to you?" "You could make them right here in my kitchen." "I prefer my own where I can find everything a lot easier. They will be ready in twenty minutes." "I'll be there just in time, unless something else comes up."

I then turned up the volume on the TV to listen to the news from Quebec.

"It will be in about two hours time that we'll have for you on this station, live from Trois-Rivières what seem to be the most famous funerals of the last century. Let's us remind you that a few days ago one of the richest man in the world, M. James Prince and his wife Danielle, a well known and most popular nurse in Trois-Rivières were most likely murdered in their own town. The investigation is not making much headway, although according to some sure information the bomb would have been deposit on the crime scene by a priest named Charles Joseph Grégoire and his accomplice, Sister Henri-Paul Toupin. We did receive hundred of calls from people saying this is ridicules and impossible. Although, many clues seem to contradict those testimonies! It won't be easy to clear this out, because there is absolutely nothing left from anybody at the scene nor a simple trace of the building where the crime took place. Many experts are saying this could be the perfect crime. According to many members of the church it would be best to wait until the investigation is completed before speculating on such a serious matter. The bishop of the diocese of Sherbrooke, Mgr Gomez thinks this could be actions from a new religion where the main goal is to bring as many people as possible in a suicidal mission with you when you die. He said that we see this mostly in the Middle-East, but we saw it lately in USA and in Canada as well. He said also to remember unfortunately the murder suicides we saw in our schools and there are more and more of those around the world. So we are inviting you to watch on our station this special event from nine forty-five. That's all for now ladies and gentlemen and be there for our next broadcast."

I'll show him a new religion, although this makes sense in a way what he's saying.

Of course, he'll do everything he can to create a diversion. Is it possible that such of diabolic religion exist? This wouldn't be from Judas, because he killed himself, but he didn't kill anybody else with him.

"Here I am, are they ready?" "Everything is ready; I'm just finishing the last one right now." "It seems that we'll have the whole show of the funerals on TV. It's not impossible that we see Janene before she comes here, you know?" "You better pray that nothing bad happens to her." "I never cease praying darling; I am in conversation almost continually with God. Maybe I should let Him take care of others too." "You seem to be at peace with what concerns Janene." "I took all the precautions I could and the rest is in the hands of God precisely. Your crepes are very good darling, but I'm full now. Are you coming to watch the show with me?" "Some of it, but I don't think I can watch to the end. This was a long day for me." "I see; you don't want to watch people bury you alive." "There is a little bit of that I guess, not too many people can see others burying you." "This is going to begin pretty soon, are you coming?" "Yes, I'm following you." "Come and give me a kiss. What would you say if we stay here a couple of months longer than we anticipated?" "The children seem to like it here. You usually have a reason for everything, what is this one?" "I would like to stay here until the hospital is completed and ready to receive patients. This would be safer for you and for Janene and I wouldn't mind to be here until the work of the hotel is well on its way before we leave." "Those seem to be reasonable reasons." "Is this mean you agree?" "Yes, I think vacations will be good for me too." "I got to go to Israel pretty soon; would you like to come with me?" "Why Israel? Do you want to make a pilgrimage?" "No, I leave this to the gentiles. I want to meet with their Prime Minister for business." "Let me guess, you want to rebuild the temple?" "No sweetie, Jews have to do that, I just want to bring in my financial contribution." "And God will give it back to you at the centuple." "When I get there I won't need anything anymore. It's starting now."

CHAPTER 15

"Good morning ladies and gentlemen. Welcome to our special report. It seems there are already thousands of people on the ground. We cannot see the end of the crowd. We have many reporters on the site and we'll let you hear some of their reports from people attending this ceremony."

"Can you hear me Julien Masseau?" "Yes, yes, I can hear you well." "Did you collect any testimonies from people attending this ceremony?" "Up till now people are very indignant that someone could kill such a generous couple."

"Excuse me sir, sir could you give me a few commentaries please?" "All I can say is this is very sad, apparently he was the writer of the chronicles about the messages of Jesus in the newspaper. That must be the reason he was killed. He himself was saying that the truth was not welcome in this world and this is the same reason our master was killed as well." "Who are you talking about when you're talking about the master?" "Don't you know that Jesus is our master?" "Who do you think did such an ugly thing?" "Every single person who wished his death is responsible for this crime sir. I got to go now." "Thank you sir, thank you for this testimony! This was very interesting"

"So there you are Marie-Claude, this is pretty well every one's opinion around here." "We'll go now on Mario's side for more testimonies."

"Can you hear me Mario?" "I can hear you very well Marie-Claude. This is a huge crowd. Did anybody have estimated the size of this one? There are many thousands people here today." "Did you collect any testimonies?" "Many people don't believe that such a horrible crime couldn't have been committed by a priest and a nun. On the other hand some people heard Father Charles Gregoire preach in church last week for the elimination of this writer in the newspaper. They say he wanted to protect his church. Opinions are different from one another." "Thanks Mario! We're going now in the center part of this ceremony where we're going to hear testimonies from people close to the deceases. Jérôme is there at this time."

"Are you there Jérôme? "Yes, I'm here Marie-Claude, but I can't talk right now, because one person very close to M. Prince is about to speak. I was right, there he is. We listen to him now."

"Good morning, good morning ladies and gentlemen. I'm not a great speaker. I'm not used to speak in public at all, but I'm going to tell you a few words about my boss and friend that is M. James Prince. He is a man who gave me one of the best jobs in the world when I was just out of jail. I was naked as a worm and he made me a millionaire. He introduced me to God when I was totally lost. In fact he got me out of hell. Just before he was killed, sort of speak; he made me understand a mystery kept secret since the beginning of the world. Hold on, because this could shock many of you today. I'm talking about the mystery of eternal life. How come people who follow Jesus will never die? John 8, 52. We all know that his disciples died long time ago and Jesus himself died on the cross. This is because between the death of someone and his judgement there is no time for this person, for that soul. One thousand, ten thousands years this is a long time for us, but for the one whose soul was taken away there is no time anymore. Zero equal nothing. This is why God's children, the ones who follow God's law like Jesus asked us to do will never die, so I can say with certainty today in front of you all that James and Danielle are still alive. Not once in seventeen years I've known him I have seen him doing something bad or wrong. I saw him doing good to thousands of people and it's not over yet. I'm asking all of James' sincere friends, rich or poor and all his relatives to come and sign the condolences book right after this ceremony. One big surprise from James is awaiting you. Thank you all for listening to me. I will now pass the microphone to my friend, Janene St Louis, a faithful spouse of late James Prince."

"People are whispering in the crowd Marie-Claude. It is possible that a lot of them didn't know that M. Prince had two wives? I got to say that he could afford to take care of them both. Now, the very pretty lady will talk to the crowd. Strange thing, she's not dressed in black, on the contrary, we can almost say that she is dressed to celebrate Easter."

"Good morning! Firstly, I want to thank you for coming in such a big number. There is so much to say that it's hard to know where to start. James is a husband like we could wish to our best friend and this is what I did eighteen years ago and since my best friend wished me the same thing, she wanted the same happiness for me. If all the women in the world were as lucky as Danielle and I have been, many lawyers would be bored to death and would find a different job. James has been for me, you cannot be more wonderful and Danielle the very best friend you can have. None is more sincere than he is, none is more generous than he is, none is more loving than he is, none is a better father than he is, there is nobody more courteous than he is. Many will tell you that there is no one smarter than he is. And I could go on and on for a long time, but I don't want to bore you with this; funerals are boring enough as it is. Don't you waste your time and energy praying for them. As Bernard said it so well, they have already been through their judgement and they are comfortably sitting down near God as I speak and probably watching what we're doing right now. I have never seen him doing anything bad either and this is the reason someone wanted to eliminate him. The devil couldn't win him on his side. Just remember the temptation of Jesus, the devil did everything he could to win Jesus over and trust me on this one, he wished he could do it before Jesus instructed his disciples, you know?" 'Throw yourself down the temple.' He said. James has started a ministry with his chronicles to make the truth known around the world and take my word for it; this ministry didn't ended with him, on the contrary. It will go on and this twice as fast as it was. If they try to kill it again we will double it again and what ever you do, you the ones responsible for this crime; there will always be someone else to continue his work. This is a work that will end with the next coming of Jesus. May God be with you, who ever loves Him with all of your heart!"

"M Sinclair, there is a man here who would like to address the public." "Ho yea and what's his name?" "He is the bishop of the diocese of Sherbrooke, Mgr Gomez." "I'm sorry but these are the funerals of the disciples of Jesus and none of the church leaders have anything in common with the people we are burying here today, especially not about the word of God." "I don't understand, he is a holy man."

"Who said this, Jesus maybe?" "These man are replacing God on earth, they have received the holy sacrament." "The ones who abused the children too! The ones who leaded the crusades and the inquisitions too! The ones who are homosexuals and commit those abominations too! The ones who accused people like James of witchcraft and condemned them to be burnt alive at the stake too! The ones who did everything in their power to get Louis Riel condemned to death too. The ones who approved the killings by Hitler of six millions Jews too! Do you want me to keep going?" "No thanks, that's enough." "Jesus said there was only one who was good and he wasn't talking about himself, but about his Father in heaven. Go read Matthew 19, 17 and open your eyes, would you?"

"Good morning Bernard!" "M. Courrois, what a pleasure to see you here. How are you?" "I am very well Bernard." "And how is your wife doing?" "She is in seventh heaven since, (pause) you know." "I am happy for both of you and I'm very glad that you came here this morning." "Do you think I could speak a word to the crowd? I want to reassure them about the chronicles in the paper." "Of course you can. Come with me, I will introduce you to the people."

"Excuse me. Ladies and gentlemen. There is a very close friend of James here who would like to tell you a few words of a major importance. He is the general director of the Newspaper and responsible for the supervision of the chronicles concerning the Jesus' disciples. Please pay attention to what he has to say."

"M. Courrois, the tribune is all yours."

"Good morning ladies and gentlemen. I won't be long, because I don't like long speeches either. The very first thing I got to say is the chronicles will continue just as usual, but before I go any farther, I want to say a few words about M. James Prince. He is a man who saved my life no later than last week. He also made a miracle happened inside my marriage, something my wife could tell you a lot more than I could. He is a man that with the help of his writing contributed to double our turnover in a very short time and his writing is in demand in fifty-three countries as I speak and growing. There are right now more than ten thousands Emails from people who want answers. That doesn't include the thousands of letters we receive every day. There is only one explanation to all of this and this is that people are thirsty for the truth and I'm one of them. I've learned more from him in a few months that I have learned in all of my life before him. This is not little to say. How could I let down so many people who want to know? So we're going to publish from now on instead than once a week, it will be once a day. I hope this way I will be able to catch up with answers that people are waiting for. If I have to risk my life for the will of God to be fulfiled, so be it. We'll simply reinforce the security for our building, but nothing will stop us. I can tell you that in the last news, the police is on the tracks of the murderers and this is only a question of few days and maybe a few hours before the guilty individuals are under arrest. Someone told me a few minutes ago that one of these monsters is here in this crowd. There is one more thing very important I have to tell you and this is that James gave all his income from the paper to some charities around the world. This will continue for as long as his succession won't advise me otherwise. That's all I had to say, thank you very much."

He was applauded for more than ten minutes while the cameras were scrutinizing the whole crowd.

"Look here on the left Danielle, these two men seem to be much in a hurry to get out of the crowd as if they were fleeing something or somebody." "You're right, but this is a church man, he's got a long white dress." "I just wonder what kind of bug has bitten them." "Maybe they need the washrooms." "According to the signs the washrooms are in the other direction. It's kind of strange that they hurry to get out of the crowd this way when everybody else is pushing the other way towards the center of the ceremony." "Do you know what James; I think we just saw the face of our killer?" "You might just be right; I'll mention it to Bernard in our next conversation. I think they'll be talking again soon."

"Are you there Marie-Claude? Have you ever witnessed such a spectacular event?" "Never in my short career have I seen such a thing. It's a sea of people and it goes farther than my eyes can see." "I think we're going to see M. Prince's mother now, I see her coming up on the stage as I speak to you. Let's listen to her."

"I would like to speak to the murderer of my son. The first thing I want to say is that you have eliminated from the earth the best man the world has known since the coming of Jesus and I think he was married to the best woman of all. Although, I want you to know that I forgive you your crime and if I can forgive you, God can too, but please turn away from your sins and turn to God. He is merciful and nothing but goodness. He can get you out of this mess if you want to. Either you know it or not, nothing is impossible to God except doing something wrong. With all of my heart I ask you to repent and give yourself up to the authorities before you do something worst yet. I'm holding in my hand here a little jar that is holding the presumed ashes of my son and those of his loved wife, because no one can tell for sure where they are. He told me one day that he wanted his ashes thrown in a lake where there is pickerel, his favourite fish. If Janene agrees this is what I'll do. I want to thank every one for coming here this morning and remember the first God's commandment. If you don't know what it is you can find it in Exodus 20 of the Bible. Don't you make an idol out of James, God wouldn't like that and neither would James. Thank you for your attention."

One more time applause were coming from every where. I recognized the one who when I was a kid let in our house my number one enemy, so he could warm up his hands when all the bugger was thinking about was to break my face. I have to say that at this moment I wondered on which side she was. She asked him then what was the reason he wanted to beat me all the time for and he told her that it was because I knew how to fight. He said it was nice to get some competition. Too bad there was no boxing ring back then in our village. Like many of my enemies he died young even though I never cursed any of them and without me lifting the little finger. Was this because they were my enemies? I cannot tell, but I found that pretty strange though.

"The last word is yours Marie-Claude. I think the ceremony is getting close to the end." "Thank you Jérôme and you're right people start going away on the ground." "Does anyone know approximately how many people were here today?" "According to my experience there were here at least twenty thousands people, which is I believe a record for a funeral in Canada. We'll have to see." "Just wait a minute Marie-Claude, there is something else going on towards the center. M. Sinclair who is the right arm of M. Prince mentioned right from the beginning of the ceremony a surprise for the relatives and close friends of the inventor. I'm curious to see what that is." "Don't forget to let us know if you find out anything Jérôme." "I am on my way over there Marie-Claude. There we are, I can see some people coming out of there with a smile on their faces, which is very odd just after a funeral."

"Hi Mrs. Can you tell me what is going on in there?" "No sir, I would prefer not to say a word about it." "Thank you just the same madam."

"Hello, Hello sir. Sir, could you tell me what is going on in there, please?" "Good morning, what do you want?" "I just want to know what is going on in there." "I only signed the condolences book and I received five thousands dollars. I always knew that M. Prince was a generous man, but this is beyond me." "Do you know why you received this money?" "It seems it's just because I am his friend and I came to the funerals." "Do you think I could get this amount too if I go in there?" "Maybe, if you can prove you are his friend, but I doubt it." "Why?" "Are you one of these people who forced the gate of his friend M. Charron?" "I didn't force the gate, but I was there with the others." "I wouldn't even try if I was you, they have everything on camera and I'm sure they have your face on it too." "To bad, I could have used some of this money." "Personally I'm very happy to be his friend and this money has nothing to do with it. He is the best man I happen to know in my life." "Thank you sir, do you mind telling me your name?" "My name is Michel Larivière." "What are you doing in life?" "I work for M. Prince like one hundred and fifty thousands other people in the world." "Aren't you lucky?" "Yes, that he is my friend."

"There we are Marie-Claude, now we know. It seems that all the relatives and close friends of M. Prince received one part of their inheritance simply for coming to the funerals.

I think it's a total new idea, because I never heard of such a thing before. I just wonder how many people will get this." "Maybe we'll know and yet maybe not, it's private matter really." "That's it for me Marie-Claude. I'm going to pack it up now, see you next time." "Thanks Jérôme. It was nice working with you again."

"There we are ladies and gentlemen; we are at the end of this report. I'm Marie-Claude Boisvert for CBK and I wish you a very good day and see you next time."

"So sweetie, we are now in the people forgotten file and frankly I don't think this is too bad of an idea." "You really think they're going to forget us this quick?" "Darling, this is what happens to people who disappeared. We remember them some time at their birth anniversary or at their death anniversary." "I wish we could inform my parents of our condition as soon as we can." "Bernard will take care of that today before they go back home." "I wish they could come spend some times here with us." "Someone would have to sleep on the boat, we don't have anymore unused bed right now." "They could take our bedroom and we can take the boat." "I'm not sure I like the waterbed this much. I will send an Email to Bernard right away so he can make them the offer before they leave for the North. I wish I could offer the same thing to Janene's parents, but I cannot trust her mother at all and there is no way we can trust her with a secret either. I'm sure Janene would agree with me too. Bernard has to work for some hours yet." "This burial will cost you a few millions." "Maybe, but I think it's worth it." "Do you think they'll find the guilty party?" "I'm sure of it and this won't take long either. I'm under the impression he will celebrate his last mass this coming Sunday. We'll put the police chief on his tracks and maybe it's already done. I'll send an Email to Bernard right away."

"Hi Bernard. I need you to offer Danielle's parents a trip over here if they want to. Here is the note that Roger will put in the collecting plate this coming Sunday. Here it is; 'This was an act from God my eye. We know who killed M. and Mrs. Prince, because father Charles Gregoire and Sister Henri-Paul Toupin spoke out before they disappeared. You only have one way out to save your soul and this is to give yourself up to the justice department to answer for your actions. It's best to pay our debt in this world, because the punishment is a lot shorter. From someone who wishes you well.'

"You'll have to tell the police chief that if he wants to know the identity of our killer he should go to the mass of the bishop and to search his quarters to find the dangerous explosives bombs that he's got made. Don't forget to warn him about the sun and any sources of dry heat otherwise I won't give much for his life. Get back to me as soon as possible." "Hi James, I got your message alright. We are up to 1.2 millions now in donations, so tell me what to do." "Make it to two millions and then start questioning a bit more about their sincerity by asking them where they've met me. Remember that I surely have more enemies than friends." "Alright and I'll ask Janene to help me identify them as well." "Good idea, she got a good judgement too." "Don't you ever forget what Jesus said on the subject in Matthew 24, 9 and Matthew 9, 22. 'You will be hated by all and by all nations because of my name.' Jesus' name means: The word of God.

This was a very long day for Janene and Bernard and for every one else who assisted them with this lazy job. All my employees from the construction and the Hair Blanket had a hard time believing in this unexpected bonus. I supposed that many of them wish I die more often.

"It's finally over James and you have given away 2.5 millions. I wonder if you knew you had so many good friends. Many of them came from far away and they never thought they will get something like this when they said being your friend. Some of them simply refused the money saying this was not the reason they came here for and they asked to give the money to charities. I suggested they do it themselves, but they said not knowing any. I think they were twenty of them. When we were done I could talk to the police chief and he appreciated our help in his investigation. He assured me that he will be at the next bishop mass and he will be in his uniform as well and siting down on the first roll. He said the house on St Euchetache was burnt to the ground and that it was from criminal activities. I checked things out with the Notary Public and he said two people came to require about your will. These were your brother and one of your sisters.

He doesn't know which one it was. I suspect they will come to claim the five thousands any minute now. You let me know what I should do in this case." "You know the conditions Bernard to be illegible for the money. If they were there they would have known.

It's just too bad for them, but it's got to be fair for everybody." "The Notary himself told me he wished he could have come, but too many obligations prevented him to do so and he wish to be able to sign the condolences book." "Alright then, you make sure he gets the money and his secretary too. I know they are friends of mine and sincere as well. I'll get in touch with him a bit later. I got to go, Raymond is contacting me now. Bring Janene over here like yesterday. What did Danielle's parents say?" "They said to be too sad to make any trip right now. I think Janene is talking to them as we speak. They'll have a hard time believing you are still alive." "I got to go, talk to you soon!"

"Yes Raymond, do you have something new?" "Yes James, the president of the electronic firm assured me full collaboration and he said the whole project will be terminated in two months at the latest. We had to offer more money to the plumbers and to the carpenters, but we doubled our workforce now. Work should be all done in approximately seven weeks." "I would like to make an offer on the property on St-Euchetache; I think that would be the perfect place to build a rest centre for paralytics. This is a big lot and not too far from our hospital. What do you think of that?" "You're right; this would be the ideal place if we can get it." "I leave this into your hands; I know you'll do your best."

I couldn't wait to hold Janene in my arms again. I had the feeling I will be able to rest in peace for a while and this was normal, because in principal, I just got buried. But life is never as simple as we wish for. One of the individuals who tried to rob my house and hold Laurent hostage recognized my face on the television and called the authorities. Fortunately Bernard was there on the site when the police came over to check this out.

They came down by helicopter on our airport run and Bernard went to meet them. During this time myself, Danielle, Henri-Paul and Charles jumped on the boat and we did nothing less then flee the site after preparing the children to morn our death. A large part of our destiny was within their hands. We prayed for their first comedy act to be the best one of their young lives. Danielle's parents and Janene were excellent as film producers. What ever happened, it worked. The police officers left satisfied with Bernard's explanation. Although; I was ready to buy their silence if I had to. Fortunately I didn't have to and I sent an offer of one billion dollars for the twenty-one neighbouring islands instead.

Roger and the Trois-Rivières police chief were at the bishop last celebrated mass, which ended up in a drama for a lot of people. Roger sent me the recording of Mgr. Gomez's last sermon. Here it is:

'My dear brothers and sisters. I will talk to you today about the power of God on earth. For since our holy church and its holy teaching were founded many years ago; there were people who tried to destroy it, but it is written that the gates of Hades will not overpower it. All the scientists of the world to this very day cannot explain what happened in a garage in Trois-Rivières this week. I can assure you that when God hit something with his mighty arm, there is nothing left. Sodom and Gomorrah are good proofs of this. I am sorry to inform you that one of our brothers and one of are sisters were sacrificed in this operation of the Holy Ghost. May God have their souls! Pray for them dear brothers. Pray and give generously, so our church continues to grow and to save lost souls around the world. This is my wish for all. May God bless you all.'

Just at the end of his speech three man passed around the silver plates collecting the money and the little envelop was deposited as well on my demand. Then this envelop addressed to the bishop was given to him. After taking a look at its content the bishop retrieved himself behind the curtain and less than a minute later every one could hear the blast. The man shot himself in the head. I personally think it's a miracle he didn't blow up the whole church when I think at the religion he was talking about earlier.

The police chief went to look quickly to what had happened and found the dead man lying in his blood on the floor holding a couple of notes in his hand. Then the respectful officer told the whole assembly that the service was over for the day and called for the coronary to come over. Then with some officers of the town he searched the house of the bishop and he found three more stainless steel little batteries and a note saying that my friend Courrois' newspaper building was another target and so was my house in Trois-Rivières. Then I realized that my little note had saved the life of many people. There were although many great questions without answers. How many accomplices were involved in this plot? Who else would be involved in this terrible conspiracy? Would I one day know the end of this threat for my family and myself? Was that the plan of only one man or a plan of a whole organization? The police had to investigate and so did I.

According to what Laurent is saying, this bomb is too expensive for one man only; especially a member of the church. So I will have to look and be shopping above the head of this bishop. I have to find the head of the beast and if this is possible, put it down before the beast put me down. My strength and my best weapon against this beast are no doubt the word of God, the very strong double edges sword. They don't really have anything against me, but against the word of God which condemns them. It is true that the word of God slices like a sharp sword. I wanted though to take a few days off all of this and go on the boat with Janene. She needed this and so did I.

Danielle was very happy with the visit of her parents and them even happier to find their daughter well and alive. Bernard had to go on many trips and Pauline was very happy to look at their future together. Raymond had more than enough with the hospital and all of his missions around the world. Samuel and Jonathan were very glad to get their dogs back. All the children are very pleased with their singing and music lessons. Charles should join us within a few days as a bran new man. Raoul and his family are on top of the world with the sonny country and the new project to build the hotel. My friend Jean Courrois is glad that I increased the security of the newspaper building and that he can count on a steady surveillance of his house. Michel said he will be happy for as long a he can keep his job. Roger is doing pretty well with all the investigations that I supply him with. He has been extremely important to us with the last investigation he was on when he found out who were making those very dangerous bombs. He thought the Cardinal was going to faint when he got out of his pocket a little stainless steel battery during a conversation about the suicide of Mgr Gomez. It was obvious to him that this man (the Cardinal) was involved in this crime too. The rest was quite easy. Although, Roger added a famous phrase from Jesus before the end of his conversation with the Cardinal. 'It would have been good for that man if he had not been born.'

This could fit a lot of people too, because Jesus also said that many are called, but few are chosen." "Too bad, because Jesus gave himself body and soul for three year without being able to rest his head to make the truth (the word of God) known to the world, this world that keeps crucifying him. In his days there were a lot of poor and people ignorant of the truth, today there are a lot of people at ease and rich who refuse the same truth. Why so many people pretending to love God are following his enemy instead. This is beyond me.

Laurent is thinking about one companion for himself and maybe two. When Charles came back nobody could recognize him. A very small operation inside his mouth and no one could recognize his voice either. He explained to the kids that he wanted a new look. I will finance him in his new career as a singer and maybe publish about fifty songs of mine that I'm sure will go a long way.

When Janene and I returned we were surprised by the children with a song they composed themselves and supervised by Henri-Paul and Charles. The song is called: My Parents.

> For you mommy, for you daddy
> We like to sing as you can see
> Because you do take care of me
> We want to sing this melody
> You watch for us all day and night

That's why we must do something right.
I know your love is pure as a dove
For your children and for our moms.

We love you much for what you do
And we are touched each time by you
This house is full of love each day
It's wonderful we like to say.

For you daddy, for you mommy
We will all sing, we will all pray
To keep you in with us always
You love your kin, we love yours ways.

Long live our dad, that's what we wish
We will be glad, we will be swish
Be there for moms, be there for us
Never be gone, be there you must.

We couldn't stop applauding them and let me tell you that it is in moments like this I realize the whole thing was worth it. Is there any use to say they brought tears of joy to my eyes?

"You know children, I made a song too lately and if you care to listen to it, I'll sing it for you." "But dad, you're not singing very well." "Maybe so, but you know what, I like to sing too and you should give me the chance to do it when I have an occasion like now. My song only last like three and a half minutes this shouldn't be that much of a sacrifice for you to listen to it."

"Do you know kids that your father composes some very nice songs? I can't wait to hear it myself, you know?" "If Henri-Paul says so it's because it's true, she knows the music and everything about singing." 👍

"Go ahead daddy sing it." "Well I'm not too sure I want to sing anymore. I'm a bit embarrassed, you know?" "Ho, come on dad, if you want we'll only listen to the words." "Well, in this case I don't risk much, do I? I called it: When Did You Last Dance With Me?"

When did we dance one night?
When were we together?
I'm sorry, but I can't remember
If I'm wrong or right, far away this memory
When did you last have a dance with me?

Remember how good it was.
Happiness to us it caused
It was great to hold you close to me
Just remember the night.
Where I held you so tight.
Someone else then took you away from me.

I was sadden by the fact
Way from me you had to act
I was hurt a long time for that
I wanted to come back
Ask you no matter what
When did you last have a dance with me?

Would you both dance tonight?
Can I hold you this tight?
To see if you can raise my heartbeat
Like you did the first night.
When I held you so tight.
And I could never return to my seat.

When did we dance one night?
When were we together?
I'm sorry, but I can't remember
If I'm wrong or right
Far away this memory
When did you last have a dance with me?
When did you last have a dance with me?

"When did you learn to sing like this dad?" "Since I exchanged singing lessons for dancing lessons with Henri-Paul. She really knows what she's doing in this field."

"But dad, you are unrecognizable."

"It hasn't been this long since we danced, has it?." "It seems to me like an eternity. Since when are you talking to me in plural?" "Since the two of you are in my life." "Nobody ever took us away from you." "What about your work?" "Darling, you say in your song being hurt and gone away from us, I would say this is not true." "Yes, but darling, I had to finish this song some how. Would you like to dance with me now?" "I cannot say no to this. That's a nice song anyway James." "Thanks sweetie! It's not my best one, but I like it anyway, mainly because it ties me to you a little more. Thanks Danielle!" "I'm the one who says thank you darling."

"Does my beautiful lady want to dance with me?" "I would have to be real sick to say no to such an offer."

"Maestro, play me a mambo for the pretty lady please?" "I'm so happy to be here with you all and I couldn't imagine my life without you. Only two days away and it was hell." "You have to forget this nightmare now sweetie, I'm sure you won't have to bury me twice. If you allow me; I will have a dance with Henri-Paul now. She's just a beginner, but she learns quite fast. I'll get you later Janene."

"Let's go dance Henri-Paul." "Me, but I'm not ready to display myself in front of everybody." "You are just as ready to dance as I was to sing. Come and give the children a lesson of courage, would you?"

"Maestro, put a cha cha on for us please?"

"Don't be nervous this is not a marriage, it's just a dance." "I would be less nervous to marry you than to dance right now." "See, it wasn't this bad after all. Let's do one more."

"Samuel, do you want to put on a foxtrot please?"

"Don't insist James, this is enough for the first time."

"Alright then, is there someone else who wants to do the foxtrot with me?" "I want to dance with you dad."

"I want to dance with my dad too." "Come Isabelle, you will do this dance with me. Be patient Mariange, this won't be very long. Jonathan you could dance with her in the mean time."

"Don't you dance Charles? You should learn. You know that the ladies like to dance with the good singers." "Danielle please; don't discourage me before I start. I'm not James and I will never be Fred Aster either." "Most of the women don't care about your steps; you know this, don't you?" "Yes, and this makes me wonder if this is not a mistake for me to sing. I just wonder if I'm not getting on the road of perdition with this singing business." "You just have to be strong every where you go, that's all. Keep God in your life and He won't leave you down." "I'll try to never forget this."

"Dad, I think I'm going to take dance lessons too." "Ho, ho. What made you change your mind about this? Henri-Paul maybe?" "I have to admit that I would like to make her dance like you did." "Dancing is one thing and sex is another, don't you forget this my son and if this is what I think it is, don't forget that she's twice your age also.

You might think she's nice and you can think she's pretty and I think you're right about this, but if you're thinking about something else then I have to warn you, it's a very slippery and dangerous ground. There are handsome young men who made their teachers fall and the lovely teachers ended up in jail. You wouldn't want this for her, do you?" "This is great to hear, but young girls my age; there is none around here." "They'll come soon enough my boy, take my word for it. I was twenty-seven when I met your mom and every one of them

I met before her even though they were pretty, they weren't worth it. It takes some time the know how to recognize the right one and every one who thinks having a lot of fun jumping one after another don't know this will play against them at the end. They will be incapable to live a happy marriage relationship and they will jump the fence at the first occasion, because this is what they always did. I would like you to go read Ecclesiastes 12, 1 when you have a chance." "I trust you dad. What does it say?" "It says: 'Young man enjoy your youth time, let yourself enjoy the pleasures of your heart and what your eyes enjoy to see when you're young, but don't forget that God will call you to account for everything you did wrong.'

"What is this mean? Have fun now and pay later?" "It's like I told you my son, if you have a crazy youth life, you'll have a crazy adult life too and all the money in the world won't be able to buy you happiness. If you want to have many blessings from God like your mom and I, you have to deserve them. Many people are forgetting that we are on earth to serve God and not the other way around. On the other hand, if you serve God like you should, you will have a hard time counting all the blessings which come your way. They will be like the sand of the sea." "This is what I see with you dad." "Just know that I wish you just as much son." "It's still true that she's desirable though." "Who's this? Henri-Paul? The least I can tell you is that you have good taste." "You too think she's very pretty?" "Can I tell you another secret?" "Of course you can dad, you know me." "It's been two weeks now that I have to push her off me regularly. She said she's in love with me, but I'm not sure she knows what love is. I think that what she's feeling is infatuation, the same thing you are feeling for her." "What is all this mean?" "It means for example that if she insults you or embarrasses you, you would start hating her right away, which would be impossible if you really love her." "She is too nice to do something like that." "Here is where you're mistaking my boy. You put her on a pedestal and you think she's an angel, but think again she is far from being an angel, believe me." "I don't understand you dad, how can you push away such a beauty?" "You'll have to remember son that adultery is no better than homosexuality or murder before God. The beauty is only superficial my boy, think about her when she's eighty. What would be left if she's not nice inside?" "You're right, old skin and old bones. But Henri-Paul is not mean." "I have met worst and I have met better. She must do what we all have to do, Jesus included, meaning she will have to eat curds and honey until she knows enough to refuse evil and choose good." "Jesus did that, him the son of God?" "This is what the scripture says. You can read it in Isaiah 7, 14-16. 'Therefore the Lord Himself will give you a sign: Behold, a virgin will be with child and bear a son and she will call his name Immanuel, he will eat curds and honey at the time he knows enough to refuse evil and choose good.'

"He lived his youth life too then?" "Many people tried to say that he was somebody else, but the references lead to Matthew 1, 23, the birth of Jesus and the reference from Matthew 1, 23 leads directly to Isaiah 7, 14. In one Bible they talk about a virgin and in the other they talk about a young girl. This is the only difference I can see." "How could you find all those things in the Bible?" "I was careful when I read and God guided me even though some people even pastors said I was lead by the devil. According to Jesus, the devil wouldn't want to destroy the devil. One thing is sure, there are thousands and thousands of pastors and priests who preached and continue to preach the lies and I wouldn't want to be in their shoes when comes the time of the judgement. It is written that the one who keeps and teaches to observe the commandments will be called great in the kingdom of heaven. God only knows how many pastors and priests who taught and keep teaching that we are not under the law anymore, but under the grace. It is an enormous lie and unfortunately too many people believed and still believe in it. They say they are under the grace and keep saying that all have sins. What a grace! See what Jesus said to the one under the grace and keep sinning in Matthew 7, 23. 'Then I will tell them plainly, I never knew you. Away from me, you evildoers.'

Learn my son, learn to know about the truth in a way that when someone lies to you you'll know that you are facing a liar. We should join the others now before they wonder if we left them for the rest of the evening."

"What would you say about listening to one of my favourite composition now sing by our new man. He's got a new name too and I like to introduce to you M. Réjean Houlet in the interpretation of my song; The Longest Highway. Please listen.

> The Longest Highway
> It's a long, long way from the birth to the end
> The longest highway surely I need a friend
>
> So be it life is the longest highway
> I've got lost often along the way
> And I've caused many people sorrow
> We don't know what will be tomorrow
> I'm asking everyone for forgiveness
> I'm asking you to come shake my hand
> I wish everybody happiness
> Please don't wait till you get at the end.
>
> It's a long, long chain from the start to the end
> It's the longest train maybe you need a friend
>
> I've crossed many rivers and the mountains
> I've been across my country so long
> Got to say that I needed a fountain
> Cause I was more than often alone
> When I left my family behind me
> I didn't ask for any permission
> I just knew I had a lot to see
> I didn't know I was on a mission.

It's a long highway I see coming the end
But I was lucky that Jesus is my friend.

So be it life is the longest highway
I've got lost often along the way
And I've caused many people sorrow
We don't know what will be tomorrow
I'm asking everyone for forgiveness
I'm asking you to come shake my hand
I wish everybody happiness
Please don't wait till you get at the end.
I am lucky that Jesus is my friend
Listen to him

After the applause, which went on for the longest time, I could hear a few commentaries around me.

"What a voice!"

"What a song!"

"It's really you dad who composed such a nice song? When did you cross the country?" "You know, I lived a few years before I met your mom."

"That's a very nice song dad and I have a hard time believing it's made by someone so close to me. How come it was never heard on the radio?" "Well you see, I don't sing good enough to sing my own song and I keep very carefully the gifts God gives me. I didn't want to give it to anybody, but all this is going to change now that I found a good singer in whom I can trust to sing them for me. If the general public likes it as much as you do, this song will go a long way and Réjean will have work to do for a long time, because I have a lot of those songs just as nice as this one."

"If someone doesn't like this song; it's because he's got poor taste." "You probably heard before my girl that tastes are not disputable, but thanks anyway for your encouragement."

"Well my husband, I think you'll never cease surprising us." "Is there anything you don't do?" "Well, now I have a real bad time all the time to do something bad." "I got to say, you know how to compose."

"I would like to hear Réjean with another one of my song. What do you say?" "Yes!"

"Yes!"

"Yes!"

"Yes!"

"It would be real hard to refuse my first fans with such acclamation. I have learned another one that I like particularly. It's a spiritual song called:

The Last Warning

Listen to this one great news sent to you today
To me it's the greatest the Lord is on his way
He has made the universe, the earth and heavens
And all that you can see has been made by his hands.
'Many times I have showed you my mighty power
I have flooded the earth but I have saved Noah
When Abram the good man has pleaded for his friends
They got out of the towns Sodom and Gomorrah.

2
Do you remember Joseph I sent to exile?
He was sold by his brothers, he was put in jail
He was to save my people from the starvation
Of a deadly famine seven years duration
And what to say of Moses drew out of water?
To guide you through the crises and lots of danger
I told him all I wanted as for you to know
He carried all my commands down to you below.

3

The wisdom of Solomon, the strength of Samson
Can just not save your soul from the lake of fire
Only Jesus the Saviour with his compassion
Left his beautiful home they took him for ransom
I sent you my loved son this for just one reason
To bring to you my word, which is sharp as a sword.
Now if you are telling Me this is not for you
Just one more thing to say I've done all I can do.
Instrumental

4

Now you are out of time and I am out of blood
Too many of my children have died for their God
Many of Jesus' good friends and his apostles
And so many others died as his disciples.
Now it is time to crown my own beloved son
He's going back to run everything that I've done
Will you be lost forever or will you be saved?
This is what you should know before you hit the grave!'

5-1

Listen to this one great news sent to you today.
To me it's the greatest the Lord is on his way.
He has made the universe, the earth and heavens.
And all that you can see has been made by his hands.
Yes, all that you can see has been made by his hands.
Thank You Lord.

This is a gift from the Lord on June 25, 1998

"But what all of you guys are crying for?" "It's so pretty dad, for sure God is talking to you and if someone tells me he's doubting this; I'll tell this person he's lost, no point to say, get lost." "That's very nice of you sweetie; you're a real darling. But just like every good thing comes to an end it is time for most of you to go to bed."

"Ho please dad, let us stay up a little bit longer?" "But it's already late."

"What do the moms have to say about this?" "Let them stay up another fifteen minutes if you don't mind, it's not every day we can give them such a nice show." "You're absolutely right and what do my in-laws think about it?" "I think that with such a good singer your songs will go a long way. They're going to cross many borders. He's a nice looking man with a golden voice and he's got everything he needs to succeed and your songs are really touching, so they are destined to reach many people around the world." "Well mother-in-law, I think I love you a bit more than yesterday." "This is what you told me yesterday." "And maybe it is what I'll say again tomorrow."

"Hold on young man, I'm here too, you know?" "Don't you worry father-in-law; I already got my limit when it comes to women, but I understand that you want to keep a steady eye on this one."

Henri-Paul didn't seem to like what I just said. I don't know yet how I will manage to make her understand that I'm already very satisfied with the two wives I already have. I'm afraid too now that she might try to achieve her aim through Samuel.

I remember when I was much younger and I couldn't get the one I like, so I went after her sister who in one way was a part of the other one. Without realizing it I caused a lot of troubles in their family. This was not too honest, but it was for me the only way to be kind of close to the one I liked. Ho yes, I too made some youth mistakes and this one was not the worst either. But I regretted them and I repented of all my wrong doing, but there will always be someone, just like a demon to come to say: 'Ho, ho, he is not better than anyone else.' But I also know that when I have repented God forgives and forgets my sins.

I often asked myself this one question as to know how could we regret something that we wanted so bad like having sex with the beautiful girlfriend we love so much? The answer was very simple. To

371

repent about something like this you have to love God with all of your
heart, all of your soul and with all of your thoughts. That's right; this
is the recipe Jesus gave us to be in peace and on good terms with God.
If we have this and on top of that we love our neighbours as ourselves,
all the commandments are then easy to follow and God have no other
choice than to bless us and this is what He does.

"You guys are doing what ever you want, but I take my beautiful
wife with me and I'm going to bed and don't you look for us, because
we'll be on the boat. We'll see you around eight in the morning for
breakfast. Good night every one!" "Good night to you too."

"The sea is calm, we should sleep well." "Is this what you want to
do, sleep?" "Don't you start something you don't have the intention to
finish." "Come on Danielle, you know me better than this, don't you?"
"Yes darling, I know you enough to know that you always finish what
ever you start, but tonight I'm very tired and I would vote for a quick
one if you don't mind." "What woman wants I want too, so just let me
know when you have enough of it."

The next day they were still talking about my songs and how much
the messages were carrying. I realized then it was time people of the world
take notice of them either they like it or not. I am conscientious of the
fact we can't please everybody. Even the greatest singer of our days, Céline
Dion whom I like very much can't please every one. The important thing
is to try. I'll do my very best to appear on a talk show; Tout Le Monde
En Parle (Everybody talks about it) just because everybody will talk about
it, of course after the crime against me and my family will be completely
elucidated. I'm sure the church will do everything in its power to hush
up the matter. Its declining is not over yet, in fact, it's just starting. The
description of its destiny is written in revelation 17 to 19. The one who
is sitting down on seven hills is Rome, see revelation 17, 5. 'The one who
has written on its forehead the mysterious name, Babylon the great, the
mother of harlots and of the abominations of the earth.'

The one who is thirsty for the blood of the saints and the blood of
the Jesus' disciples is one and the same. See revelation 17, 5-6.

Woe to the ones who don't turn away from her.

Two months later the floating wharf loaded with all the materials necessary to build the hotel was on its way to the islands. All the twenty-one islands I purchased for the amount of four billions dollars. The government was happy with the sale, but I was happier than this government to get them. Included in the deal was a complete permission to arm them with any weapon I consider fit for our defence either from up in the air or from sea.

Our hospital is basically completed and every single person who worked on this project has a special file and they are obligated to the professional secret even though all the secret codes will be renewed as soon as the operations are started.

The chronicles in the newspaper have never ceased, on the contrary, they appear now five times a week and the opinions are still diversified. The threatening letters are forward to a special investigator's office and are scrutinized very carefully. It's a real fact that a large part of the population is thirsty for the truth and this is no wonder, because it was deprived of it for nearly two thousands years.

The police chief told our family that the investigation was getting close to a happy ending. They reached the head of this criminal organization and seized a big quantity of stainless steel batteries. The makers of this illegal weapon have been arrested and the facilities are under army surveillance. I think I'll be able to come out of my coffin pretty soon. I'm afraid this is going to be the headings of the news again. I hope my spouses will think about retirement as soon as the hospital is working perfectly without them. This won't be easy at all; they have their mission at heart. I'm ending my story today, but it's not over for me yet. This is something I'm sure of.

"Janene and Danielle, would you come up here for a few minutes please? I want to introduce to you a project that I have at heart." "What is it James?" "Come up here, you'll see."

"Did he mention anything to you?" "Not at all. What about you?" "He didn't say a word to me either." "I just wonder what he's got in his bag this time." "Let's go, we'll see."

"Come in, it's opened." "What do you have for us this time?" "This might be a big surprise for both of you, I don't know." "Just a minute, this is not bad news, is it?" "I personally think it is rather good news, but I really don't know what you will think of it." "Should I sit down? I don't want to fall on my ass." "Well, sit down then, I don't want you to damage your beautiful behind." "Here we are, so go ahead." "This is our story from the very first night I met you until this minute. I wrote the whole thing almost to the smallest detail. The reason I asked you up here is because I need your permission to publish it." "You're not serious, you didn't do this?" "I do have a manuscript for each one of you if you want to relive your story from the beginning. There are almost four hundred pages. We are living a very active life you know."

"I cannot believe my own eyes and neither my own ears. As far as I am concern James; you do what you want with it, I'm not going to bloc you in any way, shape or from." "Thanks Janene, I appreciate it very much."

"Yes, yes, you have my consent too, but I have to tell you that I am completely stunned. Where and when in this world did you find the time to write all this?" "Ho, here and there, I thought our story was rather different and strange at the same time and also very special." "You are special. I'm pretty sure you are one of a kind in this whole world. You're certainly not an ordinary man. What would you say about having a third wife?" "Why would you want me to have another wife? Is one of you wants to free herself from me?" "Neither one of us would give her place even for the world, but we believe you deserve the very best. All of your children, your grand-children, your great grand-children and your great, great grand-children couldn't spent even the interests of your money even if they were all the worst spenders in the world. We both think that you should take another wife and get many more children from her." "The two of you are very special and I'm sure you're unique too, but you know very well I don't need another woman."

"God said to be fruitful, to multiply and to fill up the earth. It would be nice if there were more of your kind in this world." "I know you too well to ignore that you are serious. Should I suppose you already chose her for me?" "We cannot hide anything from you, can we?" "Are you really sure you know what you are getting into?" "Don't you worry; we're not giving up anything." "It doesn't bother you to lose your turn to someone else?" "If this is to fulfil the will of God, we are ready for this too. Either way with your new magic portion you just put up on the market you could serve all three of us the same day." "Are you going to tell me who you have in mind?" "Her name is Marianne, she is very pretty, she loves kids immensely and she is extremely in love and crazy for you." "I don't know any Marianne at all." "Where is she from?" "She is from Richelieu and tomorrow is her birthday. We both thought you would make her a very nice gift." "I don't mind making her a nice gift if she is your friend, but from this to make her my spouse there is a long way." "We think she'll be a nice wife for you and also a nice mother for your kids." "You never talk to me about her before, how long have you known her?" "We have known her for more than three months, but she's a very nice person. She's almost a virgin and she has never been with a man." "Just a minute now, you're not thinking that I'm Joseph, the father of Jesus, do you?" "You're funny sometimes James, so what do you think about this?" "I think you are off the track and you are pulling my leg, that's what I think." "Not at all, we are very serious just like the first night we met you. We talked about it for a long time and we think it's the best thing for everybody." "Do I know her?"

"Please Janene; do you want to go get her?" "Do you mean she's already in this house? Listen both of you really, I don't want another wife." "Well, now you are disappointing me a lot. You've been preaching the word of God for the longest time and saying that we have to fulfil his will. Besides, it is the only prayer that Jesus taught us; that the will of God be done on earth as it is in heaven. You know better than anyone that God wants men to be productive and it's not because Janene and I can no longer have any children that you should quit fathering and waste all of your seed." "You are twisting my arm and I hope with all of my heart you will never regret what you are proposing to me. I think I'll have a few more pages to add to this manuscript after all." "Here is Janene with our proposition. Please James, stay calm and don't react too swiftly. Take the time to assimilate all this and think about the half dozen wonderful children that will know life if you follow our plan." "But this is Henri-Paul?" "Alias Marianne Toupin! Henri and Paul were the first names of her Father and her grand-father. Henri-Paul is the name she chose when she entered the convent." "I like Marianne better; it's more feminine for a woman. You really want me to take her as a wife?" "She loves you just as much as we do and even the kids noticed this. I found out the night you danced with her. She couldn't keep her eyes off you. We'll leave you alone now and you can discuss between the two of you. Tomorrow we'll have another proposition for you." "Please, not another one, enough is enough." "Just wait, you'll see. Good night and don't pull each other hairs."

"Are you coming Janene?"

"Hey, I'm not allowed to get a hug anymore?" "We're not giving up anything. Good night!" "Good night Janene!"

"Now, let's settle this once and for all. I don't know with what magic spell you have obtained their consent, but I'm not fool enough to believe in all of this comedy. What is it? What kind of blackmailing are you exercising on them?" "Not at all, none of this is true. They have noticed that I am in love with you and I supposed they preferred sharing you with me instead of seeing you commit adultery." "Bull, they know very well I will never commit adultery with anyone. There is something else with what you holding them with and I will find out soon or later, I can guarantee you this. Do you know what I'll do? I will send you to Africa where your chances to come out of it will be very slim." "You are making a big mistake." "We'll see about that. I don't believe in your love not even a little bit. Do you know what I believe? I believe you are an instrument of the devil to torment me, that's what I believe. What ever it is, I have to get rid of you and the sooner the better. You are a thorn in my foot not to say something else." "If I'm a pain in your ass just say it." "That's exactly what I mean and I don't need this at all. As soon as tomorrow morning you'll be leaving. Go get your things ready and I will call Bernard, so he can take you in a place where there is not too much civilization, which will suit you perfectly. You're way too dangerous to stay around my family." "You are completely unfair towards me. You're not afraid of me, but you afraid of yourself. You have all the power in the world and you can do what ever you want with me. When you're at it why don't you feed me to the sharks? Nobody will ever know." "This is a very good idea. Do you want to come for a boat ride first thing in the morning? Now get out of my face, I've seen enough of you." "You are committing a big mistake." "Why don't you finish your sentence and tell me what this threat is all about?" "I don't make any threat. You're mistaking about me, I'm really in love with you." "I'm sorry, but I usually believe in the truth and I don't believe you at all. Tell me then why I see you as a threat? I'm making a big mistake for whom? Is it for me, for you, for my spouses or my whole family?" "I only say that you are making a big error of judgement about me." "Well, let me tell you that I'm ready to live with the consequences what ever they are." "You will be sorry." "Here is another threat." "You seem to forget that I contributed to save your life." "Here we are; I was expecting this one to come up sometime. Tell me how much I owe you?" "Nothing, nothing but a bit of recognition!" "You still didn't tell me how you won Danielle and Janene on you side for this scam." "Yes, I told you, they're not as blind as you are when it comes to love and they both understood that I love you more that anything in the world, more than my poor life." "Sorry, I wish I could believe you, but I can't. You have to leave before causing a disaster in my family that unfortunately I see coming too quickly." "I thought I would face resistance concerning us getting together, but I never thought it would come from you. You can do what ever you want with me, it doesn't matter anymore. I will go and you'll never hear from me again, I promise you. I'm mainly sorry for the children I adopted in my heart and they adopted me too. They are very intelligent and made progress like I have never seen before. I don't understand your attitude towards me, but I hope you understand yourself.

I'm ready to go and I want to leave before being confronted by the children if it's possible. They don't deserve the pain this will cause them." "This is very touching, but it doesn't work with me. Go and I'll see you at dawn."

I could tell she was deeply depressed, but I was not ready to get in a love relationship with a woman who has the potential to destroy everything I built in the last twenty years.

I went to the boat to discuss the matter with Danielle again. She was not worrying at all, because she was sleeping like a log. I woke her up anyway, because the matter was too serious to wait until the morning.

"Danielle, wake up. Danielle, I got to talk to you." "Whattttt? Let me sleep please?" "I got to talk to you right away." "Why? Can't it wait until the morning?" "Tomorrow might be too late already." "What is it?" "I fired Henri-Paul and she will be leaving first thing in the morning." "Why did you do such a stupid thing? The children will be mad at you for the rest of their lives." "They won't be if my judgement is right." "But what are you talking about?" "I'm talking about the plot that was made up behind my back." "What plot are you talking about?" "You're not telling me that you pushed this woman in my arms and in my bed if you're not forced to?" "James, James my love, what we told you earlier is the truth and nothing but the truth. Janene and I think that Marianne is deeply in love with you, that she'll be good for you, that she will give you some wonderful children and that you can be happy with all of us." "But Danielle, I have a hard time as it is to spend enough time with the children I have so far." "You spend more time with them than most fathers in the world do and you found the time to write our story on top of all. Making kids doesn't take this much time and we will be three mothers to take care of them." "But you and Janene are starting to work full time beginning next week already." "We were supposed to tell you this tomorrow, but since we are at it I'll tell you now. Janene and I will take six months to organize the staff at the new hospital and when everything is all set we will definitely retire. We'll only keep an eye on the operations which will take very little of our time. This will only take one or two days a month for me and Janene to take turns just like we do in bed with you. We would like that Raymond takes over the general direction, this of course if you agree, he is your employee. These few months holidays made us realized that our family is more important than all the sick people in the world and there always will be some of them. We're going to create a training centre for nurses and doctors. The province is so short of them and the centre will always be in demand. Believe me; we don't do it for the money either. As far as Marianne is concerned, just get busy making kids to her and stay here to take care of your new projects. Janene and I will go to work four days a week for now and we'll be here for our treats in the weekends. Don't you ever feel that you are obligated to make love to us, because neither one of us would like that, you know this, don't you?" "So you are sure; this is what you want?" "Yes darling, we love her like a sister and the children love her like a good mother. Go see her before she try to open her wrists." "You ask for it, but just know I didn't need this."

I went to my place and I turned on the monitors to see how Marianne was doing and mainly what she was doing. She was crying bitterly and she was holding; hold on, a stainless steel little battery in her hand. I concluded right away that this was the threat over my family and the whole house and what and who ever are in it. I couldn't see any lighter or matches around her. I realized then that I pushed her to her limits. It was hard to tell what was her intentions at that point and time. If she had a way to heat it up, she could eliminate all of us in a few seconds. Only Danielle was safe on the boat. Marianne was in such state of mind and I thought she might just be irresponsible for her actions. I have no choice I told myself; I have to go talk to her. I didn't think it will be easy to stay natural and calm.

Nock, nock, nock! "Come in, it's not locked. Is it time to go already?" "Would you allow me to sit beside you?" "It's your home, you do what you want." "It doesn't work like this with me, when I gave a bedroom, it's not mine anymore. I went to speak with Danielle and apparently I am mistaking a lot about you. I could not believe they would push me in your arms without being forced to.

A man would be very stupid not to be attracted by you; you are prettier than gorges, prettier than the day." "Before you say anymore James, I have to give you something. Don't you panic; it's completely inoffensive without heat." "Let me check if you have any fever." "You can be funny when you want to. Take this; you will know what to do with it." "What? When did you get this horrible thing?" "They gave it to me almost at the same time Charles got his." "Why didn't you give it to me sooner?" "I knew it couldn't cause any damage where I got it put away, unless I fall in a fire and I was waiting for the right moment to give it to you, but you can believe what you want like you use to." "Can you imaging what could had happened if a kid picked it up and went to play in the sunshine with this? You don't think this was irresponsible from your part?" "It was impossible for a child to find it." "How come?" "There was only one person in the world that could put his hand on it." "I don't understand! Was it hidden this well?" "It was inside of me all of this time and I would let no one but you penetrate me. Many times I offered you to discover it, but you didn't want me." "It's not that I didn't want you, it's just because I couldn't. Now it's different, someone is twisting my arms. We'll go on the boat in the morning for a ride and we'll let it explode on the water somewhere." "Don't you think it could be useful to you some day?" "Maybe so, but

I have shivers just looking at it. This is such a murderous thing." "Just think about it for a minute, you could blow up an enemy ship just with a slingshot." "As long as it doesn't fall in the water first. And what would happen if a turtle finds it and go deposit it on a beach full of people in a bright sunny day or else near our boat?" "I still think you should keep it safely hidden. If I could do it I think you can too." "I don't see myself walking with such a dangerous thing in my ass. You are even prettier when you smile. When I think that if you were the enemy you could blow us all up and our house too. We can never be careful enough. Could you ever forgive me for being so hard on you?" "I already forgave you ahead of time all the wrong you could do to me." "How many children do you want?" "As many as I could carry." "When do you want to start?" "Like three months ago! To be continued. James Prince